## Praise for

"*Malicious Intent* has an addictive plot that delves into the dangerous underworld of digital crime, and the protagonists' chemistry, brewed during a lifetime of friendship and romantic longing, positively sizzles."

*Booklist*

"Perfectly balancing chilling suspense and uplifting romance, award-winning author Lynn H. Blackburn delivers a story of revenge, greed, and overcoming that you won't want to put down no matter how late it gets."

*More Than a Review*

"This book will grab you from the beginning and keep you captivated until the end."

*Interviews & Reviews*

## Praise for *Unknown Threat*

"Blackburn's Defend and Protect series is off with a bang in *Unknown Threat*. This heart-racing romantic suspense is one for the keeper shelf! Don your tactical vests and get ready to engage a compelling story that will forbid you from abandoning its pages. Do. Not. Miss. This. One!"

**Ronie Kendig**, bestselling, award-winning author of The Tox Files

"*Unknown Threat* is a fantastic read! An action-packed opening and sharply drawn characters drew me right in and held me captive. Blackburn has an exceptional gift for weaving twisting plots with characters that walk right off the page. I absolutely adore Faith, the bright and stalwart FBI special agent. I love the attention to detail regarding Secret Service operations. The swoon-worthy romance between Faith and Luke is the perfect slow burn. *Unknown Threat* is an exciting start to a thrilling new romantic-suspense series!"

**Elizabeth Goddard**, award-winning
author of the Uncommon Justice series

"In *Unknown Threat*, Lynn Blackburn has created a page-turning novel with all the elements I've come to love in her books. The hero and heroine are unique and compelling, while surrounded by a rich cast that adds depth to the story. The suspense thread is intense and pulses with energy and pressure. And the romance? It's perfection, with tension to keep me rooting for the characters. It's a perfect read for those who love engaging stories that are threaded with hope."

**Cara Putman**, award-wining
author of *Flight Risk* and *Imperfect Justice*

"By far the best romantic suspense book I have read this year! Fans of Blackburn will not want to miss this fantastic read!"

**Write-Read-Life**

"*Unknown Threat* by Lynn H. Blackburn is a fast-paced romantic suspense read. I loved the action-packed scenes."

**Urban Lit Magazine**

"Wow, talk about an intense and riveting read. This series started with a bang and kept up a thrilling pace. I think this is my favorite book by Blackburn to date."

*Relz Reviewz*

# UNDER
# FIRE

# Books by Lynn H. Blackburn

## DIVE TEAM INVESTIGATIONS

*Beneath the Surface*
*In Too Deep*
*One Final Breath*

## DEFEND AND PROTECT

*Unknown Threat*
*Malicious Intent*
*Under Fire*

DEFEND
AND
PROTECT
3

# UNDER FIRE

## LYNN H. BLACKBURN

Revell

a division of Baker Publishing Group
Grand Rapids, Michigan

© 2023 by Lynn Huggins Blackburn

Published by Revell
a division of Baker Publishing Group
PO Box 6287, Grand Rapids, MI 49516-6287
www.revellbooks.com

Printed in the United States of America

Library of Congress Cataloging-in-Publication Data
Names: Blackburn, Lynn Huggins, author.
Title: Under fire / Lynn H. Blackburn.
Description: Grand Rapids, MI : Revell, a division of Baker Publishing Group
    [2023] | Series: Defend and protect ; 3
Identifiers: LCCN 2022028679 | ISBN 9780800737979 (paperback) | ISBN
    9780800742621 (casebound) | ISBN 9781493439676 (ebook)
Subjects: LCGFT: Novels.
Classification: LCC PS3602.L325285 U53 2023 | DDC 813/.6—dc23/eng/20220616
LC record available at https://lccn.loc.gov/2022028679

Scripture quotations are from The Holy Bible, English Standard Version® (ESV®), copyright © 2001 by Crossway, a publishing ministry of Good News Publishers. Used by permission. All rights reserved. ESV Text Edition: 2016

Baker Publishing Group publications use paper produced from sustainable forestry practices and post-consumer waste whenever possible.

23  24  25  26  27  28  29        7  6  5  4  3  2  1

# —1—

**ONE YEAR,
THREE MONTHS,
TWENTY-SEVEN DAYS EARLIER**

US Secret Service Agent Tessa Reed was no stranger to hangovers. Her head throbbed in rhythm with the beat of her heart. She didn't want to open her eyes. Didn't want to face the day. She cracked one eye enough to confirm that it was still dark. She had no idea how much longer the night would last, but she didn't fight the pull of sleep and allowed it to drag her under once more.

When she returned to consciousness, her headache was unimaginably worse. Light filtered through her closed lids and a noxious odor assaulted her with every breath.

She could power through. She'd done it before. Too many times. But the pain that radiated through her skull at the slightest movement had no equal in the vast landscape of her memories.

A few more breaths and she'd—

A cold realization flooded her as three separate sensations registered in a tsunami of horror. She was lying on top of the covers and . . . Her eyes flew open, then slammed to slits in an effort to minimize the impact of the light wedging around the edges of the curtains. She twisted, slowly, to confirm what she already knew.

Her shirt was missing.

No. No. This couldn't be happening. *Jesus, please, don't let this be happening.*

Tessa forced her eyes to open and took in her surroundings. She was in what had all the appearances of a cheap motel room. Her shirt was gone, but she still wore the rest of her clothes, including her shoes.

She had no idea where she was, how she got here, who had been with her, what they had done to her, or when they would return.

She fought the nausea and forced herself to sit, then held her head in her hands and took shallow breaths until the phantom ice pick slowed its attack on her brain.

Long before she was ready, she lifted her head and scanned the room. Her purse was on a low nightstand. Her shirt was nowhere to be seen.

What happened to her last night?

She took stock of her body. No bruises. No marks. No pain other than the hangover headache. Nothing felt numb or tender.

She reached for her purse and opened it, fully expecting it to be empty.

Her phone and keys were exactly as she'd left them.

If someone had abducted her, it was the worst kidnapping in history.

If she'd come willingly—no. She wouldn't have. Right? Could she have come here—wherever *here* was—on her own? That didn't make sense.

She strained to remember. She'd gone to Gino's. She'd sat at the bar. Then? There was something lingering on the edge of her memory, but when she tried to pin it down, it floated out of her grasp.

This was not a normal hangover.

She pulled her phone from her bag.

Dead.

If she exited this room, she'd be walking into a completely unknown, and almost certainly hostile, environment—unarmed and unprepared for whatever was out there. And she'd be doing it without a shirt.

But if she remained, there was no way to predict what, who, or how many people might come through that door.

Tessa could handle herself. Far better than most women, and men, for that matter. But again, she had no weapon. And while she was no slouch in the martial arts department, she *could* be overpowered.

She couldn't stay here. Every step sent pain ricocheting through her head, but she forced herself to check under the bed and in the drawers. Her shirt was definitely gone. She eased over to the window. Standing to the side, she peered into a parking lot. She couldn't see a sign or any distinguishing features that told her where she was.

An ancient rotary phone sat on the dresser. She backed up toward it, facing the door at all times. She lifted the receiver and listened.

A dial tone. *Oh, thank you Jesus. Thank you.*

She processed her options in the space of three breaths and made the call.

She didn't have a choice.

She waited for him to answer, knowing that with this colossal failure, the darkest parts of her soul would be forced into the light.


**US SECRET SERVICE** Special Agent Zane Thacker glanced at the phone screen. The number was local, but not one he recognized. He sent it straight to voice mail.

He had a love-hate, mostly hate, relationship with cell phones. But he kept his phone on him twenty-four hours a day, seven days a week, three hundred sixty-five (or six) days a year.

He had his reasons. Most of them were depressing. Which was why even though his phone was always nearby, not everyone who called reached him. Especially now.

Zane would have been happy if he'd gone his entire life without being shot by a grieving, revenge-driven assassin. But life hadn't exactly made a habit out of taking it easy on him. No reason to start now.

The doctor had allowed him to return to work, but he moved slow, his reaction times remained sluggish, and the pain refused to leave. Which was why he was awake, dressed, and on his second cup of coffee before 8:00 on a Saturday morning. He'd given up on sleep hours ago.

The phone rang again.

No one who knew him would call this early.

Unless they were in trouble.

He accepted the call. "Thacker."

"Zane," Tessa gasped out in a voice that trembled. "I need you to pick me up."

He had his keys and weapon before she'd finished speaking. "Where are you?"

"I . . . I don't know."

He disarmed the security system. "Are you hurt?"

"No. But I can't leave."

Everything in him iced over. "Where's your phone?"

"With me, but it's dead. I'm calling from a phone in the room."

"Hang on." He'd made it to his car and eased behind the wheel of his newish sedan. If he rushed, it would hurt, and that would slow him down. Better to move at a pace his body could manage.

Once he was settled, he opened the Find My Friends feature that all the Raleigh Secret Service agents had willingly enabled a few months earlier. When someone's trying to take out your entire office, there's a small comfort in knowing you could be found.

One glance was all it took to confirm what Zane already knew. Everyone was where they were supposed to be. Everyone except Tessa.

Tessa Reed was not in her fancy apartment. The one with high-end security cameras in every communal space and well-lit parking lot. Her phone's last tracked location was in a part of town no one should be in. Especially not someone who looked like her.

"The last GPS signal shows that you're at the Tropical Oasis Motel."

"Okay. That's probably where I am. Although there's nothing in here that has the name. And no one in their right mind would call this place an oasis."

"I'm on my way. Looks like it will take me twenty minutes to get to you."

"Okay." Tessa's whispered word held no relief or understanding.

"Is there a particular reason you chose to be there?"

"I . . . I don't know."

Zane slammed his hand on the steering wheel. He had so many things he wanted to say. But he knew better than anyone else that nothing he could say would fix this. Tessa had a problem. It was huge. It was going to cost her everything.

It might have already cost far more than she'd ever wanted to pay.

That thought sucked the anger from him. What was left was a potent combination of simmering frustration and heartbreaking compassion. "Tess, is there a reason you're still there?"

"I don't have a shirt." Her voice was so soft, he could barely hear her.

"What?"

"My shirt is missing. I've looked through the room. Under the bed. It's not here. Zane, I don't remember coming here. I don't know how I got here or why I came. I don't know what's around me or where I am." There was an edge of terror in her words that went straight from Zane's ear to his foot. He floored it.

Zane squeezed the steering wheel. *Jesus, please help me.* "Tess. I'm going to ask you again. Are you hurt? Have you been assaulted?"

"No." No hesitation or uncertainty. "My head is killing me, but aside from my shirt missing, I'm still clothed, I still have my purse, and my body has not been violated."

Zane had no words to express his relief. So he went with the easier topic. "You still have your purse? You weren't robbed?"

"No. But I don't have any cash. I don't even have my wallet. I left it at home."

None of this made any sense. "Tessa, I need you to try to remember. Last night. Where were you? What's the last thing you remember?"

"I went out for a drink."

"Yeah. I got that part." Boy, did he ever.

"At Gino's." Gino's was a newish bar in the Raleigh area. They catered to a high-end clientele. The kind of place where Tessa would fit in perfectly. The kind of place a woman would think she could get a glass of wine and not have to worry about anyone slipping something into her drink.

Or so people thought.

"Tell me everything you remember from the time you walked into Gino's until you called me this morning." She did. It didn't take long.

12

"Have you checked the room for anything left behind by whoever you were with?"

"Not really. I looked for my shirt, but then I called you as soon as I realized I can't just walk out of here. I have no money, and my cell phone is dead so I can't order an Uber. And even if I could, I have no shirt. I guess I could borrow a sheet or a towel to cover up, but again, I have no money and no cell phone. This doesn't seem like the time to go wandering around knocking on doors and asking random people for help."

"Agreed. While you're waiting for me, you need to check the room for anything that might give us a clue as to what happened."

"I will, but this phone is bolted to the desk. I can only get five feet from it. I'll have to hang up."

"No! Keep the line open but set the phone down on the desk. Say something every so often so I can hear you."

Tessa did what he asked. He heard her opening drawers and what might have been the shower curtain being pulled back. Two minutes later, she picked up the receiver. "I found a cuff link."

"Where was it?"

"Under the bed."

"Is there anything distinctive about it?"

"My head is still fuzzy, but I think this is an image of Janus."

Zane had no idea who or what Janus was. Nor did he care at the moment. "Does it look familiar? Do you remember seeing it before?"

Tessa's silence cut a gash through his soul. "No. Zane . . . I . . . I can't . . ."

"I'm almost there. Hang on."

By the time he pulled into the motel parking lot, he was vibrating with rage and fear and an intense desire to execute justice on his own terms. He didn't park in a space and kept the car in drive

13

while he scanned the building. "This place is all ground-floor units. Don't open them, but move the curtains so I can figure out which room you're in." He didn't need to tell her that this wasn't the type of establishment where the patrons were likely to be receptive to a member of law enforcement knocking on their door. When he approached, he needed to be sure he was at the right room or things could go south, well, further south than they already were.

He scanned the windows to his right and left. Nothing. He drove until another building came into view. "Move the curtain again."

This time, he saw the movement.

"I see it. I'm hanging up. Don't open the door until I knock." He parked the car and popped the trunk. Thirty seconds later he was walking to the room, a T-shirt from the stash of clothes he always kept in his vehicle in one hand, his other resting on his weapon at his waist. He reached her door and rapped his knuckles on it. "Tess? Unlock the door."

"Um. Zane. I don't—"

"Unlock the door and then go into the bathroom. I'll hand you the shirt once I'm inside."

"Right."

Zane waited ten seconds, then opened the door and bit back several words that he'd given up using a decade earlier. The place was filthy. He didn't even want to get the bottoms of his shoes dirty with the germs infesting that carpet. Tessa's hand and half of her arm stretched out of the bathroom door. He placed the shirt in her hand. "We should call the poli—"

"No. Zane. Please." Tessa emerged from the bathroom. "I'm certain nothing happened."

"Nothing happened? You woke up in a filthy hotel room without your shirt on!"

Tessa took a step back. "Please."

He should call the police. Get the place fingerprinted. Something. But Tessa was on a fine edge. She was in trouble. Big trouble. But she'd called him. He could be a law enforcement officer, or he could be her friend. But if he insisted on bringing the police in, she wouldn't call him the next time.

And if she didn't make some changes soon, there would be a next time.

"Let's go." She followed him to his car, and they didn't speak until they were back in a better part of town.

Zane pulled into a parking lot already filling with Saturday-morning shoppers. He cut the engine and turned to Tessa. He didn't have it in him to be anything but blunt. "You could have been killed."

"I know." One tear. Just one. But it broke something inside him.

All the fight in her was gone. Under different circumstances, he would be furious and do anything in his power to help her regain her strength. But in this moment, he hoped and prayed it meant she would be open to what he had to say next. "You need to go to rehab."

Time froze while he waited for her response.

"Yeah. I do. I need help."

# — 2 —

Zane stalked toward Tessa's car. The evening had started out great and ended in unmitigated disaster. His relationship with Tessa had deteriorated to the point that they couldn't even go out to eat with their friends and remain civil. One day they were fine. The next day they couldn't be in the same room without sparks flying. And not the good kind. He didn't know what her problem was, but he was done riding this roller coaster.

He reached her car. She glared at him through the window. He spoke, his voice low but loud enough for her to hear him. "We need to talk."

The glass slid down. "We do. But not here." Anger poured out of her in a flood that he could almost feel pulling him under.

"The nature trail?"

"Fine."

Zane's best friend and fellow US Secret Service agent lived in a nice enough neighborhood, but what it claimed as a nature trail wasn't much more than a glorified walking path. But it was flat and, at this time of night, probably deserted.

Tessa drove away. He jogged back inside and met four worried gazes. Luke and his fiancée, FBI Special Agent Faith Malone, sat on one side of the living room. Gil Dixon, another Secret Service agent, and his girlfriend, Dr. Ivy Collins, were cozied up in an oversized chair on the other side.

"Is she okay?" Faith managed to ask the question in a way that cast no blame on the way the evening had ended. With Tessa excusing herself and all but storming from the house after Zane asked her a simple question.

"I don't know what her problem is. But I'm about to find out."

"Zane." Luke's voice carried a warning.

"What?" Zane snapped the question.

"Be careful. With her and with yourself. You don't want to say something you can't take back."

"I'm not the one you need to be worried about." Zane grabbed his keys. He and Luke had been roommates since his house was destroyed last spring. It worked out great, most of the time. Right now, Zane would give just about anything for some privacy. "I'll be back."

He climbed in the car and kept his speed low. It was a neighborhood, and he had no plans to accidentally take out someone's family pet in his haste.

When he pulled into the parking lot of the clubhouse area, he saw that Tessa hadn't waited for him. He parked and took his time following the trail. It didn't take him long to spot Tessa's long hair whipping in the breeze, her brown skin glowing under the small trail light by the park bench set up in a curve of the path.

She stood by the bench, braced for whatever was about to happen.

*Lord, please don't let me mess this up.* He wanted to be gentle, but what came out of his mouth sounded like a cross between a growl and a snarl. "We need to talk."

Her chin came up. "We do. And if it's all the same to you, I'll go first. I'm sick and tired of your not-so-subtle attempts to manage my life. Just because you helped me find my feet as an agent when I moved here, just because you took me to rehab, just because you took care of things while I was gone—none of that gives you the right to control my life."

She took a quick breath and kept going. "I'm an alcoholic, Zane. I will always be an alcoholic. But I'm healing. I'm free. I don't want to go back to the person I was, and I'm not in immediate danger of a relapse."

"I never—"

"Don't. Don't try to explain it away. I get it. I do. Your mother never managed to hold on to her sobriety, and your childhood was a nightmare because of it. You care about me, and you're terrified I'll be like her."

He couldn't argue with that.

"But I'm *not* your mother. My life experience, and my alcoholism, is not the same as hers. I saw the path I was on, and I turned my life around before I lost everything. I'm not perfect. I'm not infallible. But I refuse to allow alcohol to steal the life God has purposed for me. I have so much to live for. So much to hope for. And I'm thankful, truly, for the way you stepped in and stayed by me for the past few months. But you are not my nanny. You are not my sponsor. And if you keep going the way you're going, you won't even be my friend." Her voice broke and the next breath she took was ragged, her next words quiet.

"Can you imagine how hard it is for me to have you hovering at every gathering? Questioning every decision? Do you really think the others didn't know exactly what you were getting at when you asked if I was going straight home?"

He wanted to deny the accusation, but the lie wouldn't come.

He dropped to the bench and rested his head in his hands. For a long minute, neither of them spoke. Then Tessa sat beside him.

"Why are we so messed up?" Her words were a whisper. "When you aren't treating me like I'm a grenade with the pin pulled halfway out, you're one of my favorite people in the world."

Zane sat up and turned toward Tessa. "You're my favorite. Hands down."

Her eyes widened.

"And that's why we're so messed up."

"I don't understand." Tessa threw up her hands. "If we like each other, what is the problem?"

"Tess." Her name on his lips was a frustrated groan.

"IT'S MY FAULT, ISN'T IT? Because of . . . what I did. Before." Even now, Tessa couldn't make herself say it out loud. At first, she'd done a great job of hiding her attraction to Zane. He had been assigned to bring her up to speed in the Raleigh office. He wasn't in her chain of command, technically, and it wouldn't have been wrong for them to get together, but Zane had never given her a hint that he might consider her to be anything other than a friend. And she hadn't wanted to make things awkward.

Until he came to her apartment one night to pick up some paperwork he wanted to get a head start on over the weekend, and she threw herself at him.

"Tessa. No." He'd been gentle but firm. "You're drunk." When she came toward him again, his voice took on a bitter edge. "Tessa. Really? I've told you about my mom. It doesn't matter how attracted I am to you or you are to me. This"—he waved a hand between them—"will never happen."

He left, and they never discussed it. Not when he took her to

rehab or visited her at rehab or brought her home after graduation from rehab.

But they had to discuss it now.

"Look." She took a deep breath, but before she could continue,
Zane took her hands.

"Tessa, the way I see it, we have two choices. We either choose
to be civil and only interact at the office, or we choose to be
friends. Just friends. Regardless of any attraction we feel toward
each other, the path to something more than friendship is one we
can't walk. You're only a few months into your sobriety, and that's
where your focus needs to stay."

"I'm well aware of what I need to do to protect myself and continue to heal. I don't need you to tell me how to live my life, Zane."

"I know." He squeezed her hands. "And I'm sorry. You're not
wrong. I can see how I've made things confusing and frustrating
for you by acting like I have some say in what you do or don't do.
Please accept my apology."

Tessa's thoughts spun, and it took her several breaths before
she could respond. "I accept your apology."

"Thank you." Zane released her hands and leaned back against
the bench.

"Where does this leave us?" Tessa asked.

"Where do you want it to leave us?" Zane's question held a
tenderness and a vulnerability she wasn't sure what to do with.
"I'm the one who's turned into a meddling control freak. I'd say
where we go from here is your call. But just to put this out there . . .
I want to be your friend."

Tessa mirrored Zane's position—back against the bench, arms
crossed. "Do you think we *can* be friends?"

Zane didn't rush to respond, and she appreciated that he took
her question seriously. "I'm not sure, but I would like to try."

# 3

"I'm going to kill the president."

US Secret Service Special Agent Tessa Reed read the threat, one of seven similar claims that had landed in her in-box courtesy of the Protective Intelligence Division, known as the PID, in Washington, DC. This batch joined the nine others the PID sent yesterday. All from social media accounts. All to be followed up on before the president's arrival in Raleigh next Friday, one week from now.

And she was the lucky agent who'd be doing the following up.

She appreciated her boss, Resident Agent in Charge Jacob Turner, trusting her with the role of liaison to the President's Protection Detail. She'd expected him to hand the assignment to either Luke or Gil, both of whom were more than qualified. Or to their new agent, Benjamin North, who was the most experienced special agent on their team and who had been on the PPD until he transferred to the Raleigh office last December.

As the least experienced agent of the team, she'd been prepared to have to wait several more years for this opportunity. But here she was.

21

"You're ready for this," Jacob had said when he called her into his office on Thursday afternoon. "Don't hesitate to ask questions. Pick Benjamin's brain. He's a resource. Use him." Then Jacob grinned widely. "And enjoy bossing Luke and Gil around for a change."

That she would do.

Her watch buzzed on her wrist and she glanced at it. Zane Thacker had left Raleigh seven months ago for the PPD. She missed him. He knew that. What he didn't know was how much she missed him. Or why. Their relationship had taken a while to settle into friendship, but once it did, their bond solidified into something she cherished. Something she wouldn't risk losing.

I hear congratulations are in order.

Tessa pulled her phone from her back pocket and replied.

I'll accept congratulations only after the job is done and POTUS is back in DC.

Fair enough. We'll celebrate next Saturday.

A tingle of anticipation trilled down her spine.

I take it you're making this trip. When do you arrive?

"Now." Zane's deep voice came from above her.

She shot to her feet and smacked his shoulder before allowing him to pull her into a quick hug. "You could have told me!"

"This was way more fun."

She glanced behind him. "Where's the rest of your team?"

"I left them in Jacob's office. Leslie is taking care of them. I wanted to see you first." He gave her a grin that was the perfect mixture of mischievous little boy and flirtatious grown man. "Without an audience."

Tessa couldn't stop herself from drinking in the fullness of him. It was more than could be experienced over the phone, or even over a video chat. Zane had a way of standing that projected confidence, stability, and security. If anyone had ever been born to protect the president, it was Zane Thacker.

His six-foot-two height and broad shoulders gave him the kind of body that made suit designers drool. His dark-blond hair had hints of auburn in it and threatened to curl at the first hint of length, but today it was trimmed close. His face was interesting and expressive, making him the kind of man who grew more handsome the longer you spent time around him.

Over the past couple of years, Tessa had catalogued everything about Zane, but her favorite feature was his eyes. They were the palest of blues at the pupils, with shards of white scattered around the middles before darkening to a deep navy rim at the edges of the irises.

And when he decided to maintain eye contact, like he was doing now, it was almost impossible to look away.

"I've missed you."

The words were a feather-light whisper, but the impact was that of a two-ton truck ramming into her heart. She hadn't seen him in person since Gil and Ivy's wedding in June. They'd spent a lot of time perfecting their friendship before he left for DC. Was this how friends greeted each other after three months apart? Long glances and heartfelt words?

"Zane! You're here! Good to see you, man!" Luke jogged down the hall and grabbed Zane in a bro hug. They slapped each other on the back several times before breaking apart. "The place isn't the same without you."

"Yeah." Gil joined them, and he and Zane repeated the hug/back-slap procedure that Tessa had long ago concluded must come encoded in the male DNA since they all knew how to do it. "There's more food in the fridge, and no one paces the halls while they're on phone calls."

"I don't pace." Zane's protest was met with three sets of "Yeah, you do." He turned to Tessa and mimed being stabbed in the heart. "*Et tu, Brute?*"

"I call it like I see it." They all laughed and spent the next few minutes catching up.

When Tessa's phone rang, she answered it with a quick "Reed."

"Tess, hon," Leslie, their office manager, said. "Jacob wants everyone in the conference room for a quick brief."

"We'll be down in a sec, Leslie. Thanks." She set the phone back in the holder and turned to see the three men who had stood by her when her mistakes almost destroyed everything she'd worked for. She adored them.

She'd do well to remember that two of them were taken, and the one she wanted didn't want her back. And if she messed that relationship up, she wouldn't just lose his friendship. She'd damage almost every meaningful relationship in her current world.

She'd gone it alone for a long time. She couldn't go back. Friendship was enough. It had to be.

ZANE ALLOWED HIMSELF one long inhale as he walked beside Tessa to the conference room. The scent he associated with only her—a hint of citrus and flowers with a faint kick of cinnamon—swirled around him.

It was good to be home.

It was torture to be home.

He wouldn't be a distraction to her. He would be a friend. Her best friend.

He, Gil, and Luke all paused to allow Tessa to enter the conference room ahead of them in a combination of chivalry and respect, both of which she deserved. And based on the smile she tossed over her shoulder at them, both of which she appreciated.

"Tessa! Come meet the guys." Benjamin North's exuberant voice carried through the door.

Zane, Luke, and Gil paused outside the conference room. "How's Benjamin working out?" Zane asked Luke and Gil.

"Great." Gil spoke, and Luke dipped his head in agreement. "He's a good fit, and he has solid investigative and protective experience. He stayed late with Tess last night, and she picked his brain about how to be the best liaison the PPD has ever seen."

No surprise there. Tessa overprepared for everything.

Luke picked up the narrative. "He's easy to work with—he's not stuffy, not proprietary, likes to have fun, pitches in when there's work to be done regardless of whether he thinks a younger agent should be handling it. He's been a real blessing since we lost you. We're still several agents short, but we've interviewed three in the last month, and they may come on board after they finish their training. If they do, he'll be invaluable. If you don't count Jacob, he's the only Phase 3 agent we have."

"The Raleigh RAIC is a great office for the first phase." Zane scanned the men in the conference room who had flown down from DC with him. Rodriguez was his least favorite agent on the PPD, but he knew his business and had never failed to do his job well. Carver was good to work with. Generally easygoing, but intense when the situation demanded it. He knew these men, but they weren't his friends outside the office.

Walking into the conference room reminded him of how much

he missed the camaraderie of the Raleigh RAIC. "When I told my mom I'd been assigned to the Raleigh RAIC, she wanted to know why they called it a 'rack office.' She thought it might have something to do with racketeering."

Luke and Gil laughed. "My mom wanted to know why we pronounce it 'rack' when there's an *i* in there." Gil's mom was an English teacher, so this didn't surprise Zane in the slightest.

"Faith thinks our terminology is ridiculous." Luke rolled his eyes. His wife of six months never failed to take the opportunity to get in a friendly dig at the Secret Service. The FBI and Secret Service didn't exactly have a track record of friendly relations, but they got along fine in Raleigh. "I told her it was faster to say 'RAIC office' than to say 'resident office' and way faster than saying 'resident agent in charge' office, but she didn't buy it."

"How close are the new agents to being ready to come to work?" Zane asked.

"Two months for one. Six months for the other two," Gil answered.

When the Secret Service hired special agents, they spent months in training, first at the Federal Law Enforcement Training Center, known as FLETC, in Georgia and then at the service's own training facility in Virginia.

After completing their training, agents entered the first phase of their career, usually in either a field office or one of the smaller resident offices throughout the country. In Phase 1, they worked more on the investigative side of the service's twofold mission to protect the president, vice president, and other high-ranking dignitaries and to investigate a variety of financial crimes, the most well-known being counterfeit currency.

Only after spending three to five years in Phase 1 were agents considered for the second phase of their career. In Phase 2, many agents were assigned protective details, either the PPD or the detail of the vice president, former presidents, or certain family members who required Secret Service protection. Others were assigned to investigative assignments focused on threats against the president.

After completing five years on the protective mission, most agents entered the third and final phase of their career. In Phase 3, they frequently took on supervisory and management roles—such as their own RAIC, Special Agent Jacob Turner—or they might return to a resident office as a senior investigator, which is what Special Agent Benjamin North had chosen to do.

Raleigh previously had several Phase 3 agents, but Jacob was the only one who'd survived the attacks on their office not so long ago. Luke was only a year or so from being considered for Phase 2, and Gil wouldn't be far behind him, so bringing in fresh agents was crucial to keeping the Raleigh RAIC strong.

The new agents would be green, but assuming they didn't balk at being sent to Raleigh, it would be a great training ground. After the office lost three agents in the space of a few weeks a year and a half ago, not many agents volunteered to move to Raleigh.

Benjamin North was the exception, but he was from North Carolina and in love with a local medical examiner, so he had more reason than most to take the risk.

"We still have a crap reputation in DC?" Luke had always been good at following Zane's train of thought, even when he hadn't spoken out loud.

"It's not as bad as it was. There's still some chatter about Raleigh attracting an inordinate amount of drama for the size of the office. Most agents go their entire careers without being shot at." Zane waved a finger in a circle to include Luke, Gil, and himself. "All three of us have actually been shot. And let's not get into the grenades and bombs."

Gil ran a hand through his hair. "Which is why the prospective agents wanted details on how safe we feel working here."

"I don't doubt it." Zane leaned against the doorjamb. "But we have an excellent investigative reputation. And we've gone almost a year without any mayhem."

"But now the president's coming to town." Luke frowned. "I hope our streak of 'days without an agent being shot at' continues."

Zane shoved away from the door and entered the conference room in time to see Rodriguez sidle up to Tessa.

Luke nudged Zane's elbow. "You can't shoot him."

There Luke went, reading his mind again. "How did you know I was thinking about that?"

"Your poker face is nonexistent when it comes to Tess. Might want to rein it in."

Maybe he was tired of reining it in.

Tessa gave Rodriguez a smile so fake, a two-year-old wouldn't be fooled by it and moved to the opposite side of the conference room table.

Her gaze landed on Zane. She widened her eyes and furrowed her brow in an expression he knew was her "what's wrong with that guy?" combined with "that guy is a creep" look. Then she looked away and resumed her professional demeanor.

Zane didn't bother to hide his laughter as he took a seat and waited for the meeting to begin.

# 4

TESSA TOOK A SEAT at the head of the conference table and pretended to scan her notes. The next few moments were critical to her success with this assignment. She was more than qualified, but there was no way around the reality that these men, every single one of them, had more experience than she did.

*Father, I need you. I need you to calm my nerves. I need you to steady my heart. I need you to help me remember everything I spent hours studying last night.*

She cleared her throat, and the room went still. All eyes on her. After introducing the other members of the advance team, Special Agents Rodriguez and Carver, to the Raleigh agents, Tessa launched into delegation mode.

"We have sixteen threats to follow up on. With more expected as we approach the president's arrival on Friday." She glanced at her notepad. "Special Agent Rodriguez—"

"Please. Call me Patrick."

She stifled a groan. She'd spent a painful minute with him prior to the meeting and had already learned that he had a real knack for making normal statements sound like come-ons. He was good-looking, he knew it, and he spoke with the self-assurance of a man who was used to being admired and assumed she would fawn over him as well.

She didn't doubt his skill. The Secret Service didn't hand out PPD positions to undeserving people. But arrogance rolled off Rodriguez like a malignant fog. Tessa gave him a smile, and he beamed at her. *If he thought that smile was genuine, I should get an Oscar for this performance.*

She flicked a glance in Luke's direction. He accepted his fate with a wink. "Rodriguez and Powell, I've sent four to your email. The PID has addresses, and all are within an hour of the event site."

Rodriguez gave her a smarmy smile. "Yes, ma'am."

Luke's smile was real, warm, and if she wasn't mistaken, proud. Of her. "Yes, ma'am."

"Carver, you and Dixon have the three the PID think are the least valid threats. They appear to have come from three different individuals, but they share an IP address and the PID suspects the individual is a minor. You'll probably get to have a fun conversation with parents."

Which was why she'd given the assignment to Gil. Gil was charming, funny, and had a disarming way of getting people to open up to him. She didn't have a read on Carver yet beyond that he was quiet and observant.

"You got it, boss." Gil's grin was full of mischief as he turned to Carver. "This just means there's something far worse in our in-box."

"That's been my experience as well." Carver inclined his head in her direction. "What else do you have for us?"

"One potential threat that may have legs. You'll need to talk to PID. They're still digging and hope to have more by the time you finish with your first objective."

She turned to Benjamin. "Please remember that you volunteered."

Benjamin's low, laughter-laced voice rumbled around the table. "I never go back on my word, Tess. I'll take care of it."

"You'll be careful while you do it."

"Yes, ma'am."

"What did you give him?" Luke asked with unveiled nosiness.

"Three ladies whose threats were of a more"—Benjamin pursed his lips—"personal nature."

"Three?" At Tessa's confirmation, Gil continued. "That seems unusual."

"Apparently they made a pact, and they intend to see it through. Indications are that there was some substance abuse involved when they made their threats. I'm hoping a quick visit will eliminate them from the board."

"What makes you the man for this particular job?" Rodriguez sounded annoyed that he didn't get the assignment. What was wrong with him?

Benjamin gave Rodriguez a flat look. "Patrick, I know you don't want to discuss what happened the last time you took one of these cases."

All the charm oozed right off Rodriguez. "Those women were nuts."

"Yeah." Benjamin agreed with his words, but not with his expression.

Was that why Benjamin had volunteered? There was a story lurking behind the words, and Tessa wanted to hear it. But not now.

"Jacob wants to go with you, Benjamin. He says it's been too long since he was out in the field."

"I'd be happy to have him along."

"Thank you." Tessa turned from Benjamin to Zane. "You and I will take the walk-through of the estate this morning, then we'll tackle the rest of the threats on the board. There's one in particular that I couldn't assign to anyone else."

Zane dropped his head and pretended to bang it on the table. "Tess. You wouldn't."

"Oh, but I would. And I did."

Gil and Luke laughed, and Luke pounded Zane on the back in mock sympathy.

"Somebody want to fill us in?" Rodriguez didn't much care for being out of the loop.

"He's a regular." Every area had them. Individuals who ran their mouths enough that the Secret Service kept them on their radar but who had been deemed to be minimal threats. They were usually attention seekers.

"He loves Zane," Luke chimed in with a laugh. "He doesn't want to talk to anyone else. Threw a can of Spam at me when I went to check on him a few months ago. I explained that Zane was in DC now, and the poor guy was so upset, I felt sorry for him. I promised him I'd have Zane check in if he was ever in town."

"He makes vague threats against the administration, random senators, representatives, and occasionally foreign heads of state. But he's been doing it for years and has never made any move to follow through." Gil turned to Tessa. "I'm so glad you saved him for Zane."

"It was the least I could do."

Zane muttered under his breath, but there was no real heat in the glare he fixed on her. "Fine. But do we have any real threats in our stack?"

"Sadly. Yes." She tapped the file in front of her. "The PID sent me an update this morning. This one isn't from social media but from chatter the NSA intercepted. From what they've sent, it looks like the prospect of the president being in a smaller venue has some people thinking it will be easier to get to him. Which is why we're starting with the walk-through. The owners have given us full access. We need to be there at ten."

Zane gave her a quick chin lift and scribbled something on his legal pad. Probably the beginnings of a list of questions he wanted to ask or things he wanted to investigate while they were there. The man loved his lists.

She looked around the room. "Please check in with me as you complete your assignments. I anticipate having more for you before the end of the day. Any questions?"

When no one asked anything, she stood. "Happy hunting."

**AN HOUR AND A PIT STOP** for lattes later, Zane and Tessa pulled onto the grounds of the Carmichael estate.

To the best of Zane's knowledge, the Carmichaels didn't refer to their home as an estate. But with a seven-thousand-square-foot main house, a guesthouse that had been the original home on the site and was now listed on the national historic register, two pools, stables, a putting green, and gardens tended by a horticulturist who used to work at the Biltmore Estate in Asheville, it wasn't difficult to understand how it had gained the grandiose moniker.

"Ever been here?" Zane asked as the gates swung open.

"No. You?"

"First week on the job. The president was the vice president at the time. It wasn't a fundraiser, and it wasn't publicly known that he was here. He came in for dinner and left. His detail handled most of it. My job was standing post at an exterior door."

"Your favorite."

"It wasn't so bad. I knew that I didn't know enough to be anywhere else on the grounds. At that stage I just tried to keep my eyes and ears open and my mouth shut."

Tessa frowned in apparent confusion. "I'm sorry, but I would need to see proof of that. Did anyone get you on video?"

"Standing post?"

"No. Of you keeping your mouth shut."

He'd walked right into that one. She flashed an impish grin, but he didn't have an opportunity to respond before the door opened.

"Agents Reed and Thacker, I presume?" The man who ushered them inside wore a suit, bow tie, and shoes polished bright enough to make a general jealous. "Mr. Carmichael is on the phone, but he asked if you would be so kind as to indulge him. He will be with you in no more than ten minutes. He would like to show you the estate personally."

"Of course." Tessa inclined her head ever so slightly in a manner that conveyed respect without in any way diminishing her own authority. It was something she had mastered prior to joining the Secret Service, and it had served her well.

"My name is Graham. Would you care for some refreshment while you wait? Coffee? Water? Tea?"

"No. But thank you."

"Please feel free to sit if you wish." Graham left them in a room the size of a small gymnasium.

"You could play basketball in here." Tessa's lips twitched.

"I was thinking the same."

"I know."

"How could you possibly know that?"

"You have a habit of sizing up spaces based on athletics. A room is the size of a racquetball court, a tennis court, or a basketball court. Outdoor spaces are the size of a baseball field or a football field."

"Do I do that?"

Her laughter, soft and low, held no censure or sarcasm. Nothing but pure amusement. "You all do it. Luke, Gil. Even Jacob."

"Huh." He'd never realized he did that.

"Although playing basketball in this room would be a crime. This is a room that calls for soft music, the tinkle of crystal, and gentle conversation."

Zane tried to see it the way she did. It was a space designed for entertaining, with chairs and sofas arranged in groupings that would allow for a few to sit and talk while leaving room for most of the guests to mingle. "I get that. This room is comfortably formal. It isn't so elegant that you'd be afraid to sit on the furniture. But it doesn't say, 'Let's sing karaoke' either."

Tessa moved around the room, pausing at random intervals to study a floral arrangement or piece of art. "The last time you were in the vicinity of a karaoke machine, I thought I was going to have to peel that blonde off you."

"As I recall, you threatened to remove her hands . . . at the wrists." Zane would never forget it. It was classic Tessa. "That poor woman probably still has nightmares."

"As she should." Tessa gave no quarter. "If anyone, male or female, says no, the answer is no. And you were being far too much of a gentleman for her to see things clearly. I"—Tessa ran a hand across a marble end table, her fingernails clicking in a soft beat as she walked by—"simply ensured that she got the message."

"By threatening dismemberment."

"I stand by it." She studied a landscape on the wall.

Zane chuckled. "Thanks for keeping me safe. You're the best."

"So you've said." Her airy tone was a stark contrast to her rigid spine.

"Tess."

"Yes?"

She continued to be absorbed in the art on the walls, so he joined her. "What's so interesting about this painting?"

"It's a print."

"Okay."

"Not a painting."

"Is that what makes it interesting?"

"Maybe. All the others are paintings. Oil. This is the only print. And I know this particular work. It's lovely, but there's no status to be claimed in exhibiting a print. The other paintings on these walls aren't by an artist I'm familiar with. Possibly someone local or someone the homeowners support. The other pieces are lovely and suit the room perfectly. This one is fine. It doesn't clash. But for some reason, it feels wrong in this space."

She shook her head, as if trying to clear it, and gave him a rueful smile. "It's probably nothing of note."

"I disagree. It is worth noting. It may not be pertinent to our mission here, but it's a detail I never would have picked up on even if you'd left me in this room for a week."

Tessa's powers of observation were well-known in the Raleigh office. By the time the president came and went, her skills would be well-known in DC as well.

Zane turned toward the door as a faint tapping of shoes on the wood floor grew louder. Tessa joined him. Marshall Carmichael strode into the room, hand outstretched toward Tessa. "Special Agent Reed." He shook her hand, then turned to Zane. "Special Agent Thacker. My apologies."

"We've been enjoying this lovely space, Mr. Carmichael." Tessa indicated a painting on the far wall. "Do you mind telling me about the artist?"

It could have been a trick of the light, or his imagination, but Zane thought there was a flicker of hesitation on Carmichael's face. "A friend. A fraternity brother, in fact. We called him Toto. He had quite a way of capturing the beauty of our state."

Carmichael pointed to the print that bothered Tessa. "His best work, in my opinion, goes there. But it was damaged by a guest and is being restored. I'm hoping it will be back in its usual position before Friday. The president was in the same fraternity and knew the artist. It's one of the last paintings Toto completed prior to his death. It's hard to explain, but I miss seeing it." He clapped his hands together. "Enough of an old man's reminiscing about the glory days. I delayed us long enough. Where would you like to begin?"

They began in the basement, moved to the ground floor, the second floor, the third floor, and then the attic before walking the grounds. Then they spent another two hours going over security details for the event.

Anyone who welcomed a sitting president into their home had to be prepared for an invasion of privacy. But when the president was joined by fifty of his most loyal—and generous—supporters, along with their plus-ones? The invasion was more of an assault that stripped everything bare.

Zane and Tessa were standing outside on the expansive front porch as they walked through the entry procedures for the president's visit when a news van pulled into the circular driveway. Zane recognized the reporter who exited the vehicle. Hank Littlefield. His cameraman barely took time to close his door before he settled the camera on his shoulder and started recording.

Tessa turned her back to the reporter, and Zane mimicked her motion.

"Special Agent Reed? Is that you? Tessa?" Littlefield called out in a loud voice.

*Tessa?* Since when did Littlefield know Tess?

Tessa made a sound that bore a suspicious resemblance to a growl before turning. "Hank. How are you?"

# 5

IF THE GROUND opened up and swallowed her whole, it would be a mercy.

Instead, Tessa pasted on a smile that she could only hope wouldn't give Hank the wrong idea. Unfortunately, in her limited experience, everything gave Hank the wrong idea.

He jogged toward them. When he was a few feet away, he opened his arms and gave her his most camera-worthy smile. No. He couldn't be planning to hug her. Could he?

He was.

She stuck out a hand in an effort to thwart him, but he never reached her.

Zane stepped between them, hand outstretched. "Hank Little-field, right? Nice to meet you."

Hank drew up short. She wanted to laugh at the way he was taken aback but was trying to hide it. He shook Zane's hand but kept his eyes on her. "Tess—"

"We're big on freedom of the press," Zane said to the camera-man, "but we'd prefer not to be included in your B-roll. Could you drop the camera for a minute, please?" The cameraman complied. "Thanks, man. You got a name?"

The cameraman frowned at Zane before replying. "Vince."

"Vince. Good to meet you. And you too, Hank."

"Tess—"

"What are you doing here, Hank?"

He winked at her in a way that seemed to indicate he was letting her in on a secret. "Heard there was a story."

"So you show up uninvited and climb out of the van with a camera rolling?"

"*You're* here."

"What does my presence here have to do with anything?"

"Come on, Tess." Hank's good-old-boy routine was about as charming as the drool dripping from an attack dog's jaws. "I can do the math. You investigate financial crimes. There must be something going on with Carmichael. That's news."

A quick look at Zane, and she could almost hear his commentary in her head. *"It's unprofessional to roll your eyes, Princess."* She dug deep and managed to keep her tone civil, if a bit chilly. "How did you get on the estate property?"

Hank grinned. "I have my ways. Come to dinner with me, and I'll share *all* my secrets."

In answer, Tessa stepped into the house and called out, "Graham?"

Graham appeared at the end of the entryway. "Ma'am? Are you in need of assistance?"

"Graham, Mr. Hank Littlefield and his cameraman are at the front door."

Graham, the urbane and sophisticated, morphed before her eyes into Graham, the ferocious and infuriated. He darted to the front door and jogged down the stairs. "Leave. Now."

Zane edged closer to Tess so they were standing shoulder to shoulder, but he made no move to stop Graham as he charged toward Hank. Technically, she and Zane had no legal right to force Littlefield from the premises. It was private property, but they weren't the owners.

Graham, however, could act on behalf of his employer.

He held up a hand when Hank tried to speak. "Mr. Littlefield, if you do not remove yourself from the property this instant, I will be forced to contact law enforcement." Graham, his demeanor both sophisticated and infuriated, glanced over his shoulder at her and Zane. "I have every confidence these agents will confirm that you have insinuated yourself where you are most assuredly not wanted."

Hank spluttered and postured, but Graham had him on the ropes. Zane leaned closer and whispered, "I'm loving this guy. Do you think we could steal him away from Carmichael?"

"For the office?"

"No. For us. I've always wanted a butler."

Hank pointed toward Tessa as he backed toward the news van. "I'll call you. We'll have a drink."

Tessa didn't bother responding. She hadn't had a drink in almost sixteen months, and she had no plans to ever have another one. But she wouldn't even sip a Coke with Hank Littlefield. Ever.

Graham stood sentry until the van drove away, then he turned smartly and marched toward them. "Special Agent Reed, Special Agent Thacker. My apologies."

"No need, Graham. You were magnificent." Tessa wanted to hug him, but the poor man might faint from the impropriety of it, so she settled for a wink.

Graham blushed.

"However, we do need to speak to Mr. Carmichael about this. And see the security footage you have of the gate. If Hank Littlefield managed to drive straight to the front door, then you have a security issue. Normally, that would be your business to handle, but under the present circumstances, we'll need to be involved."

"Of course, ma'am. Right this way."

Fifteen minutes later, they had their answer. They watched the footage as Hank Littlefield slid through the gates on the bumper of a delivery van.

"I can't make out the logo." Tessa studied the screen. "What's in the van?"

"Tables and linens for the event." Graham shook his head in disgust. "Someone on the staff gave them access but either didn't watch to ensure that no one else entered or didn't report it when Mr. Littlefield followed. Either way, it *is* a breach of our security protocol."

Tessa already knew that the security on this estate, while extensive, wasn't as heavily monitored as she had expected. It wasn't anything the Secret Service couldn't handle, but it would require more manpower.

When Graham excused himself to make a phone call, Tessa turned to Zane. "We'll need to borrow some uniforms."

"Agreed. I'll make a call when we get to the car. Local law enforcement has already been looped in, but we'll make sure they know we're going to need a heavy presence." Zane paced the small room. "I was hoping we could keep the visit under wraps, but . . ."

"No chance of that now." Tessa leaned against the desk. "Littlefield is an eager beaver. He won't leave this alone." The unmistakable *thwump-thwump* of a helicopter flying low overhead filled the room. "And we'll need that no-fly zone put in place a few days earlier than planned."

Zane pointed to the ceiling. "How much you want to bet that's the news chopper, and Hank's going to be on at four, five, six, and eleven tonight, sharing all that he doesn't know with the good people of Raleigh?"

Tessa dropped her head back. "He is such a nuisance."

"How do you know him?"

Tessa forced herself not to grin as she lifted her head and looked at Zane. He had almost managed to pull off a casual query.

Almost.

But there was raging curiosity—and if Tessa didn't know better, she would have said a strong vein of jealousy—slicing through his words.

"I was asked to provide input to the school board on their school shooting response plan. My name came up in a public meeting, and next thing I know, he's following me around town, showing up at the office, slobbering for an interview with me about what it's like to be a female in the Secret Service."

"Which you declined." There was no mistaking the delighted satisfaction in Zane's voice.

"Repeatedly."

**"THAT MAN WANTS** more than an interview." Zane could hear the grumble in his tone.

Tessa cut her eyes at him. "In my experience, most men do."

The unspoken "except you" landed softly.

She didn't know the full story, though. Sure, he'd put her health, healing, and happiness in front of his own desires. He'd traded any hope of romance for friendship. He had no regrets. It had been the right call. The honorable path.

That didn't mean he didn't wish things were different at least twenty times a day.

But, as her friend, he had the right to hassle her about this.

Didn't he? Luke would. So would Gil. If they knew. He'd have to ask Luke tonight.

Before he could question her further, Carmichael entered the room, Graham close on his heels. The next two hours were spent in intense discussion. The security situation turned out to be a simple case of the guard monitoring the gate needing to answer the call of nature. Apparently he left his post a few times a day, and it had never been an issue before.

For the next week, all entry codes would be deactivated. No one would be allowed in unless the guard opened the gate. If he wasn't available, the guest would have to wait.

After the president left, the codes would be reset and a new procedure put in place.

Mr. Carmichael walked Tessa and Zane to their car. "I'm embarrassed by what happened today, Agents. But also weirdly relieved. This is something that needed to be brought into the light and resolved."

"There's no need for embarrassment, Mr. Carmichael." Tessa pointed toward the house. "This is your home, and your security is designed to accommodate a busy household. There's nothing about this that we can't handle with regard to the president's visit. We're used to venues with significantly less security in place. The real issue is that Hank Littlefield seems to think he has permission to come onto private property in search of a story."

"Yes." Carmichael's friendly demeanor shifted into that of the shrewd businessman he undoubtedly was. "My lawyer is already drafting a complaint to the news station. And a cease-and-desist order for the sheriff's department to enforce. Mr. Littlefield will rue this day. I'll make sure of it."

They said their goodbyes, and neither spoke until Tessa drove through the gate.

"Remind me never to tick off Marshall Carmichael." Zane pulled his phone from his pocket.

Tessa's tense laughter broke off as her phone buzzed on the console. "Would you see who that is?"

Zane grabbed her phone and entered the password. She hadn't changed it since she'd handed it to him the day he drove her to rehab. He should suggest she choose a new one, but he liked that she hid nothing from him.

Or did she?

Dinner tonight?

The text, and the sender, mocked him. He took a few seconds to breathe. He wasn't her keeper. He was her friend. "Someone with the initials RK wants to know if you'd like to have dinner tonight."

Tessa blew out a slow, exasperated breath. "What does it take?" She executed a left turn. "I want to know. What does it take for a man to get the point? I'm not interested. I'm not going to be interested. I don't think it's a cute game we're playing."

"Who is he?"

"A guy I met at a meeting."

"I thought you weren't supposed to see people from meetings. Socially."

"I wish it was prohibited. It would make my life a lot easier."

So would having a wedding band on her finger. It wouldn't stop everyone, but it would serve as a deterrent. Zane's stomach clenched at the thought of anyone staking that kind of claim on Tess.

*She's mine.*

The thought pinged through his brain and heart and left him staring out the window. They'd agreed. Friendship. Nothing more.

She didn't have to worry about him hitting on her or things getting weird.

It would be okay. He just had to get through this week. When he returned to DC, he'd throw himself into his work and she'd never be the wiser. It was easier to behave like her friend and not some overprotective Neanderthal over texts and phone calls.

"Zane? Hello?"

"Huh?"

"Where'd you go?" Tessa's query was tinged with laughter. "I wasn't ranting to hear myself talk. I want an answer."

"Sorry. Brain's in overdrive."

"That's okay."

The silence stretched as he struggled to remember what she had asked him that had brought on his moment of terrible clarity.

"Well?"

"Well what?"

"Is it a state secret or something? Do they pull you aside when you're fifteen and tell you it's part of the bro code that you can never share the key to getting a guy to back off?"

Ah. That's what she wanted to know. "Of course not. Kids are growing up faster, so that conversation happens at twelve these days."

She smacked his arm. "I'm serious."

"You think there's a supersecret bro code?"

She flexed her hands on the steering wheel, and he stifled a laugh.

This he could do. Verbal sparring, teasing, messing around. This was safe territory. "Okay, fine. I know you were joking. But you already know what the problem is. You're too nice."

"I am *not* too nice."

"You are. That's why you have so many admirers. Rodriguez,

Hank, and this RK guy. You're nice, and guys are attracted to that."

Her hands spasmed on the wheel. "I told him I wasn't interested. I shouldn't have to be cruel to get my point across."

"I agree. How often is he asking you out?"

She waved a hand toward the phone he still held in his hand. "Look for yourself."

He scrolled through the texts. "He's been asking you once every couple of weeks for months."

"Yes."

"And you stopped responding last month. After"—Zane glanced at the phone—"warning him that you had nothing further to say."

"Yes."

"Block him."

"He comes to meetings. Every week. He's hard to avoid. He acts like we've had a conversation when all I've done is said hello or good morning."

"I think blunt honesty would be wise in this case. Tell him you aren't interested and won't be interested and that his texts bother you. Tell him if they continue, you'll block his number. And speak to your sponsor about helping to keep him away from you at meetings."

"Yeah."

"Want me to do it?" It would be his pleasure.

"No. I'll do it later. Thanks."

They rode in silence for a minute before Zane asked, "So, what *are* you doing for dinner?"

# 6

"I HAVE PLANS." Tessa didn't look at Zane, but she knew him well enough to know that he didn't like her answer. She thought about torturing him further but couldn't do it. "So do you."

"I do?"

"Yes. Luke's place. Gil's cooking, I think. I wasn't clear on the details. As long as Faith isn't cooking, we're safe."

"Gil would never do that to me. Neither would Luke."

"True." Faith was one of Tessa's best friends, but she couldn't cook to save her life. She tried, bless her, but there was a reason Luke had taken cooking lessons from Gil before he and Faith were married.

"I thought we might as well eat there, and Faith and Ivy are anxious to see you. But I warned them that I'm planning to go back to the office after dinner."

"Sounds good. I need to go over my notes and send a report back to DC."

They pulled into Luke's driveway ten minutes later.

Faith stood in the doorway and waved at them, her motions indicating that they should hurry inside.

Zane joined Tessa as they half walked, half jogged to the door.

His hand was on her lower back. "This isn't giving me the warm, fuzzy feeling I was hoping for." His breath tickled her ear, and she fought the tremble that threatened to betray her.

"I really hope this doesn't ruin your dinner," Faith said in greeting as they reached the front porch. "Gil's outdone himself."

"What's going on?" Tessa asked.

"TV."

Tessa turned to Zane. "I'm going to kill him."

"I'll help you." His hand moved from her lower back to her elbow, and she wasn't sure if it was for her benefit or his. Regardless, they entered the den and found the entire gang in a semicircle around the TV mounted on the wall.

A few muttered greetings were exchanged as Luke hit Play. Then the room was silent except for Hank Littlefield's grating voice. How long had he been filming? The first shots came from the helicopter footage and showed the estate, before switching to a view of her and Zane standing at the front door. Badges gleaming. Weapons clearly visible.

"The Carmichael estate is the scene of an investigation by the US Secret Service." Hank Littlefield's voice-over continued as the footage shifted to a close-up of Tessa. Her hair was blowing back from her face, and her expression was one of intense focus.

Ivy Collins, Gil's wife and the CEO of her own cutting-edge prosthetics design firm, was on Tessa's right. She bumped her elbow and whispered, "It's like you're a supermodel agent."

Tessa didn't respond. She'd lost the capacity for speech. Hank Littlefield mentioned her name four times in the few seconds the footage rolled. This wasn't news. The only fact he had available to him was that the Secret Service had agents on the property.

"We've been able to confirm that Special Agent Reed and her associate remained on the premises for several hours. We're still working to confirm the details regarding the case against Marshall Carmichael and will report it as soon as our investigation is complete."

Littlefield signed off, and the news switched to a story about a local knitting group.

Luke and Gil stood in matching poses. Hands on their waists. Expressions somber. "Tess." Luke had nominated himself as spokesperson, but the others were clearly in agreement. "We've given him a long leash. We're done."

Tessa appreciated their big-brother attitudes. She'd always wanted a brother, and the last place she'd expected to find one was at her job. She'd expected coworkers and brothers-in-arms—and Luke, Gil, and now Benjamin were that. But they were more. They respected her abilities but also looked out for her. Not because she was a woman. They all did it. She looked out for them too. And if the roles were reversed, she would be livid and ready to act on their behalf.

"I appreciate it. I do. But Carmichael already talked to his lawyers this afternoon. My guess is this will be pulled from the air and the internet, and I wouldn't be surprised to see an apology issued."

"And that has what to do with you, exactly?" Gil frowned in mock confusion. "I'm not worried about his professional life. I'm worried about you."

"What do you want me to do? Get a restraining order? I can take care of myself. He has no chance with me. He'll figure that out. Eventually."

"I'm starting to think he won't." Luke turned to Zane. "This guy is a problem."

Zane was a statue beside her. "I got that. The question is why I'm just now getting it."

Gil and Luke exchanged a look. "The situation devolved rapidly, and you were out of the country."

Luke picked up the thread from Gil. "We'd planned to discuss it with you this week."

What was going on? Were they checking up on her and reporting to Zane? "Please tell me you're joking right now." She focused on Zane.

"What?"

"Do you expect them"—she waved a hand at Luke and Gil—"to tell you what's going on in my life?"

"No. But I assumed they would let me know if there was an issue."

"Why is that, exactly?"

"For the same reason I would expect Luke to rat on Gil. Or for you to rat on Luke. We're a team. We don't have to live in the same state for that to be the case."

Faith stepped into the small circle that the four of them had made. "Tess. No one is going behind your back. But we've all been concerned about Hank Littlefield. And yes, these guys are looking out for you. And yes, they are telling Zane how they think you're doing. But you're doing the same thing. Last week you told Luke how tired Zane is and that you're worried he's working too many hours."

Zane turned to her. "You did what?"

Before Tessa could defend herself, Gil squeezed between her and Zane. "Bottom line, we're all nosy, bossy control freaks who have come too close to losing each other, and we're all up in each other's business. I'm not sure why either of you are surprised by this. But you can work that out on your own time. I've cooked a fabulous meal, and I don't want it ruined." He started walking them toward the dining room. "Sit. Eat."

**THIRTY MINUTES LATER,** Zane leaned back in his chair and groaned. "I'm going to have to run an extra five miles in the morning."

Luke, Gil, and Benjamin all mimicked his position. Faith sipped her water and tilted the glass in Gil's direction. "Delicious, as always."

No one spoke for a solid minute. No tension. No stress. Just good friends enjoying one another's company enough that there was no need to fill every moment of silence with chatter.

Tessa scooted her chair away from the table, breaking the moment. "Duty calls."

"What's got a burr under your saddle, Tess?" Benjamin asked from the far end of the table. "You're doing great. And you can't do anything about the news coverage. It is what it is. Let it go."

Zane watched the exchange with interest. He didn't know Benjamin well, but he did know Tessa respected him as an agent and liked him as a person.

"Thank you." She inclined her head in his direction. "I appreciate it. But I didn't intend to be at the Carmichael estate all afternoon. I have about two hours of work to do that can't wait, because there's a good chance tomorrow will be as random as today was."

"True enough." Benjamin settled his arm around the back of the chair where his wife, Dr. Sharon Oliver, sat. "But this week is going to be a marathon. You'll need to prioritize rest whenever you can."

"I'm going back to the office with her." Zane stood. "I'll make sure she goes home."

Tessa's eyes flashed with something that was not good-natured teasing. "You'll . . . make sure?"

He held his hands up in surrender. "I'll strongly encourage you to make that decision for yourself."

"Better." She shared a look with Faith and Ivy that he couldn't quite make sense of. She was exasperated, but not angry, but maybe a little hurt, and he had no idea where that was coming from.

This was not like her. Tessa was all over the emotional map tonight. One minute she was teasing him and conversation was easy. Then she was taking everything he said the wrong way and biting his head off over nothing. He wasn't looking forward to working for several more hours, but if it gave him an opportunity to get to the bottom of her mood, he'd take it.

They said their goodbyes, and he climbed into the car beside her. He closed the door, snapped his seat belt, and turned to face her.

"I'm not your apprentice." Tessa was calm. Her tone measured. "I'm not a child. I do not need to be managed. Not by anyone, but especially not by you. That"—she flung a hand toward the house—"was embarrassing."

Zane sat back in his seat. "Tess, that's not—"

"And that nonsense about Luke and Gil not telling you about Hank Littlefield? Please. You really are checking up on me, aren't you? What's the deal? Don't think I can hack it without you here? Or is it that you don't trust me to stay sober if there's a hint of adversity in my life, so you're trying to manage me from afar?"

She put the car in reverse with enough force that Zane wouldn't have been surprised if the gearshift had bent.

"Tess—"

"Is that what the past six months have been to you? All the texts and phone calls? Was that a way to check up on me to be sure I hadn't strayed from the path or gotten into a situation where I was in danger of taking a drink?"

There was the hurt.

"Tess. Pull over. Please."

"No."

"Tess. You can't dump all this on me and not give me an opportunity to say something."

She didn't speak, but she pulled into the clubhouse parking lot of Luke and Faith's subdivision and slammed the car into park. "Fine. I'm all ears."

Zane got out of the car, walked around to the driver's side, and opened Tessa's door. "Walk with me?"

Her eyes widened, but she climbed from the car and joined him on the small walking path.

"Tess?" Zane paused to see if she would interrupt again. But she remained quiet. "Where is this coming from? We're friends. I'm not your keeper. I'm not your sponsor. And I'm not trying to manage you. Why do you think I am? You sound hurt and angry, and frankly, I don't think I deserve either of those things. If I've done something to earn your anger, please tell me what it is, because I can assure you it hasn't been intentional."

She kept her face tilted away from him, and she didn't respond immediately. He gave her time. She was here. She was walking beside him. She would talk when she was ready.

It was five minutes before she spoke. "I overreacted."

"Okay."

"I apologize."

"Apology accepted."

She blew out a long sigh. "I know what's wrong, but I'm not ready to discuss it."

Her words sent a chill through Zane's veins. "I'm safe, Tessa. We . . . I . . . I'll listen to anything. Help with anything."

"I know."

"Can I ask you something?"

"You can ask."

"Do you know when you'll be ready to discuss it? Can I expect us to talk this out this week while I'm here?"

She huffed. "I know you can't stand for anything to be unresolved. I won't make you wait forever. I need some time to process what I'm thinking and feeling. It's too soon."

This made no sense. None. What could be so bad that she had to process it before she shared it with him? They'd been sharing everything for months. Bad, good, goofy, somber. But she hadn't shut him out.

Or had she?

How would he know if she had? Phone calls and texts weren't the same as doing life with someone day in and day out. Maybe she was hiding more than he could imagine. "Can I say one more thing before we go back to the car?"

"Of course."

"There's nothing you can say to me that will break us."

She didn't respond, but the bleak expression on her face told him everything he needed to know.

She didn't believe him.

# —7—

**THERE WAS NO SHORTAGE** of idiocy in the world.

But the client for this job had received an extra healthy helping. How did any man who aspired to power not realize that his actions had consequences? And yet, time and time again, the rich, powerful, and influential made choices to engage in reckless and harmful behaviors.

And time and time again, their sins surely found them out.

A photo of Special Agent Tessa Reed stared back from the computer. Successful in a stressful, male-dominated profession. Physically stunning by any standard. The kind of woman men found highly desirable. And women found intimidating.

It was a shame, really.

The phone rang. The voice on the other end of the line was as familiar as a favorite sweater and as annoying as a scratchy scarf at the throat. "Did you get the information?"

"Yes."

"Will you take care of it?"

"Don't I always?"

TESSA NEEDED to get away from Zane. Far, far away. She was acting like an idiot.

No. She was acting like a girl with her first crush. She was so happy to see him, so thrilled to be with him, so angry at the thought that he was just staying connected to her because he wanted to keep an eye on her.

Because he didn't trust her not to fall into addiction again.

And if he didn't trust her, there was no hope for them. He'd told her about his mom, showed her the photographs that portrayed his mom's disintegration in full color. His mom had been vibrant. Now? She was shattered. Her mind fragmented by years and years of substance abuse. Her son loved her still, but he would never tie himself to a woman who couldn't stay sober.

But Tessa wasn't his mother. Her fall had been huge, but she'd seen it for what it was and stopped the descent before she lost everything. She took it seriously. She went to meetings. But her life was no longer controlled by the driving need for another drink.

And she thought he trusted her.

She also thought maybe she could be brave enough to test the waters of their friendship. To see if there was room for something more.

But she was deluding herself. The distance and space between them had given her a false sense of security. He would always see her as the broken bird he'd found and nursed back to health. Not as a woman who could take care of herself. And not as a woman who could lay claim to his heart.

The ache splintered through her chest. She hadn't realized how much she'd begun to hope. She'd always talked herself out of it before. But today, working with him, laughing with him. She'd thought maybe there was a chance.

Now she had to survive this week.

And she would have to tell him.

Zane didn't shy away from conflict. He took it head-on. Dealt with it. Moved on to the next thing. He wouldn't forget this conversation, and there was no way for her to avoid him.

She'd go home tonight. And pray for the strength to let him go.

**"GREG, HOW'S IT GOING?"** Zane bumped fists with the evening security guard before turning to Tessa. "I'll catch up in a second."

Tessa said hello to Greg but didn't stop. She was on a mission tonight. Hank Littlefield was going to go down. Zane didn't know how or when, but he knew Tess. She was furious, and she was going to make Littlefield pay.

"Heard you were back in town." Greg tilted his head toward the hall where Tessa had disappeared. "I'm guessing she's floating on the clouds now. You two look as cozy as ever."

Zane didn't bother to correct Greg. Lots of people thought they were together. "It's going to be a crazy week."

"So I hear."

"Did you catch the news tonight?"

"I don't watch the news. It's all bad, biased, or bogus."

Zane couldn't argue with him. "Okay. But do you know who Hank Littlefield is?"

"Pretty-boy reporter. Sure."

"He's not welcome on the property."

That got Greg's attention. "What's up?"

"He filmed us today. Tess is ticked. He'll probably have to issue some sort of retraction, but the damage is done. I doubt he would approach the building, but he seems to think he's got some kind of inside track with Tessa. If you see him, even if he's sitting in his car in the parking lot, let her know. Yeah?"

Greg quirked an eyebrow. "Let her know, or let you know?"

"Her first. Then me. If it's next week after I'm gone, make sure Leslie knows. She'll spread the word."

"You got it."

Five minutes later, Zane found Tessa in her cubicle. "I told Greg to let you know if he spots Hank Littlefield anywhere on the premises. And made sure Greg knows Hank isn't welcome."

"Good idea." She rubbed her eyes. "I cannot believe he got on the property. And then had the audacity to air something so . . . so nonexistent. What could he possibly be thinking? I was never going to go out with him before, but if I'd had any thoughts of saying yes, this would have quashed them. Permanently."

She was looking at him like she expected an answer. "Tess. There's no understanding him. Don't waste brain cells trying to apply logic to an illogical scenario."

"He irks me."

"Yeah. I got that."

She straightened in her chair. "I have work to do. I'm assuming you do too?"

"Yes. I'll stay as long as you do. Can you swing me by the hotel on your way home?"

"Of course."

They worked for the next ninety minutes in companionable silence. He'd always liked being in the office with Tess. She was smart and funny and could work circles around any agent he'd ever come across. Luke and Gil were excellent agents, but both of them had to take a break every hour or so. And he had to get up and walk. He couldn't think sitting or standing still.

But Tess could sit in that chair for hours. And when she did get up to get a drink or a snack, she could return to that place of focused effort almost immediately. He had no idea how she did it, but it made her very productive and effective.

"This is interesting." Tessa's voice floated to him through the cubicle walls.

Zane walked around the wall they shared. "What's interesting?"

She pointed to her screen. "This threat."

He leaned over her shoulder and fought the unexpected but intense urge to play with her hair while he read the email. Three lines in and all sense of play deserted him. "This is a threat against you."

"Yeah. I got that part."

He read the words again.

*To Whom It May Concern: The president of the United States deserves to be protected with diligence and courage, by men who respect the office and are willing to lay down their lives to preserve the life of the man legally chosen by the people of the United States of America. While we respect the efforts of the United States Secret Service, allowing women to fill this crucial role is beneath the dignity of the office they are called upon to protect. We saw the woman on the news tonight. She looks like a Barbie doll. What is she supposed to do? Bat her eyelashes at the bad guys until they give up? This is the only warning we will give. Remove the female agent from the protection detail on the president's visit to Raleigh, NC, or we will make sure she is unavailable to serve.*

Tessa pointed to herself. "In what universe do *I* look like a Barbie doll?"

There was no way he was going to answer that question, but when he didn't respond, she turned to face him. "Well?"

"I think the more important question is why that's the part of the threat you're fixated on. Who cares if they think you look like a Barbie doll? They're threatening to make sure you're unavailable to serve."

Tessa conceded the point, but her expression made it clear she wasn't happy about it. "Fine, but don't think you've gotten away with anything. You don't want to talk about the Barbie doll comment because you're afraid anything you say will get you in trouble."

There was no point in denying it. "You are one hundred percent correct."

She grumbled under her breath as she spun her chair to face her monitor, "I'm not a Barbie doll."

"So, I'm guessing calling you Barbie is out?"

Tessa straightened in her seat and responded with a clipped, "Do you have a death wish?"

Now wasn't the time to bring up that he only started calling her Princess after he overheard a young student at an elementary school tell Tessa that she looked like a Disney princess. Tessa had taken the remark as the compliment the little girl had intended, and while she never admitted it, he was almost certain she didn't mind him calling her Princess for the same reason. It was one of many secrets they shared, but unlike the painful events he held close and would never share, this was more of an inside joke. He knew for sure he was the only one who would ever call her that and get away with it. But he didn't say it often, because every time he did, and every time she accepted it as the endearment it was meant to be, it was like Cupid had released a crossbow bolt with precision aim at his heart.

Zane wanted to get to the bottom of why the Barbie comment bothered her so much, and normally he'd push to do that. But in the past year of their friendship, he'd learned that sometimes the full-force approach backfired.

Badly.

Subtlety wasn't his specialty, but he was capable of it. He was also not above changing the subject for no reason other than that he didn't want to fight with her. "Do you think I'd lose my job if I shot Hank Littlefield?"

Tessa didn't turn, but her shoulders shook in amusement.

"Note, I didn't say I would kill him. I wouldn't do that. Just take a little skin off. Probably from his rear."

Tessa's entire body was bouncing now, and her stifled laughter escaped in a muted giggle.

"You think I'm joking."

"In answer to the question you originally asked"—she gave him a pointed look that told him he wasn't off the hook for dodging the Barbie doll question—"yes, you would lose your job. And go to jail."

"Killjoy."

"That doesn't mean you can't find some other, less violent way of delivering appropriate retribution."

"Do you have something in mind?"

"No, but give me time. I'll come up with something."

"Fine. We'll do it your way." He tapped the back of her chair. "What do you want to do about the threat?"

"Constant vigilance?"

Now it was Zane's turn to laugh. "I was thinking something more like letting your team know. Tonight. And then taking reasonable precautions."

Tessa had her phone, and he could see her typing out a message to the other agents on the team. "And what would you consider to be reasonable?"

"Nothing too crazy."

Tessa cut her eyes to him and continued texting. "Not buying it."

"Fine. I don't think you should be alone."

She ignored him, hit Send on the text, and stood. "There's not much more I can do tonight. You ready to head out?" Tessa rolled her neck to the left, then to the right, then dropped her chin to her chest while she waited for him to gather his things. "I need a massage. Remind me to schedule one for next week."

Zane set his things back on the desk.

"Come here."

"What?"

He didn't wait for her to come to him. He took the two steps needed to reach her, spun her around so her back was to him, and settled his hands on her shoulders. "Relax."

She pulled in a deep breath, blew it out, and her shoulders dropped a good two inches. He kneaded the base of her neck. "Good grief. You weren't joking. How are you even able to move your arms? You're all knotted up."

"Hazards of the job." She angled her neck to give him better access to a tight spot. "And I carry all my stress in my neck and shoulders. Always have."

"I can tell." He moved his hands from her shoulders. "Come on. Sit. Let me work on you for a few minutes before we leave. You'll rest better."

She sat at her desk and flipped her hair so it fell in a wavy cascade over the back of the chair.

Zane swallowed. This was dangerous territory. They were alone, and he was touching her. Had that ever happened? He cleared his throat. "Besides the threat on you—which, by the way, we have not finished discussing—what have you been working on tonight?"

He tackled a pesky tight spot in her left shoulder.

"I reviewed what everyone did today. And lined up a new schedule for tomorrow that includes the visits we didn't get to and the new threats the PID forwarded this afternoon. The president is reasonably popular here, but there are a few bizarre ones in this bunch."

"I've only been in DC for seven months, and trust me—if you can imagine it, someone has threatened the president with it. One guy in the Midwest said he was going to drown the president in a grain silo."

Tessa dropped her head to the right. "How did he propose to get him into the silo?"

"Unclear."

"What else?"

"A group in Florida seemed to think the Everglades would be a great place for a long walk."

He found another knot and she winced. "I'm not a fan of swamps."

"Spent a lot of time in swamps, have you?"

"Fair point. To clarify, there's nothing about swamps that I find appealing."

"What? You don't want to wander around in one hundred percent humidity while mutant mosquitos suck your blood and alligators stalk your every move?"

"It's not the alligators. Or the mosquitos. Although neither of those sound great."

"Then what is it?"

"Snakes."

She shuddered, and Zane couldn't stop himself from laughing. He'd seen Tess afraid only once, and he never would have imagined she would have such a visceral reaction to a reptile. "How did I not know this about you?"

"I have no idea."

"You do realize that you're bigger than they are. And they're more afraid of you than you are of them."

"Nope. I'm definitely more afraid of them. I know there are good snakes." She made air quotes around the word *good* and spoke with the cadence of schoolchildren repeating memorized facts. "Snakes eat rodents and bugs. You should leave them alone if you find one in your garden."

"That's true."

"I don't care. That knowledge changes nothing. I cannot stand them. I don't even like thinking about them." Another tremor went through her. "One summer when we were in India, a friend and I were outside. There was a whole group of us playing a hide-and-seek game. We scattered to hide. I thought I'd found the best spot, so when the boy who was doing the seeking started yelling, I ignored him at first. I thought he was trying to cheat and make us come out before he found us, and I didn't want to give away my spot. But then I realized he wasn't joking. My friend had been bitten by a snake. She died that night."

Zane wrapped a hand around her neck, his thumb no longer pressing into the tight spots but sweeping back and forth across her nape. "I had no idea. I'm so sorry. And I'm sorry I made light of it. You have every right to your fear."

"It's okay." Her words were husky. She swallowed again, and the room suddenly felt too small, too hot, and far, far too intimate.

He should remove his hand from her neck and return to the safe ground of deep and abiding friendship.

He was usually good at doing what he should.

Why couldn't he do it now?

# — 8 —

ZANE HAD MAGIC HANDS. That was all there was to it. There was nothing inappropriate about what he was doing. Gil had picked up some tips from his physical therapist sister, Emily, and he was always willing to help work out a few kinks. Friends did this. Right?

Except, when Gil did it, he didn't stand so close. And he was usually saying something that made her laugh. Or she was threatening to kill him when he dug his thumb into a tight muscle.

Gil's hands never made her feel so safe that she was compelled to share her darkest secrets and deepest fears.

This was . . . other. She never wanted Zane to stop.

But she needed him to stop immediately before she turned around in her seat and did something she could never take back.

Why couldn't the phone ring? Or someone walk in and interrupt them? That's what always happened in books and movies. Where was a good old-fashioned interruption when she needed one?

But no. She was going to have to get out of this on her own. Drum up some willpower and pull away. Come up with something witty to say that would prevent any awkwardness later.

Zane moved his hands, and his thumbs pressed into her skull.

Her attempt at stifling a moan was wildly unsuccessful and his hands froze, then continued. So much for making things less weird. *Think about work. About the reason Zane is here. Say something. Anything.*

"How—" she started.

"What—" Zane spoke at the same time. They both laughed, and whatever was thickening the air with temptation and possibilities best left unexplored released its hold. He gave her neck one soft squeeze. "Better?"

"Yes. Much. Thanks."

"Anytime." He stepped back, and she got out of the way so he could get his stuff from the desk. She picked up the bag she'd dropped on the floor when Zane decided on the impromptu neck massage.

"What were you going to ask me?"

It took her a few seconds to remember. "Oh. I was going to ask if this level of threat and the types of threats we're seeing, if it seems high to you. Or if it's par for the course."

Zane joined her and they walked toward the exit. "I wish I could tell you it's normal, but there's something about it that feels off. There are threats all the time, but this seems excessive. The president is popular enough. He hasn't done anything rash or gone too far toward any particular ideology, but this threat we're tackling tomorrow has a darker undercurrent. Sometimes people spout off because we have free speech and they feel like they can say whatever they want. There's no intent behind it. But this? I don't like it."

"I agree. And I have a bad feeling Hank's stunt today may have poured fuel on the fire. And I'm not talking about the threat against me. I'm talking about the threats against the president."

"You're probably right."

"I was kind of hoping you'd give me all the reasons I'm wrong."

"Sorry. But if they didn't already know where the event will be taking place, anyone paying attention would be able to figure it out. In fact, it doesn't say much for Hank's supposed investigative skills that he thought we were there for a financial investigation."

"True."

What a lot of people didn't realize was that the agents on the protective detail didn't do financial investigations. They protected. That was it. The PID and local agents did most of the investigative work, even related to the threats that came up. And advance agents were involved in the investigations only on the front end as they tried to weed out the real threats from bogus ones. To anyone with an understanding of Secret Service methods, Zane's presence at the Carmichael estate could only mean one thing. The president of the United States was coming for a visit.

On top of that, when the local office was asked to assist on a protective assignment, all other work ceased. The Raleigh RAIC had only one objective for the next seven days. Protect the president. When he returned to DC in a week, the agents would resume work on their current cases, but until then, those investigations would wait. No one was interested in any financial crimes the Carmichaels may or may not have committed. Not this week, anyway.

And to Tessa's knowledge, the Carmichaels were clean. They were influential. And while they had some friends who walked the fine edge of shady, there was no evidence that the Carmichaels were anything other than what they appeared to be.

Zane waved at Greg but didn't slow down for a chat as they exited the building. "The president and Marshall Carmichael were fraternity brothers. They speak regularly and rarely about politics. It's all about their families and people they both know. Catching up. The way normal people do with someone they genuinely like. Carmichael will give us access to whatever we need. He wants the president to visit, and while I'm sure he'll benefit from it socially, financially, and professionally, I think he mostly wants to give his friend an easy evening. Some of these fundraisers are ridiculously stressful. The president has to be prepared to cover all kinds of topics and also keep the base happy. But this? A small number of already committed supporters, in the home of a decades-long friend? This should be a home run."

Zane had talked all the way to the car, but Tessa wasn't fooled. He was scanning the parking lot, searching for any sign of a threat.

"Zane, nothing's going to happen tonight."

"What makes you so sure?"

"The threat came in a few minutes ago. They'll need some time to pull it all together."

They discussed what kind of person would make such a ridiculous threat as Tessa drove Zane to the hotel. When she pulled into the circular drive and stopped in front of the valet station, she had a brief flashback to the last time they'd been here. They'd all been staying on the top floor as a protective measure. She and Zane had a huge fight. If she'd listened to him then, she could have spared both of them a lot of hurt. And maybe made it possible for them to explore something beyond friendship.

"Thanks for the ride." Zane climbed from the car. "I'll come in with Rodriguez and Carver tomorrow."

"Sounds like a plan. Good night."

"Night." He gave her a small salute and walked into the hotel lobby.

Tessa pulled away from the curb, but she didn't go straight home. It took her five minutes to spot the tail. She'd thought it was there earlier, but now she was sure. It might be pointless to lose them. It wouldn't be that difficult for anyone to discover where she lived, but she wasn't going to idiotproof it for them.

She lost the tail in four turns. It would be easy to think it was because of her prodigious driving skills, but it had more to do with the fact that she knew Raleigh roads better than most. She'd been intentional about learning them, and the effort served her well tonight.

She drove around for another fifteen minutes before she pulled into her parking garage. She paid a lot of money for her space and had considered dropping it. Right now, she was thankful for its proximity to the lobby. She walked in, nodded to the doorman, and took the elevator.

When the doors opened, the hall was clear. Her door appeared to be unmolested. She entered with her keycard and made short work of clearing every room. Only then did she slide out of her shoes and jacket. She dropped her badge and keys in the small bowl on the shelf by the door where she usually left them, but for now, she kept her weapon.

She should tell the guys. Not because she couldn't take care of herself, but because they were a team. She would string them up if they had a tail and didn't share. She walked to the fridge, grabbed a bottle of water, and guzzled it. Then she sat in her favorite chair and pulled out her phone.

**ZANE'S PHONE BUZZED,** and he yanked it off the nightstand by the bed. This group text hadn't been active in several months. It included Tessa, Luke, Gil, Benjamin, and him.

> Tessa
> Picked up a tail after dropping Zane off. Lost it fast. Not skilled. Took my time getting home. No evidence of anyone having been around. Apartment secure.

**Luke**
Want company?

> **Tessa**
> Thanks, but no. I'm going to call the doorman.
> Make sure he knows I'm not expecting guests.

**Gil**
What time are you planning to come in
tomorrow?

> **Tessa**
> I was planning to go for a bike ride first and
> come in around seven.

**Benjamin**
Do we really need to tell you not to do that?

> **Tessa**
> No. But I would still like to be in around seven.

**Luke**
I'll have Faith drop me off at 6:45. Don't shoot
me. And check in when you get up.

**Benjamin**
And if you wake up during the night.

**Gil**
Maybe you should take Luke up on his offer.

> **Tessa**
> Maybe you should all go to sleep now. I'm fine.
> I'll text you when I wake up. And I won't leave
> until Luke arrives.

Zane stared at his phone and forced himself not to open the

Uber app. She didn't need help. That didn't mean he didn't want to help. Or just be in the same space.

He opened a separate text to Tessa.

> Thanks for including me. You know I'll be there in a heartbeat.

I know. But I'm good. Why are you still up? You should be asleep.

> Whatever. Swing by here after Luke gets there. We'll ride in together. Spoke to Carver. He and Rodriguez don't plan to arrive until 8.

Will do. Go to bed.

> Bossy.

I'm putting my phone down. Good night.

> Night.

He dropped the phone on the nightstand and ran his hands over his face. He'd expected sleep to be elusive, but he slept hard until three. He checked his phone and found that the group text had continued after he'd gone to sleep, mostly with the guys checking on Tess at random points after midnight. The last text was from her and had come through ten minutes earlier.

> You're all idiots. I'm fine.

With that confirmation, he rolled over and slept until his alarm jerked him to consciousness three hours later. He hit snooze, then checked for texts. Nothing. Good. He rolled over and fell back asleep until the alarm went off nine minutes later.

He forced himself to get out of bed. Still no text from Tessa. She was supposed to text when she woke up. He stared at the phone.

He was being ridiculous. An idiot. What was wrong with him?

He didn't need to answer that. He already knew. With a frustrated groan at the cruelties of the world, he called Tessa.

"I literally just opened my eyes." Her sleep-smudged voice confirmed her statement.

The relief at hearing her voice sent his mood soaring. "Good morning to you too, Princess."

"Why do you hate me?" Her sleepy question was followed by a sound that could have been her getting out of bed but was more likely her settling back into a comfortable spot *in* the bed.

"I thought you planned to be in the office at seven?"

"So?"

"Doesn't it take you an hour to get ready?"

"It does not."

It so did. Zane waited.

"Shoot! It's already 6:10. Why didn't you call me earlier?"

"Ha. Ha." She didn't disconnect the call, and neither did he. He put her on speaker, and he could tell she'd done the same. "Sleep okay?"

"I did." A huge yawn. "Although we're going to need to have a chat today about overprotectiveness in the workplace."

"Sorry, Princess. We left coworkers behind a long time ago."

"I thought Luke and Gil were bad."

"Luke is the worst." Zane had personal experience with Luke's special brand of hovering.

"You'd think he would be. But you haven't spent much time with Benjamin."

"Does he hover?"

"No." The sound of the refrigerator opening followed by coffee splashing into a mug muffled her words. "But he likes the fact that we look out for each other outside the office. He fell right in with that. Luke twisted an ankle running last week and then drove himself to the doctor. It wasn't a big deal, but Benjamin read him the riot act when he finally checked in."

"Ha. Serves him right." Luke *did* hover. If you were his friend, he took that as tacit permission to get all up in your business. Especially if you got shot. Or blown up. Or had your house burn down. So, maybe Luke had some basis for his worry. "He wasn't limping yesterday."

"It was super minor. But Faith has a zero-tolerance policy for unreported injuries. He knew he needed to get the okay from the doctor or she'd never let him hear the end of it."

"That's why I love her." Zane adored Luke's wife, both for who she was as a person and for the way she loved his friend. Luke was a lucky man. Fortunately, Luke knew it and loved Faith with an intensity that had surprised all of them, perhaps Luke most of all.

"Me too." Faith and Tessa were close, and it wasn't unusual for them to combine a shopping trip with a stop at the shooting range.

Zane had pulled out his clothes for the day and draped them over the edge of the bed. "I have to get ready."

"Same."

"Call you back in ten."

"Make it fifteen."

"Deal."

When he called Tessa fifteen minutes later, she answered with a laugh. "You know I'm going to see you in twenty minutes."

"True. Do you want me to call ahead to The Chipped Saucer?"

"I already did."

"What did you order for me?"

"Your usual. And I added a blueberry muffin top for fun." There was a definite hint of smugness in her statement.

Zane had no problem with that at all. "You know me so well."

"I do. I also know you won't have time to get breakfast at the hotel."

"What are the chances of Gil bringing something to the office?"

"He made sourdough earlier this week and brought it in warm, with whipped butter and homemade strawberry jam and blackberry jelly."

He moaned. "You're killing me, Princess."

Her laughter held a bite to it. "I'm not sorry. And as a reminder, if you call me that in the office—"

"I would never." He held up a hand in a vow, even though she couldn't see it.

"Luke's here. I'll call you when we get there."

"Tess?"

"Yeah."

"Be careful."

"You're the worst one of the bunch." She wasn't wrong, but based on the humor and gentleness in her voice, she also didn't care.

"Your point?"

"I'm hanging up now." She was full-on laughing when the call disconnected.

# 9

TESSA PULLED ONTO the highway with Luke in the passenger seat. "Is there a reason Faith is tailing us?"

Luke grabbed his phone and started texting. "She's going to be so mad. It took you less than fifteen seconds."

"It took less than five." Tessa turned right. "I was debating whether to mention it."

"She's going to back off now and see if she notices anyone following us."

"Lovely." Tessa didn't succeed in hiding her annoyance.

"Don't be that way. We're all worried about you."

"I get it." She did. Early in her career, this would have made her mad. She had so much to prove then. Such a driving need to be seen as competent and capable. Now? She still needed to be seen that way, but she understood that accepting the help of friends didn't make her less. It made her more.

They drove in silence for a few minutes. The road, a split four-lane highway, was busy with morning traffic, and Tessa checked her mirrors on a regular rotation.

Luke shifted in his seat. "I was surprised Zane didn't chime in last night."

"Subtle." She didn't attempt to hide her sarcasm.

He didn't laugh, and he didn't drop it. "You included him in the text. He didn't respond. What's up?"

Tessa could have told him to let it go. He was being nosy, but there was an undercurrent of concern there too. Luke loved her. She knew that. But what Luke and Zane had was special. And Zane had kept her secrets, even from Luke. She never wanted to come between their friendship. "He texted me off the loop and volunteered to come to my place. I told him I was fine. I've already talked to him this morning." For almost an hour. "He'll be waiting for us."

She could feel the relief coming off Luke. "It's none of my business—"

"No. It isn't."

"I need to say this. Then I'll hush. I don't know what the deal is with you two. But I know it's important to him. And to you. So whatever it is, thank you for letting me know it's good. I didn't like to see him hurting. Didn't like seeing you hurting either. And I don't want to go back to that."

She kept her eyes firmly on the road. "Thanks. We're good. Promise."

"Good." Luke turned toward her. "So, what *is* the deal with the two of you anyway?"

Before she could come up with a witty response, the Camry two cars ahead of them slammed on its brakes. What was that idiot doing? Instead of changing lanes or turning, the car came to a complete stop.

The domino effect was unavoidable. The car directly in front of Tessa crashed into the back of the vehicle that had inexplicably decided to turn a busy road into a parking lot. Tessa spun the wheel and squeezed onto the shoulder a half second before the truck behind her barreled past where she'd been and straight into the car that had been in front of her. It rolled up onto the trunk, shattered the back glass, and pushed both cars forward another twenty feet before coming to a stop in the middle of two lanes of traffic.

The air filled with the cacophony of screeching brakes and crumpled metal as the vehicles in the lanes behind the accident swerved and spun in an attempt to avoid the heap of twisted automobiles now blocking the road.

There was nothing she could do but wait it out. When silence finally descended, Tessa had to pry her hands from the steering wheel. "You okay?" Tessa turned to Luke, whose only readable emotion was fury, before turning around to look behind her. "Where's Faith?"

Luke's phone rang, and he answered with the speaker on. "We're okay. Where are you?"

Faith's voice came through. "Fifty yards back. Mass of cars between us. I'm fine. I'll call it in. I love you. Stay sharp."

The first faint whine of a siren filtered through the morning air. Followed by another. Tessa scanned the chaos. "I want to check on the people in the cars, but—"

"But you think this might have been directed at you?" Luke finished her thought.

"Yeah. Does that make me sound conceited?"

"Nope. Makes you sound smart."

She looked at each face that moved around the vehicles, trying to memorize them. "Whoever is behind the threats, they wouldn't be the ones in the car."

"No, but they'd be nearby."

"Shooting me would be rather obvious, don't you think?"

"I do. Doesn't mean I think you should hop out and make yourself a target."

"Agreed. But I'll have to get out eventually."

Luke grunted. "Where's your vest?"

"In the back."

Luke unbuckled and clambered over the seats. "You are freakishly organized, Special Agent Reed."

She knew he was trying to lighten the mood, and she appreciated the attempt. But . . .

"Hey." Luke passed Tessa's vest to her. "I get it. I know what it's like to have a target on your back."

"I know you do."

"Can I make a suggestion?"

"Sure."

He slid across the back seats toward the door. "Focus on what you can control."

"Which is what, exactly?"

"You."

Tessa adjusted her seat back so she could maneuver. "And how does that help me?"

"You do what you know to do. Trust us to do what we know to do."

Luke eased out of his door and walked to the back of the vehicle while Tessa strapped on her vest. Then she sent Zane a quick text so he wouldn't stress when they didn't arrive in the next five minutes.

She watched in the side mirror as Luke squeezed himself between her car and the car beside them and approached Tessa's window. She rolled it down. "There are three other cars on the shoulder now behind you." Luke pointed to the road behind them. "At least fifteen cars with damage ranging from minor to total loss."

"Injuries?"

"Hard to tell." He looked her over. She had the vest on and her weapon and badge in full view on her belt.

"I'm going to see if I can help with the injured."

"Tess—"

"I can't sit here and do nothing." She tapped the vest. "I've taken precautions. Now I'm going to be useful."

She didn't need to be a mind reader to know that Luke didn't like her plan. She could see the argument behind his eyes, and then the moment he knew it would be a waste of breath to try to talk her out of it. "Text Zane."

She waved her phone at him. "I already did."

"I'm coming with you."

She rolled up her window, turned off the car, and squeezed out beside Luke. "Let's go."

They made their way to the car that had started this whole mess. The driver's-side door was open.

The seat was empty.

ZANE OPENED the car door before Gil pulled to a complete stop. He ignored Gil's shouted "Are you crazy?" and ran along the shoulder toward the collection of law enforcement vehicles, ambulances, and fire trucks.

They were a good half mile from the wreck. It was as close as Gil could get with the traffic stopped to stare at the carnage on the other side of the highway. Zane scrambled across to the now-empty lanes of traffic and ran.

He paused long enough to flash his badge at the first officer he came to and kept going. He had one goal.

Tessa.

He spotted her a minute later, and a piece of him relaxed that he hadn't realized he was holding tight. She wore a forensics hat and a Raleigh Police Department jacket engulfed her frame, but he knew it was her.

He stopped when he reached her side but didn't interrupt the conversation she was having with Luke, Faith, and their "not so favorite but always there in a pinch detective," Daniel Morris.

It was Morris's jacket that graced Tessa's shoulders. Smart move to make an effort to disguise her identity.

Morris, Luke, and Faith all acknowledged Zane's presence with a chin lift. Tessa didn't look at him, but she moved toward him. It was subtle. A small shift of her feet that almost looked like she was doing nothing more than adjusting her stance. But when she came to a stop, her left arm brushed against his right.

"We have to get this road open." Morris waved a hand toward the highway. "But I've instructed the uniforms to have the car towed to the forensics guys. They'll go over it from top to toe."

"That would be great." Tessa shrugged out of the jacket and handed it to Morris. "Thanks for the camouflage. We'll get out of your hair."

Morris took the jacket. "I don't like this, Tessa. Keep an eye out. Yeah?"

"I will."

Morris strode off in the direction of the flashing lights.

Zane wrapped a hand around Tessa's elbow. "What doesn't he like?"

"The car that started all this." Tessa pointed to a gray Toyota Camry, or what was left of one. "It came to a stop in the middle of the road. By the time we got here, the driver was gone. No one remembers seeing anything. We have no description. The driver could have been in a T-Rex costume and no one would have noticed."

Tessa's aggravation put a gruffness in her voice. "There's no way this was an accident. Someone decided to snarl traffic this morning. It's possible our presence was a coincidence, but I find that hard to believe."

Gil joined them, sides heaving, as Luke said, "Let's take this to the office."

"Are you kidding me?" Gil wiped a bead of sweat from his temple. "I just got here."

"If you'd run more often instead of spending all your time in the pool—"

Gil punched Luke's shoulder. "We'll see who comes out on top the next time there's—"

"A what?" Faith teased. "We don't get a lot of opportunities to *swim* to the rescue around here."

Gil wrapped an arm around her shoulders as they moved toward his car. "Not many opportunities to *row* to the rescue either, Mrs. Powell."

The trio ahead of them were laughing and not paying one bit of attention when Zane pulled Tessa into his arms. He had things to say, but all that came out of his mouth was, "Princess."

He'd intended the hug to be quick, but now that he had her in his arms, he couldn't find the motivation to release her. This was not a friendly embrace. He knew it, and by the way her breathing had accelerated, she knew it too.

This was dangerous. For both of them. They'd agreed on friendship and nothing more.

But . . . they hadn't said friends forever. They'd said friends for now. That had been some time ago.

Friendship was still the safest choice, but was it still the best choice?

Tessa's hands squeezed his waist, and she lifted her head. He looked down. If he moved an inch, and she moved an inch . . .

Her smile was conflicted, and she took a half step back. "We're going to need to have a long talk, but this isn't the time or place."

"Agreed." He slid his hands along her arms until they found her fingers. "But we will be talking. Soon." Her eyes widened as he laced his fingers with hers and squeezed before releasing them.

He stayed close as they wound through the chaos, and if his hand occasionally brushed hers, and if hers randomly flitted across his, that couldn't be helped.

They climbed into her SUV, and due to their location near the front of the backup, and with the help of the responding officers, they were one of the first to slip through when a lane was cleared enough to allow for passage. They didn't talk until Tessa stopped at The Chipped Saucer. "The coffees will be cold, but I ordered them. I need to pay the bill."

Zane didn't say anything as he followed her inside. "Special Agent Reed," the twentysomething male barista called out when the bell rang over the door. "Thanks for having that agent call and give us the word. We held off on the drinks. Give me ten minutes and we'll have you ready to roll."

"Thank you, Toby." She pointed to two chairs in a cozy corner. "We'll wait here."

"Sure thing!"

When they sat down, she studied Zane's face. "You called him."

"I did."

"Thank you."

"You're welcome."

"What are we doing, Zane?"

The question wasn't rhetorical, but he had no good answer. "I don't know."

She stared at a random spot on the floor. "Just to be clear, I can't deal with messing us up."

She'd voiced his deepest fear. "I can't either."

After another minute of silence, she dropped her head back and her gaze went to the ceiling. "Do you think the wreck was intended to impact me? Because that seems . . . I don't know. I can't get my brain around it. What would be the benefit of me having a car wreck? There could be no guarantee it would kill me. As messy as the accident was, there were no fatalities on the scene. The worst thing I saw was a broken leg. Not that I want to have a broken leg, but what's the point?"

She looked at him then. "This isn't like what happened with you, Luke, and Gil. That man shot at you. He tried to kill you. Not that we knew who was behind the attacks at the time, but still. Someone shoots at you, you can usually assume they're trying to put you in the ground. Someone stages a wreck? What are they hoping to gain from it?"

Before he could answer, she continued. "And yes, I appreciate how much of a *princess* I sound like, assuming everything is about me."

"You aren't that kind of princess."

She grumbled something unintelligible, but it was followed by a low laugh that ended in a long sigh. "What now?"

"Coffee. Muffins. Office. The PID will have loaded your in-box by now with threats that need to be chased down. We work. We prepare for the president's visit. We encase you in Bubble Wrap and don't let you go anywhere alone until we figure out what's happening."

Tessa made a show of tapping the weapon at her waist, but whatever she was planning to say was interrupted by Toby yelling across the shop. "Got your order ready, Special Agent Reed."

Zane stood and hauled her up beside him, then took two of the carrying trays loaded with coffee, leaving her one tray and a bag of pastries.

"Did you get coffees for the DC guys too?"

"Yeah. Had Leslie ask them for their order yesterday."

"They'll love you forever."

They kept their own coffees, and Zane rummaged through the bag to find his muffin top before they placed the remaining beverages in the back of Tessa's SUV. Tessa did the coffee run so often, she had special boxes that held the coffee in place while she drove. When they were on the road, she tapped her steering wheel and asked, "What do you think of Rodriguez?"

"Not much." He made it a point not to badmouth his fellow agents, but this was Tess. He wasn't going to lie to her. Not about this. Not about anything.

"Hmm."

A dreadful suspicion curled in his gut. "Why?"

She didn't respond immediately. "He has my number. I gave it to him and Carver yesterday so they could reach me."

"Yeah."

"He asked me out."

"What? When?"

# — 10 —

TESSA TRIED NOT TO LAUGH at Zane's blatant aggravation. He didn't like Rodriguez. She could tell when she watched them interact yesterday.

"Are you messing with me?" Zane had way too much hope in his voice for him to be truly teasing her.

"Nope. Asked me out last night. When I declined, he put forth several reasons I should reconsider."

"What did you do?"

She tapped her phone. "See for yourself."

The tension flowed out of him as he grabbed her phone and scrolled. She kept her eyes firmly on the road, but she didn't need to see him to know when he got to the pertinent texts.

"He's an idiot."

"Is he dating anyone?"

"The correct question is, 'How many women is he currently dating?' or you could go with, 'How many women did he date last week?' or—"

"I get the picture. But this still surprises me."

Zane put the phone back on the console. "You're surprised he asked you out? Or you're surprised he didn't take no for an answer?"

"Both."

"Please. Tess, you get asked out all the time."

He wasn't wrong. But . . . "Not by coworkers."

"Is that what surprises you? That he asked you out while you're working?"

"Yes. Doesn't this reek of unprofessional behavior? I haven't even known him twenty-four hours. Which tells me exactly what he sees in me. It's not like he wants to get together to discuss protection tactics or investigative strategies."

Zane's hands were fisted on his thighs. "No. I'm sure that is not what he's interested in."

"I'm not opposed to workplace romance. Where else are we going to meet people? Especially with the kind of hours we work. Luke met Faith through work. And even Gil and Ivy reconnected because of work."

"Rodriguez is nothing like Luke or Gil. He's a player. He goes through women the way Faith goes through Cherry Coke." Given the level of Faith's Cherry Coke obsession, Zane's words painted a disturbing image. "And he's used to women saying yes. To hear him tell it, it's rare for him to get shot down."

She would bet he got shot down a lot more than anyone knew. "There's one good thing about Rodriguez."

"What's that?"

"He's given me new appreciation for our team. I've never felt anything but respected and accepted here. And no one has ever made me uncomfortable."

"Liar." Zane took a bite of his muffin and mumbled, "You weren't my biggest fan for a while."

Tessa couldn't believe he'd brought that up. This was a season of their relationship they never discussed. "That was different."

"Not by much. I wasn't trying to go out with you, but I was all up in your personal business."

"You were trying to help. And you weren't creepy about it. I knew where you were coming from. And while I didn't appreciate it then, I do now."

He swallowed and turned to her. "I wasn't angling for gratitude."

"I know. But that's the difference between what he's doing and what you did. What you did was for my benefit. Not yours."

"That's not entirely true."

What did he mean by that? Before she could ask, he changed the subject. "We're three minutes from the office. It's time to get your game face on."

"I never should have told you that." It had slipped out one morning while they were chatting on the way to work, him in DC, her in Raleigh. She called it her game face, a tiny ritual she went through before walking into the office. She reminded herself that she was an agent, that her mission was to defend and protect, and that it wasn't about her, it was about those impacted by crime, deceit, and evil. Then she prayed for strength and creativity for the day. It helped her shake off whatever personal problems she carried and made it easier to focus on the work at hand.

She pulled into a parking spot and cut the ignition. Zane unbuckled but made no move to climb from the car. "Can I pray for us today?"

"Yes, please."

He used to do this a lot, and she missed it. Zane bowed his head, and she followed his example. Before he began, she heard him take a deep breath. As he blew it out, his hand cradled hers. "Holy Father, we come to you as your children. Your servants. Your hands and feet in the world. We know you've gone before us, and you already know what today holds. Please give us grace and strength specific for whatever is coming. And help us trust you to be enough, no matter what happens. We know you've promised to give wisdom to those who ask, so would you give us eyes to see what we cannot see without the power of the Spirit at work in us and give us wisdom in our dealings with others, as well as in our efforts to prevent violence and evil from touching those we've sworn to protect? Thank you for being bigger than anything we will face. We love you. We trust you. Thank you for giving us this day to serve you. In Jesus's name, amen."

"Amen."

ZANE HELPED CARRY in the coffees and pastries. The second they walked in, Rodriguez wolf-whistled at Tessa. And if Zane hadn't had his hands full, he would have found it difficult not to cram his fist into the other man's throat. Clearly God was already at work in their day, protecting him from doing something stupid.

He wasn't generally a violent man. He was calm. Contained. Thoughtful. Everyone said so.

But not when it came to Tessa.

Rodriguez walked up to Tessa. "Come to me, you beautiful angel."

Luke stepped forward to take the coffee from Tessa and gave Rodriguez a death glare. "I don't know how y'all do things in DC, but that won't fly in Raleigh."

Rodriguez was pure innocence. "Man, I was talking about the coffee."

No one bought it. But Rodriguez did shut up.

After everyone had settled in the conference room with their coffees, Tessa divvied up the threat assessments the PID had sent out and confirmed Rodriguez's and Carver's plans for the day, which included liaising with local officials, traveling to the airport, and developing multiple routes for the motorcade. She made sure everyone knew to avoid Hank Littlefield at all costs but didn't bring up the threat that was directed at her.

Zane didn't mind her keeping Rodriguez and Carver out of the loop at this point, but if she didn't bring it up with the rest of the team, he was going to have to insist they discuss it.

When Rodriguez and Carver left, Gil, Luke, and Benjamin gathered around. "That guy is not right." Gil looked ready to punch a wall. "What's his deal?"

"He's not popular in DC either," Benjamin said. "I know he's been written up several times, but this is a bit over the top, even for him."

Tessa flashed what Luke had once, and only once, called her beauty-queen smile. "Thanks for looking out for me, guys, but I'm fine. Not my first rodeo. Now, let's figure out what's going on with these threats."

Tessa was all business as she mirrored her computer screen on the large TV in the corner so everyone could follow along. "We have two threats that have some teeth." She tapped on the computer and a photograph appeared. "This one has everyone in DC on edge. Craig Brown is a forty-two-year-old white male. He lives forty-five minutes outside of Raleigh, in Carrington County. He has two weapons registered in his name, both hunting rifles, but his social media accounts indicate that he has access to an arsenal and he's a UAV enthusiast."

"Why can't we just call them drones?" Gil grumbled.

"Craig Brown has a treatise on that if you'd like to read it. It's six pages long. At least twenty percent of the words are expletives. The rest of them seem to indicate that, in his opinion, referring to an unmanned aerial vehicle as a drone is disrespectful."

"Seriously?" Gil shook his head. "I'm still calling them drones."

"What's his beef with the president?" Benjamin asked.

"Years ago, a Texas jury found a man named Calvin Cross guilty on eight counts of murder and an assortment of other charges, including sexual assault and battery. It was appealed, of course, but the verdict was upheld. Ultimately, when all appeals had been exhausted, they petitioned the governor for a stay of execution. The president, who was the governor of Texas at the time, refused to sign it and Cross was executed."

Zane remembered hearing about the case. "Wasn't that the one where there was video and DNA evidence?"

"Yes. It was the definition of an open-and-shut case. But Craig Brown was part of a group who insisted that Cross was innocent. There are always people who protest because of a moral conviction regarding the death penalty, but that's not what this group was about. They had concocted an elaborate conspiracy theory that Cross had been set up to protect someone else. The state brought numerous witnesses to confirm the veracity of the video and DNA evidence, but they couldn't be dissuaded. When Cross was executed, they vowed that justice would be served."

"They've been a thorn in the side of the President's Protection Detail since he was on the campaign trail." Benjamin pointed toward the screen. "I haven't come across this guy, but I've seen some of them at various events. They show up with these neon-green crosses on their jackets or shirts. There's nothing stealth about them. It's like they're trying to get some kind of vengeance by intimidation. The First Lady is terrified of them."

Tessa pulled up a report and it flashed on the screen. "According to this, they've shown up at eighty-three events in the past four years. That includes his appearances as governor, then on the campaign trail, and now as president." She turned to Zane. "Have you seen them?"

"No, but I've heard about them."

"Well, you'll get to see one member in a few hours. You and I are going to pay Craig Brown a friendly visit today."

"Sounds fun."

Tessa turned to Luke, Gil, and Benjamin. "I need you three to run down the rest of the social media threats and follow up on anything that requires a presence. And when you're done, I'd appreciate it if you could spend some time on the threat directed at me."

Benjamin rested both forearms on the table. "How about we reverse that order?"

**"THE PRESIDENT IS THE PRIORITY."** The four men at the table gave Tessa nearly identical looks that she didn't have to be an expert on body language to read. Nothing she said was going to stop them from doing what they felt they needed to do. They were going to find out who had threatened her, and the lunatics who thought she was too pretty to protect the president were going to find it difficult to eliminate her from the equation.

"Fine. I don't care what order you do them in." And just like that, they all relaxed. "But"—she held each one's gaze in turn—"if you don't have those presidential threats removed from the board by tonight, you'll have to stay late to finish them."

"I guess she told us." Benjamin looked at Luke and Gil. "How do y'all want to do this?"

As the three men divvied up the threats, Zane stood and walked toward her. "Where are we starting today?"

He was all business and she was so thankful, she could have kissed him. She needed to get them solidly back into the friend zone. The zone they were in right now was confusing and complicated, and she didn't have time for that. "We need to go see Bruce."

Zane pretended to bang his head on the wall. "Why me?"

Tessa knew why. Zane could be fierce and deadly, but he had a gentle roughness about him that appealed to certain people on the margins of society. He spoke to them with respect even as he told them that if they didn't cut it out, they'd go to jail.

Bruce was a classic example. He was mentally ill but refused medication. He preferred to sleep outdoors and only went to a shelter when it was bitterly cold. Despite this, he always had the latest cell phone and never seemed to run out of data. He had social media accounts under random names and used those platforms to rant about the president, making threats he had no hope of carrying out.

Zane had taken Tessa to meet Bruce her first month on the job after Bruce sent a threat to blow up the White House. She'd expected Zane to be harsh, but Zane leaned against the telephone pole beside Bruce's current habitation and said, "Dude, if you want to talk to me, all you have to do is call. You keep pulling this crap and I'm going to have to arrest you."

Bruce gave Tessa a cheeky smile and whispered, "He doesn't want to let on, but he loves me."

That was two years ago.

"Let's get it over with. Bruce first. Then Craig Brown."

Tessa didn't let on that she knew Zane had looked for Bruce before he left for DC, but Bruce had disappeared. Or that he'd asked Leslie, their office manager, to let him know if Bruce popped up. "Okay. Let's go."

It took them thirty minutes to find Bruce, who was lounging on a bench in a local park. "Special Agent Thacker. It is about time." Bruce had a voice for radio. Deep and melodic, with crisp diction and no discernable accent. And when his mind was clear, he spoke like the English professor he'd once been. "And Special

Agent Reed. Always a pleasure. Please, sit." He gestured to his bench, and Tessa took a seat.

"Where did you run off to?" Zane stood above Tessa, blocking the sun so she could see.

Bruce pointed to a scar on his arm. "Ran into some miscreants and determined that it would be best to avoid their company for a time."

Tessa patted Bruce's arm. "Maybe you should avoid their company indefinitely."

Bruce gave her a sly grin. "Perhaps." When he turned back to Zane, his expression altered, and Tessa braced for the possibility that he was losing his hold on the present. "I should confess that my own threats were nothing more than the rantings of an old man. But you have some real problems to deal with, young man."

"I do?"

"Indeed. I hear things."

Zane kept his posture relaxed, but Tessa noticed the slight narrowing of his eyes. Bruce had his undivided attention. "What kind of things have you heard this week?"

Bruce shuddered beside her and put one hand on her knee. "You need to watch out for your girl, Special Agent Thacker."

# 11

ZANE STUDIED BRUCE. His eyes were clear and focused. His hand on Tessa's knee wasn't shaking. His voice was always deep, but when he was lost in his delusions, his words were halting and his thoughts fractured. Today, Bruce spoke with crisp clarity.

"You must be careful, Special Agent Reed."

"What have you heard, Bruce?" It took effort, but Zane kept his voice low and calm.

"Someone has declared open season on the 'pretty Secret Service agent.'" Bruce shook his head in obvious disgust. "As if that's an appropriate description. How are they supposed to know which pretty agent to go after? Criminals these days. No one appreciates the importance of a well-written hit."

Bruce leaned into Tessa's shoulder. "Don't be alarmed. We know you are the prettiest of them all. But lucky for you, your brain is even more beautiful than your face. And the pretty boys you work with have decent minds."

Zane chose not to be offended that his brain was only deemed "decent" by Bruce.

"More important, they have honor and bravery. As do you. Be

cautious, young warrior. The truest sign of courage isn't to ignore the threat but to prepare for it."

"Thank you, Bruce." Tessa leaned into Bruce's arm with no apparent concern for the dirt and germs that would transfer to her. "I will."

Bruce turned his penetrating gaze on Zane. "You have survived much in your young life, but I fear for you if anything happens to her. Take care."

How had this insight come from a man who spent much of his time locked inside a mental landscape where no one could wander with him? Zane didn't want to do anything that would push him back into that place, but he had to ask. "Do you know where the threat originated?"

"It was on the wind," Bruce said. "The wind knows."

Tessa met his gaze, and he saw the truth in her eyes. Bruce was fading. "I owe you a great debt, Bruce."

"Then perhaps you'll tell the president to leave me alone and quit making it hard for me to get my check. Yeah?"

"Sure thing, Bruce. You need anything?"

"I'm free. I'm good."

Zane fought the surge of anger that always accompanied his visits with Bruce. He kept it contained until he and Tess were back at her car.

She bumped his arm with hers. "There's nothing you can do, Zane."

"And why is that?" He growled the words and slammed his hand on the top of her car. Tessa didn't flinch. She leaned against the car and watched him but made no effort to talk him out of his fury. "The man is intelligent. Brilliant. He was a professor of English at UNC in Carrington. I've heard him quote Shakespeare. I don't even like Shakespeare, and it was so beautiful I almost cried."

Tessa nodded.

"He's not free. He's not fine. He's broken. He's alone. How is that okay?" This was the real reason Zane hadn't wanted to see Bruce. He was relieved the man was still around but at the same time wished for him to finally be at peace.

"I don't understand this stuff, Tess. I know God is in control. I also know he is love. But then you have people like Bruce. I've never been able to find out what happened, but it was something bad enough that it literally broke his mind. His family doesn't try to contact him. They've given up on him. But he's still in there. Enough to know to toss out a random threat to get me to come see him. Enough to know that he didn't need to mess around today because his threat wasn't real, but the threat to you is. He should be with people who care for him. How is this okay?"

He shut his mouth. He was ranting, and he didn't rant. He discussed, calmly and rationally. Tessa never moved from the position she'd taken beside the car, but he couldn't stay still. He paced from one end of the car to the other.

No matter what condition he was in, visits to Bruce always made him think about his mother. The main difference between the two was that Bruce was the way he was because of a tragedy. His mother? He had no idea.

He understood addiction as an adult. Understood the power of it. But there would always be a part of him that was the terrified kid who couldn't understand why his mother wouldn't wake up when he needed to go to school or why she disappeared for hours, sometimes days, at a time. That kid wondered why God had given him the mother he had when other kids got mothers like Gil's. That kid—okay, that adult—never understood why he'd had to fend for himself for so long.

And he knew that was a big part of the reason his heart was still so fragile that he couldn't give it to the woman who stood waiting for him. He stopped beside her and whispered, "Sorry about that."

She cocked her head to one side and traced his jaw with her finger. "Never apologize for being the man you are, Zane." She dropped her hand and walked to the driver's side. "Let's update the guys on the info we got from Bruce, then head to Carrington."

Zane looked back toward the bench where Bruce now sat, face to the sun, eyes closed. *Father, I want to fix him. I want to fix my mom. You have the power to fix both. I'll never understand why you don't.*

He climbed into the car and slammed the door. "You drive. I'll call Luke."

**TESSA DROVE IN SILENCE** as Zane talked to Luke. He stuck to the facts, shared what Bruce had told them, and ended the call. When he spoke, he was back to his calm, collected self. "Have you called anyone in Carrington to let them know we're coming?"

"Yes. Adam is going to meet us in a church parking lot that he says is a mile from the house." Adam Campbell was a white-collar crimes investigator in Carrington County. "Jacob called their captain yesterday and cleared everything."

"How's the Carrington crowd doing?" The Raleigh RAIC and the Carrington Dive Team had developed a close bond over the past few years.

"All good as far as I know. Leigh just had a baby, and Sabrina is pregnant."

That got Zane's attention. "Sabrina? Pregnant?" Leigh was a nurse practitioner, married to homicide investigator Ryan Parker. It was no struggle to imagine Leigh as a mother. She mothered everybody. Dr. Sabrina Fleming-Campbell, however, was a cyber forensics expert who taught at UNC Carrington and assisted law enforcement all over the country. She didn't have a mean bone in her body, but she could be blunt, and she didn't come across as particularly maternal.

Tessa laughed at Zane's shocked expression. "Pregnant and giddy about it. Adam is already showing off ultrasound pictures. It's so cute. Sabrina sent us a video last week of the nursery, which is not decorated but is fully equipped with sound and video monitoring."

"Of course it is." Zane's laughter sounded unforced, and Tessa relaxed. The rest of the drive was easy, the way it usually was between them. When they stopped in the church parking lot, Adam was waiting.

Zane bounded from the car, and he and Adam met in a bro hug.

"Have you heard our news?" Adam held out his phone, and Tessa didn't need to be close to know it was an ultrasound picture.

"That's amazing. Congratulations!"

Adam pulled Tessa into a quick hug when she approached. "Hey there. You good?"

"Yeah. Thanks."

They took a few minutes to catch up before turning to the reason that brought them to Carrington.

"I assume Craig Brown has been on your radar before now?" Tessa pointed to the file Adam had set on the trunk of his car.

"That man is a pain in the rear."

Something about Adam's tone set Tessa's intuition pinging. "Other than about the death penalty case?"

"Oh yeah. He's a crusader. If you can find an unworthy cause, he's probably championing it." Adam began ticking off examples on his fingers. He tapped his first finger. "A few years ago he opposed a historic preservation group that was attempting to purchase an old farmhouse. No one, including the owners of the property, was opposed. Everyone thought it was a great idea. Everyone except Brown. He protested it on the grounds of it being governmental overreach, but there was no government input at all. It was a private group, seeking private money. And the farmhouse is a beloved landmark in the community. Even some of our biggest land developers wanted it preserved."

Adam tapped his middle finger. "We have him on video at protest rallies during the last election cycle. That wouldn't be a big deal except that he protested both parties, the Electoral College, the Constitution, and was a loud voice at a tiny protest that declared the Supreme Court should be abolished. All within a two-week period."

"Is he a protestor-for-hire?" Zane asked. "Or just angry at everything?"

"He'll take payment when it's offered, but we've come to the conclusion that he's an attention seeker. If he thinks it will get someone to look at him, listen to him, or better yet, interview him on local TV? He's all in. And the more scandalous or outlandish the better."

"Anything else we need to know before we say hi?" Tessa asked.

Adam rubbed the back of his neck and cleared his throat. "Yeah. Probably."

Tessa waited.

Zane was less patient. "Spit it out, man."

Adam gave her an apologetic smile. "He's not big on women in law enforcement."

"Of course he isn't." Tessa did not make any attempt to hide her annoyance.

"If it makes you feel any better, he's not big on women, period." Adam twisted the wedding band on his left hand. "His mother was an abusive addict."

Tessa sensed Zane's tension beside her and was unsurprised when he took a few steps to the side and then came back toward her. He couldn't stay still when he was calm. When he was agitated, he moved nonstop.

"His grandmother was abusive, and we believe his older sister was too. His childhood was full of drugs, sex, and violence. And the people who should have protected and nurtured him used him as an outlet for their own anger."

"How do you know all this?" Zane asked.

"His mother moved here with his grandmother and sister when he was in his midteens. A few officers on the force went to high school with him and say he wasn't bullied, but he was a loner."

"The kind of kid we'd watch closely these days?" Tessa was deeply involved in the Secret Service's efforts to prevent school shootings. She knew what to look for.

"Definitely. He disappeared off the radar for a few years, but then he became a frequent flyer at the jail. He gets picked up with some regularity for drunk and disorderly. Nothing that would keep him incarcerated for any length of time. But enough that some of the officers who deal with him the most often started digging."

"Good cops," Zane muttered.

"Yeah. Some of the best. One of our female beat cops is the one who found out about the abuse. She asked him if he needed anything, and he went off on her. By the time he'd spewed his story, she said she felt too sorry for him to be offended."

"Where's the mom and grandmother?" Zane asked.

"Deceased. Grandmother died of a stroke. Mother died of an overdose."

"The sister?"

Adam shook his head. "Married a man who beat her to death."

"Good grief."

"Yeah. Needless to say, Craig Brown did not hit the family lottery. And it doesn't take a degree in psychology to figure out that his childhood has made him distrustful of all authority. He's the type who's looking for a purpose, something to make him feel like he's worth something."

"Are you trying to make me feel sorry for him?" Tessa didn't succeed in keeping the grumble out of her voice.

"Nope." Adam pointed to her. "You beat back your addiction. You live with the knowledge of it every day, and you no longer let it control you." He pointed to Zane. "And what little I know of your childhood, you didn't exactly hit the family jackpot yourself."

Zane acknowledged the remark with a frown. "That's an understatement."

"I don't want you to feel sorry for him. But I do want you to understand him. I'm not convinced he doesn't have an undiagnosed mental illness, but it's no question that there's deep childhood trauma that he never healed from. It doesn't excuse his behavior, but if you can see where he's coming from, it might help you prevent a tragedy."

"That's the goal." Tessa caught Zane's eye, reading the emotion and determination in his expression before turning back to Adam. "Thank you for the insight. It's helpful."

"You're welcome."

"How do you feel about leading the conversation?" Tessa didn't want to put it on Zane's shoulders, and if Craig didn't like women, there was no point in antagonizing him.

"I'm fine with it if you are."

"I think it would be best." Tessa nodded at Zane. "We'll chime in as needed."

"Sounds like a plan." Adam clapped his hands. "Let's go stop a domestic terrorist."

# 12

TEN MINUTES LATER, Zane fought the desire to pull Tessa behind him as Craig Brown greeted them on his front porch, rifle in hand. While Adam Campbell tried to convince him to set the weapon down so they could have a civil conversation, Zane and Tessa remained several feet away.

Tessa stood beside him and muttered, "Don't even think about it."

"What?"

"Bubble Wrap."

"I'm going to buy it by the truckload."

She scoffed but said no more, and Zane returned his focus to the contrasting images of Craig Brown and Adam Campbell. Adam looked like an actor portraying a local detective. He could have walked right off a photo shoot.

Craig had the look of a man at least two decades older than his forty-two years. His hair was thinning and greasy. His shirt needed to be laundered a month ago. His pants were beyond redemption. His bare feet were several shades darker than his natural skin tone. His hands yellowed from nicotine. Zane didn't relish getting close enough to take a whiff.

But for all that, it was Craig Brown's eyes that gave Zane pause. They held a dangerous glint when he spoke to Adam, but when his gaze landed on Tessa, they filled with a predatory gleam that put every protective instinct in Zane's body on red alert.

"I don't have to talk to you." Craig pitched his voice loud enough to carry to the neighbor's, a quarter mile away. "I haven't done anything wrong."

"You are part of a group that has publicly and repeatedly threatened the president of the United States." Adam leaned against the porch post. "Put the gun away, Craig, or I'll have to add threatening a law enforcement officer to the mix."

Craig sneered at Adam. "I know who you are, pretty-boy cop. You have no idea what it's like to have the powerful turn against you. You've never needed to rely on others to support you. You don't know the meaning of loyalty. We're loyal beyond the grave. We're going to be sure no one else dies at the hands of a twisted legal system."

"So, are you saying you plan to attack the president of the United States?" Adam's question was so conversational, Zane thought he might get Craig to admit it on the spot.

But Craig's eyes lit with harsh humor, and he laughed until his lungs protested. He wound up coughing for a solid thirty seconds. "You're funny. I don't plan anything, Investigator Campbell. I go where the wind takes me."

Adam took a step closer to Craig. "Make sure the wind doesn't take you to Raleigh anytime soon."

"Is that a threat? You trying to limit my freedoms?"

"No." Adam's smile was chilling, and Zane saw the steel of the man behind the pretty-boy façade. "I believe we're all free to make our own decisions. But if you decide to go to Raleigh, you'll be detained. That isn't a threat. That's a fact."

Adam jerked his thumb toward the bottom of the steps where Zane stood with Tessa. "Those two don't play. If you want to continue to be free to protest anything and everything, I suggest you pay attention. This is the only warning you'll receive."

"Get off my property, Officer." Craig hitched the rifle onto his hip. "Unless you have a warrant for my arrest, we're done."

Adam backed down the steps but paused at the bottom. "Oh, Mr. Brown?"

"What?" The question was harsh and guttural.

"See my car over there?"

"What about it?"

"My car belongs to the Carrington County Sheriff's Office. We have dash cams in every vehicle."

"So what?" Craig's tone had lost some of its earlier bravado.

"Nothing much. Just making sure you know what's at stake."

Craig's response was to step back inside and slam the door.

Adam didn't speak until they were all in his car. Tessa took shotgun. Zane climbed in behind Adam. "That went about as well as expected."

"He's a real charmer." Tessa turned in her seat to see Zane. "Did you catch that, about the wind?"

"I don't like it." Zane filled Adam in on Bruce's warning.

"I don't like it either." Adam pulled to a stop in the church parking lot beside Tessa's car. "I'll keep an ear out. And if it's okay with you, I'll share with our investigators."

"We'll take all the help we can get." Tessa climbed from the car. "Thanks for the assist."

"Anytime. Let us know if you need us for anything else. We'll be keeping a close eye on Craig, and we'll contact you if we notice any suspicious behavior."

"Appreciate it." Zane shook Adam's hand and waited as Adam gave Tessa a gentle hug and whispered something in her ear that had her smiling softly.

When they were headed back to Raleigh, Zane couldn't contain his curiosity any longer. "What did Adam say to you?"

Tessa tapped her fingers on the steering wheel. "It was nothing. Adam's not as overtly protective as some people." She emphasized that with a quick glance in his direction that left no confusion as to who she was referring to. "He said he had my back. And access to a private plane if I need to make a quick getaway."

Zane snorted. "As if you'd ever have enough sense to get on the plane."

"I'm confident the offer was made with the full knowledge that I would share it with you, and that *you* would put me on a plane in a heartbeat if it became necessary."

"True. But I wouldn't trust you not to jump out." Tessa's entire body went rigid. "If I ever put you on a plane, I'll be staying on it with you."

"I'm not dumb enough to jump out." Tessa's low mumble sounded genuinely frustrated.

"Okay, but if you really wanted to be on the ground, you might overpower the pilot and fly the plane back, right into the middle of whatever we were escaping from."

"I don't have a death wish, Zane."

Her tone was harsh, and it was then that he realized he'd hit a nerve, and he hadn't meant to. "I was messing with you, Tess."

She didn't say anything for five miles. Zane was prepared to let it go another five when she said, "Isn't Adam adorable? About the baby?"

Where had that come from? "Um. Sure?"

"Oh, come on. He's precious."

"Yeah, see, guys don't use words like *adorable* and *precious* when they talk about other guys."

"What words would you use?"

"We wouldn't."

Tessa gave him a quick glare. "You didn't notice how excited he was?"

"Yes. But what is there to discuss? He's excited, as he should be. If he wasn't excited, that would be disturbing. As it is? I'm happy for him and Sabrina."

Tessa mumbled something unintelligible.

"Let's get back to your lack of a death wish."

Her hands flexed on the steering wheel. "I'm not sure if you noticed, but I changed the subject."

"Oh, I noticed. I'm still recovering from the conversational whiplash."

"I don't want to discuss it." Tessa's words were clipped.

"I figured that out all on my own."

"Then why did you bring it up?" Her exasperation bled through every word.

Was she being intentionally difficult, or did she truly not understand? "Your reaction didn't make sense to me. We've been through a lot together. Some of it was bad. Some of it was horrible. Some of it was tragic. But I've never entertained the notion that you might have a death wish. It should have been a safe thing to tease you about because I thought it was obvious that it was ridiculous. But you went porcupine on me, and I want to know why."

"Went porcupine?"

She was messing with him, but he wasn't going to let her make him mad. "Yeah. All bristly. Quills everywhere. Ready to stab me if I got too close."

Tessa's hands relaxed on the wheel. "I did do that. I apologize."

Zane made an effort to keep his voice gentle. "I don't need an apology, Tess. I need to understand."

"Why?"

"Why? Because we're friends? Because I care about you? Because obviously at some point in your life, the idea of having a death wish hurt you, and I want to know if I need to kill someone? How many more reasons do you need?"

Rather than bristling further, she laughed, although her laughter had a brittle edge. "You have a bloodthirsty streak."

"Only when it comes to the people I care about."

TESSA COULDN'T DISPUTE Zane's sincerity. She also wasn't sure how to get out of this conversation without telling him. It wasn't that it was some dark secret or she minded him knowing. But she'd overreacted, he'd called her on it, and now she'd rather jump out of the car than answer him.

"Tess?"

She had to say something. "It's not that big of a deal. It hit me wrong for some reason. Not your fault. And not anything you need to worry about."

"I prefer to decide for myself when it comes to whether or not I should worry about something. Particularly when it comes to you."

There were several ways she could go with that response, but before she could stop herself, she decided to focus on the part that most intrigued her. "Why do I get special treatment?"

Now it was Zane's turn to go quiet.

"Zane?"

"You know why, Tess."

Zane's declaration sent a wave of warmth through her system, chased by a terror so cold she fought a shiver. Because she did know. But she also knew that while Zane was acknowledging the powerful connection between them, he was also fully aware of how fragile it was.

All of a sudden dredging up old family hurts didn't seem like such a bad idea. She'd talk about anything to avoid the one conversation she wasn't ready to have with Zane. Might not ever be ready for.

"My grandparents moved to Texas when my dad was two. He grew up returning to India every two or three years for the summer. He spoke the language, ate the food, and in their home they were a traditional Indian family. But he also went to public school, spoke English without an accent, and had strong opinions about everything from college football to salsa."

Tessa almost never talked about her dad. Even with Zane. So she had his full attention. "My mom was half Indian. Her dad, my grandfather, could trace his genealogy back to Norway in the 1800s. He was blond and blue-eyed." That tidbit put a smug grin on Zane's face. He ran his hand through his own reddish-blond hair and flashed his baby blues at her. "Anyway, when he fell in love with my grandmother, it caused quite a stir. She was born in India and hadn't moved to the States until she was nine. She spoke with heavily accented English and had very traditional parents. They'd planned to arrange a marriage to a nice Indian boy."

Zane was hanging on her every word. "How did they meet?"

"My grandfather was an engineer. My grandmother was an accountant at the plant where he worked. They started having lunch dates and staying late at work. She knew her family wouldn't approve. They had indulged her desire to get a degree and start work, but they expected her to marry by the age of twenty-five and had begun bringing men around at dinner."

"Uh-oh."

"Apparently my grandfather did not like that at all. But there were plenty of family members on his side who wouldn't approve either. So they kept their relationship a secret. The way my grandmother told the story, no one knew until they returned from Vegas, married."

"They eloped?" Zane laughed with unhidden delight. "Good for them. How did the families react?"

"My grandmother told me once that she never regretted falling in love with my grandfather, but the first few years of their marriage were tough. Her parents were furious. His were hurt. But my grandparents had stayed in Vegas long enough that everything was legal, the marriage had been consummated, and there wasn't anything anyone could do about it."

"Wow."

"Then my half-Indian mother went and married an Indian with a very traditional family. My grandmother couldn't believe it. Told her that she was in for a lot of heartache, but that if she loved him, she'd never be sorry."

Tessa's voice broke. "My mother told me at Dad's funeral that she'd do it all over again. She loved my father. They were sure of who they were to each other, they made an effort to treat the various family members with respect, and they taught us to do the same. My siblings and I learned all the traditional dances and customs. We spent several summers in India with family and have close ties to both my mom's and dad's Indian relatives there. It was a beautiful way to grow up, with rich heritage on all sides."

Zane took a few minutes to absorb everything, and Tessa didn't interrupt his thoughts. "So, you told me this story now because you wanted me to know you come from a long line of hopeless romantics who believe true love can conquer any obstacle?" He steepled his fingers. "Or to distract me from the death-wish conversation you continue to avoid?"

"Zane!"

Zane's laughter filled the car.

Tessa waited until he got control of himself to continue. "Can't it be both?"

"No, Princess. It can't." The words were serious, but with a deep thrum of humor and an undeniable vein of affection. "Spit it out."

"I have two cousins who I'm close to. They don't understand my choices. When I went to India for the funeral, they pulled me aside and begged me to find different employment. Something safer. Went on and on about how if I loved my mother and my family, I'd do whatever I could to protect myself. And that if I refused to do this, they had to wonder if I had some kind of death wish. Was I depressed? Was I trying to hurt everyone with my early demise?"

"Wow."

"Yeah. And, as you know, I was slipping further and further into my alcoholism at the time, so the words hit me in a tender place. And that place hasn't healed."

There was not a trace of humor when Zane spoke. "I never believed you had a death wish. Not even when I knew you were hungover. Not when I could see you losing your hold. Not when you called me to get you from that hotel. Do you believe me?"

"Yes." She didn't have to ponder that. She knew he meant every word. "I think it hurts because I wonder if there's some truth to it. If I chose to push boundaries and drive myself to be the best I could possibly be in a dangerous profession because I figured I would either succeed or die in the attempt. And that if I failed, death would be preferable to living with the failure."

Zane shifted in his seat. "Do you think that now? Death is better than failure?"

Tessa took a few moments to consider Zane's question. She couldn't give him a flippant answer. Not about this. "No. I don't. I know I'm valued for who I am, not for what I accomplish. And the people in my life who know me, who love me, will continue to do so regardless of whether I guard the president or a junkyard. But it has taken a while to get to this point."

Zane glanced at his watch and then stretched his hands in front of him. "You know what we need?"

"What?"

"Milkshakes."

"Milkshakes?"

He gave her a pleading look. "Come on, Tess. You know you want one. It's not that far out of the way."

"Are we getting them to go?"

"No." Zane's response was quick. "We're going to order them and enjoy them. And then when we're done, we're going to walk around the metropolis of Pittsboro and enjoy the sunshine of a beautiful fall day. Then we'll drive back to Raleigh and deal with whatever we're facing."

"Zane—"

"I'm not ready to go back. Can't we take an hour to just be together?"

His words knocked the emotional wind out of her. She had no idea what was happening. Didn't want to give herself permission to even think about it too much or it might disappear like a mirage. But if Zane Thacker wanted to spend time alone with her, she wasn't going to try to talk him out of it. "Milkshakes it is."

# —13—

ZANE HAD NO IDEA what he was doing. Was he on a date with Tessa? No.

But maybe yes?

No.

Except when they sat down at the soda shop in Pittsboro—a tiny town with the best milkshakes in the state—Zane had to fight the urge to reach across the table and tug on Tessa's hand until she intertwined her fingers with his.

The planned shakes turned into cheeseburgers, fries, and shakes, because neither of them had eaten enough over the past few hours. The tension in the car, the heavy topics, the words said and unsaid—none of that joined them at the table. Tessa relaxed, and when she relaxed, she could be hilarious. She had a sly sense of humor. One that had made him enjoy verbally sparring with her from the first day.

"Tell me how it's going in DC, and don't make me drag it out of you. I don't want any of your macho manspeak." She pointed her milkshake at him. "I want the truth."

"You can't handle the truth."

Tessa rolled her eyes at his pitiful Jack Nicholson impression. "Spit. It. Out."

"It's fine."

"Wow." She widened her eyes in mock surprise. "With that ringing endorsement, it's a wonder we don't all pack up and move to DC immediately."

"Has anyone ever told you that you have a smart mouth?"

"*Moi?*" Tessa's French accent was flawless. Her fluttering hand at her throat and eye-batting added to the drama.

"*Oui, oui, mademoiselle.*" Zane exhausted his French vocabulary with that retort.

Tessa took a sip of her shake and stared at him.

He relented. "It's fine. But it isn't home."

"I can see that. You made Raleigh home. You left behind a lot of friends here."

"I did. And a larger sense of belonging that I don't have in DC. But I don't see that changing anytime soon. I'm always traveling. I haven't been home long enough to make my house into anything more than the place I sleep and do laundry."

Tessa furrowed her brow. "You've unpacked, though."

"Mostly."

"Zane, I hate to have to remind you, but you didn't have that much to begin with. How is it possible you've been there six months and haven't unpacked?"

He dragged a fry through ketchup before responding. "There's no real reason to."

"But it's your home."

"I'm never there, so what does it matter? I have a bed. I have a TV. I have clothes. I sometimes have food in the fridge. I have coffee. So I'm good."

"Do you have any pictures out?"

That stopped him. Because he did. But not any he was prepared to share with Tessa. "A few."

"Larger than eight by ten?"

"No."

"Zane! Have you done nothing? Do you have furniture? Towels?"

"You do realize that I'm a guy, right? I don't care."

Tessa shook her head. "That's not true. You had all of that at your house here."

She wasn't wrong. Although, now that he thought about it, most of the homey aspects had been a result of Luke, Gil, or Tessa deciding he needed something and insisting he purchase it. But thanks to their prompting, he had put effort into his place. Nothing elaborate, but it'd had a few nice touches.

Until it burned to the ground.

"Tess, I haven't had time to do anything more than sleep, eat, and run. When I'm there, the last thing I want to think about is whether the shower curtain matches the paint."

"Zane, your home should be your safe space. The place you retreat to when life gets to be too much." She dipped her French fry into her milkshake and nibbled the end of it. "I get that you're a guy." She gave him a very intense look, from head to, well, to as far as she could see before the table got in the way. "No doubt about it."

Was she flirting with him? Before he could follow that up, she continued. "And I can understand being too busy to think about turning your place into a real home, but you need to. You'll unwind and recharge so much better if your home is somewhere you want to be."

He took a bite of his burger to give himself a few seconds to respond. He could be flippant. Or he could open up in the same way she'd opened up to him earlier. "Home is a complicated thing for me, Tess."

"I know."

They'd discussed his childhood at length. Growing up, home wasn't a safe space. It wasn't a retreat. He never invited friends to his house because there was no telling what condition his mom would be in. He learned how to do laundry because that was the only way he had clean clothes. He learned how to make a grilled cheese sandwich from a friend's mom, how to scramble eggs from another one. He ate a lot of canned food—ravioli and random canned meats—not a lot of veggies.

She nudged his plate. "Eat. It will get cold."

He obeyed. Chewed. Swallowed. "The only reason I have a clue what a normal home life looks like is because of what I experienced from my friends growing up, and then watching you, Gil, and Luke make your homes into places of refuge. I appreciate it, and I agree that it's something I should do. But I'm not sure I have the capacity to."

"You know what you need?" Tessa asked after swallowing a huge bite of cheeseburger.

"I'm sure you're going to tell me."

"You need me to come to DC and set up your house." Tess crammed a fry into her mouth. It almost disguised the vulnerable expression on her face.

But he saw it, and he knew he could hurt her right now. He could tell her no, and she would smile and say something glib about how he shouldn't complain about his living conditions if he wouldn't accept assistance. She wouldn't make a big deal out of the fact that she was wounded. She never did.

But they were past the point where he could wound her, even

if it was for her own good. His heart simply refused to consider it. "You have to stay in budget."

Her eyes widened in unmistakable delight, but the glee morphed into a haughty, albeit fake, response. "I'm the queen of discount. The empress of clearance. The czarina of markdown. I never exceed my budget."

They talked specifics while they finished their food. Tessa grinned at him as they left the soda shop. "You won't be sorry."

"I've seen your place, Tess. I know I won't." Her apartment was his favorite spot in Raleigh. It was cozy, restful, clean, uncluttered, and screamed "Tessa lives here" to anyone paying attention. "I retain veto rights on colors and patterns. I'm not putting a floral duvet cover on my bed. There will be no pink, no lavender, and I'm not a huge fan of green."

Tessa linked her arm through his as they walked and discussed his home. He didn't think she even realized they were walking so close that their hips occasionally brushed. Or maybe she did, and she didn't care. He certainly didn't mind.

"You need to make your living room a place you can unwind at the end of the day. Your kitchen needs to have the basic necessities for quick, healthy meals, and your bedroom needs to be an oasis."

"My bedroom needs to be a place I can sleep. That's all I care about."

"That won't work." Tessa squeezed his arm. "It's the first thing you see in the morning, the last thing you see at night. It should be a space that speaks to your soul, calms your nerves, and enables you to fully relax. You need rich wood tones, navy bedding, gray walls, photographs of waterfalls and mountain ranges, and if there's room, a chair with a reading lamp."

Zane's mind filled with the image her words created. The mental picture had him slowing their pace until he brought them to a stop on the sidewalk. "It sounds perfect. How do you know that's what it should be?"

She smiled. "Because I know you. You love blue, you love nature, you had two huge photographs of waterfalls in your place before the fire." Tessa kept her left hand wrapped around his bicep and gestured with her right. "I don't see you with white, light wood or painted furniture. No fabric-tufted headboards."

"That's a definite no."

"I picture a bed frame made of mahogany. Maybe a deep cherry or walnut."

"That sounds a bit harsh."

"No. It sounds warm and solid. Like you. Because the bed is the foundation for the room. I'll find a bedspread that's all masculine lines, but we'll soften it with a plush throw at the foot and a couple of throw pillows—"

"You do realize that I'm going to veto the throw pillows."

"You can't veto them before you've seen them."

"Pretty sure I can."

"You're going to love it."

He would. He had no doubt. And then he would hate it, because at every turn he would see Tessa's touch.

# 14

TESSA DIDN'T GIVE UP on the throw pillows or her idea of using orange in Zane's hall bathroom for a pop of color in the otherwise muted color scheme she had in mind, and the debate raged all the way from Pittsboro to Raleigh.

The afternoon had turned into an almost-date with Zane. He bought her meal. They flirted (a little), talked (a lot), and made plans for the future that involved her spending hours with him in DC. That last part caused tenuous hope to skitter through her system.

The time she'd spent with Zane, time intentionally not thinking about work, had been a needed respite, but Tessa felt the weight of responsibility settle on her shoulders as she walked into the office.

"Special Agent Reed." Greg held up a hand as she scanned herself in, Zane behind her.

She liked Greg fine but she wasn't in the mood to chat, so she kept walking as she said, "Greg, how's it going?"

"Good. Except for when your friend came by."

That stopped her. "Who?"

"Littlefield."

She closed her eyes and took three calming breaths before she opened them. Zane was beside her, his pulse throbbing in his neck. She waited for him to look at her. "Okay?"

He didn't answer her and instead focused on Greg. "Please give us the good news that he's in jail."

"Sorry. Though it wasn't for lack of trying on my part."

"What happened?" Tessa asked. "Start at the beginning. Please."

Greg leaned against his desk. "He showed up around one thirty p.m. with a big basket."

"Do we want to know what was in the basket?" Zane asked.

"He left it, so you can see for yourself."

"What?" Zane looked around Greg's desk area. "Where is it?"

Tessa put her hand on Zane's arm. "Focus. We'll worry about the basket in a minute. Let's get the whole story first." She turned to Greg. "Please, continue."

"Right." Greg pointed out the window. "I saw him getting out of his car, so I called Ms. Leslie to let her know we had some unwanted company and for her to stay put for a few minutes."

"Thank you." Tessa and Zane spoke at the same time.

"Ah. Wasn't nothing. We all love Ms. Leslie. I didn't want her to decide to head home and get caught in the middle of everything, especially since she was in here on a Saturday."

She'd have to remember to add Greg to her coffee rotation when he was in the office. The man could be a scoundrel when it came to his dating life, but he knew his job and did it well.

"Anyway, he came to the door and walked right up to my desk as bold as could be."

"Was his photojournalist with him?" Tessa asked.

"The cameraman? No. It was just Littlefield. He had this basket of stuff. Said he knew you were working today, and that it was an apology gift."

Tessa shared a look with Zane. Sounded like Littlefield had

gotten his rear kicked over the report Friday evening and was trying to make amends.

"I told him he was welcome to leave the basket, but that he
couldn't go any farther. He got all yappy then. Rambling about
freedom of information and freedom of the press. None of it made
sense. I think he throws words like that around to try to intimidate
people. I have a degree in political science and history. I know the
Constitution. I also know the law as it relates to the presence of
a reporter at a federal agency."

*Definitely adding Greg to the coffee club.*

"I repeated myself. Kept my voice calm. Told him no one was
allowed in without prior authorization, which he didn't have. I
did not mention that he was persona non grata. Didn't seem to
be the kind of thing he needed to know. But I did tell him if he
wanted to speak to Special Agent Reed, he should call the office
and schedule an appointment."

Zane leaned against the wall. "How'd he take it?"

"'Bout as well as you might expect. There were several more
minutes of blustering followed by his claiming he would be back
with permission to enter." Greg pointed to the cameras mounted
in the corners of the room. "It's all on video if you want to
watch."

"We'll want to do that. Thanks." Tessa could not believe this was
happening. Wasn't it enough that she had a viable threat against the
president? But now she had to deal with Hank Littlefield's idiocy?

"He left the basket. Said it was for you, and that he would be
calling later."

"Oh, joy."

Greg chortled at her remark. "I hope you don't mind, but I went
through the basket. Took everything out. Scanned it. I haven't had
a dog come, but we can do that."

Tessa couldn't stop herself. She reached for Greg and took his hand. "Thank you for looking out for me."

Did Greg blush? He had a pink tinge to his cheeks as he said, "Gotta take care of my people." He cleared his throat and pointed to the office behind him. "Basket's in there."

"Mind if we take a look?" Tessa asked.

"It's all yours." Greg unlocked the door and stood to the side as Zane and Tessa entered. "I'll be at my desk. Holler if you need anything."

"Will do." Zane shook Greg's hand. "Thanks, man."

Greg closed the door as he left.

Tessa stared at the contents of the basket.

"Zane—"

"I know. I see." Zane was half beside her, half behind her, his body pressed against her back and side. One hand at her waist. "We'll figure this out."

"How could he know any of this?" Tessa pulled out a bag of individually wrapped butterscotch candies. Then a bag of Red Hots. Followed by a container filled with Pixy Stix. A note was written on a card attached to the side of the basket filled with an assortment of candy. In bold block letters it said, "Sweets for the Sweet."

"Have you given any interviews? Talked to anybody about your favorite things?" Zane's body was a wall of heat and tension at her side, and it took all her self-control not to lean into him and let him hold her.

"No."

"Grocery delivery?"

"I don't use a grocery delivery service. I'm too paranoid. I want to pick up the food myself."

They stared at the basket for a long moment before Zane said, "We'll figure it out."

"It's creepy, though. Right? I mean, it isn't me overreacting to—"

Zane leaned into her, his lips at her ear. "It is twisted and sick. You aren't overreacting. This isn't a basket begging for forgiveness. This is a message telling you that he's been watching you for a while. I can't say whether he means it to be a threat. It's possible he's clueless enough to imagine this would flatter you."

"It makes me want to take a shower." Tessa stared at the basket and groaned. "If he's ruined Pixy Stix for me—"

"I'll buy you some on the way home tonight."

She turned into him then. His arms slipped around her, one hand at her waist, one at the back of her head holding her close. "I've got you."

"WE'LL GET TO THE BOTTOM OF IT. You aren't alone." Zane whispered the words against Tessa's hair as he held her tight to him. Tessa rarely showed fear, and even more rarely admitted to needing any kind of comfort. He hated the cause of her distress, but he was so glad he was the one with her as she dealt with it.

He would have held her forever, but a tap on the door made him step back. Not far. He wouldn't leave her to deal with this alone.

Tess, for all her courage and drive, was an intensely private person. When she chose to share something about herself, it was a gift to be cherished. For someone to snoop around and take that from her, take the choice to share or not to share? It only proved how little Hank Littlefield knew Tessa Reed.

"Hey. Greg told us what happened." Luke entered the room, with Gil and Ben following.

"What are we looking at?" Benjamin picked up a box of old-fashioned peppermint sticks.

"This basket is filled with Tessa's favorite candies." Zane

wanted to take the entire basket and toss it into an incinerator, but that would not solve anything.

"Are they poisoned?" Benjamin asked. "Laced with explosives? I'm sorry. I'm not understanding what's got you riled up. It's a basket of candy. Good stuff. If someone brought me a basket of my favorite candy, I'd probably kiss them on the mouth and invite them to Sunday dinner."

Gil leaned toward Luke. "Make a note to never bring Benjamin anything. Ever."

Luke nodded. "Noted."

"Does Sharon know this about you?" Tessa widened her eyes in overdone concern.

"Of course." He waggled his eyebrows at her. "Why do you think she brings me my favorite candy on a regular basis?"

When Tessa turned back to the basket, Benjamin made eye contact with Zane, then mouthed, "She okay?"

To which Zane gave nothing more than a barely there shake of his head. Luke and Gil were talking to Tessa but paying attention to him and Benjamin. Concern on every face. They were taking this seriously, but their banter had lightened the mood and seemed to snap Tessa out of the dark mental space she'd been in.

How was he blessed enough to work with these men? Before he went back to DC, he would have to be sure to tell them how much it meant to him to know they had Tessa's back.

"This came from Hank Littlefield?" Gil removed a box of Bit-O-Honey from the basket. "Did he buy every candy at Mast General Store?"

They didn't have a Mast General in Raleigh, but there was one in Winston-Salem. The store had barrels filled with all manner of candies, including everything from chocolate-covered pretzels to old-fashioned, individually wrapped hard candies. Tessa made it a point to stop there anytime she was in the area. Zane knew that. As did Gil and Luke. Benjamin might have.

But how would Hank Littlefield know about Tessa's deep love for all forms of candy? And not just any candy. He'd created a basket filled with her favorites. Was he following her? Stalking her?

"Looks like it." Luke examined the box of peppermint sticks. "Still sealed."

Tessa finally spoke, her voice rough. "I'm not touching any of it."

"Oh, we're tossing all of it." Gil picked up another bag filled with strawberry bonbons. "But not until we know where it came from and how he could have known that our Tessa has a sweet tooth."

"*I* have a sweet tooth," Benjamin all but growled. "Tessa has a highly advanced sweet obsession. I'd never seen anyone as giddy as she was the day that package came with the Zero bars in it."

Luke and Gil both grinned huge. Tessa kept her eyes on the basket. Benjamin went on, oblivious to the sudden shift of the mood in the room. "You'd have thought someone had given her tickets to the Super Bowl. She hugged the box."

"Did she?" Zane tried to keep his own grin from breaking free.

"Wait." Benjamin turned to Tessa. "They weren't from Littlefield, were they?"

"No."

"Who sent those?" Benjamin asked.

Tessa gave him a tight smile. "Zero bars are hard to find around here. Zane found them and mailed them to me."

Now it was Benjamin's turn to grin, and his grin came with a healthy helping of sly innocence. "Wow. Zane. That was so nice of you."

Zane took back every positive thought he'd ever had about Benjamin North. "Can we get back to the fact that Littlefield showed up here bearing gifts for Tessa?"

"He's a moron." Tessa stood with her arms wrapped around herself as if she were trying to keep from flying apart. "But it's hard for me to see him as a threat. Unless his idiocy has been a long-term ploy to make himself appear too stupid to pull off anything so he can get close and successfully implement an attack."

"We need to get the contents of this basket tested." Luke piled everything back inside. "I'll call CCBI and see what they can do for us."

The City-County Bureau of Identification was unique to Wake County and one of the best forensic teams anywhere. They'd be able to get answers.

"Until we have results, we proceed with caution." Everyone agreed with Luke's remark. "We assume he's either part of the plan to take Tessa out, or he's being used by the people who want her out. If we're wrong, and this is nothing more than a misguided attempt at courting, then we can point out the error of his ways after this is over."

"Do we have to?" Gil tapped the basket. "I mean, wouldn't it be a disservice to all humankind if this man married and reproduced? It would be wrong to unleash someone like him on humanity. If he carries on like this, he'll keep himself out of the dating pool indefinitely."

"Good point. We'll revisit it later." Luke looked around the room. "All agreed?"

A chorus of yeses was the response.

"Excellent. Let's get this stuff out of here, debrief, and go home." Luke picked up the basket. "I'm tired, and I'd like to see my wife before midnight."

"Me too. *My* wife, that is. Not yours." Gil opened the door as laughter filled the room. They filed out and went down the hall to their offices, each with a wave or salute to Greg.

**WHEN THEY REACHED** the conference room, Luke and Gil veered off to log the offending basket in to evidence. Benjamin's phone rang, and he disappeared into the cubicles to answer it.

Tessa was left alone with Zane. There were so many things she wanted to say. Needed to say. But now wasn't the time or the place. So she settled for the barest minimum acceptable response. "Thank you."

"Anytime, Princess."

Princess. She would gut anyone else for using the nickname, but she'd never been able to deny how much she loved it when Zane called her that.

Before she could say anything else, Rodriguez and Carver returned and filled her and Zane in on their day.

"Your local law enforcement is quite accommodating," Carver observed when they had finished bringing her up to speed. "It's clear they have an excellent working relationship with this office."

"We've worked hard to make it so." Tessa made a note to pass the words along to Jacob.

"One detective there today seemed mighty interested in you, Tessa." Rodriguez took a seat and lounged, his long legs stretched out in front of him, crossed at the ankles. He was a good-looking man, but he did nothing for her.

"Was it Morris?" she asked.

"It was. So you know him? He seems a little old for you."

"He is a little old for me." Tessa did not want to get into a discussion about this with Rodriguez. "He's helped us with multiple investigations and is an excellent law enforcement officer and friend to our office. You've misinterpreted friendship for something else."

"Well, your *friend* seemed awfully protective of you. Are you sure he isn't looking for more than a professional relationship?"

"Quite." Tessa kept her voice calm, if it was a bit clipped. She didn't know what game he was playing, but she didn't have any inclination to discover how his mind worked. Rodriguez opened his mouth to say something else, but Benjamin, Luke, and Gil returned to the conference room and Tessa took advantage of the distraction to bring them back to things that mattered, like how they were going to keep the president safe when he arrived on Friday.

They covered everything each group had accomplished, which aside from the successful meeting with local law enforcement, added up to a whole lot of not much.

Benjamin must have sensed her frustration, because he spoke up when she asked if anyone had anything else to add. "We only eliminated a handful of threats today, but we also know where to best direct our resources. That's progress. It's part of what makes this job so frustrating. You can spend hours and hours and get to the end of the day with little to show for it. Then the next day you clear the board in thirty minutes."

"I doubt we'll get that lucky tomorrow, but thanks for the pep talk." Tessa dismissed everyone and requested that they return tomorrow by one. "Go to church, sleep in, grab brunch, whatever you need to do. We're facing a long week, and we need to be able to give it all we've got."

"Yes, ma'am." Rodriguez snapped her a salute before turning to the others. "What's the nightlife like in Raleigh?"

Benjamin, Luke, and Gil gave him blank stares.

"You're on your own, Rodriguez." Zane pointed to the other three men. "They have wives. New-to-them wives. They aren't interested in partying."

"Add me to that list," Carver said. "My wife expects me to sit quietly in my hotel room all evening, and I don't plan to disappoint her."

Rodriguez turned to Tessa. "How about it?"

She was done with this. It was time to shut him down. Now. "Rodriguez, I'm not interested in spending the evening with you under any circumstances. Like Zane said, if you want to party, you're on your own." She stood. "Have fun, but don't do anything to bring dishonor to the agency. I have enough to deal with this week."

With that, she left the conference room and walked to her desk.

The howls of laughter that followed her down the hall weren't enough to make her even consider a smile.

Why was this happening? Hank Littlefield had always struck her as clueless but harmless. But that candy basket was eerily accurate. Almost every candy in there was one she indulged in.

She'd always had a sweet tooth. It was something she shared with her dad. He would call her or text her a video anytime he discovered a new candy. If she couldn't find it, he'd mail it to her.

While she was in India after his death, she considered never eating candy again as a type of tribute to him. But then she realized that was ridiculous. Instead, she would honor his memory by continuing the tradition, even if he wasn't there to enjoy it with her. She would pick up new candies, try exotic flavors, experiment with the weird in hopes of finding the wonderful. And that's what she did.

After she returned from India, she talked to Zane about it. He helped her find the best candy shops in the city, and he paid attention. He knew which ones were her favorites, which ones were her dad's favorites that she chose specifically to remember him, and which ones she had tried but didn't like.

She'd never explained it to anyone else. They just thought she really liked candy.

"Hey." She turned to find Zane leaning against the doorway to her cubicle. "You ready to call it a day?"

"It's only seven. I should stay here. Work some more."

"Or," Zane said, "we could get out of here. Stop by the store to grab some candy to clear your emotional palate. Get you settled in at your place."

The words sounded lovely, but she knew the motive behind them. "Nice try, Thacker."

"What?" Zane was innocence personified.

"You're trying to get me behind the security systems at my apartment before you go out with the guys tonight."

"You must have me confused with some other overprotective friend. Didn't you hear Gil and Luke? They're going home to their wives."

"Have you forgotten that their wives are my best friends?"

Zane kept up the charade. "What does that have to do with anything?"

"It means I know they want to see their wives. They didn't lie. But I also know they have plans to go out with you tonight. Dinner and some time in the batting cages if I'm not mistaken?"

"Maybe?" Zane dropped the act. "Under the circumstances, none of us are okay with leaving you here alone."

She knew a guilt trip when she saw one. This one had neon signs flashing all around it. Zane was here for only a few days. The guys had missed him and were looking forward to tonight. She could cause a stink about it, or she could go home.

Alone.

Which wasn't as pitiful as it sounded. Tessa liked being alone. Faith and Ivy had volunteered to hang out with her this evening, but she needed a quiet night in.

"Fine. I'll go home. Happy?"

"Deliriously."

She packed up her things, and he fell in step with her as she left the office. "Zane?"

"Hmm?"

"What are you doing?"

"I'm coming with you."

She stopped in the hall. "Why? Aren't you going out with Luke and Gil?"

"Tess. I can't go home with either of them. They weren't kidding about wanting to see their wives. I don't want to be a third wheel. I'm going with you. We're stopping for candy. Then any groceries you might need or any other stops you need to make. Then I'll hang out with you at your place until they come by to pick me up. They'll drop me back at my hotel tonight."

"Did it ever occur to you to ask me if I was in favor of that plan? Maybe I want to go home alone. Maybe I don't want you hovering over me in full protective mode until you're sure I'm safely behind the security walls of my apartment complex."

She was prepared for Zane to argue. Prepared for a snappy comeback. Prepared for a well-reasoned argument about why this plan was the best plan and she should roll with it.

She was not prepared for Zane to step toward her, put one hand on her waist, and lean close to whisper, "I promised you we'd get candy on the way home. It's important to me. Please let me do this."

This was the second time today that Zane had asked her for something. Asked to spend time with her. Asked to do something for her.

And she found that she couldn't tell him no. Not when he laid his feelings out there and made no effort to hide what he wanted.

"Fine. Candy. My place. Then you go smack some baseballs around until you and Luke are mad at Gil for being better than you."

"Thanks, Tess."

# 15

ZANE WOKE IN HIS HOTEL room on Tuesday morning and grabbed his phone to call Tess.

"Hey." Her answer was warm, and he got the impression that she'd been waiting for his call. As she should, since he'd called her at the same time every morning since he'd been in town.

"Sleep okay?" He put the phone on speaker, then climbed out of the bed and made it. He always made his bed first thing, and he never got regular housekeeping while in a hotel. The last thing he wanted was someone entering his room when he wasn't there.

Her yawn proceeded a muffled, "No."

"Why not?"

"Brain wouldn't shut off." He didn't give her any tips to improve her sleep health. She'd sleep fine once the president had come and gone. And once the people behind the threats against her had been apprehended. "How'd you sleep?"

"Fine. I woke up twice but went right back to sleep." After checking his phone to be sure he hadn't missed any messages. "It's a survival mechanism. I've learned to sleep when I can, wherever I can."

They avoided speaking of the twelve hours they worked on

Sunday, the eighteen on Monday, the security protocols they were following up on today, the fact that they had less than forty-eight hours before Raleigh was invaded by the president's advance teams, or that last night they received word that Craig Brown, their "person most likely to try to assassinate the president on this trip," was seen in Charlotte . . . at a drone expo.

No. They talked about the ridiculous bike ride she was training for. The Assault on Mt. Mitchell began in the Upstate of South Carolina and covered over one hundred miles, a painful majority of it uphill, until it ended at the top of Mt. Mitchell, the highest peak east of the Mississippi. She expected it to take her a few years to be ready, but she was determined to pull it off.

He had no doubt she would succeed. Right now, however, her work hours made consistent training difficult if not impossible, and the lockdown they'd put her in since the threats on her life began had further impeded her ability to ride. She'd squeezed in an indoor ride Sunday morning, but it would be the weekend before she got in another one.

"I don't have to do it this year, or even next year," she said. "But I need a goal. It keeps me motivated."

"I'd rather run a marathon than ride a bike that far."

"That's because you're weird." Before he could argue, she said, "Gil's here. See you in a few."

"Be careful."

"Always."

ZANE WAS WAITING by the curb when Gil and Tessa pulled in to pick him up. He opened the door. "Morning."

Gil gave him a small salute. "Tessa is already bossing me around."

"What's new?" Zane slid into the seat behind Tessa and gently tugged the fall of wavy hair that flowed down the seat. He leaned toward her and whispered, "Morning, Princess."

She turned enough so he could catch her glare before she picked up the conversation she and Gil had been in the middle of. "I'm saying that you don't have a leg to stand on. You need to butt out."

"She's my sister." Gil turned in the opposite direction of the office. "And they haven't been dating that long."

"They've been dating almost a year." Tessa held up a hand when Gil went to protest. "Let's see. You reunited with Ivy in October, was it? You proposed at Christmas. And then you married her in, wait, let me think. Oh, that's right. June of the following year. Is that correct?"

"That was different. I'd known Ivy almost my entire life."

"You hadn't spoken to her since you were seventeen!" Tessa's hair swayed as she shook her head. "Emily and Liam have been together for almost a year, and he just now popped the question."

"He's been working a detail for that year. They've barely seen each other."

Zane didn't comment. Gil wasn't wrong. Neither was Tessa. And Emily, Gil's twin sister, would do whatever she wanted.

"Gil." Up to this point, Tessa's arguments had been light-hearted, but her tone was serious now. "She loves you. She doesn't need your approval, but she wants it. Don't give her a hard time. Trust her to know her own mind and heart. You can go a little big brother on her, but be careful that you don't overdo it."

Gil dropped his head back against the headrest. "Why do you do this to me?"

"Do what?"

"Make me see reason?"

"That's my job."

Their shared laughter settled over Zane, and he waited until it had died down to ask, "Where are we going?"

"It's Tuesday." Gil said this as if that explained everything.

"He doesn't know." Tessa twisted in her seat enough that he could see her face. "I found a new place. It's called The Slam Dunk."

Understanding dawned. "What's their specialty?"

Tessa sighed in a potent mixture of anticipation and delight that gave him a glimpse of what she had looked like when she was an innocent girl who'd never experienced any pain or trauma. "Doughnuts." Her eyes were closed, her expression pure bliss. "And on Tuesday, they have a crème brûlée doughnut with vanilla custard, and they torch the top."

"Every Tuesday," Gil said. "We had to increase our weekly coffee club dues to pay for the doughnuts, not that any of us are complaining. They have a peanut butter and jelly doughnut that will make you think you're headed to kindergarten instead of the office. You'll start looking for your little desk with the pencil holder at the top."

"Peanut butter and jelly?" Zane didn't try to hide his skepticism. He was a doughnut purist. Plain. Glazed. Krispy Kreme. Done.

"I ordered several of everything today." Tessa had a light in her eyes that some might call rabid. Not that he would say that out loud. "Zane has to try them all. They have the best glazed yeast doughnuts, but their sourdough with the chocolate and hazelnuts?"

"Ivy's favorite. And Emily's." Gil flicked on the blinker. "Here we go. Zane, get ready for a sugar overload. The last time I went in here with Tessa, I gained five pounds before I got back to the car."

They walked in and the aroma of sugar, yeast, and coffee, with hints of chocolate and cinnamon, permeated the air. Tessa bumped his arm. "You'll smell like this place for a few hours. Hope you don't mind."

"Remind me not to come in here before the president arrives."

"Your order is ready, Special Agent Reed." A young woman stood behind the counter. "We added the extra coffees and doughnuts you requested for this week."

"Thank you, Cherry." Tessa handed over her credit card.

Cherry leaned toward her, and Zane didn't pretend not to eavesdrop. "I saw you on the news Friday night. You're famous!"

Tessa's smile was genuine, her words full of a big-sister warmth when she replied. "Thanks. But don't believe everything you see on the news. The only part of the story he got right was my name."

"But you were at the Carmichael estate. Right?" Cherry returned the credit card to Tessa. "I've always wanted to see inside. It's supposed to be gorgeous."

"How do you know about the Carmichaels?" Tessa framed the question as one would when mildly curious.

"Oh, their children are the same age as my aunt. She went to middle school with one of them. She went to a couple of birthday parties at the house and says the place was unbelievable. But, of course, she doesn't remember a lot of details."

"I can confirm that it is a stunning home. Beautifully furnished and quite elegant. But I can't say more."

Cherry's wonder was evident on her face. "You have the coolest job."

"Some days it is." Tessa took the coffees one of the baristas handed her. "But you have a cool job too. Coming here is one of the highlights of my week. You make people happy. Don't ever minimize the importance of that. There are not nearly enough happy people in the world, so you're doing a good thing."

Cherry's eyes were glistening as she whispered her thanks. It

took Gil, Zane, and Tessa to carry out the coffees and the three—
yes, three—bags of doughnuts.

"Do I want to know how many doughnuts you bought?" Zane
asked.

Tessa hugged two of the bags to her. "I suggest you don't ask
questions you don't want the answers to." Her tone was frosty,
but her smile was like an iced tea on a hot day.

Zane followed behind Tessa, with Gil splitting off to go to the
driver's side. But before they made it to the car, an extended-cab
pickup pulled in and parked beside their vehicle. There were four
other open spaces. Why did he park so close? The driver opened
his door and temporarily pinned Tessa in the space between the
car and the truck. He hopped down and moved to close his door,
which left him inches away from Tessa.

And that was when Zane saw the knife.

TESSA'S ANNOYANCE at the truck driver's rudeness morphed
into fury when he stepped toward her, knife in hand.

This was getting old. How much of a weakling did they think
she was? She was a trained federal officer. She wasn't about to be
taken out by a knife-wielding imbecile. Before he took another
step, Tessa threw the doughnuts at the man. It startled him long
enough for her to adjust her position in the tight space between
vehicles and aim a kick at his knee.

Her foot connected, and that knee would never be the same.
His scream tainted the cool morning air and almost covered the
sound of the knife hitting the pavement. Her would-be attacker
sagged against Gil's car before he slid to the ground with his hands
clutched around his damaged leg.

By the time he was down, Gil was on the other side of the narrow gap between the truck and the car, weapon drawn.

Zane was a warm presence at her back, and she didn't need to look to know that he also had a weapon drawn.

They had the man covered, so she knelt beside the bag of doughnuts that had landed near the driver's-side door of the truck. She opened it and removed a napkin from the top. She swiveled to her right and, with the napkin, lifted the knife from its location a foot underneath Gil's car.

She stood and did nothing to hide her disgust. "This knife is filthy."

Zane stepped back enough for her to slide out from between the vehicles, and she showed him the knife. "When am I going to get attacked by a classy criminal?"

Zane didn't crack a smile.

"I'll call it in."

TWO HOURS AND NO DOUGHNUTS LATER, she walked into her office with Zane on one side, Gil on the other, Luke in front, Benjamin behind. They'd put her in a bubble the moment she exited the car in the parking lot, and they'd refused to listen to reason. She argued against their overprotective behavior, but when Benjamin made an unveiled threat about shoving her back in the car and returning her to the warm embrace of Detective Morris, she gave in.

Morris was apoplectic when he arrived at The Slam Dunk. If she got within ten feet of him now, he'd snatch her up and put her in protective custody. As it was, she wouldn't want to be in her would-be assailant's shoes today. The Raleigh police were less than thrilled to have him in custody, partly because the FBI was insisting on keeping their fingers in the pie. The Raleigh PD, FBI, Secret Service, CCBI, and other law enforcement/forensic entities in the city got along reasonably well. But no one loved having representatives from another agency on their turf.

Greg stood at the security desk, hands on his hips and his expression set to "don't mess with me today."

"Greg, if I should feel compelled to run screaming from the building, would you attempt to stop me?" Tessa asked in lieu of a greeting.

"No, ma'am." He pointed at her entourage. "But I wouldn't stop them from coming after you either."

"You're no help." She waved and tried to smile enough so he would know there were no hard feelings.

His response was a curt nod to her and extended eye contact with Zane. If she'd had any doubt, it was gone. Any escape attempts on her part, and Greg would rat her out to Zane in a heartbeat.

Not that she planned to escape. She wasn't an idiot. And as she'd told Zane, she didn't have a death wish. She liked her head on her shoulders where it belonged. She also had an intense desire to remain hole-free for the duration of her career and beyond.

But whoever was behind these attacks was either an evil genius or a few crumbs short of a biscuit. The people coming after her were doing such a bad job of it, she was almost embarrassed for them.

Her protective bubble popped when they reached their cubicles, and everyone separated to go to their own desks.

Zane paused at her cubicle, and she dropped her bag into the bottom desk drawer, then turned to face him.

He took a small step back. "You're mad."

"You're just now figuring that out? I may need to downgrade my estimation of your intelligence."

"Burn!" The word came from the other side of her wall, and tense but real laughter floated through the room on its heels.

"We love you, Tessa," Gil called out in a singsong voice that could have come from one of the elementary-aged ballplayers he coached.

"We do," Luke agreed.

She couldn't stay mad at them. But that didn't mean she could give in too easily. She crossed her arms and leaned back against her desk. "What? Nothing from Benjamin?"

Benjamin came around the side of the cubicle, and one look at him sent a chill straight to her bones. "What happened?" she asked.

Benjamin swallowed. "He's dead."

"Who?"

"The assailant from this morning."

Before Tessa could wrap her mind around the news, her phone rang. She let it go to voice mail, but when the ringing stopped, it began almost immediately in Gil's cubicle. He ignored it. But then Luke's phone rang. That couldn't be a coincidence.

"Powell." Luke's voice carried through the walls. A pause, then, "You cannot be serious. Does he have a death wish?" Another pause. "Yeah. I'll tell her. Hang tight."

Luke joined Benjamin outside her cubicle, Gil hot on his heels. Luke pointed down the hall. "Care to guess who's here wanting to talk to you about the incident this morning and the dead assailant?"

Tessa dropped her chin to her neck. "Littlefield."

"The one and only." Luke rubbed his chin.

"How could he possibly know about the guy being dead? We found out five seconds ago!" Gil had a baseball in his hands and tossed it to Luke.

Luke tossed it back. "I say we let Jacob deal with him."

"I'll—"

Whatever Zane was going to say was cut off when Luke grabbed his arm. "*You* are the last person who needs to go out there."

Zane didn't contest Luke's assertion. "Where's Jacob?"

Gil waved his phone in their direction with one hand, then put it to his ear. "Jacob? Yeah." Gil walked away, filling Jacob in on what was going on.

Zane, Luke, and Benjamin stepped a few feet away but didn't go far.

Tessa ignored all of them and sat down at her desk, closed her eyes, and inhaled. Then she concentrated on every body part. First she focused on her feet in her favorite boots. They were the unicorn of boots that she'd searched for years to find. They were not only fashionable but also comfortable, and she could run in them if necessary. And as this morning's events had proven, she could kick the tendons and ligaments out of a knee while wearing them.

She wiggled her toes, then pressed them down on the floor. Next she rotated her ankles before settling her feet once again. She worked her way up, tensing and releasing her calf muscles, flexing her legs at the knees, squeezing her quads, concentrating on her abdominals, inhaling slowly and deeply to feel her chest expand before pressing her shoulders back to tighten and then relax her upper back. To complete the exercise, she rolled her head in a slow circle. After three rotations in one direction, she reversed course. All four of her fellow agents had returned to her doorway while she was rolling out her neck, but they'd seen her do this before and didn't interrupt.

Taking a minute to zero in on her body and breathing gave her the ability to focus past the frustration that had spiked at the one-two punch of a dead assailant and a very much alive and in the way

Hank Littlefield. And that brought some clarity to her thoughts. "Is it possible someone has Littlefield on a leash?"

Her question got the attention of the three men in her doorway. Gil spoke first. "You think he could be connected to the attacks?"

"I think it's interesting that he keeps showing up. One time, fine. But unless he's truly delusional, and I'm not ruling that out as a possibility, nothing about my behavior toward him can explain this level of infatuation."

"Infatuation isn't rational." Zane paced back and forth, coming in and out of her vision as he crossed in front of her cubicle. "But it's an interesting hypothesis. We need to add him to our list of possibles."

Gil checked his watch. "Jacob should be here any minute. He's going to chat with Littlefield, and when they talk, he's going to mention that if Hank interferes with an ongoing investigation, we'll throw the entire weight of the federal government behind his prosecution. There may be a few words like *aiding and abetting* and *collusion* headed his way. Also words like *sexual harassment* and a few observations regarding how incredibly awkward it would be for him if we let it slip that one of our agents took out a restraining order against him."

"I haven't done anything of the sort." Tessa sat straighter in her chair. "I can handle him."

"He needs to know we're taking this seriously." Gil was implacable. "We don't take chances. We'd do the same thing if it was a female reporter chasing after one of us."

Tessa couldn't argue with that, but she didn't want to think about it anymore. "Can we get back to our dead assailant? Benjamin? What happened? Last time I checked, blown knees aren't fatal."

"Sorry, Tessa. Morris didn't have much time, but he was able to tell me that they took our assailant to the hospital, where he was seen by medical staff prior to his incarceration. They put his knee in a brace and sent him on to jail. They all knew he'd need surgery in a few days, but that was no reason to keep him in the hospital. Any regular citizen with a similar knee injury would be sent home until the swelling went down, then surgery a few days to a week later."

"Okay." Tessa was following the narrative, but she still didn't see how any of that could have killed him.

"They did their usual intake, put him in a cell alone. They have cameras all over the place, and the officer on duty noticed that our guy was twitchy. Assumed it was from pain. Maybe nerves. Then the guy's twitching turned into full-body spasms. The officer called reinforcements and the paramedics. They did all they could, but the guy was dead by the time they got him to the hospital."

"That sounds like poison or drugs."

"Agreed. Morris couldn't give me any more details and said he would let us know when he had more. And"—Benjamin looked at the floor, and when he returned his gaze to hers, there was a wicked gleam in his eyes—"to lock you down."

Tessa would have been angry if she'd thought he was serious. Well, okay, he was serious, but he wouldn't follow through. Still, she couldn't let it go without some kind of response. "Morris is dead to me. Tell him that when he calls back."

# 16

JACOB ARRIVED, and Gil, Luke, and Benjamin slipped away to eavesdrop on his conversation with Littlefield. Tessa declined to join them, and Zane waved them away.

They took the hint, and for the first time all day, Zane and Tessa were alone.

"You were magnificent. That kick." Zane shuddered. "Perfection."

Tessa huffed. "Yeah."

"You feel bad that he's dead." He didn't frame it as a question.

"I have the sense that he was being used. And whoever used him killed him." Tessa pressed her palms to her temples and held the tension for several seconds. "We're missing something big, and people are dying."

"You aren't pulling the trigger. You aren't ordering the hits. There is a reason, but you aren't it."

Tessa didn't speak.

"I have something for you that might cheer you up." Zane waited for Tessa to look at him.

When she did, there was a trace of curiosity in her expression. "You got me a surprise?"

"I did."

"When did you have time?"

"I'm sneaky."

That earned him narrowed eyes and blatant skepticism. "What is it?"

"Sit tight." He jogged to Luke's desk and retrieved the small bag he'd had Luke carry in. He returned to Tessa and extended the bag to her.

She took it. "Thank you."

"You don't even know what's inside. You might hate it."

"Unlikely. You give good gifts."

He hadn't known she thought that about him. "Then I hope I haven't set the bar too high. As you said, there wasn't much time."

She opened the bag and peered inside. A small gasp escaped as she removed the crème brûlée doughnut and studied it. "How did you get this? They were sold out."

By the time she, Zane, and Gil had the opportunity to go back inside, the crème brûlée doughnuts were gone, the doughnut case empty. The doughnuts they'd already purchased had been scarfed down by grateful first responders, law enforcement officers, and FBI agents, but Zane had acted long before then. "I may have run inside and asked Cherry to set one aside for you."

"Thank you. I could kiss you right now!"

His gaze flicked from the doughnut to her mouth, a mouth that was hanging open, the doughnut forgotten as she stared at him.

"Anytime."

Her eyes flared and she turned to her desk, opened a drawer, and removed a plastic knife and a napkin. That drawer was Tessa's version of a Mary Poppins bag. She had everything in there.

Ten seconds later, the moment was over, the doughnut had been cut, and she handed him half.

"No. You eat it. I got it for you." Zane tried to give it back, but she refused to listen.

"Please. I wanted *you* to try it. I can't sit here and eat the whole thing while you watch."

"Fine." He took the doughnut, then tapped it to her half in a toast. "To a week of questions that can be answered."

"Amen." She took a bite and sighed. "Perfection."

He took a bite and had a moment of regret that he hadn't asked Cherry to hold back a dozen. "This," he said around another mouthful, "is amazing."

"I know, right?" Tessa told him about how she'd discovered The Slam Dunk and how she'd made it her personal mission to make sure everyone knew they existed.

"I've told people at church, in my cycling club, at my AA meetings, and in my apartment building about them. I even sent some to Detective Morris for his birthday. He's now devoted. I have yet to find anyone who's tried them and hasn't fallen in love." Her eyes met his, and a spark of something flashed between them. She cleared her throat. "With the doughnuts."

He wiped his mouth with a corner of a napkin. "That's a relief. For a second I thought you meant they infused their doughnuts with a love potion."

She tossed a wadded-up napkin at him, and her laughter was real and unforced, her eyes clear, and her mood lighter than it had been all day. "Can you imagine the chaos? People falling in love with random strangers because their lemon-filled doughnut made them? No thank you."

"I don't know. It might not be so bad. You might fall in love with a millionaire who wants to whisk you away to the Amalfi Coast."

She snorted. "With my luck, the guy would be running some kind of scam and living in a van down by the river."

145

Zane laughed, but before he could comment further, Jacob called from down the hall. "Zane? Tessa? Could you come here, please?" Jacob's yell told Zane two things. Littlefield was long gone, and Jacob had enjoyed getting rid of him.

Tessa stood and joined Zane as they headed down the hall.

"So to be clear, you're a firm no on love potions?"

"That is correct." She nudged his arm with hers and leaned close. "Besides, who needs a love potion when you have doughnuts?"

He had no time to respond. Not that he was currently in a position to say anything. Because the look in her eyes told him she'd seen right through him. Clearly, he wasn't being as subtle and sneaky as he thought he was. Being with her was breaking down the walls he'd erected to protect himself and making him forget all the reasons he'd put those walls up in the first place. Did she have any idea how desperately he missed her? Or how much he wished he hadn't friend-zoned her at the beginning of their relationship? Or how even though she had a past that terrified him, he believed her future was bright and would give anything to share it with her?

Whether she did or didn't, now wasn't the time for any declarations. They joined the group standing near Leslie's desk, and he forced himself to pay attention to Jacob and not the woman standing an inch from his left shoulder.

"I believe I made my point to Mr. Littlefield." Jacob rubbed a hand over his head. "It's hard for me to believe anyone that imbecilic ever made it on the air, but if he's faking it, he deserves a Tony, an Emmy, *and* an Oscar."

"Come on, Jacob." Gil patted him on the back. "Tell us how you really feel."

"I feel like filling his rear with buckshot if he shows up on the property again. But I won't." There was no mistaking the regret in Jacob's tone. "However, if he gets anywhere near Tessa, I won't quibble if he finds himself on the wrong end of a few well-placed kicks." Jacob stage-whispered to Tessa. "If you take out *his* knees, he won't be able to follow you around."

"I'll keep that in mind."

"Good. But since he doesn't have the good sense the Lord surely tried to give him, I made a phone call to the station and spoke to the general manager. He assured me he would rein Littlefield in."

"Do you believe him?" Tessa asked.

"Not even a little. Which is why I also alerted the FBI and the Raleigh PD. Littlefield isn't welcome anywhere. He'll have to get his information from other sources, but they won't be official ones. Not that it's likely to stop him, but it should slow him down. A little."

"Unless he's working for whoever is behind the attacks on Tessa." Zane didn't know how he could be, but they couldn't rule it out.

"If he is, he'll out himself soon enough. The man is persona non grata in this building or anywhere near Tessa. Greg knows, and he'll pass it along to the rest of the security team." Jacob turned to Tessa. "I'd like a word with you in my office."

Tessa didn't flinch. "Yes, sir."

**TESSA FOLLOWED** Jacob into his office.

"Have a seat, Tessa."

"Yes, sir."

"It's just us. You can drop the 'sir' stuff." He sat, not behind his desk but in the chair beside her.

"Habit, sir. I mean . . . just habit." She was taught early and often to use her manners.

"I know." Jacob shook his head, his smile warm and indulgent. "But please relax. You aren't in trouble. You aren't about to lose your role. You aren't even going to be asked stupid questions about how you're holding up, because I know you're frustrated, but you're holding up fine. And I trust you to come to me or your fellow agents if that isn't the case."

Tessa did relax at Jacob's no-nonsense summation of the situation. "So . . ."

"I need a favor."

He'd said that to her before. Tessa rubbed her hands together and made no effort to hide her glee. "What's my budget?"

"How do you know I want you to spend my money?" Jacob frowned, but there was no real frustration in it.

"Because that's how you asked me to help you find the diamond earrings your wife wanted. And the best deal on flights to Mexico. And that furniture for your parents, and—"

"Okay. Fine. Point made. It's your own fault. It's like you walk into stores and the best deals magically appear before you. You get online and, presto, the same thing I was going to buy for a thousand dollars is now in the cart for five hundred. Now I can't make any large purchases without thinking, *Could Tessa find this for less?*"

Tessa laughed at Jacob's obvious ploy to butter her up. "My mother is the master. I learned everything I know from her. Her motto was that if my father was going to make a bunch of money, she was going to make the effort to spend as little of it as possible. She's always wheeling and dealing, bartering, trading, and finding the best deals. She would skin me alive if I paid full price for anything."

"The next time I see your mother, I'm going to tell her that not only are you one of the finest agents I've ever had the privilege to work with, but you've also single-handedly saved me thousands of dollars and made me look like a hero to my wife and family. I might have to give her a kiss on the cheek."

"She would be delighted."

The truth was, her mom would probably be prouder of the fact that Tessa knew how to save a buck than she was about her being an excellent agent. But Tessa had long learned to deal with her mom's version of approval.

"Excellent. I know you're busy, obviously, but I also wanted you to start thinking about this. I want to take the family to Florida, the 30A area, for spring break. Still months away, but I know those places book fast."

"I know several people who own rentals there." Tessa's mind was already categorizing the locations. "Do you want to be right on the ocean? Or just in the area?"

They chatted for a few more minutes, and when she stood to leave, Jacob placed a big hand on her forearm. "Tessa?"

The serious tone in his voice had her responding in kind. "Jacob?"

His hand flexed on her arm. "Be careful. I can't lose anyone else."

"I will." She placed her hand over his. "I promise."

She was almost out of his office when he called her again. "Tessa?"

"Yes, sir?"

He pointed to the door. "I'm not the only one who wouldn't make it if we lost you. You know that, right?"

Tessa couldn't be certain if Jacob meant the entire group of men who were waiting for her at Leslie's desk or the one man who watched her with narrowed eyes and didn't relax until she gave him a smile that she hoped conveyed that everything was okay. But either way, she knew he was right.

Zane pulled away from the knot of agents and met her halfway down the hall. "Everything okay?" He stood in front of her, preventing her from walking down the hall and blocking the others' view of her as they spoke.

"Yes. I don't think Jacob meant to be so dramatic. He's planning a trip. Wants some help finding a good deal."

"That's it?" Zane didn't move.

"For the most part."

"Right. And what about the other part?"

"A brief conversation that can be summed up with, 'Don't get dead or we'll fall apart,' and I promised I'd do my best."

Zane nodded and stepped aside. She had a similar conversation with Luke, Gil, Benjamin, and Leslie before she was able to return to her desk. Leslie, bless her, had ordered lunch. And because Leslie ran their office with the skill of a CEO and the heart of Mother Teresa, she'd ordered Tessa's favorite. Chicken salad on sourdough. Lettuce, tomato, salt, pepper, and a hint of mayo. Kettle chips. Fruit cup instead of a cookie. Large unsweetened tea. And a sticky note on the box.

*Let not your heart faint. Do not fear or panic or be in dread of them, for the Lord your God is he who goes with you to fight for you against your enemies, to give you the victory.*

Leslie had a knack for finding the perfect Bible verses for the moment. Today was no exception. Tessa bowed her head and thanked God for her food and for his presence. Then she got back to work.

When Morris called two hours later, Tessa answered with, "What do you have for me?"

"I don't have this officially. But I'm passing it along because I think you need to know. The ME told me he believes our dead guy was dead before you ever destroyed his knee."

"Is that supposed to bother me?"

"Which part? The dead guy being dead. Yeah. That part's weird. But scaring off these guys? No. You shouldn't be bothered. You should be proud. They aren't good enough. And if they get scared off by a woman who knows how to defend herself, good riddance."

"Then we're on the same page. Talk to me about the dead guy."

Morris heaved a sigh. "The medical examiner had some students in today and thought this was an excellent opportunity for them, so he bumped our guy to the head of the line."

Tessa made a note to thank the ME later. "What did he see that makes him think our guy was a dead man walking?"

"Two pills in the stomach that hadn't fully dissolved. ME says that happens sometimes with a slow-release medicine. They're designed to dissolve slowly. The ME doesn't have toxicology yet, but based on the manner of death and something about the way the stomach looked, he strongly suspects poison."

"Seems strange for the ME to share something like that. They're usually pretty by the book over there. No results that aren't confirmed." Tessa had spent enough time with Benjamin's wife, Dr. Sharon Oliver, to know that this was not normal procedure. Sharon would never release information this way.

"It is highly unusual, but the ME mentioned it because he's seen this before."

Tessa straightened in her chair. "We don't get a lot of poisonings in Raleigh."

"We don't. But this particular ME remembers a similar situation. Two years ago."

"How similar?" Tessa's mind raced with possibilities.

"Similar stomach contents. Otherwise healthy woman. Dead of what turned out to be strychnine poisoning."

"Strychnine? What is this, an Agatha Christie novel?"

Morris snorted. "That's what made the ME take notice. Because that first death was never solved. There was no doubt that the strychnine killed her, and that was listed as her cause of death. But no one could confirm whether she died by suicide or ingested the pills under false pretenses."

"So someone is running around Raleigh putting strychnine in slow-release capsules and killing people with it? How do they get them to take the pills in the first place?"

"That's where I come in, Special Agent Reed." Morris could be a dog with a bone when something didn't make sense to him. "Tox is being rushed, but it'll be a few weeks at best before we know for sure if it's the same MO. But I've already requested the case files on the death the ME told me about. There's something here. I can feel it."

Morris was a curmudgeon 98 percent of the time. But he was an excellent detective 100 percent of the time. He would run this down.

"Bottom line for now is that they sent this guy to kill me and planned to kill him regardless."

"Close. They had *already* killed him before they sent him after you. He just wasn't dead yet."

"DID YOU KILL HIM?"

The Fixer wasn't surprised by the anger in the voice. The question, however, was unusual. This client had never appreciated that the work done on his behalf was often messy. He never got his hands dirty, and he lived in blissful oblivion. He never wanted to know. Plausible deniability was the name of the game.

How he'd become so powerful and influential remained a mystery.

Or maybe not. When all your problems magically disappeared, climbing the social and political ladders was easy.

"You and I have an agreement. You give me the jobs. I do them the way I see fit. You stay out of it. Are you interested in renegotiating our business relationship?"

"Of course not. But if *I'm* wondering if you killed him, then others are too."

"No, they aren't." The sound of liquid splashed over ice, and the cubes clinked against crystal. "No one in Raleigh knows about me. That's why I'm so good at what I do."

"But—"

"Everyone else is trying to solve a puzzle without having a clue what the final image will be. We are the only two people who have the whole picture." At least that was true as far as this client knew. Others had a vested interest in this mess, but the Fixer had no plans to share that information. Ever.

The client moaned. "She could ruin everything."

Yes, she could. But taking her out directly was too big a risk and one the Fixer would attempt only if there was no other option. "I didn't get where I am by making foolish mistakes or taking unnecessary risks. I'm covered. You're covered. She'll be out of the picture soon."

"Before Friday."

"That's the plan. Stick to it. Continue your normal activities. You've done nothing wrong." Lately. "You know nothing about the threats made against her or the attacks that have been dogging her steps."

"That's true."

"And if someone should speak to you about it, you're not the kind of man to take issue with a woman in a position of power. You have daughters. You can't imagine why anyone would quibble about a female agent."

"Exactly."

"I trust you can run with that?"

"Yes."

"One more thing. Stop calling. I'll call you the next time we need to chat."

"But—"

"I don't want anything tying our businesses together. It's in your best interest."

*And mine.*

# 17

"I KNOW IT'S ALREADY BEEN a long day and it isn't even three o'clock, but we need to look at all the outstanding threats against the president." Tessa had gathered the team in the conference room. She acknowledged the tight expressions on their faces and added, "And the threats against me. We have three days until he arrives, and I don't want to risk anything falling through the cracks while we're sorting out the chaos. So let's start with the smaller cases."

She turned to Gil. "What happened with the threat to blow up the Beast?" The Beast was the name the Secret Service used for the presidential limo. Blowing up the Beast wasn't necessarily impossible, but almost.

Gil pulled a file from the stack he had in front of him. "Handled. They were kids. Dumb. One of them almost vomited when I showed them my badge. They had no clue that all threats against the president are taken seriously. I think they assumed we'd know it wasn't real. They have almost no resources. They couldn't pull off an attack on a parade float, much less plan and execute an attack against the Beast." He set the file to the side.

"Wow. Open and shut. A miracle." Tessa worked through the rest of the smaller threats, all of which had been addressed satisfactorily. Carver and Rodriguez returned as she pulled out the Craig Brown file.

"Heard you had an interesting day." Rodriguez scanned her from head to toe, then repeated the trip in reverse.

"Rodriguez." Her voice snapped like a whip.

"Yes, ma'am."

Was he trying to purr? It made him sound demented.

"I'm sharing this with you because it's clear no one has ever taken the time to educate you properly when it comes to how you should look at your fellow agents. That look"—she pointed at him—"is the way agents like you wind up unable to father children."

Carver nearly choked on the water he'd been swigging.

"Keep your eyes on my face. If you don't, I can't promise I won't put these boots to good use for the second time today. Are we clear?"

Rodriguez blinked at her a few times before he recovered. "We're clear."

"Great." She opened the file. "Craig Brown."

It seemed her handling of Rodriguez had struck all six men mute. They stared at her with expressions that ranged from glee to fury. "Does anyone have an update on Craig Brown?"

Zane snapped out of it first. "I had a message earlier from the Carrington County Sheriff's Office. They confirmed that it was him in Charlotte. He was with several others, and they spent hours at the expo but made no purchases. There's also been an uptick in activity at his home. At least three cars parked overnight. Three, maybe five people staying in the house. That's all they have for us."

"Do we have photos of these people?"

"Not yet, but they're working on it."

Tessa made a note to follow up on the photos tomorrow. "Do we have anything else?"

Carver spoke up. "Nothing on our end. We talked to the local agencies today. None of them had anything actionable. We've made them aware of the threat."

"I'd love to take care of it before POTUS sets foot in North Carolina," Tessa said.

"Wish it worked that way, but it rarely does." Carver gave her a sympathetic shrug. "And given the way your luck's been going this week, I don't hold out much hope myself."

"Don't hold back, Carver." Benjamin shot him a death glare.

Carver raised his hands in a gesture of innocence. "Agent Reed has made it clear that she neither needs nor wants anyone to take it easy on her. We have a job to do. We're doing it. I'm calling it the way I see it. I never believed the scuttlebutt about this office being jinxed, but I'm starting to see the validity of the argument."

"I wish I could refute your assertion," Tessa said. "But we don't do calm and sedate around here."

"Clearly. I just want to get out of here alive." Carver knocked on the wooden table for luck.

"No one has you in their sights," Gil told Carver, then pointed at Tessa. "But we can't say the same for you."

"We'll talk about me in a few minutes." After Carver and Rodriguez left for the evening. "Right now I want to get through the rest of these threats."

It took another hour. When they were done, she checked her inbox for any last-minute reports. "PID says we're supposed to have a firm guest and staff list and photos of all attendees by tonight. I'll forward them to you when they become available."

Everyone nodded. "Okay. Rodriguez, Carver, are you still on board to meet with the officers who will be on duty Friday night?"

Carver checked his watch. "Yep. We'll have to head out soon. We're supposed to be there by six."

Tessa wasn't sorry to see them go. "Then you'll need to get

moving. Morning meeting tomorrow at seven. Everyone else, let's take ten minutes, then we'll discuss what happened today."

Luke, Gil, and Benjamin pulled their phones from pockets and left the room.

Rodriguez tossed a cup toward the trash and missed. When he went to retrieve it, he paused by Zane. "Hey, Thacker, whatever happened with that pretty little accountant you were dating?"

Tessa kept her face neutral and carefully avoided looking at Zane as she typed a reply to the PID investigator who'd emailed her about the photos.

Had Zane dated an accountant since being in DC? Because if he had, he'd never brought her up. She and Zane were friends. Best friends. Didn't friends share that kind of thing?

"I don't think a single date counts as dating." Zane's confirmation of the mystery accountant, and of the fact that he'd spent time with her, was an ice pick through Tessa's chest.

"What happened?" Rodriguez pressed. "She turn you down when you asked her out again? Or did you decide you preferred the Spanish teacher? Or was she a French teacher? You know, the one Matthews set you up with."

"Rodriguez." Zane's tone was harsh.

"What?" Rodriguez had the nerve to laugh. "Sore subject?"

Tessa continued typing, even as the pain in her chest slithered up to her neck and down her spine.

"I don't discuss my personal life with people who haven't earned the right to the information."

"Ouch." Rodriguez stood and walked to the minifridge in the corner. "Don't hold back, Thacker."

Luke and Gil reentered the room, coming to flank her on either side. How much had they heard? Or did they already know Zane was in DC dating accountants and teachers and who knew who else?

Why would Zane have kept this from her?

No. She knew why. They had agreed that dating each other wasn't an option, but he wasn't oblivious to how much she liked him. And it sounded like while he was happy to be friends with her, he was ready to find someone to date.

But was that the truth? Because one thing she could be sure of was that Zane did care about her. He wouldn't fake an attraction to her. He wouldn't hurt her that way.

And he *had* been flirting with her today. And all week since he'd been here.

Would he do that if he wasn't interested?

She didn't think he would. But she also hadn't thought he was dating anyone, and it sounded like he'd been dating a revolving door of women in DC.

She bit down on the inside of her lip at the thought of anyone touching him, holding his hand, snuggling against him as they walked, or . . . kissing him.

Unbidden, the image of Zane with a beautiful blonde in his arms, lips trailing a line of kisses down her jaw, filled her mind. She forced it out. Tried to replace it with an image of him holding her. The image was warm and real, but it wouldn't last.

When they were together, they were attracted to each other, smoldering embers waiting to burst into flame. But when they were apart? What then?

In her peripheral vision, she saw Carver leave the room. Rodriguez paused in the doorway. "Have a great evening, Special Agent Reed." Manners dictated a reply. She met his gaze. Rodriguez's expression was cold and calculating. He knew he'd scored a direct hit, and he was enjoying every second of it. "I'm sure I will, Special Agent Rodriguez."

Her voice didn't shake, and he seemed disconcerted by the smile she flashed his way. Not so sure of himself anymore, was he?

Zane, however, looked like he'd consumed some bad seafood. Lies of omission were still lies. The guilty expression on his face spoke volumes. It hadn't been her imagination that he'd been flirting this week, walking that line between friendship and more, teasing and tempting her heart to believe they could rewrite the past. But he wasn't serious about her. Zane might not ever be serious about anyone.

His heart had taken a beating as a child. And while his capacity to love was enormous, his ability to receive love was minuscule. His need for love? For someone to be his person, his forever, his rock in a storm? That was off the scale, but that didn't mean he would ever acknowledge it.

Thankfully, Benjamin returned to the conference room, and everyone took a seat. Tessa turned to the four men who, Zane's deception notwithstanding, she knew would always have her back. "First, thank you all for today. You were wonderful."

"We didn't do anything, Tess. You took the guy out on your own." Gil grinned at her. "And I'm officially afraid of those boots."

Tessa wasn't in the mood for anything light and fluffy. Not tonight. "Thanks. I appreciate that you have my back." She filled them in on everything Morris had shared with her.

"You mean to tell me someone has killed someone with strychnine before? In Raleigh?" Luke rubbed his temples. "I'm tired of people putting targets on us."

They discussed the possibilities and ramifications for another thirty minutes. By the time Tessa had an opportunity to rein everyone in, it was almost seven. "Look, we need to get out of here. We all need a good night's rest. And while I know you all want to come riding to my rescue, there's nothing we can do right now. Morris is tracking down leads. The ME is all over this. The best thing any of us can do is refuel and recharge."

No one disagreed, and they began chatting with each other. All except for Zane. He'd kept his eyes on the table and hadn't made true eye contact with her since Rodriguez had left the office.

She gathered her computer and walked to her cubicle. Zane, Gil, Luke, and Benjamin stayed behind to restore order to the conference room. Leslie was a marshmallow—the kind that was sweet and gooey but also capable of scalding the skin off the roof of your mouth if you didn't put the markers away where they belonged.

The guys were talking, and it didn't sound like their conversation was winding down. This was her only chance. She grabbed her bag and her keys and slipped out the back door that opened into a service hallway and dumped her out on the opposite side of Greg's desk.

"You headed out?" Greg asked.

"Long day. Need to get home and get some rest. Thanks for everything."

"You leaving alone?" Greg stood and leaned against the door.

"I'm a federal agent, Greg. I can take care of myself. But thanks."

"Okay. Good night."

Once outside, she jogged to her car, opened the door, threw her bag across to the passenger seat, and climbed in.

She fired off a quick text to Luke.

> I need to head out. Can you be sure Zane gets to his hotel? Thx.

She was out of the parking lot thirty seconds later.

The tears she'd held back broke free before she got a mile down the road.

# 18

ZANE HIT THE PARKING LOT in time to see Tessa's brake lights. Luke slapped him on the back. "Come on."

"Where are we going?"

"Tessa's." The "Where else?" was implied. "Walk back inside with me, get your stuff. I'll take you there, and I won't leave you until I know she's going to let you in."

Gil and Benjamin joined them inside the building. "I'm going to kill Rodriguez," Zane said as they walked past an obviously curious Greg.

"Get in line," Benjamin said.

"Rodriguez's original plan may have been to make Tessa so mad at Zane that she'd go out with him to get back at him. But then after she smacked him down this afternoon, I think he did it for spite." Gil's anger was an unsheathed blade, and he turned it on Zane. "When are you going to get your act together and fix this? You two have danced around each other for as long as Tessa has been here. It's obvious to everyone that she's it for you. When are you going to do something about it?"

Benjamin raised a hand. "Okay, so maybe not obvious to everyone? But the picture is coming in clearer."

"I don't have time to talk about this right now." Zane grabbed his laptop and shoved it into his bag.

"Gil's right." Luke's quiet confirmation sliced another cut through Zane's defenses.

Zane turned to his best friend. "You *know* how complicated this is."

Benjamin rubbed his chin. "Yeah. See, you're looking at three men who are living lives of marital bliss with women who probably could have done a lot better than us, but for some reason, they love us."

"Ben—"

"Don't worry. We aren't going to get into a big discussion about our feelings."

"Thank heaven."

"But trust me on this, no matter how complicated it is, if you can win her heart, it will change your life."

"That's the thing, Benjamin," Gil said. "We're pretty sure he's already won her heart. He just doesn't seem to know what to do with it."

"We're not doing this." Zane turned to Luke. "Take me to Tessa's. Please."

"Let's go."

TESSA DROVE STRAIGHT HOME. It was a coping mechanism she'd learned early on in her recovery. Home was safe, so when she was upset, tired, frustrated, overwhelmed, or anxious, she went home. She didn't go shopping. She didn't go to a movie. She didn't go for a drive.

She went home. She took a different route than her usual one. It would add a few minutes to her overall time, but it served two purposes. It would be easier to spot a tail, and if workers were still digging up the road they'd been working on for the past week in preparation for a widening project, it would help her avoid being delayed by road construction.

Zane would not be happy that she cut out without talking to him, but he'd check to see where she was. He would see that she was at home, and he'd go to his hotel. He'd text her at some point. She'd reply in a few hours with a lame "I don't know how I missed this," and by tomorrow she'd have an excuse for her abrupt departure. He wouldn't believe it, but he'd pretend to buy it because he wanted her friendship. And that would have to be enough for both of them.

She never should have let herself—not even the tiny, fragmented parts of her—believe she could have Zane. He needed a nice girl from a nice family with a nice past. Not one who had lost hours, days, weeks of her life to alcohol. He'd told her so, not long after they met.

They'd been sitting in the car for hours watching an informant. It was dark, and they were both bored senseless. To pass the time, they covered their life histories. She told him about her dad, who was sick at the time. He told her about his mom. He didn't get into details, not then. That came later. But he made a throwaway comment that she'd never forgotten.

"I don't think I could ever trust a woman who drinks. It's a slippery slope. One day I might wake up in love with a woman who needs alcohol more than she needs me. I'm not going to put myself through that."

She didn't know if he remembered saying that, but she knew his concern that she would lose the fight to alcohol was there, between them, every time he looked at her. Thought of her.

She was safe as a friend. Nothing more.

Tessa grabbed a tissue from the console and dabbed the moisture from her eyes. Then grabbed another to blow her nose. This crying jag wasn't over. Not even close. But she couldn't walk into her apartment lobby with tears streaming down her face. The security team that guarded the doors had developed a fondness for her over the past few years. In part because she brought them chocolate chip cookies warm from her oven, but also because they were good men and women.

She could probably get past them like this. But she'd never make it if she walked in sobbing.

She put a fresh tissue in her hand and with one last sniffle, exited her car. She wasn't proud of it, but she faked a sneeze as she walked in the door and threw up a hand in greeting as she hurried to the elevator.

The ruse might not have been necessary, but it hadn't hurt. She made it all the way to her door without being accosted by any well-meaning neighbors or security guards.

Every part of her relaxed as she entered her apartment. She hung her bag on the hook by the door, slipped off her shoes, and tossed her car keys, keycard, and badge into the bowl in her small entryway.

The tears she'd held back pressed against her eyes, and she gave up the fight as she entered her bedroom. She fumbled with the gun at her waist and dropped it into her nightstand drawer. She could barely see through the flood but made it to her bed, where she fell face-first and released all the hurt into a pillow.

She cried until her eyes pulsed with every heartbeat. Then she lay on the bed while the tears dried on her cheeks and left her skin tight and burning.

She stayed there in an exhausted stupor, unwilling to give in to sleep, reluctant to return to the world that waited for her. Her phone had dinged multiple times, probably texts from Zane, Luke, Gil, Benjamin, Faith, Ivy, and Sharon. Emily and Hope might know by now.

They denied it, but the men in her office gossiped like old women. They were probably on a group text right now, discussing what had happened and how they were going to handle it.

She closed her eyes. Maybe sleep was the best solution. Everyone would be waiting for her tomorrow.

**THE RIDE TO TESSA'S APARTMENT** was silent. Zane took advantage of the quiet to text Tessa.

> We need to talk. Where are you?

When she didn't respond, he texted again.

> You know I'm not going to back off.

Crickets.

Ten minutes later, there had been no response, and they were still three miles from Tessa's place.

"What's going on here?" Zane leaned forward in his seat. They were in a line of cars that stretched as far as he could see ahead of them, taillights shining red, brake lights flickering on and off in the stop-and-go traffic.

"Sorry. Forgot about this mess. They're widening the road. Way overdue."

He opened the Find My Friends feature on his phone. If Tessa didn't want him to know where she was, all she had to do was block his access. But she never had before.

And she hadn't now.

Her location blinked back at him. She was at home. Unless she'd left her phone in her apartment, she was there now. And based on how long her phone had been at home, she hadn't been caught in this ridiculous traffic jam.

Zane stared out the window. "Did you do this on purpose?"

"You need to give her some time."

Zane had always appreciated how Luke had stood by him when he'd made the decision to place Tessa firmly in the friend zone. Zane had never betrayed Tessa's confidence about the night she wound up in a creepy hotel room, but other than that, Luke knew the whole story.

Luke understood how important it was for her to heal and focus on her recovery and not a long-distance relationship. But Zane knew that what Luke and all of them wanted was the same thing he wanted. For Tessa to be his.

Both for his sake and hers.

So he didn't lose his temper with Luke. He was a good friend. The best. And right now he was trying to be a good friend to two friends who needed to sort themselves out. Or, more specifically, one friend who needed to grovel and another friend who hopefully would find the capacity to understand his reasoning.

The traffic eased as soon as they passed the construction, but it had cost them a solid twenty minutes. He checked the phone. She was still at home.

"Rodriguez is slime." Luke turned into the circle at the entry to Tessa's apartment. "He's petty and small. She'll see the ploy for what it was."

"I hope you're right. And thanks for not saying it."

"Saying what?"

"I told you so."

"No need." Luke had told Zane he should tell Tessa about his dates. That it would come back to haunt him if he didn't. "Although, if you don't fix this, she'll be mad at all of us. We all knew and didn't tell her."

"You were trying not to hurt her."

"Don't think she'll see it that way."

Zane opened the door. "Go home to Faith."

"Faith would not be happy with me for leaving you stranded here. There's no guarantee Tessa will let you in. You may not make it past the guards."

"If I'm unsuccessful, I'll Uber to my hotel."

"Zane—"

"You've always been there for me, man. You literally dragged me away from an exploding car and covered me with your own body. I know you love me." Zane tried to smile at Luke. "But you can't help me with this."

"Wanna bet?" Luke set his jaw. "Faith—"

"No. Keep Faith out of it. If Tessa calls her, fine. Otherwise, please tell Faith to stand down."

"I don't like this."

"I know."

Their standoff lasted a full thirty seconds before Luke dropped his head in defeat. "Fine. I'll be praying. For both of you."

"Thanks."

Zane stepped from the car, and Luke called out, "Text me. Either way."

"Yeah." Zane watched as Luke drove away. Then he pulled the keycard to Tessa's apartment from his wallet. He wasn't worried about getting past the guards. He already had access to the building, the elevator, and the door to her hallway. No one would stop him.

He wouldn't enter her apartment without her permission. But if she wouldn't let him in tonight, she had to leave eventually, and when she did, he would be waiting.


THE SOFT SNICK of the front door filtered through the haze in her mind.

Zane.

She was going to take that keycard away from him as soon as she finished telling him off for invading her private space. She'd given him that card knowing he would never use it without her consent. But he'd walked right in. No knock. No called-out greeting.

She heard him pause at the door to her room.

"You've got some ner—" The words died on her lips as a man charged toward her. He was tall. He was blond. He had blue eyes.

But he was not Zane.

Tessa threw an arm up to block a blow that would have knocked her out and left her to this man's mercy. His forward momentum sent him flying over her bed. She scrambled to the other side, but before she could reach the nightstand, he came at her and took her to the floor. He was heavy. Outweighed her by at least a hundred pounds. Maybe more.

He got a hand around her throat. Another hand pinned her left hand to the floor.

She thrashed underneath him, bucking her hips and twisting her legs. With her free hand, she tried to force his fingers to release her neck.

Her vision had clouded, air a commodity she would never again take for granted, when her assailant messed up. He shifted his position and came up on a knee. That was all the room she needed. She pulled her own knees to her chest and shoved outward. One leg caught his stomach. One foot made solid contact with a far more sensitive area of his body. The man crumpled on her but loosened his hold, and she was able to wriggle out from underneath him.

She ran straight to her nightstand and retrieved her weapon. She pointed it at her attacker. "Do not even think of moving," she said to the man who lay curled in on himself on her floor, her voice a low rasp. "I will not hesitate to use this."

# 19

THE KNOCK ON HER DOOR was unexpected, loud, and for a split-second, terrifying.

Then she heard his voice, muffled through the nearly soundproof door. "Tessa? I know you're home. Open up. We need to talk."

"Use your key." Her words were too low, her throat too bruised from the attack, to project her voice enough for Zane to hear her. The soundproofing of the apartment—keeping outside sounds out and inside sounds in—had been a huge perk when she was looking for a home. She never considered a scenario where she would want someone in the hall to hear her. Zane must be yelling at full volume for her to be able to hear him.

He had a key, and because he was the kind of man he was, he wouldn't use it. She knew that. Had always known that. But she'd let her anger twist the truth into a lie. If she hadn't been so sure it was Zane coming in, she would have been armed before the intruder reached her bedroom door.

She wanted Zane in here with her, but she wasn't going to leave her assailant, whose breathing had settled into a more natural rhythm, just so she could open the door.

"Come on, Tess. Please."

Tessa called out, "Hey, Siri, text Zane Thacker."

She could have cried in relief when the computerized voice with a plummy British accent responded. "What would you like to say to Zane Thacker?"

"Use your key."

Siri repeated the message, then asked, "Ready to send it?"

"Yes." Tessa never took her eyes away from the intruder, but she backed toward her bedroom door.

After what felt like an hour but was more like thirty seconds, she heard the lock disengage and Zane walk in. "Tess?"

"In here. Got a suspect on the floor. Bring your gun."

"Tess? What's wro—" Zane pulled his weapon from his waist and aimed it at the man on the floor. With his free hand, he tugged Tessa until she stood partly behind him. "Talk to me."

"I don't know how he got in. He attacked me."

Zane never took his eyes from the man. "What did he do?"

"Tried to hit me. I dodged. Then he tackled me. Tried to strangle me."

His gaze flashed to her neck before he asked, "How'd you incapacitate him?"

"Knee to the gut. Foot to the—"

"Yeah. I can see that. Have you called 911?"

"Not yet. I had just taken care of him when you knocked."

"Do you still have cuffs in the kitchen?"

"Yes."

"I'll get them. You good?"

She refocused on the man on the floor. "Yes."

Zane was back in seconds with the cuffs. He handed them to her. "Want to do the honors?"

"I'd love to." She trusted Zane to cover her, so she slid her weapon into the waistband of her pants at her back and approached the assailant. "On your belly. Hands behind your back."

The man cooperated, albeit with a fair amount of groaning. Once he was prone, she knelt over him, careful not to put herself in a position where he could lash out, and cuffed him. "Stay there."

She rose and retrieved her phone. Dialed 911. Dealt with the dispatcher. Refused to remain on the line. Called down to the security desk. Explained that the police were en route and that they should allow them access to her floor. Again refused to remain on the line.

Then she called Luke.

"Powell."

"Luke."

"Did you shoot Zane? I'm not saying he didn't deserve it, but it will be messy dealing with the paperwork." Luke's brand of protectiveness, for both her and Zane, chased away some of the chill that had set up residence in her bones.

"No. But I do have an intruder in handcuffs."

Luke was all business when he spoke. "Maybe you should start at the beginning."

By the time she'd explained the situation, Luke and Faith were in their car headed her way. They promised to fill in the others.

She rejoined Zane and couldn't resist asking a few questions of the man on the floor. "Who are you?"

Nothing. No surprise.

"How did you get in my apartment?"

Again, nothing.

"Do you realize you've attacked a federal agent?" Zane's question carried far more bite than hers had, and this time the man reacted. It was brief, but there was a flicker of something. Not fear. More like anger? Annoyance?

It was possible he hadn't known who she was and what she could do, which would explain how he'd muffed the takedown. If he hadn't made that one mistake, he could have killed her while Zane stood outside begging her to let him in.

A shiver raced up her spine. It was too much to hope that Zane wouldn't notice. His free arm came around her, and he pulled her toward him until her cheek rested on his shoulder. It was the same position they'd taken in the security office on Saturday.

But then she thought they were moving toward . . . something. Not what they had, but something more.

Now?

The image of the French teacher had her stiffening, then pulling away.

"Tess?"

She gave him her best smile. "If you have him, I'm going to go wait at the door to let the others in."

"No. Tess. I—"

"It's okay." Now was not the time for this conversation. Oh, they'd have it, because Zane wasn't the type to avoid important conversations, but even he had to know they couldn't get into this now.

"Princess—"

"I think maybe we should retire Princess, okay?"

The endearment, one she had always loved, cut her deep and she'd responded without attempting to hide her hurt. She didn't give him a chance to argue, but before she turned, she caught the hurt in his eyes, the pain on his face. And now *she* felt guilty for hurting *him*.

No. That was not how this was going to play out. He'd gutted her today. She knew it was unintentional, but accidental wounds still bled. She was doing what she needed to do to protect herself and to ensure that nothing got in the way of her healing and recovery.

She opened the door and came face to chin with Detective Morris. "Are you always on call?"

Morris gave her his usual "don't mess with me" look. "I'll have you know that I heard what was happening and volunteered."

"Oh." She hadn't expected that. "Thank you."

"You're welcome. May I come in?"

"Yes. Of course." She stepped to the side and Morris scanned the room, nodded at Zane, and walked through every room in her apartment before joining Zane at Tessa's bedroom door.

"This my criminal?" Morris sounded as enthused as if he'd been presented with a bag of dirty laundry.

"Yes." Zane sounded like he needed to yell at someone, and if Morris didn't watch it, he'd be the lucky recipient of Zane's fury.

Morris made a call, and the next hour was a circus of police, FBI, Secret Service, and the apartment complex security personnel all vying for their piece of the investigative pie.

They'd turned Tessa's office space into the interview room. She'd told the story six times. If she had to tell it again, she was going to start making things up like, "Then Mickey Mouse strolled by and blew me a kiss," just to see if anyone noticed.

She knew the drill. Knew they were doing their jobs. Knew she would continue to cooperate until the last person had left and she was finally, blissfully alone.

But the idea of being alone didn't hold the appeal it usually did. How could she sleep, knowing someone had entered her apartment with a keycard?

That was the part of the story that had everyone confused and, even though they were trying hard to hide it, alarmed.

Luke, Gil, Benjamin, Jacob, and, for better or worse, Zane were huddled together in her kitchen planning how they would protect her whether or not she wanted them to. She knew that's what was happening, because if anyone else had been attacked in their home, she would have been in a huddle doing the same thing.

The CCBI had fingerprinted everything on the assumption that it was possible the assailant had been inside earlier and returned.

Her attacker was in police custody. So far, he wasn't talking.

Faith was making a strong case that the investigation into an attack on a Secret Service agent fell under FBI jurisdiction. It was unlikely that they would give Faith the lead on the case because of her relationship with Tessa, but by tomorrow, the FBI would be in charge.

Jacob walked in and closed the door. He squatted down beside her and shook his head. "I cannot believe this happened, Tessa. And I'm sorry it has."

"Thanks."

"How's the throat?"

"I'm fine."

Jacob's relief was evident. "Good. Good."

She knew why he was in here, and when he said what he'd come to say, it was going to be the second time tonight that someone ripped her heart out and stomped it.

Jacob stood, and Tessa braced for what was coming. "Do you want me to pull you from the president's visit?"

Wait. What? He was asking?

"Because no one would blame you. Not one agent would find fault. You've been threatened and attacked in your home. There's no shame in stepping aside."

She shook her head. "I can do my job, Jacob."

"I know you can. That's never been in doubt." His words chased away some of the chill. "I told you this before. You're one of the best agents I've ever had. You deserve this chance, and I'm not going to take it away from you."

"You aren't?"

"No. I've talked to the team. We're in agreement. You're running this, you're doing a great job, and you'll continue to do a great job."

"Thank you, sir."

Jacob held up a hand. "You'll have to accept that we're not going to let you out of our sights for the next few weeks. Not until we have this taken care of. And if you fight me on that, I *will* yank you from this assignment and put you in a safe house for the duration. Is that clear?"

"Yes, sir."

"They're working out a rotation right now. Forensics is done and said there's no reason you can't stay here tonight. But you won't be alone."

That was not a surprise. She knew they'd never leave her. Not tonight. "What about building security?"

Jacob ran a hand over his head. "For now? We don't trust them. We've made that clear. They have a leak somewhere. Their own security logs show that you entered your home, then thirty minutes later, someone else entered. Five minutes after that, another person entered. We know you were the first. We know Zane was the last. The keycards are both in your name. The one in the middle—the one used by the attacker—was under the name of Martin Swain."

"I know Martin! He's one of the best on the security team. That wasn't Martin."

"Mr. Swain has been contacted. He claims that he has his card to enter the building on his person. And that his card to enter the individual apartments should be locked up in the office."

"Was it?"

"Yes."

"Wait. Martin's cards were where they're supposed to be?"

"Yes."

"Then my attacker had a forged set?"

"So it would seem."

The ramifications were staggering. Someone was walking around with the ability to enter any apartment at any time? Someone who wasn't supposed to have access?

"I didn't use my secondary security measures." Tessa shook her head. "I have a dead bolt and a third lock. I always set them before I go to bed, but I've gotten out of the habit of using them otherwise. If I'd had the door bolted from the inside, he wouldn't have been able to get in."

"No. It was a gamble on his part. He may have thought he could try your door and if it was locked, he'd disappear down the hall and you'd never know. Or he may not have realized you were home and was planning to hide and wait for you to arrive."

"Cheery thought. Thanks for that."

Jacob didn't fall for her crabby attitude. "No point in keeping the truth from you. You would have gotten there on your own when the chaos settled."

She slapped her hands on her thighs and stood. "If you're sure, then I would like to continue my assignment. Whatever game they're playing, I don't want to let them win."

Jacob pointed to the office door. "Then I suggest you find out what your friends have planned. There was some discussion of bulletproof vests, helmets, and even a motion that you only leave the house in full body armor."

"You'll protect me from their protection, won't you?" Tessa opened the door and exited into her living room.

"I'll do my best." Jacob followed her to the kitchen, where the guys were giving a great imitation of the Four Horsemen of the Apocalypse.

# 20

ZANE FORCED HIMSELF to stay put when Tessa entered the kitchen. He wanted to pull her into his arms, drag her into a room where no one was around, and hold her.

Unfortunately, he had no right to do that.

But that was going to change. And soon. He was done pretending he was okay with the status quo. Done pretending that his feelings for her were platonic. Done with keeping his distance. Done with secrets. And done with trying to find anyone who could take her place.

She slid onto a stool at the bar. With her eyes on the counter, she asked, "What's the verdict?"

His so-called friends all dropped their eyes to the floor, then to him. Great. So he was going to have to be the one to tell her? Fine. "Twenty-four-hour companionship. You don't go anywhere alone. You're either at work or home or one of our homes. If you're here, someone is with you. If you're at work, you don't leave the office without a shadow. If you need to go to the grocery store, make a list. Someone will pick up whatever you need. This continues until we've agreed the danger has passed."

Tessa looked at each man. Each man, that was, except Zane. "I expected as much."

"We care about you, Tessa." Gil walked around the counter and stood beside her. Luke took her other side. Benjamin stood in front of her. Zane maintained his position, holding up the refrigerator.

"These guys"—Benjamin pointed at Luke and Gil—"tell me that you have no room to argue with our gross overstepping of all reasonable boundaries, given that you yourself have, in the not-so-distant past, undertaken extreme measures to keep them safe. Is this true?"

A grin flirted on the edges of Tessa's mouth. "Maybe."

Luke and Gil both reacted with gasps and shakes of their heads. "Maybe?" Gil said. "If you can't remember the way you drove by my house in the middle of the night when Ivy was in trouble or the way you refused to leave Zane's hospital room in case he woke up and needed an ice chip, then we need to have a chat about your mental capacity."

She still looked wan, exhausted, and her eyes were red and puffy, but her shoulders had dropped and her hands were no longer clenched, the affection and humor all around her having the expected effect on her stress level. "My mental capacity is fine, and you'd do well to remember that. Especially if you want me to use my brain the next time you're ready to buy your wives gifts and you come to me wanting assistance. I may have to conveniently forget exactly which type of oar Faith was hoping would be under the tree."

Luke winced.

"Or the earrings Ivy showed me a few weeks ago that would make the perfect 'just because I adore you' gift."

Gil groaned.

"As for you"—she turned her attention to Benjamin—"your wife is hoping for some new vinyl records to add to her collection."

"I know." Benjamin sounded smug.

"Do you know which one she wants most? Or where it can be purchased for half the regular price?"

Benjamin bowed his head. "You are the queen of savings and good deals and gifts, and we, your humble servants, want you to know that we will do whatever we can to keep you safe so you can continue to make us look good to our wives."

The four of them burst into laughter. And for the first time since he'd been back in Raleigh, Zane felt the sting of being on the outside looking in.

When the laughter ended, they all pitched in to clean up Tessa's apartment. Ivy and Sharon had come with Gil and Benjamin, and they made short work of the fingerprint dust. Faith and Luke restored order in the living area. Zane and Benjamin put the bedroom back to rights.

When everything was done, they all said their goodbyes. Hugs and whispered promises of protection and vengeance were bestowed on Tessa while Zane kept himself occupied in the kitchen.

Faith and Luke were the last to leave, and he heard Tessa ask, "So who gets babysitting duty tonight?"

The response was too low for Zane to hear. The fact that the conversation was taken to the hall confirmed that Tessa had not approved of the decision.

But there was no way Zane was leaving her. Not tonight. He knew she was exhausted, and if she didn't want to talk about what happened, he wouldn't push. Yet. But she would know that he cared about her safety. That he was going to be there for her no matter what. He wasn't going to let her push him away.

He knew how she felt about him. If she hadn't cared about his dating, maybe it would be different. But she'd given herself away tonight.

He'd never meant to hurt her. And as far as he was concerned, it wasn't an issue she ever needed to worry about coming up again.

He was off the market.

The door opened, then closed, but no sound of approaching footsteps reached him.

One minute passed. Then two. Zane stepped around the counter, expecting to see Tessa leaning against the door.

No Tessa.

His nerves sparked like he'd closed his hand on an electric fence. He ran to the door and yanked it open. Tessa sat in the hallway across from her door. Eyes open but staring at nothing.

He knelt beside her. "Tess?"

No response.

He tried a different approach. "Princess? Talk to me, baby. Why are you in the hall?"

Nothing.

Zane couldn't make sense of what was going on. Was this some sort of delayed shock? Her breathing rate was normal. Her pulse, which he could see in her neck, wasn't particularly elevated.

He sat beside her. She didn't flinch or move away. A minute later, he scooted closer so their arms and legs touched. She didn't move, but she also didn't speak.

Was this her version of the silent treatment? He'd never known her to be this way, but maybe? If so, he had to admit it was wildly effective. He was prepared to spill all his darkest secrets if it would get her to talk.

He leaned toward her and whispered in her ear. "If you want me to tell you everything in the hall where we have a full audience of nosy security guards, I will. It would be fair penance for my sins. But I feel I should give you fair warning. I intend to tell you some things tonight that I should have told you a long time ago. And there's a good possibility that before this night is out, I'm going to kiss you, and I'm going to keep kissing you until I'm convinced you're okay."

She didn't look at him, but she did get to her feet, her movements lithe and graceful. She opened her door, and when he approached, she held up a hand. "I don't recall saying you could come in."

He froze. Then took a step back. Then another, until he was pressed against the far wall.

The way she studied him made him feel like a virus under a microscope. Her words, when they finally came, were the last thing he ever wanted to hear.

"I'm not sure if I can let you in again."

She closed the door.

A moment later, the dead bolt clicked into place.


SHE WAS OVERREACTING. She knew it. Before tonight, she hadn't cried in months. No, longer than that. The last time she cried was on the anniversary of her dad's death. She was on a Zoom call with her sister, cousins, mother, and grandparents. They mostly laughed as they remembered, but they also shed some tears.

Zane had made her cry.

She dropped onto a chair in her den. Everything hurt. Her head, her eyes, her throat.

Her heart.

The phone buzzed. She didn't want to look, but she'd promised she would stay available to the people who loved her. It was Ivy.

Gil tells me you've locked Zane out of your apartment. Want to talk about it?

Did she?

No. Thanks though.

Okay. If you change your mind, I'm here.

And while I'm thinking about it, remind me to
tell you sometime how one of the ways I knew
I could believe Gil loved me was how jealous he
was of Ab. You give so few people the power
to hurt you, so the fact that he can just proves
how much you care.

Tessa stared at her phone and sent another text. This one was
not to Ivy.

Why?

The three dots that told her he was replying came immediately,
but it took a few minutes for the text to come through.

Aside from being an imbecile, I would say that
the short version is that I was afraid. Afraid of
what it would do to me if you knew and didn't
care. More afraid of what it would do to me if
you did care. The longer version isn't something
I'm willing to discuss via text because I'm thirty-
five, not thirteen, even if I do, on occasion,
behave like a teenage boy with a still-developing
brain.

Tessa held her phone to her chest. If she let him in, he would
want to talk. She wasn't sure she could handle it, but she couldn't
avoid it forever either. She had a job to do, and the emotional
turmoil she experienced around Zane was not helping.

Who was she kidding? She knew she couldn't leave him sitting out in the hall all night any more than she could keep herself from forgiving him. He was too important. But this was too important to let it go.

> You hurt me.

> I'm sorry. I wish I could say I'll never do it again,
> but I'm sure I will. I'm human, a sinner, and at
> times, an idiot.

She opened the door. He stood against the wall but made no move to join her until she stepped back and waved him in.

He held her gaze when he entered. She could feel his eyes on her when she locked the door.

She turned, and instead of moving farther into her apartment, he walked to her. "Let's get this all out in the open. I've gone on three dates since I moved to DC. The first one, Heather, was a woman I met at church. She asked me out. I didn't want to go, I didn't have a good time, I didn't touch her beyond the absolute necessities of politeness, and I declined when she asked again."

"Za—"

"The accountant, Carla, lives in my apartment complex. I asked her about the Friday night social time. I wasn't trying to ask her out, but she took it that way. I enjoyed talking to her, so I decided not to make an issue of it. She's beautiful, funny, charming, and I'm sure she will make someone very happy. But that someone is not me."

"Okay." Tessa wasn't quite buying it. How did one accidentally wind up on a date?

"The third, the Spanish teacher, Jamie, was a setup made by Matthews, one of the agents in the office. Again, I wasn't looking, but she was interested and had asked Matthews about me. I wasn't in a relationship, and I had no viable reason to say no. Jamie was hilarious. Full of energy. I laughed with her more than I had the entire time I'd been in DC."

This was not helping. How could he possibly think she wanted to hear this?

"But while Jamie was fun to be with, when I dropped her off, my mind couldn't stay focused on her. I don't wonder what she's doing during the day or if she's sleeping well at night. I don't think of things to share with her. I don't miss her. I don't wake up in the morning before my alarm goes off because I'm excited to hear her voice."

Zane took a step closer. "It's important that you understand this. No, I didn't tell you about any of the dates. I felt guilty about them, and I felt like I was cheating on you when I was with them, even though as far as you were concerned, we were just friends."

"Then why did you go out with them?" She had to know.

"Because I have no desire to date."

"That doesn't make sense. If you don't want to date, why date?" Tessa braced for what was about to come.

"It's nice to have a beautiful woman want to spend time with you, laugh at your jokes, admire your profession, and make it clear that she's attracted to you."

Tessa fought the urge to hunt down Heather, Carla, and the effervescent Jamie and make it clear that if they wanted to admire Zane Thacker, they could do so from afar.

Zane reached toward her and twisted a lock of hair around his fingers. "I thought maybe God was trying to give me some of the happiness I've seen Luke and Gil find, but I was being too stubborn to accept it because I was carrying a torch for you. I've prayed for the strength to be your friend, to never ask you for more than you're willing or able to give, and to be content with whatever I could have of you in my life."

Zane reached for her hand and laced his fingers through hers. "I knew that someday you'd find someone, and when you did, I'd lose you. Because I knew I could never just be friends with you. Not really. But I also knew I'd never let you go until I had no other choice."

He tugged on her hand, and she stepped toward him. Only a few inches separated them now. He took their entwined hands and twisted them up to press a kiss to her fingers. "I've known all week that the time had come. I can't lie to you. Not about how I feel or what I want. There will be no more dates for me, Tessa. Not unless they're with you."

Tessa believed him. She was still jealous beyond belief about the time he'd spent with those women, but she was no longer angry. At least not very angry. But the whole "no more dates" thing? She wasn't sure she believed that.

"You told me once you couldn't be with a woman who drank."

His brow furrowed. "I don't remember that. But it's a moot point. You don't drink."

"I'm an alcoholic, Zane. I always will be."

He traced the line of her chin. "And I'm the son of an alcoholic. I always will be. Do you know how messed up I am? Really? My mother taught me that women can't be trusted. That I'm the only one I can rely on. That I'm not important enough to sacrifice for. I know none of those things are true, but they're imbedded deep within me. They're not ever going to go away. And statistically speaking, it means I'm more likely to become an alcoholic. And studies indicate that some of the trauma from being raised in an alcoholic home doesn't fully come to light until you're in your forties. Which means there's no telling who I'll be in five to ten years."

Tessa had no idea what to say.

"Does that mean I don't deserve to fall in love? To have a chance to break the cycle? Do I have to settle for someone else? Someone who doesn't make me smile just by texting me an emoji of a taco every single Tuesday morning?"

"You insisted, that night in the park, that friendship was the only path open to us."

Zane blew out a long breath. "At the time, it was. You were only a few months out of rehab. You needed a year, minimum, before you entered into any romantic relationship. I knew you were attracted to me. I knew I was attracted to you. But the tension between us was tearing us apart. I couldn't in good conscience ask you out or confess how much I wanted to see where things could go for us. From where I stood, at that point we had two choices. Friendship or nothing at all. And while I was strong enough, barely, to hold back from asking for more from you, I wasn't strong enough to stay completely out of your life."

Tessa leaned into the palm he now had pressed against her cheek.

"I will always be your friend. You're never going to lose that, Princess. But I want more than friendship. I want your love. I want your heart. I want all of you."

# 21

TESSA SLID HER ARMS around Zane's waist and leaned into him. They stood that way long enough that their breathing synced. Zane was holding her. Zane wanted her. Zane's timing was truly horrible.

He pulled back and tilted her face up. "I'm loving having you in my arms, Princess, but do you think you could fill me in on what you're thinking right now? Are you going to break my heart or make me happier than I've ever dared to be before?"

Tessa stared into eyes so blue that it was like looking up into a clear sky. "I would never break your heart. It's mine, and I protect what's mi—"

Zane's lips were on hers before she got out the final word. His kiss was a gentle inferno. Slow but engulfing. And when they finally broke apart, his name was emblazoned on her soul.

He brushed her cheeks with his thumbs and whispered, "My princess," before he kissed her again.

When they eventually made it to the kitchen, Zane insisted that she needed food, then sleep. "I'm not as good as Gil," he said as he opened her refrigerator. "But I make a mean omelet."

"I know."

His smile was almost shy. Was he nervous? Now? A spike of fear shot through her. What if, despite the feelings they already had for each other, they messed it all up?

She stood at the counter and watched as Zane diced onions and tossed them into a sauté pan before turning to the other ingredients. She didn't need to tell him what she liked. He knew. The same way he knew she liked sparkling water with lime when she went out to eat, and that as much as she loved coffee, she also loved chai tea at midday. She knew a lot about him too. She knew he had zero tolerance for unresolved conflict, but not because he was afraid of it. He simply couldn't leave things up in the air. He needed to know where he stood, even if it was on the opposite side of an issue.

But for her, he'd lived in the tension of their friendship that wasn't just a friendship. And he'd lived with it for almost two years. She so didn't deserve him. She didn't realize she'd let out a huge sigh until Zane came around the counter and took her hands in his. "Regrets already?"

"No regrets. No doubts. But some . . . trepidation. I don't know how to be your . . . ." What was she? His girlfriend? That seemed . . . not quite right. They hadn't even been on a date. Officially.

"I don't think we have to put a name to it yet."

She couldn't explain the sense of both relief and concern his words generated. "Are you planning to keep us a secret?"

"Absolutely not. If I didn't think you'd shoot me, I'd put up billboards all over Raleigh that read, 'Have you seen this woman? She's mine.'"

She laughed and the tension broke.

"Don't be scared of us, Tess. We're exactly who we were an hour ago. The only difference is that we're not pretending to just be friends." A sly wink. "And we kiss."

She leaned toward him and pressed a quick peck to his lips. "Kissing is good."

"It is." He pressed a finger to her lips before she could kiss him again. "But if you keep that up, I'll burn the onions." He squeezed her knee. "We're going to be okay. We'll figure it out as we go. Sometimes it will be easy. Sometimes it will be tough. But have you ever known me to give up on anything?"

She shook her head.

"Do you think I'll ever give up on us?"

"No," she whispered.

"Me neither." He went back to the stove, and she leaned against the counter as he cracked eggs and whisked them in a small bowl. "I do want you to think about something tonight, though."

"What's that?"

"If you want to tell everyone tomorrow or if you want to wait."

Tessa sat on a barstool. "I thought you said you didn't want to keep us a secret."

"I don't. I'm asking about what you want."

"Why wouldn't we tell them?"

"You have a lot going on this week. The president will be here in less than seventy-two hours. You were attacked a few hours ago in your own home. You're under a lot of stress. A better man would have waited to confess his feelings until Saturday."

"You leave Saturday. I think you chose well."

He poured the eggs into the pan and frowned at them. "Good point. But regardless, think about it. You won't hurt my feelings if you want to tell them we resolved our differences, talked it out, and everything's fine." He spun the pan around on the burner before flipping the omelet. "As long as you understand that we're coming out on Saturday as a couple."

"Right." She wouldn't complain. She was still in shock that he'd broken through the walls they'd built and captured her heart in the process. Being claimed by him? No. She had no issue with that.

He slid the omelet in front of her, then grabbed a fork from the drawer and placed it by her plate. "Pray first. I'll get you some water in a minute." Then he pulled her hand into his.

"Father, thank you for the food before me and the man beside me. Amen."

She opened her eyes to a smile. He squeezed her hand. "Eat while it's hot." The words weren't a command, more a plea. If he talked to her like that all the time, he'd be able to get his way with just about anything.

She took a bite. Then another. Then a third. She hadn't realized how hungry she was, and the eggs were soft as they slid down her bruised throat. By the time she finished the omelet, Zane had made his and put her kettle on. He placed a tea bag in a mug and ate standing up while he waited for the tea to brew. "We don't have to talk about it tonight, but at some point we need to discuss what happened."

"Which part? The part where someone waltzed into my apartment and tried to kill me? Or the part where you kissed me senseless at the front door?"

He pointed his fork at her. "You're trouble, Reed. I knew it from the first day."

She dug through her candy dish and unwrapped a butterscotch. "I don't want to talk about it right now. Later?" She popped the butterscotch into her mouth.

"Yeah. Later is fine. Why don't you get a shower, get ready for bed? I'll clean up in here."

"Are you going to sleep?"

"Nope."

She knew it. "Then I won't either."

"Wrong answer."

His flip response crawled all over her. "You're not my boss, Zane Thacker. If you start thinking I'll do whatever you tell me to, then we're going to be in couples therapy before we go on our first date."

Zane pinched his lips together but didn't succeed in hiding his smile. "Couples therapy?"

"It's a thing." Tessa wasn't ready to let this go. "We probably already need it."

"Maybe." Zane took his last bite of omelet. He must have been starving.

"Do you want another omelet?" Tessa stood and made it one step toward the kitchen before Zane caught her around the waist and pulled her against him.

"No. I'm good." His lips were at her ear. "I'm sorry. I'm not trying to be bossy. I'm trying to keep you alive long enough to need couples therapy. And I need you to go to bed because I don't think it would be wise for you to stay up all night with me. Do you understand?"

Tessa shivered. "Yes."

"Do you forgive me?"

"Yes."

"Thank you."

"Thank *you* for the omelet."

"You're most welcome."

She slipped from his arms and didn't turn around until she tried to close the bedroom door and discovered she couldn't do it. She pulled back until she could see him. "Zane?"

"Yes?"

"I'm going to need to leave the bedroom door open." If she closed that door, she would lose the grasp she had on her calm.

"Okay. Whatever you need. Do you want to leave? We could go to the hotel. Or to Luke and Faith's. They have plenty of room."

"No. I need to stay here and face my demons. I'm just not ready to shut myself in there alone."

**ZANE CLEANED UP THE KITCHEN,** prepped the coffeepot, and returned to the living room. He sat on the sofa. That lasted approximately two seconds before he was up and walking around the apartment.

He walked, and he prayed.

*Lord? Um. Wow. I'm not even sure what to say right now. Thank you seems woefully inadequate, but maybe if I say it every day for the next sixty years it will finally be enough.*

He paused to pick up a framed photo. It was of him, Luke, and Thad Baker, a colleague who died under tragic circumstances not long after Tessa came to their team.

*I don't know how it works, Lord, but if you could let Thad know? He'd love to see this. He prayed for this. Please don't let me hurt her ever again. Help me never forget how extraordinary she is, how blessed I am, and how my job is to make sure she knows that every single day.*

His phone buzzed. Morris. He answered immediately. "What do you have for me?"

"How's Tessa?" Morris tended to growl more than speak, and he was in a growly mood right now. Enough that Zane had no desire to mess with him.

"Good. She ate an omelet, and she's getting ready for bed now."

"Good. She going to be okay staying there tonight?"

And that was why he liked Morris even though the man had the personality of a ticked-off hedgehog. He knew what mattered, and he cared. "She wants to stay. We'll see how it goes."

"Fair enough. I didn't want to call her number in case she was asleep."

Tessa emerged from her room, hair up in a messy bun, bare feet peeking out of the bottom of flowy pajama pants that looked like a trip hazard to Zane. "Who is it?"

"Morris, I'm going to put you on speaker." Zane did that and nudged Tessa toward the oversized chair in the corner.

They sat together and listened as Morris brought them up to speed. "We have a name," Morris said.

Tessa's entire body went solid beside him. "Anyone we should know?"

"I doubt it. Name's Perry Loth. His record is long. Most of it's petty. But he's done time for assault, and he's currently out on parole after having his sentence reduced."

"What was he in for this time?"

"Rape."

Zane had an intense desire to turn back time and accidentally ensure that Loth would find it impossible to ever perform that particular crime again. He put his arm around Tessa's shoulders, and she wrapped an arm around his waist, then rested her face against his chest. Natural. Easy. Like they'd been sitting this way for years.

"Is he talking?" Tessa burrowed closer to him.

"No. And by no, I mean not a single word. He hasn't requested a lawyer. He hasn't requested a phone call. He hasn't even requested a trip to the toilet."

"I don't suppose you've had him checked for pills of dubious origin, have you?" Tessa shifted in the chair. "Could they even check for that? Seems like there wouldn't be much you could do short of pumping his stomach."

Morris snorted. "He was doing his supersilent act when we

asked him if he'd taken any medication in the last four hours. So, I casually mentioned we were asking this now because we had an inmate die from poison they'd ingested prior to committing their crime and that I'd hate for him to kick the bucket in one of my cells. The paperwork. You wouldn't even believe."

"He bought it?" Tessa asked.

"Not entirely, but he did give me a very firm shake of the head. And those eyes. He's one bad dude. I don't know who sent him after you, Tessa. But my guess is whoever they are should watch their back. If he ever breathes free air again, he'll be going after them. I have no doubt."

"Do you need us at the station tonight?" The last place Zane wanted to be was the police station, but he trusted that Morris was fond enough of Tessa not to ask unless it was necessary.

"Nah. Captain kind of wanted Tess to come in, try to rattle Loth. But I told him it could wait."

"You think he'll live through the night?" Tessa asked the question Zane was thinking.

"Honestly? I give him fifty-fifty odds. I don't think he took any meds, and I think if he had, he would have requested medical assistance. This man is stone cold, but I don't get the sense that he's ready to end his life. So the next question is, what could our mystery person have done to him that he isn't aware of? It could be nothing, but our boy is sweating right now. We put him in isolation for his own protection. He had no complaints."

The sound of a chair creaking came through the phone. "I'm going to attempt to get a few hours of shut-eye. If this waste of oxygen does something stupid or goes to his eternal reward, I'll get a call, and you can be sure I'll be rousing you from your slumber."

"Something to look forward to." Tessa reached for the phone. "Thanks for the call, Daniel."

"We've got your back, Tess. Sleep the sleep of the righteous."

The phone disconnected. "Daniel?" Zane asked. "I've never heard anyone call him by his first name."

Tessa gave him a "whatever" look. "He likes me."

Zane did not doubt that for a second.

"And he's sweet."

"I'm sorry? Daniel Morris? The guy on the phone?"

Tessa's expression was a hair too close to dreamy for Zane's comfort level. She was his. There was no way she was interested in Morris. But—

"He has a crush on a dispatcher. It's adorable. The dispatcher bought Ivy's old house, and now Ivy's determined to get her and Morris together. Faith thinks she's cracked. But I think Ivy might manage it. It would be like the grumpy cat falling in love with a golden retriever puppy, but . . ." Tessa frowned at him. "Were you . . . jealous?"

"No. But he seemed too familiar with you. He called you Tess."

"Lots of people call me Tess."

Tessa held his gaze. He didn't know what she saw, but whatever it was had her pinching her lips together and doing a poor job of stifling laughter. After a few seconds, she gave up and laughed full-out. "Zane! Really?"

"I was an only child. I never learned to share. And as previously discussed, I sometimes behave badly."

"I have a sister. I got tired of sharing a long time ago. And I would eviscerate anyone who tried to get between us."

Zane sat up straighter. "Well, that escalated quickly."

"I'm playing for keeps." The words were soft. "Just so we're clear."

"That's the only way I know to play."

"Good." She dropped her head and studied her hands. "Is this going to be weird? I'm not sure how to be with you right now. If this was yesterday, I wouldn't be sitting this close to you. I'd be at one end of the sofa and you'd be at the other end, probably pelting me with popcorn."

"We'll find our way, Princess. Tell me if something is strange. If it's too much, too fast, too anything, we'll back way off."

Her expression was pensive as she stood. "I should go to bed."

He watched her walk to her room, pause at the door, then turn to face him. "I'm going to leave the door open." A minute later, he heard the covers being pulled back, a pillow being fluffed, and the unmistakable click of a round being chambered.

That was his princess.

# 22

WHEN TESSA WOKE on Wednesday morning, her first thought was that she must have dreamed the events of the previous evening. Had she really been attacked in her own home? Based on the soreness in her muscles, the answer was a definite yes.

But body aches aside, the more pressing question was about Zane. Had he really kissed her?

She rolled over. The clock read 9:17.

That couldn't be right. She grabbed her phone. 9:18. How could Zane have let her sleep so late?

She scrambled out of bed and pulled on a robe.

The unmistakable sound of her refrigerator door closing reached her right before a deep voice called out. "I hear you rushing around in there."

Luke?

He continued talking. "You might as well chill. No one's in the office anyway."

What was Luke doing here? And where was Zane?

She walked into her kitchen and found Luke standing there, hip to the counter, coffee cup in hand. "Morning."

A swell of disappointment and confusion crashed over her. Zane wasn't here. Why did he leave without saying goodbye?

Luke took a sip of coffee. "Don't be mad. We didn't do it on purpose."

"What didn't you do?"

"Sleep late."

"So the entire office slept in?"

Luke pointed to himself. "Not me. But everyone else did. Well, not Zane, but he should be asleep in his hotel. I didn't tell him last night, but the rest of us worked out that part of the plan. In my experience, sometimes the best way to get Zane to do something he needs to do is to not give him any choice in the matter. So I showed up at five thirty and told him to get out of here and catch some shut-eye."

Tessa had a nearly irresistible urge to slug Luke in the gut. That would wipe the self-satisfied look off his face.

Luke's expression morphed from "Aren't I awesome?" to "Um, what did I do wrong?" in the space of the few heartbeats it took for her to rein in her violent impulses. "Tess?"

She walked around the counter to the coffeepot. Luke had made enough for four normal people, not two. Wise move on his part. She jerked the carafe from the machine with so much force that some spilled down the sides. "That was a good idea, for Zane to get some sleep. But it doesn't explain why you didn't wake me up at a normal time. Or why my alarms didn't go off."

"I can answer both questions." Luke spoke in a way that reminded Tessa of how she'd once heard a horse whisperer settle an angry stallion. "Zane snuck in there and turned them off before he left. He texted you. Did you not look at your phone when you woke up?"

Tessa cleaned up the mess she'd made and added cream to her

coffee. "No. I woke up and looked at my clock and nearly died on the spot. It would have been a real kick in the pants to have survived the week I've had, only to keel over from the shock of being late to work for the first time in my life." Her voice had risen in both volume and pitch as she spoke.

Luke nodded solemnly as she passed him. "I can see your point. But you've had a horrible week, and you were sleeping. Zane almost woke you up to say goodbye, but he said he couldn't bring himself to do it. You're tired. More tired than you realize, considering Zane wandered around your bedroom and it didn't set off your internal warning system. You needed the sleep. So did Zane. The only way I was able to convince him to leave was by promising that I wouldn't wake you before ten."

Tessa took her coffee with her and returned to her room. She went straight to the phone sitting on the charger on her nightstand. Zane's text popped up on the screen.

> Don't be mad.

Huh. Fat chance.

> I wanted to be there when you woke up,
> but more than that, I want to be there for
> you today, tomorrow, and so on. Luke's
> overprotective streak has kicked into high gear,
> but he's not wrong. We both need the sleep.
> Call me when you wake up. Please.

What followed was a string of GIFs ranging from kittens begging for forgiveness with their tiny paws in the air to grown men sobbing fake tears. These were followed by random pictures of candy.

It wasn't fair to fight with kittens and candy. At the rate they were going, she would never win an argument with this man.

I'm never speaking to you again.

Call me when you wake up so I can give you the
silent treatment while I'm getting ready.

Luke's face appeared around her doorframe. "Is it safe to enter?"

"I don't like being managed, Luke. No one does."

He shrugged. "This is one of those times when you were overruled by everyone, including Jacob. Before we left here last night, he told everyone to stay out of the office until eleven. He passed that along to Rodriguez and Carver."

"Why not tell me?"

"You're going to try to convince me that you wouldn't have rolled in around eight anyway? Maybe earlier?"

"Maybe."

"Thou shalt not lie, Ms. Reed." Luke patted his phone. "I have calls to make. I'm going to your office. Holler when you're ready, and we'll head out."

Zane didn't call while she was getting ready. And she found herself in a predicament. If she didn't call him, he would probably be frustrated with her, the same way she was frustrated with all of them. But he did need sleep. Wasn't letting him sleep the more loving thing to do? Especially considering that what she wanted was for him to show up at her front door with flowers, candy, and promises that neither of them were ready to make or keep.

She finished her hair. No call. No text.

Then her makeup. No call. No text.

She fought her rising unease the only way she knew how. *Jesus, I know you love me. I know my ultimate happiness is in you, not in anything else, and definitely not in a relationship with a man. Even a man like Zane. But now that you've given me Zane, I'm going to need your help to fight this insecurity. It hasn't even been twenty-four hours, and I'm stressed out over the fact that he hasn't called. That's not who I want to be. Help me keep my trust in you. Help me keep you as the focus. Help me remember that I'm yours and because I'm yours, I'm already loved perfectly and completely and forever.*

With her heart and mind calmer, she threw a handful of pillows onto the bed and remembered Zane's intense reaction to the idea of throw pillows. He was going to have to get over that.

She checked her phone. Still nothing. She opened the door, walked to her office, and pasted on her best smile as she faced Luke. "Can we go to work now?"

"Sure thing." Luke followed her out of her apartment and watched as she locked the door. While they waited for the elevator, he nudged her arm with his. "Tessa?"

"Yeah?"

"Zane, he, uh, he said everything was okay. That y'all were cool."

"We are."

"You sure?"

"I'm sure. Don't worry about us. We're good."

Luke dropped it, but Tessa didn't think for a second that he was convinced. What was she supposed to say? "We're better than good. I've been half in love with him since the day we met, and he kissed me last night, and I think if I don't die from worrying that I'll mess it up that I might die from happiness"?

Yeah. No. That was not ever coming out of her mouth. Her phone rang when they hit the lobby, and her entire body thrummed in anticipation. "Hello."

"I can't believe I slept through our morning routine," Zane grumbled. "Especially not today, of all days."

Her fear and annoyance evaporated at the frustration in his voice. "You needed to sleep."

"Luke needs to quit micromanaging us."

"I said something similar when I discovered him in my living room this morning."

The sound of something—a shirt, maybe?—being pulled off a hanger. "I wish the circumstances had been different. None of this is playing out the way I'd imagined it."

"You had imagined it?" The question popped out before she remembered that she had an inquisitive audience.

Luke came to a complete stop in front of her, eyebrows raised nearly to his hairline. "Should I give you some privacy?"

She shook her head and stepped around him. He chuckled as he jogged a few steps and fell back in beside her.

Zane, oblivious to all this, answered. "Oh yeah. It went more like me getting up the nerve to ask you out. Taking you on a long bike ride, then dinner, then maybe an evening stroll where we would talk and laugh and at some point, kiss."

"That sounds lovely."

"Yeah. A lot more romantic than the way it actually went down."

Why hadn't he called while she was still in her apartment? She wanted to say so many things, none of which were an option with Luke shamelessly eavesdropping. "I'm not complaining."

Zane was quiet a half second too long. "You aren't alone."

"Nope. Luke and I are almost to my car."

"Tell Luke to mind his own business."

"Has Luke ever minded his own business?"

Luke paused by her car. "Go ahead. Talk trash about me. I know you love me." He motioned for her to wait while he checked under the car. "You are bomb-free."

"Good to know. Thank you." Luke gave her a small bow and walked to his car that he'd parked two spaces down. "Zane, Luke has declared my car bomb-free. Give me a minute, and I'll continue this conversation over the Bluetooth."

"That sounds like an excellent idea." There was humor and anticipation in his voice, all earlier hints of grumpiness evaporated.

She opened her door.

And screamed.


ZANE HAD NEVER HEARD anything like the terror in Tessa's cry.

"Tessa! Baby, talk to me!"

"I'm okay."

She was not okay. She was gasping for air, and her voice trembled. "Where's Luke?" Wasn't it in the best friend bro code that a man had to be there for his friend's . . . whatever Tessa was to him? Why wasn't he taking care of her?

"He's . . ." She blew out a breath. Then another. "Sorry. I'm okay. He's—Luke! Be careful. Stop!"

"Tessa! What is going on?" Zane had never put much thought into what superpower he would want to have, but in this moment he would give almost anything to have the ability to teleport to Tessa's side.

"Snakes."

"Snakes?"

"In my car." A tiny scream came through the phone. "I have issues with snakes."

So she'd said. Clearly, she hadn't been kidding. "Tessa. Please concentrate. Have you been bitten?"

When she replied, her voice was stronger. "No. I'm fine. I would like Luke to get away from my car until animal control can come get these vile creatures. Then we will have to burn my car."

The words were so matter-of-fact that it took Zane a moment to capture the ridiculousness of her response. The only option he could see was to agree with her. "I'm sure Jacob will approve the ritual sacrifice of your sedan."

"Good. I'm glad you see the wisdom of my plan."

She wasn't laughing, but if she was making wisecracks, she was going to be fine. That didn't change the fact that Zane wanted—no, he needed—to be with her. "Tessa, do not leave. I'm coming to you."

"Right. Okay. I'll call you back in a few minutes."

"Tessa?"

"Yes."

"You decide what and when we share. Okay?"

"Okay."

"Now, any chance I could talk to Luke?"

"Hang on."

Thirty seconds later, Luke said, "You're coming here?"

"I am. What's going on?"

"For starters, I just learned that Tessa is pathologically afraid of snakes."

"I know. She has reason. She lost a friend to a snakebite when she was young. She was with the friend when it happened."

"That would explain it. And that's a problem, because I count six snakes in her car."

"Come again?"

"You heard me. There might be more. It's hard to tell because a few of them are slithering over each other."

"Is Tessa okay?"

Luke didn't answer immediately, and it sounded like he was moving. When he replied, his voice was hushed. "Man, she was freaked out. I've never seen her react to anything like that. She's holding it together, but I thought she was going to have a full-blown panic attack at first. I'm not sure how she found the strength to reverse it. But if she'd been in the car and one of those things had appeared? She would have wrecked. I have no doubt about it."

Zane's thoughts were running along the same path. "How on earth did someone get inside her vehicle? That place has cameras and security everywhere. And beyond that, how did they know to use snakes?"

"Maybe they didn't know." Luke's voice was reasonable. It annoyed Zane but also helped him focus. "Not many people are fond of snakes. I'd say it would make most people flip if they were driving along and suddenly had a snake join them around the brake pedal."

"Valid observation." Zane could not believe someone had done this. "Stay close to her until I get there. Don't leave her alone. Okay?"

"You know you don't have to ask. I've got her."

"Thanks." Zane disconnected, ordered an Uber, and raced down to the lobby. His Uber driver was an eighteen-year-old girl with green hair. He didn't care about her age or her hair color. He did care that she talked the entire way to Tessa's. When she pulled into the circular drive, she commented, "Wow. There's a lot of activity for this time of day. Wonder what's going on."

Zane replied with a noncommittal shrug. "Thanks for the ride." He escaped the car and jogged to the parking garage.

Tessa stood against a wall fifty feet from her car. She was talking to two men wearing animal control jackets. Two deputies stood by her car talking to Luke. Gil and Faith stood at the back of Gil's car looking at something on Faith's ever-present iPad.

Tessa saw him coming and said something he couldn't hear to the two men. They stepped away. She came toward him.

He expected her to stop a few feet away, but Tessa walked straight into his arms and clung to him. He was more than happy to hold her, but he couldn't ignore the watchful eyes all around them. He turned his mouth to her ear. "Princess, we have an audience."

"I don't care." The words came out muffled against his neck, but there was no hesitation in them.

"Your call." He wrapped one arm around her waist, while his other hand went to the back of her head and his cheek against her hair.

She snuggled against him for a glorious thirty seconds before she pulled away, sucked in a long, slow breath, straightened her shoulders, and met his eyes. "Thank you."

"Anytime."

The police officers approached with wary expressions. "Special Agent Reed," Deputy Andrews said. "We're going to have the animal control officers remove the snakes. Then we'll have CCBI check the vehicle for prints and any weird forensics stuff they might know to do related to snakes."

"That's fine." Tessa was pure poise and composure.

The officer waved a hand to the animal control officers, and they approached the car. "Do you have anything in your vehicle that you need?"

Tessa shook her head. "I keep a bag in the trunk, but I don't want it."

She probably planned to burn it, along with the car.

"In that case, you're free to go. I understand you have other priorities today, and we don't want to keep you. We'll be in touch."

"Thank you. I appreciate that."

The deputies sent chin lifts in Zane's direction and walked back to the car. It did not escape his notice that Deputy Andrews did not get closer to the car than twenty feet or that his hand strayed to his weapon on more than one occasion. Zane nudged Tessa's arm. "Pretty sure you and Deputy Andrews have something in common."

His remark elicited a small but genuine smile from Tessa. "Yes. He told me he drew the short straw when they got the call. At one point he was sweating so much, I was afraid we might need an ambulance."

Faith joined them and threaded her arm through Tessa's. "Can I walk up to your apartment with you?"

"Of course."

Tessa turned back to Zane. "We have an appointment at the Carmichael estate at one. I don't want to miss it."

"Okay."

She held out a fist to Luke, then Gil. "Thanks for having my back."

"Anytime," both men said in unison.

With one last look at Zane, she left the parking garage with Faith. When they were out of earshot, Gil and Luke converged on him.

Gil turned to Luke and tapped a finger to his chin, his expression one of deep concentration. "Luke, help me out here. But last night when we left, it wasn't my imagination, was it, that they"—he waved a hand in Zane's direction—"were not in what one would call a good place?"

"That was my assessment as well." Luke turned to Zane. "What exactly happened last night after we left?"

Zane studied the ground. "Gentlemen, that is a conversation for another time."

Gil turned to Luke. "We should have expected this. Zane's not the type to kiss and tell."

"Nice try, Dixon." Zane laughed at Gil's crestfallen expression. "But my secrets are not so easily unveiled."

Luke shrugged. "We'll know soon enough. Faith will get the scoop before they get back down here. She'll tell me. I'll tell everyone else. Done and done."

Gil extended his hand to Luke. "Good man." Luke shook it.

He didn't bother to tell them that he didn't care. If Tessa told Faith, that was fine. But all they'd done so far publicly was share a hug after an intense experience. They might have done that regardless.

Zane checked his watch. "We need to get to the office, but before we do, I want to put this out there." Luke and Gil gave him their full attention. "I don't know what this is, but I don't think it was done by the same people who complained about a woman guarding the president."

"Why not?" Gil asked.

"The candy. The snakes. These are very specific to Tessa, but at the same time, they are things she might, theoretically, share with someone in casual conversation."

Luke picked up Zane's train of thought. "They're personal but not private."

"Exactly. Which means whoever is behind these attacks has either spent time with Tessa or has talked to someone who has. It's unlikely our misogynists have that kind of access to her."

Gil frowned. "Are you telling me you think someone is after her, and it's a coincidence that it's this week while she's preparing for a presidential visit?"

"No. I don't think any of this is coincidence. I think there's a pattern, a plan, something that ties it all together that we aren't seeing yet. But it definitely has Tessa at the center."

## 23

ZANE TOOK LUKE'S CAR and drove Tessa to the Carmichael estate. She'd left instructions with Luke and Gil, called Carver and Rodriguez and checked on their status, and had a five-minute phone call with Benjamin that involved her saying two words and listening the rest of the time. Whatever he said to her, the effect was positive, so Zane was good with it.

They passed through security with no difficulty and parked in the circular drive. Graham waited for them at the door and whisked them inside immediately. No hanging around outside where any pesky reporters could snag a photo today.

"Please wait here." Graham left them in the same room they'd been in on Friday.

"Look. The painting is back." Tessa walked over to the spot where the print had been on Friday. She studied it and smiled. "It fits the room better." She leaned closer to one corner, eyes narrowed, expression blank.

He joined her. "Is something wrong?"

"No. Not a thing." Her voice, her bearing, her expression all matched her words. Her eyes told a different story. She walked the room, much as she had on Friday, and examined the paintings again. Then she pulled her phone from her pocket.

Seconds later, his phone buzzed. He stepped away from her and waited a minute before taking a look.

There's a Janus in the bottom right corner of every painting.

Janus. Zane would never forget the first time he'd heard of Janus. The Roman god of portals and doorways, he was frequently depicted as having two faces, and it was his image on the cuff link Tessa found in the hotel room. In the time since, Zane had done everything he could to find out more about Janus and if he was a symbol for any particular group, but all his efforts had come up empty.

Zane made it a point to remain casual as he wandered through the room. This time he saw what Tessa had seen. The symbol was small and easily missed on most of the images. But on the restored painting, it was brighter and larger.

A signature.

But the signature of a dead man. Carmichael had made it clear that the artist, a man he called Toto, had passed away. And that this painting had been one of his last.

Toto had been in the same fraternity as the president and Carmichael. Was it possible that the man who'd been with Tessa that night had also been a member?

Tessa was a rock star over the next three hours. She interacted with Carmichael like the professional she was, and with no hint of the dual dramas Zane knew she was dealing with.

When they left, it was with the assurance that the guest list had been completed, the file was being emailed to them, and Carmichael was ready and excited to receive the president on Friday.

Tessa didn't speak until they were two miles away from the estate. When she did, it was to say, "Not in the car. Not now. Later."

He didn't push her. He did, however, reach for her hand and was rewarded with her immediate acceptance of his touch. They rode with fingers laced and thoughts their own until Zane pulled the car to a stop in the parking area of his and Luke's Monday morning run. "Walk with me?"

"Okay."

He climbed from the car and jogged to her door as she opened it but before she climbed out. He blocked her in the seat. "Tessa."

"Yeah."

"I get the doors."

She raised her eyebrows. "Since when?"

"Since last night."

She considered his words and then extended her hand with an imperious look. He took it and helped her from the car.

"Thank you."

He couldn't stand it anymore. He pressed a quick kiss to her lips. "I've been wanting to do that all day."

This time her smile was mischievous. "I almost kissed you in the parking garage, but I restrained myself. I'd already screamed like a frightened toddler. I didn't want to look any less professional than I already did." On those words, she rose on her tiptoes and kissed him.

Hers was not quick.

"Wow." He tucked her hand in the bend of his arm and walked with her toward the trail.

She dropped her head to his arm, and they walked for ten minutes before she pointed to a small bench. "Let's sit here."

He joined her on the bench. "Talk to me."

"Janus, the symbol, it's not always the same. If it was Janus,

212

but a different design, I would be inclined to think it was a bizarre coincidence. But it wasn't. It was identical. Either the artist copied the symbol and used it in his art, or he designed it in the first place."

"Janus wasn't a Greek god. He was Roman." Zane pulled up every bit of random mythological information he'd learned about Janus in the weeks after Tessa's abduction. Because no matter what she chose to think, he remained convinced that she'd been abducted that night. "The fraternities are big on their Greek background. I don't know if they would have used Janus."

"Maybe. Not everyone knows he was Roman, so it could have been a mistake and once it was done, they ran with it. Or it could have other meanings. To the Romans, Janus was the god of doorways, pathways, and portals. Maybe they used his image in a symbolic way?" Tessa dropped her head into her hands. "I cannot believe this is happening now."

Zane rubbed her back. "I'm not prepared to stake my life on it, but even if it's somehow associated with their fraternity, I think we can rule out both Carmichael and the president."

"Why?"

"For starters, the president was being guarded by none other than Benjamin North two years ago. If there had been any weirdness, he would have said something."

"You think he would have? We keep secrets, Zane. It's part of the job."

"It is, but Benjamin wouldn't throw you to the wolves. If he had reason to believe you needed to stay away from the president, he never would have been so enthusiastic about you running the protection preparation."

"True."

"As for Carmichael, I did some background research on him

while I was still in DC. He's not perfect, but he's a family man. And he doesn't drink. He's been sober for over thirty years."

"Plenty of people go to bars to hang out with friends and don't drink a thing. That doesn't rule him out."

"True, but the fact that he was with his wife in Aruba that weekend does."

"That would do it. But there are way too many ifs in this situation. We don't even know for sure when that cuff link was lost. It could be unrelated to me. That place was a pigsty. Anyone could have left it at anytime."

"It's possible." Zane couldn't argue that point.

"But if it is connected, I can't keep everyone in the dark. It isn't safe."

"True."

"I may need to tell everyone on the team about what happened that night, and about Janus and the cuff link. I'm not ready to do it yet. But I'll pray about it. And if I have to speak up, I will. I won't risk any of them over my own pride."

"Fair enough." It wasn't the answer he wanted, but it was a step in the right direction.

"For now, we need to get back to the office. I want to go over the guest list."

"Your wish, my command."

Tessa leaned her head against Zane's shoulder. "Maybe we could stay here a few more minutes?"

He slid his arm around her. "When you're ready to go, let me know." He played with her hair, almost unable to believe that this moment, this woman in his arms, was real. "Fair warning. If you don't say anything, we'll sit out here forever, because I'm never going to choose to let you go."

**HIS WARMTH,** his gentleness, his compassion, his strength, everything that was Zane being Zane all worked to loosen the knot of dread that had her insides in a snarl.

And the fact that he liked to play with her hair? Bliss.

It took fifteen minutes for her to find the willpower to insist that they return to work. Zane held her hand until they pulled into a space in the parking lot, then he climbed out and opened her door. He walked closer than ever before, but he didn't touch her.

When they entered the conference room, they came face-to-face with three sets of curious eyes.

Luke checked his watch, then turned to Benjamin. "Time."

Gil laughed. "Luke wins. I take second. Benjamin comes in last."

"Do we want to know?" Tessa asked as she took her seat at the head of the table. Zane settled into the seat on her right.

"No wager was involved." Gil opened his laptop. "But we all made a guess as to when you two would turn up."

"Why?" Tessa glanced up in time to catch Luke give Zane a questioning look and Zane reply with a barely there shake of his head.

Luke bit back a grin but didn't say anything.

Benjamin leaned forward in his chair. "It seems you two have some explaining to do."

"About what?" Tessa asked with all the innocence she could muster. She didn't care if they knew. But watching them try to pull it out of her was too much fun to short-circuit.

Benjamin wasn't fooled. "Oh, I don't know. But maybe you could share with the class how it is that you blazed out of here last night with your shorts in a twist because Rodriguez jerked your chain about Zane dating other women." He paused to give Zane a reproachful look. "And then Zane insisted that Luke leave you at your place because it turned out he had a key?"

Tessa didn't respond to the bait.

"And then after you were attacked in your own home, Zane pulled rank and insisted he be the one to stay with you, but after everyone went home, you left him sweating out in the hall for a while." This time, the censorial gaze was directed at her.

"But eventually you let him in, and when Luke got there this morning, he had to insist that Zane go to the hotel to get some sleep because Zane didn't want to leave you?"

Although it took a Herculean effort, Tessa refused to let herself look at Zane. She kept her eyes on Benjamin and tried to maintain a placid expression.

"And then you were talking to him when the snakes were discovered, and he burned rubber to get to you. And according to people who were there and saw it with their own eyes, you two were locked in each other's arms for several *minutes*."

He took a breath. "Then you went straight to the Carmichael estate, but you left there an hour ago, and I hate to have to point this out, kiddies, but it doesn't take an hour to get back to the office. So inquiring minds want to know exactly what you've been up to."

"What he said," Luke chimed in when Benjamin stopped talking.

"Ditto." Gil grinned at her. "Come on, Tessa. Spill. I saw Ivy's text to you last night. And I know what I saw this morning." When she didn't respond, he turned his attention to Zane. "You two are friends. Good friends. But I've never once in my life held a *friend* the way you held her this morning."

"I'm not sure what you guys are on about." Tessa tapped the table. "We have work to do. And the sooner we finish it, the sooner Zane and I can go somewhere where we can make out without an audience."

216

Her skin heated as four sets of eyes turned on her in shock right before the room erupted in hoots of laughter.

When the chaos settled, her eyes met Luke's and the fierce joy she saw nearly overwhelmed her. "About time," he said. "I'm happy for you both."

"Thank you. Now that we're done gossiping like middle schoolers, let's see if we can get this guest list sorted."

Of the ninety-two people on the guest list, the Secret Service had detailed information about fifty-seven of them due to their known connection to the president or previous attendance at fundraising events. That left thirty-five individuals they had to create basic profiles for. Twenty-eight of the thirty-five were couples, which would make that part of the process easier.

Tessa assigned all the couples to Benjamin, Luke, and Gil. She kept the seven singles for herself. Zane was busy working on the plan for the arrival of the Beast and going over the route for the motorcade.

They ordered pizzas and worked while they ate. The couples on the list were mostly local families, registered voters with high net worth and a history of supporting the president either financially or in business ventures.

Morris showed up and accepted the offered pizza while he filled them in on Tessa's assailant. "He's still alive. He's also met with his public defender. They did speak, but it was a brief conversation. Of course, since it was privileged communication, we have no idea what they discussed. The public defender is a good guy, but he's young and inexperienced. With that said, I got the distinct impression that he was not happy about their conversation. I'm tempted to say that Loth scared him, but that's conjecture on my part."

Tessa closed her eyes and for a split second was back in her room, his hot breath on her neck, fear flooding her system with adrenaline. Zane's low "Tess?" was accompanied by his hand on her neck and a gentle squeeze.

She opened her eyes and shot him an appreciative glance. "I wish I could understand how he got in. I realize he had forged Martin's security cards, but how did he get them?"

"We're still working on that, but we do have one possible lead," Morris said around a bite of pizza.

"Do share." Zane hadn't moved his hand, and Tessa was fine with that.

"We showed his picture to everyone on staff today, including part-time help. Nothing until the assistant manager said he looked familiar, but he couldn't quite place him."

"What about Devin?"

"Is Devin the head of security?" Morris asked.

"Yes."

Morris tore the crust of his pizza in half. "See, that's where this gets interesting."

Tessa could almost taste the wild energy burning off Zane, but he didn't interrupt Morris.

"It turns out that your head of security is on a primitive back-packing trip in Wyoming. Minimal cell coverage but calls his wife every couple of days when he's in an area with a phone."

"That doesn't make any sense." Tessa swiveled in her seat. "I'm not much of a hiker, but Gil's brother-in-law-to-be is into that stuff. He went on a trip to Montana not long ago. He was completely out of pocket for six days. He was with a guy who had a sat phone, but apparently the rule is that you only use it if there's an emergency."

Morris nodded. "Matches with what I've always thought. My understanding is that once you hike out of civilization, you're out until you hike back in. And here's the real kicker. He wasn't supposed to be on this trip at all. Won it through some outdoor magazine he subscribes to. Found out about it Saturday morning, left town on Sunday."

Zane still didn't speak, but his silence was a threatening storm. Tessa had no doubt he had already reached the same conclusion she had.

Morris continued. "I've left word that when he connects again, he's to call me no matter what, day or night. But I find the timing of this excursion to be suspect."

"Do you think he's on the trip, or is he lying low?" Tessa fought the urge to place a hand on Zane's thigh. He was abnormally still, and if he didn't get up and start pacing the room soon, she was going to have to intervene before he ruptured something.

"Hard to say. The wife is a cute little thing. She was so excited for him. I hate to imagine how she'll react if he turns out to be the lowlife scumbag he's looking to be." Morris gave them a rueful grin. "Because if our friend Devin got on an airplane on Sunday, he did it under a different name."

Zane came out of his chair like someone had pulled the ejection handle and hurtled him into the room. "There's no way that's a coincidence." The words were spoken through gritted teeth.

Morris grabbed another slice, his fourth, and raised it toward Zane. "Which is why I'm here. I know you don't have the man-power to join in the hunt, but I've got good people looking for him. Right now, my money is on him helping your intruder get set up with the forged security access card and then taking this supposed vacation long enough to be unavailable for questioning."

Tessa pushed back the sorrow that lingered around the edges of her heart. "Devin has always been kind, thoughtful. Sweet, even."

"He may have owed someone a favor." Zane wore a path in the carpet between the door and the table. "We need to talk to Bruce again. He might have heard something more. Or this might be what he originally heard about."

Morris polished off his pizza and stood. "I have to get back to work. Thanks for the food. I'll call if we get anything. In the meantime, Tessa, if you see Devin, you should assume he's not your friend."

"Got it." Tessa stood. "I'll walk you out."

Morris didn't say anything until they were past the security desk. "People do all sorts of things for all sorts of reasons. We're digging into Devin. You stay focused on staying safe. I'm kind of counting on the lot of y'all having kids named Daniel and Danielle. Maybe Daniella? I'm good with any of them."

Tessa gave him a quick side hug. "You know, you could still have a few yourself."

"Nah. I'm too mean." He gave her a small salute and strode to his car.

Tessa returned to the conference room to find that in the two minutes she'd been gone, Zane had rallied the troops and was giving them a full briefing. She retook her seat and listened to his summation.

"Someone is willing to do just about anything to get to Tessa. We're going to need to increase our vigilance and trust no one who isn't in the inner circle. No one and no place can be assumed safe."

Tessa looked at the faces of four very angry men. "I'm going to my desk. Y'all plan whatever you want to plan. I trust you to keep me safe. I have to figure out who is or isn't going to try to kill the president."

It was twenty minutes before the guys returned to their desks. Zane came up behind her and began massaging her shoulders. "We'll get to the bottom of this."

"Are you trying to convince me or yourself?"

His hands tightened. "Both of us?"

"Fair enough."

He brushed a kiss to her forehead and went back to the cubicle that he'd claimed as his while he was in town. They all worked with few interruptions until 10:00 p.m.

"It's time to call it a night, guys. We all need some rest."

Five minutes later, and with minimal commentary, Luke, Gil, and Benjamin said hurried good-nights and exited the building.

"That was weird," Tessa said to Zane as she packed her bag.

"That was them giving us some privacy." Zane crowded her against her desk. "Because the three of them got me alone earlier when you went to the restroom and, after threatening me with bodily harm if I ever hurt you, insisted that I return to the hotel to get a full night's sleep."

He ran his fingers through her hair. "I know they're right, but I don't like it."

"I don't like it either."

"Then you're going to hate this next part." Zane smirked. "Morris called. He has some concerns that we're all burning both ends, and he's got some overtime approved and some officers who want it. Which means you'll have a guard outside your door tonight."

"If I have a guard outside, I don't need anyone inside."

"Nice try, Princess. We aren't leaving you to the tender care of a wet-behind-the-ears cop. But it does mean Gil will get to sleep tonight."

"Gil's my babysitter?"

"Gil's one of a very small number of people I trust enough to stay with you while I go to sleep in another part of town when your life is being threatened," Zane murmured against her ear. "I want to be there, but we both need sleep, and Gil will bully you into going to bed as soon as you get home, while I would be okay with keeping you up for a while."

He kissed the tip of her ear. Then her nose. Then placed the lightest of kisses on her lips.

"I want more time with you." Tessa pressed her palm to his cheek. "We only have three more days before you go back to DC."

Zane's smile was so big, she could feel it under her hand. "I put in a request this afternoon, and it's been approved. I'm staying through Wednesday of next week."

"Seriously?"

"I can't leave town without taking you on our first date."

# 24

ZANE WALKED INTO THE OFFICE at 7:22 a.m. and found Tessa already at her desk. Gil came around the corner, saw Zane, and made a show of turning around. "I'll go stand in another room for a little while. Someone let me know when I can come back."

Tessa twisted in her chair to face him, and her expression was not one of welcome and affection.

"Tess?"

She turned back to her computer and pointed to her screen. "This man. He'll be there Friday night."

Zane rested one hand on her desk, one hand on the back of her chair, and leaned closer to look. A cold finger of trepidation traced his spine. "Is that . . . Tyson Monteith?" The man had a reputation in political and business circles as a gatekeeper. If you wanted to get something done, or get yourself noticed, you went to Tyson Monteith. If he decided your proposal was worthwhile, he could utilize his vast array of connections to open doors that normally remained closed.

"Yes." Tessa flipped to another photo. "This is Yancy Mc-Cloud." Another photo appeared. "And this is Wheeler Meadows."

She leaned back in her chair. "All three will be there on Friday."

She pointed to her list. "Monteith is attending alone. He was on my list. But after I saw him, I did a quick scan of the other photos. McCloud and Meadows are married and plan to attend with their wives. They were on Luke and Gil's list."

"Okay." He had no idea what had Tessa so tweaked, but his sense of impending doom didn't lessen. *Father, whatever bomb she's about to drop, give me the strength to handle the damage.*

"Look carefully." She returned to the photo of Tyson Monteith and zoomed in—not on his face, but on his hand.

And that's when he saw the cuff link. Tessa clicked to the other photos. All three men wore the distinctive cuff links.

"These photos are two years old. They were taken at an event in DC. Which means it could have been any one of them. Or none of them. These are not the kind of men who hang out in hourly motels in bad parts of town. But right now, I think we have to assume that multiple members of this Janus society will be present, and any one of them could have been with me that night."

He moved his hand to her neck and squeezed. "Tess."

Tessa dropped her head. "I have to tell the others. Tonight. Even if these men weren't there, it's possible they know the truth about what happened that night. They might even recognize me." Her voice held horror, despair, embarrassment, and shame. "I know I should have reported it when it happened. I . . . I was a mess."

Zane couldn't disagree. She'd been hungover, confused, afraid, and so horrified by what had happened that it was hours before she would even make eye contact with him. Despite his encouragement, she refused to file a police report. Which left them with little to no information about who she'd been with. He traced circles on her neck with his thumb. "Have you remembered anything more?"

"Not really. Every now and then there's a flash of something. A man in nice clothes. Not fancy. Nice as in expensive. High-end brands but casual. A wealthy man in casual attire. But that does us no good. That could apply to every single male present at the event this weekend. Beyond that? Nothing. No hair color, eye color, build. Nothing."

Zane had done his best to piece together the events of the evening, but the only thing they knew for sure was that she'd gone to Gino's. The security cameras—which should have captured her movements, who she spoke to, and most importantly, who she left with—had malfunctioned that night. A fact Zane had always found to be all too convenient, despite the bartender's assertion that the system was a piece of junk and was on the fritz more than it was functional.

"Can I make a suggestion?" he asked.

"Sure."

"We were already planning to split up tonight—guys at Luke and Faith's house, girls at your place. Leave the plans as they are. You tell the girls. I'll tell the guys." He pulled far enough away that he could massage the tight line of her neck.

"It was my mistake, Zane. My failure. My addiction. Why should you take on the responsibility of telling them?"

This probably wasn't the best time to tell her there was a good chance Luke and Gil might throw a punch when they found out what he'd done—or more precisely, not done. Faith would be equally angry, but while she would never resort to physical violence against Tessa, he couldn't rule out the possibility that she would punch him the next time she saw him.

He gave her another reason, and it was true enough. "Tessa, they're going to be freaked out. Given the delicate nature of where and how you woke up that day, it could be awkward for everyone if you tell that story in mixed company."

She shuddered under his hands. "Okay. Tonight, then."

"The truth will set you free, Princess."

"Even if I remembered details, Zane, which I don't, it would be my word against theirs. And based on where we've seen this Janus symbol, it's safe to assume that the person who was with me that night has a lot to lose if I were to go public with an accusation."

"I'm not saying you have to go public. But within our circle of friends, the truth will free you from some of the shame and guilt you're still fighting to release. And this Janus symbol is something we can investigate."

"Not now. It's waited this long. It can wait until the president is back in DC. I won't pull resources for this."

Zane wanted to argue, but her point was valid. "I can't disagree, but when this is over, I think we need to consider talking to Sabrina. She's an expert at finding photos and video. She might be able to find what we need."

"I'll consider it." Tessa pulled away from his hand. "I can't help but feel like this will never truly go away. That I'll spend my entire life wondering if the man who won't quit looking at me in a restaurant is doing so because he finds me attractive or because he once drugged my drink and hauled me off to a hotel room, then left before anything happened."

Tessa's words punched through Zane. "Just for the record, anytime a man won't quit looking at you, feel free to start saying things about your superhot Secret Service agent boyfriend who protects the president and considers your continued health and safety to be his highest priority."

"Is that what you are?" Tessa turned her head and looked up at him.

"I think it's a good place to start." Zane brushed a thumb across her cheek. "Is that okay with you?"

Tessa shrugged. "Yes. But I think there should be a word for someone who is more."

"We have words for that."

"Oh?"

"Sure. There's fiancé, which generally leads to husband."

"True. But I've known people who are engaged or married who don't have the same kind of connection we have."

She was killing him. Was she going to profess her love while they were in her cubicle? Hardly the most romantic locale.

She leaned into his touch. "Soul mate sounds too . . . romance novel."

He chuckled. "True, but I think if I walked around introducing you as the pulse of my heart, we would get a few weird looks."

"Probably."

"And I'm guessing you might object if I said something like, 'This is Special Agent Tessa Reed. She's mine.'"

She surprised him with a small shrug. "So long as you know that goes both ways."

Before he could explore that intriguing concept further, her phone rang and the day took off at breakneck speed.

Between final meetings with local law enforcement, driving the motorcade route four times, and checking in with the local trauma center to be sure the appropriate medical staff were on standby, Zane barely saw Tessa until late afternoon.

"I'm going to see Bruce," he told her when he caught her in the conference room. "Want to come with me?"

"I would, but I'm waiting on a phone call about the flight plans for tomorrow, and I'm waiting for someone in Carrington to update me about Craig."

"Okay. I'll touch base with you after I see him."

"Sounds good."

"HOW DO YOU PLAN TO FIX THIS?" A disturbing trace of anger laced the voice on the secure line.

"We've discussed this. Stop calling me and let me do my job."

"You're my fixer, not my CEO. Don't forget that."

"You never fail to make that distinction, and you seem to forget that I'm not just your fixer. I'm *the* fixer. You and all your cronies turn to me when you've made a mess you can't clean up on your own. If you'd like to sever our business association, say the word. I won't be going hungry."

"If I leave, so do they." The threat was unmistakable.

"Do you honestly think I'm stupid enough to work for only one group of overgrown juveniles who don't know how to hold their liquor, keep their pants up, or mind their manners on social media?"

Silence.

"Now, here's how this is going to work. You're going to keep your mouth shut. You're going to stay on the guest list, but you are *not* going to show. You'll give the president your apologies and assure him that you expect the stomach bug to pass quickly."

"Now, listen—"

"No. You did this. You bought this mess. I cannot protect you from being devoured if you insist on walking into the lion's den."

"I'm going. I'm paying you to make sure there's no blowback—"

"We left blowback behind three days ago. You cannot be anywhere near her. We don't know what she remembers, and her profile is too high. There will be other opportunities for you to rub shoulders with the president." Why was this so difficult for him to understand? He could be difficult, but he'd never been this intractable. "Is there something you haven't told me?"

A long sigh. "I don't answer to you."

"No, but you pay me to help you avoid doing stupid things,

and I'm telling you that going to this event will be the highlight of your personal stupidity reel."

"The president has requested that I attend."

"I got that when he sent you an invitation."

"You don't understand. He called and personally asked me to attend."

"Again, he doesn't want a stomach bug. You've known him since you were sixteen. Send him your sincere apologies and tell him you'll visit him in DC as soon as he spends more than three consecutive nights in the White House."

"I'm going. Make sure she isn't there."

"If you insist on going, then I'll have to insist on going with you."

A taut silence, then, "I'll make the call."

The phone disconnected.

ZANE FOUND BRUCE in the third spot he checked. Bruce waved him over and patted the space beside him on the park bench he'd commandeered, probably for the evening.

Zane took a seat and noted the tremor in Bruce's hands. It was more pronounced than it had been last year. "How's it going, Bruce?"

"I've been better. I've been worse. You?"

"I've been worse. Can't say I've been much better."

Bruce's lined face split into a huge grin. "You kissed that girl and she didn't throw you off a high-rise. Congratulations!"

Zane chuckled. "Did you expect her to throw me off a high-rise?"

"Not if you did it right."

Zane leaned forward and rested his elbows on his thighs. "I've missed you, Bruce. You sure know how to make me feel like I have my life together."

Bruce patted his back. "I'm here to keep you humble. Men who start thinking they're invincible screw up their lives and the lives of those they love. I would spare you that if I could."

"One of these days I'm going to write down all your words of wisdom and publish them."

"Bah." Bruce coughed, a deep, scraping sound that set all of Zane's protective instincts into overdrive. When he could breathe again, Bruce wiped the corners of his mouth with a handkerchief he'd pulled from a pocket. "Most people would say that a man who lives on the streets can't be wise."

"That's because most people assume that if someone makes choices they don't understand or agree with, they don't have anything to offer."

"I think you learned a long time ago that people are far more than their address or their addiction."

"Or one bad decision," Zane added.

Bruce cut his eyes toward Zane, and they held a million shadows. "Some decisions lead a man down an irreversible path."

"No one is beyond redemption, Bruce." They'd had this discussion many times.

"You believe in a God who forgives anything."

"I do."

"I wonder"—Bruce took a deep breath—"if you knew the truth about me, if you'd still say that."

Zane tried not to react. This was the closest Bruce had ever come to sharing what he'd done that had led him away from the halls of academia to life on the streets.

"I would. Forgiveness doesn't mean there are no consequences.

I can forgive my dad for splitting, or my mom for caring more about her next drink than about my next meal, but—"

"She doesn't get a relationship with you." Bruce shook his head in grim acknowledgment. "She's missing out, young man. Truly."

"I'm not sure if she cares, to be honest." Zane had no idea why he talked to Bruce about his mom when he rarely spoke of her to anyone. "But regardless, if she asks for forgiveness, it will be given. I know that."

"So, you think there's hope for an old reprobate like me?" Bruce's tone held a solid core of disbelief but also a tiny vein of longing.

"I don't know that you're a reprobate, but I know there's hope for you."

Bruce didn't speak for a while, and Zane didn't attempt to push the conversation. *Lord, I'm convinced you're drawing Bruce to you. Help me trust you to continue the work you began.*

When Bruce spoke again, he was all business. "You get any more details on the threat against your lady?"

"None of it makes sense." Zane leaned back against the park bench. "The threats about her being too pretty to protect the president just came up after the news reports aired last weekend. But the person or persons behind the threats have too much knowledge about her. They've put a lot of thought behind what they're doing, and the attacks have hit her in very personal ways. It makes me think they've been planning this for a while. But that doesn't make sense either. Tessa has worked a few high-profile cases, but not anything that would generate this kind of revenge."

As he said the words out loud, something too faint to catch whispered through his mind. Zane didn't fight to hold on to the idea. It would come back.

"I've been listening to the wind," Bruce said.

"And?"

"The wind is angry."

"Yeah. I got that part." What was with Bruce and the wind? Was his brain truly degenerating? He'd never been this far detached from reality.

"She knows something, your Tessa."

Zane sat straight and turned to Bruce. "What?"

"Maybe she doesn't know she knows? But she has knowledge that she shouldn't have."

"Where did you hear that?"

"The wind says she can't be allowed to see. If she sees, all is lost."

Zane dropped his head in his hands. "Bruce, you're killing me, man. What does she know? What can't she see?"

Bruce patted Zane's back. "Only the wind knows, and the wind keeps her secrets."

Zane bit back a groan. Maybe the reason he'd felt so compelled to talk to Bruce today was because God knew Bruce would be receptive to what Zane had to say about forgiveness. Zane was thankful for that, but he'd been hoping for information that would help him protect Tessa. It was too much to hope that the wind had given Bruce any suggestions, but he had to ask. "Any advice?"

Bruce inclined his head toward him, the aged professor prepared to share with the ready pupil. "Keep her close. Make sure she knows how you feel about her. Don't leave it until it's too late. You'll regret it if you do."

"More words of wisdom for the book?"

"If you want." Bruce's smile was a little wicked. "I'm here all week."

Zane had to laugh. "I'm only here until next Wednesday. I'll look for you before I head back to DC."

"You do that. And bring Tessa when you do."

"You got it, Bruce. Take care of yourself." Zane slipped some cash into Bruce's bag. Bruce pretended not to notice. That was how they made this work. "And stay out of that angry wind. I don't want you to get blown away."

Bruce smiled. "Now who's sharing words of wisdom?"

Zane mulled over their conversation as he drove back toward the office. Back to Tessa. But no epiphanies illuminated his understanding, and when he found her in the conference room, she was surrounded by agents giving her their final reports. The president arrived tomorrow, and the groundwork was done. This was hardly their first rodeo, and Tessa had managed everything with grace and professionalism.

They were as ready as they could be.

# 25

TESSA PULLED UP THE SPREADSHEET that currently held the contents of her brain. Everything she could control was done. Assignments had been made for every checkpoint and every post in the home and on the grounds. She knew where each agent would be, from the snipers to the K-9 officers. And, much to her chagrin, every single person on the guest list, including the three she considered to be the most likely to be hiding past criminal activities involving Secret Service agents, had cleared the security screenings and was approved to attend.

There were some hints of impropriety, usually of the financial or business variety. But nothing that would eliminate them from attending. And not a single one of them had any known affiliation to Craig Brown or Calvin Cross.

The spreadsheet and every piece of information that filled the cells on it said that the president would be safe at the Carmichael estate.

But Tessa couldn't shake the feeling that she was missing something. Something big.

**TWO HOURS LATER,** she tossed the final remnants of the Chinese take-out containers into the trash. The women who had joined her for the evening—Faith, Ivy, Hope, and Sharon—were some of the finest women she knew. Of the group, the only one who needed to know now was Faith. Faith would be present tomorrow night, and it was critical for her to be in the loop.

As for the others, there might never be a better opportunity to share the details of the night that changed everything. And the truth was, she needed them to know. Needed to stop carrying the shame of it all. Needed to trust them with this part of her that no one but Zane knew.

But how was she supposed to initiate the conversation? What was she supposed to say?

"Okay, everybody." Faith clapped her hands. "We all know that there's something on Tessa's mind, so let's take a seat and let her unload on us."

She should have known that Faith would have her back on this. Everyone laughed at Faith's blunt approach to the situation and sat around her in a loose circle, cups of hot tea, hot chocolate, and decaf coffee scattered on the tables around them.

Tessa looked at each of them, who had nothing but love and compassion in their expressions, and had to blink back tears. "I don't know how to do this." The pending confession had all four women leaning toward her.

Ivy slid to her knees and took her hand. "Maybe we could start with prayer?"

Tessa squeezed her hand. "Yes."

Ivy reached for Faith, who reached for Sharon, who reached for Hope, who reached for Tessa. Only when the circle was complete did Ivy begin. "Father, we are so thankful for the bonds of friendship and family that have joined our hearts together. We also know that when two or more are gathered, you are in our midst. We're so thankful for you. For your love, your mercy, your grace, your forgiveness, and most of all for the gift of your Son and the freedom to walk into the future knowing that our pasts, whatever they hold, have been redeemed in Jesus. That we are clean and spotless before you. And that we are held in you, not by our own strength, but by yours. Please calm our hearts and give us wisdom to respond as you would have us respond. Give Tessa the courage to say what's on her heart. In Jesus's name. Amen."

The murmur of "amen" filled the room, and everyone resettled into their seats. But before Tessa could begin, Sharon raised her hand. Ivy and Hope laughed, but Sharon widened her eyes at them while keeping her hand up.

"Sharon, do you have a question?" Tessa asked.

"More like a request."

"Okay."

"Given that I'm the most out of the loop on pretty much everything, and I'm not sure what you're planning to share, could you possibly start at the beginning and give me the time line of events that have led up to this point?"

"I would appreciate that as well," Ivy said.

Tessa took a sip from her water bottle. "Fair enough. If I'm going to start at the beginning, I would have to go way back. I remember the first time I took a drink. I was in middle school. I had a wine cooler, and one wasn't enough. I didn't realize it then, but I know now that I'm not someone who can ever have alcohol, because I will always want more."

The women gave her encouraging smiles.

"I kept it reasonably in check while I was in my twenties, but sometimes I drank too much on the weekend, woke up with a hangover, swore I'd never do it again, and usually managed to hold it to one glass of wine a night for a while after. But then a few months after I moved to Raleigh, my dad died."

She closed her eyes, the piercing pain of her dad's death still a throbbing bruise on her heart two years later.

"He wanted to be buried in India, so I took some leave and did all the things I needed to do for my family during that time. There was a lot of pressure from my extended family while I was in India. Pressure to marry. Pressure to have kids. None of which was stuff my dad cared about. He loved me. I loved him. He was proud of me. He wasn't thrilled when I decided on law enforcement over law school, but he never stopped supporting me."

"I'm sorry you lost him," Ivy said, her eyes shimmering. Ivy knew the pain of losing a dad.

"Thank you. Our relationship was complicated, but at the core I knew he had my back. With him gone, some of my extended family got all up in my business, even after I returned home. When I came back to work, I was grieving my father and already fending off well-meaning but misplaced advances from random men that my family kept trying to set me up with. The first night I was back in my apartment, I got completely trashed."

Her skin heated at the memory. "I was so hungover the next morning that I could barely see straight. Zane ran into me in the grocery store. I'd dragged myself there to get the basics, and he knew."

"Zane is annoyingly perceptive." Faith's remark was met with general agreement.

"Yes. And Zane's mother is an alcoholic. He has far more experience than anyone should have with hangovers."

Understanding flashed in Faith's and Ivy's eyes. Concern in everyone else's. Tessa assumed from those reactions that Zane had shared about his mother with Gil and Luke, and while they had shared with their significant others, it had gone no further.

237

"Needless to say, he kept a close watch on me after that. I didn't get wasted again, but between my grief, the family drama, and then Thad's death and everything that came with that, I was drinking more and more each night."

Faith popped her palm to her forehead. "That's what you guys were fighting about at the hotel when we were under guard after Jared and Michael were killed."

"Yeah. I'd had a drink. Not much. But I was at the point where I couldn't cope without it, even though I was denying it. Zane was furious. I was terrified."

"I wish you'd have told me," Faith whispered.

"I didn't tell anyone but God," Tessa said. "Until Zane found out, no one else knew. I prayed and prayed and tried, but I couldn't heal myself, and I couldn't get it under control. And when everything went so very wrong and my coworkers were all dying or getting shot, I held it together until it was all over."

She put her head in her hands. *Jesus, please help me get through this.*

"Tessa?" Hope's voice was a whisper of warmth and comfort. "You don't have to tell us more. We get it."

"Thank you, but I'm just getting to the part that applies to our current situation."

"We'll hold whatever you tell us as a sacred trust." Ivy's eyes still glistened, but her smile was genuine. "I won't even tell Gil."

"It's okay. Zane and I discussed it this morning. He's telling the guys tonight. Everyone will be on the same page by tomorrow. Although I would appreciate it if we could keep it to this group." She looked at Ivy. "I do expect you and Gil to tell Emily. Or I can tell her. It doesn't matter."

Ivy nodded.

Tessa took another sip of water. "This next part is where it gets messy. It wasn't long after Jared and Michael died. Faith and Luke had just officially become a couple. We were all at Luke's place. Me, Zane, Gil, Emily, Luke, Faith, and Hope. We'd ordered pizza because Gil was still having headaches from getting shot, and everyone was still recovering.

"Despite Gil's mood—and, as I recall, Zane's as well—we had a great night, but I was about to jump out of my skin. I needed a drink, and I left around nine. I think I used the excuse that everyone needed to get their beauty sleep. I knew Emily would take care of Gil. Faith planned to stay until Luke and Zane were settled, and then she was going to crash with Hope because her house was still not her favorite place to be."

"Everyone had someone to be with, except for you." Faith frowned. "Tessa, I'm so sorry. I never made that connection."

"You were busy making googly eyes at Luke." Faith didn't deny it. "And all of us were so shell-shocked and relieved that we were alive, it wasn't anyone's fault that I left alone. I could have gone with you and Hope. I knew it then. All I had to do was say something, and we would have made it into a girls' night. But I didn't want to. I wanted to drink."

Tessa took a sip of her water. "I went home and left everything that could identify me as an agent. I didn't have my weapon, my badge, my access card to the building. Nothing like that. All I took was my phone, some lipstick, and cash in a small purse. I'd been to this bar before. I knew the bartender wouldn't ask me for my ID. It's not a dive. It's a nice place. And while I wasn't planning on getting drunk, I was planning on being intoxicated enough not to drive, so I took an Uber over there. I settled in to listen to the music and drink."

Tessa clasped her hands together and took a deep breath. "I woke up the next morning alone in a nasty hotel room with my shirt missing."

"Tess." She couldn't tell who had spoken. Several of them had said her name. Ivy had whispered a soft, "Christ have mercy." Sharon was full-on crying, and Sharon almost never cried.

"I'm going to tell you all of it, but let me jump ahead on one point. I wasn't raped. There was no evidence of sexual assault of any kind."

"You were taken from a bar to a sleazy hotel, and you have no memory of how you got there?" Faith's voice vibrated.

"Yes. It could have been much, much worse. But I had no bruises, no injuries. I wasn't beaten. And . . . once I realized where I was and what had happened, I called Zane."

No one seemed surprised by that.

Relief mingled with sorrow for her and anger toward whoever had taken her to the hotel made the air in the room pulse with an energy Tessa couldn't describe. She felt no sense that these women thought they were better than she was. Tessa was ashamed, but she knew that the shame was self-imposed. These women only wanted to see justice for her. It broke something inside her and began the process of mending it all at the same time.

"But let me back up to before I called Zane. I still have no real memory of what happened. Nothing from ten p.m. until I woke up. Sometimes I get a vague flash. A well-dressed man, the bar, but no matter how hard I try, I can't get his face to come into focus. I was alone on a bed, and there was no sign of a struggle. The blankets weren't even wrinkled. My purse was still there, but my phone was dead. The phone in the room was an old rotary, and I knew I could call any of you. But Luke and Faith were planning to spend the day building the ramp for Hope to be able to access the house. Emily and Gil were driving to meet their parents in Asheville. And none of you knew about my drinking except for Zane. So I called him."

"What did he do?" Hope asked.

"He tracked my phone from my last known location, found me, took me to get some food, and came back to my apartment with me. I was so embarrassed. So ashamed. I could barely look at him, but he stayed with me the rest of the day. I told him everything. At that point, there was no sense in trying to hide the truth. He went with me to talk to Jacob. Then he told me about this rehab center that he'd already looked into. And the following Monday, he drove me to rehab even though he was barely recovered enough to drive. It had only been a few weeks since he'd been shot, but he insisted, and I wasn't in a position to argue."

"Wow." Sharon shook her head. "I had no idea. I mean, I knew about the rehab, but I had no idea what led to it."

"I was in rehab all summer. When I got out"—Tessa smiled at the women in the circle—"none of you asked me for details or got nosy. You simply accepted me back. And I appreciated that you were going to let me talk about it when I was ready. But then we went to the Outer Banks, and we went diving, and I was tentatively excited about living life as someone healed and whole. I didn't want to talk about the past. I kept thinking that I would tell you all the details eventually, but the time never seemed right. And the longer time passed without discussing it, I guess I thought I could just forget it had happened and move on with my life."

Ivy raised a hand. "Is that how Zane got a keycard to your apartment?"

"Yes. He took care of my plants while I was gone. He watered them every few days. Checked my mail. Paid my bills. Even drove my car around every so often. When I got out, I asked him to keep the keycard. In case he ever needed it." Tessa couldn't resist teasing Ivy on this one. "I never imagined he would need it so soon. But I was glad he had access to my home the day you needed a safe place." Zane hadn't hesitated to take Ivy to Tessa's apartment when they'd needed to get her out of the line of fire, but his familiarity with her apartment, and easy access to it, had raised a lot of eyebrows at the time.

"So was I," Ivy said. "This place is awesome."

Hope shifted in her chair and lifted a finger. "I get everything you're saying, but Zane was a bear when we went to the Outer Banks. We all concluded that something had gone very wrong between the two of you, but then when Ivy had her drama, the two of you seemed closer than before. We were all very confused."

"So were we," Tessa admitted. "I'm afraid that before the night in question, Zane saw me several times while I was drunk. And once"—she gulped in a breath and then went on as fast as she could—"I made a pass at him."

"Oh." Hope widened her eyes. "That would explain a lot."

"Yes, it does," Ivy agreed. "Zane would never catch a pass made by a drunk woman."

"Definitely not." Faith frowned. "And with his childhood, growing up with an alcoholic mom, I'm guessing that didn't exactly endear you to him."

"You could say that." Tessa forced herself to continue. The embarrassing parts were almost over. "The bottom line is that I'd made no secret of the fact that I was extremely attracted to him. And then it was awkward, because in my mind, he didn't reciprocate those feelings. But then he came to my rescue and promised he wouldn't abandon me. And he didn't. He drove me to rehab. Took care of my stuff while I was gone. Wrote me letters, sent cards and care packages, et cetera. He came to my graduation from rehab and was so proud of me. But when I first got home, it took us a while to figure out who we were to each other. Things were tense, and there was a lot of emotion between us. I was so thankful for everything he'd done, but I also felt like he was being controlling now that I was out. It was complicated and confusing."

Tessa tried to choose her next words carefully because she wouldn't hurt these women for anything in the world. "After Ivy and Gil got together, everyone was paired off. Emily started dating Liam a few weeks after Ivy and Gil's situation. Hope finally realized how perfect Charles was not long after that."

Hope shrugged. "It's true."

"Everyone had a person."

Faith dropped her head. "Except for you and Zane."

"We were both so happy for each of you. But we also wanted to give you some space and time to be alone. You didn't need us tagging along on all your dates."

"We never minded." Ivy reached for her hand and squeezed. "I'm an expert at being a third wheel, and we never would have made you feel that way."

"I know, but there were a lot of nights after everyone had gone home to be with their person that Zane and I wound up together. We'd both work late, partly because we had nothing else to do, and it was always a little weird, until one night we laid it all out."

All four women leaned toward her. She could tell their curiosity was burning high. "The bottom line is that we acknowledged our mutual attraction, but we also agreed that the timing simply wouldn't work. I needed to focus on being the healthy and healed person I was becoming. Anyone serious about recovery knows that it's wise to wait a year, bare minimum, before considering any new relationships. I knew it. Zane knew it. And we were both serious and committed to my recovery. So we decided to be friends."

"Did that work?" Sharon didn't try to hide her skepticism.

"It was a little awkward at first, but we figured it out. We always went dutch, we never went to my apartment, we drove two cars and met when we went out to eat. It was never a date. So while all of y'all were falling in love, we were eating out, going to movies, walking or riding bikes, that kind of thing."

"And you never . . ." Faith let the words trail off, but her meaning was clear.

"No. Nothing physical. We became friends. Best friends. We talk a lot. Text too much. We read books together so we can discuss them. Since he's been in DC, it's been harder, but sometimes we even watch shows together with the phone on speaker."

Faith and Ivy shared a look.

"What?" Tessa asked.

Ivy shrugged. "I hear what you're saying, about agreeing to be friends and everything, but Tessa, guys don't watch shows like that."

"What do you mean?"

"I mean that's something a girl might do with her girlfriends. But a guy doesn't do that with his guy friends. If a guy is doing that? He's into that girl."

Sharon waded in. "I realize I'm new to this party, but I've seen the way he looks at you. And that is not how a guy looks at his friends. Male or female. He looks at Faith and Ivy like they are friends. I think he might think of Hope and Emily as his surrogate little sisters. But the way he looks at you is neither friendly nor familial. He looks at you the way a drowning man looks at a life raft as it floats away."

# —26—

ZANE PRAYED THE GIRLS were going easier on Tessa than the guys were going on him. He'd stood the entire time, but now Luke and Gil were also both on their feet.

"What kind of an idiot are you?" Luke's fury was big, bold, and blistering.

"You should have insisted she go to the cops." Gil's anger simmered on the edge of a full boil.

"This is messed up." Benjamin's head was down, his elbows on his knees, with the burden of knowledge heavy on his shoulders.

Charles leaned back in his chair and muttered, "I do not understand women."

No one had punched him, so Zane figured these reactions were as good as he could have hoped for.

"She's telling the girls?" Luke asked.

"Yes."

"And Jacob knows?"

"He knew when it happened," Zane confirmed. "She left out a few details, but he knew enough."

"So we need to have Jacob's head examined too?" Gil asked.

And even though he'd expected their anger and censure, Zane

lost it. "She didn't call *you*. Okay? She called *me*. And I made the call. Jacob agreed. At that moment, she was willing to admit she had a problem and willing to go to rehab. If we'd insisted she file a report, what guarantee could we have had that she wouldn't drink to escape the pain of it all?"

Zane pointed at Gil, decades of hurt fueling his diatribe. "*You* have no idea. *You* grew up with the blasted Cleavers for parents. I'm not convinced that your mom isn't an angel sent to earth. She mailed me buckeyes when I was recovering. Did you know that? *Your* mom. Do you know where my mom was during that time?"

Gil shook his head.

"No. You don't. Because I don't either. My mom has never realized how messed up she is. She's never faced her need, never been willing to do the hard work to heal. She's never cared enough about me to bother. So, no, I didn't insist that Tessa go to the cops. I helped her get into rehab, I drove her there, I took care of everything for her so she wouldn't have to worry about anything except her treatment, and when she got out, I ignored how much my feelings went way beyond friendly because what she needed from me was for me not to fall in love with her but to like her for the extraordinary woman she is."

Four sets of eyes stared at him. Then one by one, four gazes dropped to the floor.

Zane tried to breathe around the rage riding him. Tried to re-member that these men were his friends, his brothers, his anchors. He'd had eighteen months to come to terms with what had hap-pened that night. They'd had ten minutes. "I need some air." He turned and walked to the front door. But when he went to close it behind him, Luke was there. Zane ignored him and leaned against a porch rail. "I'm not kidding, Luke. Give me some space."

"Can't do it, brother." Luke tugged on his shoulders and wrapped him up in a bear hug. "I'm sorry. I was out of line."

The door opened and Gil came out, Charles and Benjamin hot on his heels. Gil joined the hug, and when they broke apart, he said, "It isn't an excuse, Zane, but you have to understand. We love her too. Not the same way you do, apparently, but . . ."

Gil barely dodged the punch Zane aimed at his shoulder. "You're all a bunch of idiots."

Benjamin shook his head. "I would like the record to show that I stand by what I said. This is messed up. But, like you said, she called you. And she's been sober ever since. I've only ever known her sober, but it would gut me if I had to watch her descending into the clutches of an addiction, so I can only imagine what it was like for you."

Charles leaned against the door and said, "I feel like I might be tossing a live grenade into this bro lovefest y'all have going, but right now what I want to know is why it was so important for you to share this with us tonight."

Luke, Gil, and Benjamin all focused on Zane.

"Let's go back inside." Zane's suggestion was met with grumbles but also with slaps on the back before everyone headed in.

Luke held back. "Zane. Really. I'm sorry."

"No need. I was prepared for you to punch me, so all things considered, I think you exercised impressive restraint."

"I'd like to punch somebody."

"Yeah. Maybe hang on to that thought."

Luke followed Zane inside, and as soon as they resumed their seats, he said, "Explain."

Zane explained about the cuff link, the Janus symbol, the paintings in the Carmichael estate, and the photos of Monteith, Meadows, and McCloud.

"Do we have anyone looking into this Janus group?" Charles asked.

"Not yet. Tessa agreed with me this morning that we need to investigate it further, but she didn't want to divert any resources until after the president is back in DC."

Luke, Gil, and Benjamin groaned. Charles snorted. "Again, I do not understand women. What I do understand is that not one of us fell in love with a woman who doesn't have a razor-sharp mind of her own, a stubborn streak ten miles wide, and a heart bigger than the Milky Way. Tessa's made up her mind, and getting mad at her won't change it."

"Point to Charles." Zane shrugged. "For now, it's crucial that you know what's happening and you're aware of the possible ramifications of members of this Janus society being present tomorrow night. Tessa still has nothing but a few fuzzy memories of that night, but she studied those photographs today hoping she could place any of them at the bar. No luck."

"Can Sabrina help us?" Gil asked.

"Possibly, but she's working with the Carrington officers to track the Calvin Cross protestors, who are currently the most likely threat we have against the president."

"Tessa will be devastated if anything happens to the president tomorrow night. But if she thought that she'd been a distraction to the investigation or the protective detail, it would destroy her." Benjamin rubbed a hand over his face. "Charles is right. She's stubborn. But she's one of the best agents I've ever worked with. I'm willing to give her this." He looked at Zane. "But to be clear, I will not leave this alone. Once POTUS is back in DC, we dig deep into this Janus situation."

"Agreed." Luke nodded.

"Definitely." Gil looked at Zane. "We've got her back, man."

"I know. Thank you."

Benjamin blew out a long breath. "So, I'm not sure I want to do this right now, but just so we're clear on one point, you *are* in love with Tessa. Am I right?"

Zane started to speak. Stopped. Started again. Stopped again.

Charles leaned toward Benjamin. "Pretty sure that's a yes."

Gil took a sip of his Coke. "That's been a yes since she walked in the door."

Luke laughed so hard he choked. "Worst-kept secret ever."

Zane pointed to each of them in turn. "I hate all of you."

"Sure you do." Luke stood. "Now, why don't you text Tessa and tell her you survived and find out how she's doing."

Zane didn't need to be told twice.

> Done here. How's it going there?

> Good. They're all furious, of course, but they love me. How's it going there?

> Good. They're ready to go for blood. But they'll follow your lead for now. You should expect them to be all over it next week.

> I guess that's to be expected.

> It is. I'll text you again when I head your way.

> You're coming here?

He sent a GIF of a boy rolling his eyes and saying, "Duh."

She replied with a GIF of a little girl waving a hand and saying, "Whatever."

"All good?" Luke asked.

"Yeah. She said they were furious, but they love her."

"And that, friends, is the summary of the evening." Gil stood. "Might as well go to Tessa's so we can all tell her that we love her too, and she's an idiot for not sharing it with us sooner. Then we need to sleep, because if I know Tessa, she's going to plan to be in the office around four a.m., and someone's going to have to go with her."

"We'll sleep next week." Benjamin grabbed his jacket. "Let's go."

TESSA SLID HER PHONE into her pocket. "The guys are coming here."

The women around her grinned.

"Then that means we only have a few minutes." Hope rubbed her hands together in obvious glee. "You shared the hard stuff, but I think we all know we want to end the evening on a positive note. Spill."

Tessa kept her face a mask of calm. "I'm sorry, Hope. I don't know what you want me to share."

The entire room exploded in laughter. "I know what I saw in the parking garage." Faith pointed at her. "And I know that Zane was not holding you the way he would hold a friend after a traumatic incident."

Tessa slouched in her chair. "I don't know what to say, and I'm not ready to talk about it. It's too . . . too . . ."

"Private?" Hope suggested.

"New?" Ivy added.

"Yes. I . . . we . . . it's terrifying. He's my friend. I cherish that. If I mess this up, mess us up? I don't even want to think about it."

"I hate to have to point this out, but I think you left friendship behind a long time ago." Faith's statement was met with agreement from the others. "And, honestly, could you watch him fall in love with someone else?"

"No." Tessa didn't need time to process her response. "Knowing he'd been on a few dates in DC made me lose my mind. I told him his dating days are over."

Ivy nudged Hope and said in a stage whisper, "She doesn't seem terrified to me. Am I missing something here?" Ivy's attempt at seriousness failed when she and Hope dissolved into giggles.

"Laugh it up." Tessa was spared having to answer more questions by the buzzing at her door.

She opened her door to find a group of men with their arms crossed and expressions that all but screamed their annoyance and frustration. Luke and Gil were each tapping a foot. "Tessa Reed, if you ever do anything like that again"—Luke paused and took in a deliberate breath and blew it out—"we will still love you forever."

He pulled her into his arms and whispered into her ear. "But don't you dare."

She was passed from Luke to Gil to Benjamin. Even Charles, the newest of the group, gave her a quick hug and said, "You're a gift, Tessa. Not a burden. Never a burden."

And then everyone was inside, and she was in the hall with Zane. "Thank you for doing that for me."

He pulled her to him. "Anything for you."

The door opened, and Faith stuck her head out. "I would think by now the two of you would understand how this works. Come inside and kiss where we can see you."

"Go away, Faith." Zane didn't release Tessa and didn't move from his position. "You're messing with my game."

"Game?" Luke joined Faith at the door. "Since when do you have game?"

"He doesn't need game!" Gil yelled from somewhere inside.

Tessa pulled away enough to look into Zane's face. "If we go in, maybe we can get them to leave."

"Good point. Let's go." Zane tugged her hand, and they were inside and settled in an oversized squashy chair moments later.

"Since the gang's all here, can we get an update on the status of things for tomorrow?" Faith asked.

Ivy stood. "Go ahead and talk about protecting the president of the United States. Hope and I are going to the other room to discuss *important* things, like where to find the best sushi in Raleigh and the new Broadway series coming to the performing arts center."

"Oh yeah, that's what we'll be talking about. We wouldn't dream of talking about Zane and Tessa finally figuring themselves out." Hope moved to join Ivy, her grin full of mischief.

"You don't have to go." Tessa hated for them to remove themselves from the conversation.

"It's okay." Hope reached a hand up toward Charles as he leaned toward her to place a kiss on her forehead.

Ivy and Hope left the room, and when they closed the door to Tessa's office, the mood in the living room took a decided turn to the serious. Charles took a seat by Faith. "What do we need to know?"

Before Tessa could speak, Gil asked Zane, "Did you get anything more from Bruce?"

"A whole lot of how Tessa's in danger and how the wind is angry, whatever that means."

Zane's frustration was a low thrum of tension Tessa could sense running through him. She shifted in the chair so her right leg was pressed against his left and experienced a little thrill when he relaxed against her. She knew who she was dealing with. A man like Zane would always try to protect her from anything and anyone that sought to do her harm. But he would learn soon enough that while she might utilize them differently, her protective instincts were as finely honed as his.

"Most of the advance team is in town. The motorcade route is set. The locals and state police have everything ready. The biggest unknown is Craig Brown and his merry band of protesters for hire." Tessa ran a hand through her hair. "I'm confident that we've hunted down every known threat, but I think he's up to something. I'm not sure what it is, but I'm convinced they'll try something tomorrow."

"Do we still have eyes on them?" This from Luke.

"Yes and no." Tessa wished she could scream her frustration, but it would serve no purpose. "Craig is still in his home. The Carrington County Sheriff's Office has gone over and above when it comes to keeping an eye on him. But given that we have no proof of anything, and despite Adam's threats to the contrary, we can't stop him if he chooses to leave. And as of five this afternoon, there were four cars, two trucks, and get this, six RVs on the property."

Zane was a coiled spring beside her. She squeezed his thigh and whispered low in his ear, "Go ahead."

His expression morphed from confusion to understanding to amusement to affection. And then he leaned over and kissed her on the tip of her nose. "I won't go far." With that, he stood and paced behind the chair she now occupied alone.

Tessa caught Luke's eye and saw something she suspected was joy, but he stayed on task. "Do we have Brown's description in the hands of the local LEOs?"

"Yes. And the Carrington sheriff's promise that if there is a mass exodus tomorrow, they'll do everything they can to provide descriptions, license plate numbers, et cetera so we know who to look for." Tessa dropped her head to the back of the chair. "I hope it's enough."

"What about Sabrina? Will she be involved?" This came from Faith.

"She's all over it," Tessa said. "I set up a Zoom call with her and an agent on the advance team yesterday. It took him about three minutes to appreciate the brilliance that is Sabrina, and when I left the room, he had already asked if he could loop in his counterpart in DC."

"Interagency cooperation at its finest." Gil slapped his hands on his knees. "Probably helps that she isn't part of any agency. No one gets into too much of a turf war. Sabrina doesn't care who gets the credit. She just wants to catch the bad guys."

"I'd like to catch a few myself." Charles's muttered statement generated grumbles of agreement. "So how do we do that in regard to this Janus situation and the whole danger on the wind thing?"

"For starters, we keep a close eye on anyone who walks in the door wearing those cuff links." Zane leaned over the back of Tessa's chair. "And we make sure Tessa is never isolated. Short of locking her in a room until everything is over, the best way to keep her safe is to keep her highly visible."

"Agreed." Benjamin tapped his watch. "And we also need to get some rest. Tomorrow starts early and runs late. If this event goes anything like the last one I was involved in, POTUS won't be wheels up until after midnight."

Which meant tomorrow would be a twenty-hour day, minimum.

They said their good-nights, with Tessa finding herself on the receiving end of extra-long hugs from everyone except Faith and Luke, who hadn't moved. They made themselves comfortable in her living room, while Zane took the pullout sofa in her office.

Zane cornered her in the kitchen before he called it a night. His arms slid around her and pulled her against his chest. Her soul sighed in contentment. "I need to tell you something."

His tone ruined her mellow mood. "Okay."

"On my way here tonight, I got a call from the detail leader. Carmichael has been quite impressed with us."

"Why do I get the feeling that there's a huge 'but' coming?"

"Not a but. A request. He spoke to the president, singing our praises, and the president has requested that I be on his personal detail tomorrow night."

"Oh. That's not a bad thing, is it?"

"Normally? No. But I would prefer to have a bit more flexibility in my assignment for the evening."

"You mean you'd prefer to be able to keep an eye on me. But you'll be focused on the president, and that has you stressed."

"Do you blame me?" He cuddled her closer, and she didn't complain.

"This is what we do. It's who we are. Tomorrow night isn't about keeping me safe. It's about making sure the president's visit goes off without a hitch. Obviously, I won't be taking any chances, but once everyone is on-site and the party has started, it will be very difficult for anyone to come after me without getting caught in the security bubble we have in place."

"True. I'll still be glad when it's Saturday and we can catch our breath. Maybe I can even talk you into going on a real date Saturday night."

Tessa tilted her head to the side. "Have you actually asked me out yet?"

Zane rubbed his cheek against hers. "Tessa?"

"Hmm?"

"Would you please go out with me Saturday night?"

"I'll consider it on one condition."

"What's the condition?"

"That that was the last time you'll ever ask a girl out for the first time."

# — 27 —

WITH TESSA'S GOOD-NIGHT KISS lingering on his lips, Zane fell asleep approximately ten seconds after he went horizontal. He'd set his alarm for 4:30 a.m., but when his phone blared at him, he was on his feet before he was fully conscious.

The clock in the corner of the room said 3:22.

He found his phone and tapped the screen to accept the call. "Thacker."

The voice on the other end didn't bother with an introduction. "Craig Brown is on the move."

"Why didn't you call Tessa?"

"We're calling everybody." The voice registered as Gabe Chavez, a Carrington County Sheriff's investigator and a friend. "Anissa's on the phone with Tessa now. Ryan's got Gil. You get the idea."

"Yeah. Thanks. You sound like you're on the road."

"I am. Felt like making a middle-of-the-night drive to Raleigh for absolutely no reason."

"You're a good man."

"I'll be in touch."

Zane put the sofa back to rights and entered Tessa's living room to find everyone awake and moving. Tessa was in the kitchen with a phone to her ear, four travel mugs on the counter, and coffee brewing. He walked to her and pressed a kiss to her other ear before he took his turn in the bathroom.

In ten minutes, they were all dressed and in the process of being caffeinated. But before they walked out, Tessa tugged on his arm. "Hang on. I know time is critical, but I think we should pray before we go."

Without another word, they formed a circle and Zane began, "Father, we need you to give us wisdom, insight, courage, and strength to face the day. Protect us and those we have sworn to protect from harm."

Faith picked up the thread. "Please protect the Carrington officers who are currently following Craig Brown and his cronies."

Luke added, "And please protect the innocent who could come under fire in the chaos."

Tessa squeezed Zane's hand as she closed. "We trust in your love and power and will for our lives. Give us the courage to do what we've trained to do and what you've called us to do, and help us remember that you have gone before us into whatever we face today."

All four said a soft "amen" and walked out to face whatever the day held.

Zane drove to their office while Tessa made and received phone calls. Luke was behind them. Faith was on her way to the FBI office. Every law enforcement agency in Raleigh—local, state, and federal—had responsibilities today. Some as mundane as crowd control along the motorcade. Some as up close and personal as wanding every person who stepped onto the Carmichael estate. All with one focus—to make sure the president came and went with no complications.

And no one felt the pressure more intensely than the Raleigh

Secret Service agents. Despite having an impressive case-closure record, excellent interagency cooperation with their counterparts, and a reputation for professionalism whether they were giving a presentation at a school or filling a position on a counterterrorism task force, their office had become the butt of many dark jokes within the service.

This was their opportunity for a bit of redemption. And Craig Brown's crew was not going to mess that up.

Tessa's phone rang again. She answered it with the speaker on. "Reed."

"Tessa, Anissa." Anissa Bell-Chavez, another Carrington County investigator, spoke with an urgency that set Zane's nerves tingling. "We didn't have enough manpower to follow every vehicle, but we have four of them. Two are on the grounds of a warehouse three miles from the airport. We don't have a location on the other two yet, but we're keeping a close eye on them. Sabrina has all the license plates, and she's doing the best she can to track everyone. But we suspect they made their move in the middle of the night not only to make it harder for us to follow them, but also because it would be more difficult to track them using traffic cameras."

"Thanks for the heads-up—and for following them. What were y'all doing out there tonight?"

Anissa chuckled. "Gabe and I haven't been on a stakeout in a while. We figured we'd take two cars and stay close enough to keep an eye on things. When we got hints of activity, we called in a few patrol officers in unmarked vehicles. That's how we managed to keep up with four of them."

"We're going to owe you for this." Tessa's gratitude poured through every word.

"Nah. You'd do the same for us. But we need to plan a Saturday where we can all hang out. We'll even let Zane join in on the fun."

"I'm right here, Bell."

"I know." Anissa's laughter was filled with teasing. "Gabe told me the two of you were together. Stay sharp. I'll be in touch."

Tessa dropped her phone into her lap. "Three miles from the airport. It's doable with some of the drones they have on hand."

"Yeah, but attacking the motorcade? That only works in the movies."

When the president came to town, nothing was left to chance. Roads would be closed. Snipers positioned on rooftops and in buildings. Counterintelligence agents would be in the crowds watching for any hint of a threat. Even if they flew in drones carrying explosive payloads, the risk to the president was minimal. No drone could carry enough explosive material to destroy the Beast. But the risk to the men, women, and children who lined the motorcade route? That was a different story altogether.

"Is it possible these people are crazy enough to want to harm innocent bystanders just to make a point?" Zane asked.

"I've spent hours studying this group, and I'm not sure they're entirely rational." Weariness filled Tessa's voice. "I'm not opposed to nonviolent protests, but when your actions harm innocents, you've lost my respect and any protection under free speech or right of assembly or any other freedom we hold dear." She rolled her head in a slow circle. "Part of what makes these people so frustrating is their lack of logic. It's difficult to predict what an irrational person will do next."

"And even harder to predict what a group that is feeding off each other will do."

It took a little over an hour to get all the parties in place to discuss the next steps. The Carrington investigators had followed the remaining two vehicles to a private home located five miles by road but only two miles as the crow flies from the Carmichael estate. Given that Gabe and Anissa had no jurisdiction in Raleigh, they'd returned to Carrington after the Wake County Sheriff's Office took over surveillance.

Tessa stood beside the conference room table, the phone in the middle, as the Raleigh agents and advance agents gathered around to speak to agents still in DC, the sheriff's office, the FBI office, and at least five other local and state law enforcement agencies. "Can we get a warrant?" Zane had no idea who had asked the question. "Do we have a judge who would be willing?"

"We have no hard evidence. None."

"Can we get hard evidence?"

The conversation continued in circles for another thirty minutes, with the final decision coming from the protective detail lead agent, Supervisory Special Agent Duane Ledbetter. "We work on getting that hard evidence, but until then, we keep people close and make sure the snipers know to be on the look-out for UAVs. And we double the foot patrols along the river, both sides."

Unmanned aerial vehicles had progressed so much in the last decade that it made it possible for them to carry anything from an incendiary device to a biological weapon. Which made shooting them down potentially problematic.

"Special Agent Reed?" Ledbetter's voice was calm and crisp.

Tessa didn't flinch. "Yes, sir?"

"I want to commend you on your prior preparation and incredible response time tonight. Or I guess it's this morning. It's obvious you have a handle on this threat and have prepared for any eventuality. Good work."

"Thank you, sir."

Zane had never been so happy to not be on a video call. He gave Tess a discreet thumbs-up, and she responded with a small shrug and a smile that he knew wanted to go full voltage but she kept to barely there levels.

"The rest of the advance team will be wheels up in two hours. We'll see you soon. Good work, Raleigh."

**WHEN THE PHONE CALL ENDED,** Tessa didn't relax. She couldn't. Not only were her own coworkers and fellow agents in the room, but Rodriguez, Carver, and seven other advance agents were present. This was not the time to give in to the full mental and physical exhaustion that had her in a vise. If she lived through the next twenty-four hours, she was going to put on her comfiest pajamas, curl up with Zane on her sofa, and sleep until Monday. Then she was going to eat a ton of carbs and go back to sleep.

She took a sip of coffee and went to her office to try to figure out what was going on and how to prevent it. Of course, it would be a lot easier to prevent it if she knew what it was.

Dawn hadn't broken when her phone rang with an incoming call from Detective Morris. "Morris, you're up early."

"Yeah. And I'm not happy about it, Reed, so don't mess with me."

"Thanks for the warning. I can't really tell any difference between this and your normally grumpy self, so I might have misread the cues and accidentally been insufferable."

She infused her words with all the false cheeriness she could muster and had the satisfaction of hearing Morris groan. "Why do I put up with you? Why?"

"Doughnuts."

"Yeah. That's it. But I didn't call so you could harass me. I called because we got a phone call from a concerned citizen who is convinced she saw three UFOs in the field behind her house.

And it so happens that the Wake County Sheriff's Office has some deputies nearby. As in, right on the other side of that field."

All weariness fled as adrenaline spiked through Tessa's system.

"Part of her concern was that her neighbors told her they would be in Arizona for the month and the house is supposed to be empty. So she asked us to go check things out."

*Oh, thank you, Lord. Thank you.*

"Raleigh PD, Wake County Sheriff's Office, and SBI are working together to cover this, and I thought, in the interest of interagency cooperation and all, that you might like to be involved as well."

Tessa was thankful. So very thankful, but it felt a little bit too much like a coincidence. "Morris?"

"Yeah?"

"Is the phone call legit?"

"Now, Special Agent Reed, I'm offended that you would ask such a thing." Morris spoke with so much faux outrage, it almost made Tessa laugh. "However, as it seems you and I think a lot alike, I feel compelled to tell you that I asked the same question, and I have been assured that it is real."

Whether it was or wasn't, Tessa had done her due diligence, and there was no way she was going to miss out on seeing what was inside that house or flying around in that field. "Where do you want to meet?"

TWO HOURS LATER, Tessa was in a bulletproof vest, a helmet, full body armor . . . and a very bad mood. "Are we ever going to get inside?"

Zane stood beside her. He hadn't moved in twenty minutes. She kept checking to see if he was breathing. Nothing moved but his eyes.

"What's the matter?" he asked. "Is there a pea under your mattress, Princess?"

She glared at him. "I want to finish this." When he didn't respond, she nudged him with her elbow. "Since when do you stand so still that someone might mistake you for a mannequin?"

"I'm conserving my energy." Another quick glance in her direction. "You should try it."

"Why? Is it relaxing?"

"Nope. I'm about to jump out of my skin."

She didn't get to question him further because the signal she'd been waiting for finally came through her earpiece. It was time.

The sheriff's office had a highly decorated SWAT team made up of mostly retired special forces operators. They had the skill, experience, and legal authority to take the lead in this situation. Tessa, Zane, Rodriguez, Carver, and the other advance agents were on the right side of the house nearest the driveway. Gil, Luke, Benjamin, and four FBI agents were on the left side of the house. A team from the North Carolina State Bureau of Investigation's Tactical Services Unit had the rear covered. The NCSBI officers were experienced with high-risk warrants and searches, and Tessa had every confidence in their ability to contain anyone who attempted to leave the property.

The homes on either side of the residence had been evacuated, and a perimeter was in place, manned by local officers. The neighbor at the back who'd called in the report had been delighted to have officers take positions in her backyard.

Regardless of the outcome of this search, most of these same agents, officers, and deputies would be working all day and into the night. As she tensed for the moment of truth, all Tessa could think was that if she was wrong about this location, this threat, she would never recover from the professional backlash.

At least she hadn't had to be the one to make the call on how to handle the situation. Someone from NCSBI had found a willing judge, and they had a warrant to search the premises. Now to see how the people inside would respond.

Four officers armed to the teeth approached the door. They knocked.

Knocked again.

In the early morning stillness, a low voice carried with ease. "NC State Bureau of Investigation. We have a warrant to search the premises. Open up."

Nothing.

The tension lingered for a full minute. Then a voice came over the earpiece. "We have a window being opened. Upstairs. Back of the house." A pause followed by a calm observation. "UAV deployed. Payload unknown."

Why didn't the bad guys ever just say, "You know, this plan was stupid. We're idiots. You caught us. We give." But no. They had to fly a weaponized drone out the window.

*Lord, protect us.*

"Hold your fire." The incident commander's voice came over the coms.

The drone flew over the backyard and hovered. A female called out from the front of the house. "We don't want to hurt anyone, and we aren't doing anything illegal. We have permission from the homeowners to be here."

"Come out with your hands up." Under normal, non-life-threatening situations, the incident commander had the kind of voice that frightened babies. Now? He sounded like he was about to call down fire from heaven and burn the whole place up.

Zane spoke in a low murmur. "Would you believe he's married and has four girls?"

Tessa kept her eyes on the house. "I bet they have him wrapped around their little fingers."

"Every last one."

A drone appeared over the top of the house right as a new voice came through the coms. "Another UAV deployed from the opposite side of the house. Payload unknown but is visually similar. That makes two UAVs. One in the backyard, one flying into the front yard."

The incident commander's tone was a spike of fury. "Land the UAVs or we'll shoot them out of the sky. Come out of the house with your hands in the air."

The drone Tessa could see hovered in the middle of the yard. She wouldn't consider herself an expert, but she knew enough about UAVs to see that this one was not the kind you bought off the store shelf. This model could easily go for $50K. Maybe double. And whoever was operating it knew what they were doing. The flight was smooth, the hover alarmingly steady.

"We have heat signatures." Tessa assumed that was coming from either the SWAT or the SBI team. "Six people inside. All appear to be in the center of the house. Upstairs. No one is moving to exit the residence."

They'd dug in? Six people against a host of law enforcement? Wha—

Tessa lifted her phone and made a call. "What's the status at the warehouse by the airport?" she asked the woman who answered. She didn't know her name but knew she was the communications specialist for this op.

"Updated thirty seconds ago. All quiet."

"Thank you." Tessa disconnected and directed her next question to Zane. "Is it possible they think we're onto them at this location but not at the other? That if they keep us tied up here, we won't be able to do anything about the warehouse near the airport?"

"Maybe?"

"We've got movement inside." The voice in her ear was calm. Relaying facts without emotion. But that didn't prevent Tessa's pulse from spiking. "Looks like we've got another UAV being launched. This one is significantly larger. Hang on."

Tessa knew it wasn't possible, but she was so sensitized to what was going on around her that it felt like her hair was tingling.

"We've got spray nozzles." The words had barely come through the coms when the air above them filled with red mist.

"Take cover!" Everyone on the far edge of the mist turned and ran. Those directly underneath the mist scrambled into or under cars if they could.

Everyone else, including Tessa, pulled jackets over their heads. She felt one small drop on her hand before she got it tucked under her coat. Situationally blind under the jacket, she suddenly felt a large, warm body covering her. She didn't need to see him to know who it was.

"Zane!"

"Be still! I'm covered. Don't move."

He was covered only as long as whatever this stuff was didn't eat through their clothes.

They stayed still until they heard, "The drones are empty. Nothing new coming down." Followed by. "I think it's water."

What?

"Did he say 'water'?" Zane's voice rumbled in her ear.

Tessa twisted her head enough to speak to him. "Are you burning anywhere? How do you feel?"

He stood, then pulled her up beside him. All around them, agents and officers emerged from wherever they'd taken shelter.

"We have six in custody." The SBI and SWAT teams had taken advantage of the chaos to breach the house. "The UAVs were filled with water and red food coloring. It looks like a bloodbath in here."

Tessa groaned. They'd just run an entire operation to track down drones armed with water?

Then, "We've got bleach and ammonia in bulk. And ten more drones. Looks like they were in the process of filling them. It's a miracle these idiots didn't blow themselves up."

# 28

"WE HAVE TO GET TO THE AIRPORT SITE." Tessa was already moving. "Can you imagine the terror if the other team were to get those drones in the air over the crowds?"

Zane checked his watch. "We'll have a hard time getting there. There were people lining up along the motorcade route two hours ago. The crowds will be much larger by now."

Tessa ran straight to the incident commander. "We have to get to the other site."

"It looks like most of their arsenal is here," he countered. "And they could dump a vat of bleach on the Beast, and it won't harm the president."

"I don't think they ever planned to hit the president."

"With all due respect, have you been reading the same reports I've been reading this week? Because their threats have specifically been against the president."

"I've memorized every single one. And if you read them carefully, they don't say they're going to kill him. Or even harm him. They say they're going to be sure he can't be at the fundraiser. They say they're going to disrupt everything. They say it will be bloody and brutal. We assumed they meant to come after him directly. But I think this was their plan all along."

He narrowed his eyes at her. "Explain."

"It's bugged me ever since we learned about the drones." Tessa pointed to the house. "This crowd has a serious beef with the president, but they've never shown any indication that they would kill him. Killing him—or anyone—goes against everything they claim to stand for."

"Okay. I'm following you."

"We assumed they'd gotten fed up and were prepared to take things to the next level. But what if their 'next level' was simply to incite fear and panic, but not to harm anyone?"

"They have bleach and ammonia in there. That would hurt. It could burn. Or explode."

"Yes. It could. But they also had a lot of water, and the drones that came after us were just water. I'm not so sure they want to hurt anyone. But bleach and ammonia stink to high heaven, and it doesn't take much to get the odor. You add a little bit of either to that red water, then spray it over a crowd?"

He clearly wasn't convinced. "You're making a lot of assumptions."

"My assumptions are based on spending a week immersed in this crowd's previous activities. It's possible they knew that if they picked a location closer to tonight's event, we would focus there. Which we did. But what if that was their goal all along? To distract us here long enough so they could have the drones ready to go along the motorcade route. The president is still two hours out, but the streets are crowded. They don't have to attack the president directly. They wait until Air Force One is en route. Maybe even until it's ready to land. Then they send out the drones and panic everyone in the streets."

She looked at Zane. "What would happen if the president landed and Raleigh was in chaos?"

Zane took time to think about her question. "It wouldn't be a given that they'd cancel. He's highly motivated to attend tonight's event, but he might turn around and go back."

Tessa turned back to the incident commander. "And just like that, they would have succeeded."

"But how could they hope to get away with it?"

Tessa snorted. "They've been arrested so many times it's a wonder they have anyone left in their organization to stage a protest. It's like a badge of honor with them. The people here probably volunteered, knowing there was a high likelihood they would be caught but believing the disruption would be worth it."

Zane had to hand it to Tessa. Her theory had merit. In fact, after a week of confusion, it was the only version of events that came close to making sense.

"Sir, we have to get to that site and keep them from deploying those drones." Tessa wasn't pleading, but there was a passion in her eyes that couldn't be denied.

The incident commander turned to his second-in-command, a fierce woman who kind of scared Zane. "Get me . . . everybody."

At that vague order, she smirked and said, "Yes, sir."


IT TOOK AN HOUR to regroup and reset the teams outside the warehouse. "It took too long," Tessa fumed. "A smaller force could have gotten in and—"

"Gotten themselves killed." Zane stood in front of Tessa. "They haven't deployed the drones yet. And now that we have a good idea of what they're carrying, we can shoot them out of the sky if necessary."

Snipers were in position along the entire motorcade route, but two of the best had been relocated to positions in the vicinity of the warehouse. A newfangled drone defense device was also ready to be deployed. No one would explain how it worked, but SBI was confident it could stop the drones in the air. Apparently SBI had had it ready to go at the first site, but without knowing for sure what the drones were carrying, no one had wanted to risk an explosion. Now, the techs in charge were itching to test out their new toy.

"I need this resolved, Zane." Tessa paced in a tight circle around him. "I can't have the president land in this mess. I'm not sure if I could recover from the failure."

"He won't land in a mess." Zane kept his tone calm, even though the depth of her trust in him—her willingness to be vulnerable with him, to share the truth of who she was—staggered him. "And even if he did, it would not be your personal failure. You've been all over this. You're still all over it. You're the reason the visit tonight will go off without a hitch."

Her smile was gentle, but when she spoke, it was clear she remained unconvinced. "I hate to have to point this out, but you may be a little bit biased."

"I'm not a little bit biased." When she went to argue with him, he held up a hand. "I am intensely and completely biased. Doesn't make me wrong."

Everything went silent as the SWAT and SBI teams approached the warehouse. The decision had been made to breach the building without any warning. After what happened at the house, no one was in the mood to go gentle. But before they got inside, six drones flew from the roof and into the airspace around the warehouse. All were carrying an unknown payload, but from the ground it looked like the same setup as what they'd faced earlier.

Before the drones were a hundred yards from the warehouse, two exploded in midair in a spray of red and then rained down in tiny fragments. Sniper shots. Two others hovered, then dropped out of the sky as if they'd lost communication with their flight controllers. Both shattered on impact, and large puddles of red fluid leaked from them onto the ground.

Then a small drone took flight from the SBI command vehicle, and a brief dogfight took place over the warehouse, ending in both drones crashing into the roof.

The last drone met the same fate as the first two. It wouldn't surprise Zane to learn that the snipers had been arguing over who got to take the final shot.

As before, the chaos of the drone attacks had provided cover for the teams entering the warehouse.

"You know, if these guys were serious about causing any real damage, they should get someone with some military experience to help them plan their missions."

Tessa's acerbic comment was too much for Zane to resist, and he took a step closer and ran a hand across her shoulders. "I'm sorry they didn't present a bigger challenge for you, Princess."

"Oh, hush."

A new voice over the coms. "Ten individuals. All contained. Similar setup inside. Bleach, ammonia, water, drones."

Tessa shook her head in disgust. "Did they really think this was going to work?"

Zane squeezed her shoulder. "It could have. You're not giving yourself enough credit."

Tessa frowned. "Right now, the only thing that will make me happy is if Craig Brown is in there. If he isn't and I have to spend next week hunting him down so we can arrest him, I'm going to be seriously ticked off."

Five minutes later, Craig Brown was loud and proud as he was escorted from the building. "He'll never show now. Not after all the chaos we caused! We made our point! He will have to listen to our demands now!" The rhetoric continued until the door of the patrol car closed and thankfully muted the sound of his voice.

"Idiots," Tessa grumbled as they walked back to her car. "All of them. Blooming idiots."

Zane pulled her to a stop. "Let me get this straight. First you were worried they were going to succeed. Now you're mad they weren't a big enough challenge?"

She scrunched her entire face and hissed. "That would be ridiculous."

Zane laughed as they resumed their walk. "I realize this may sound backward, but sometimes it's the morons who succeed. They don't have enough sense to know something can't be done, they don't set up their attack in a logical fashion, and it's their unpredictability that gives them an edge."

Tessa didn't agree, but she didn't disagree.

"And, as you so eloquently pointed out earlier, this was no lame attempt. The crowds would have panicked. And depending on the concentration of ammonia or chlorine, some could have been harmed. Those who weren't would have been furious—either at having their clothing ruined or because they ran screaming from what was essentially red rain. Not to mention the danger a stampeding crowd is to the young, elderly, and disabled."

"True."

Her disgruntled tone had him reaching for her hand. She didn't shy away when he pulled her close and whispered in her ear. "Tess. Look." He paused by an agent who had the local news pulled up on his laptop. The camera angle showed an overpass filled with people. At least half of them were children. They were laughing and having a grand time. "Those people will never know that today could have ended in tragedy. When those kids grow up and think about this afternoon, they'll remember the joy, not the trauma. You did that, baby. I'm proud of you. Your team is proud of you. And if they knew what you'd done, your country would be proud of you too."

Tessa studied the crowd. "They do look happy."

Zane knew that was as much as Tessa would give him. At least for now. Her perfectionist tendencies were never going to go away. And he didn't want them to. They were part of what made her *his* Tessa. And if he had his way, he'd be hassling her at her ninetieth birthday party about that time she complained that the bad guys didn't present a big enough challenge.

"What are you thinking?"

He hadn't realized she'd turned her all-too-perceptive gaze on him, but it didn't matter. His secrets were hers. "How this will bug you until you're ninety."

She laughed. "Yeah. It will." This time she was the one tugging on his hand. "Come on. I have to get you to the airport and then get back to the Carmichaels'. This day is nowhere close to over."

# 29

**TWO HOURS LATER,** Tessa entered the room the PPD had chosen to make its command center for the night. It was a small room Graham said had once been used as an art studio by one of the Carmichael daughters during her "starving artist" phase. The room had huge windows that provided an abundance of natural light, and it boasted a ridiculous amount of lighting options, including black lights and UV. Even though the windows were currently blocked by shutters, the space was lit up like an operating theater.

There was an exterior door that would make it easy for agents to come in and out unobtrusively as they rotated between the indoor and outdoor seating areas for the event. This room also shared a wall with the main dining area. Shared walls made it easy to run discreet wiring without drilling holes in the home. Always a plus. But in this case, there was even a hidden door. This room was originally designed to be an oversized butler's pantry, which made it possible for household staff to come and go without disrupting the homeowners and their guests during parties.

Zane was with the president, and they were scheduled to arrive in ten minutes. Which meant she didn't have much time.

"Do you need something, Tessa?" Richard Carver walked over

to join her. She liked Carver, but unfortunately his question caught the attention of Rodriguez, and he sauntered over with a huge smile on his face and a look in his eyes that made Tessa want to shower.

"Yes, Tess. How can we help?"

Tessa fought to remain professional. "I saw a woman enter a few moments ago. In her thirties. Blond. Curvy. She was with Tyson Monteith."

"Okay?" Carver shrugged. "Wife? Mistress?"

"No idea. That's what bothers me. I memorized the guest list. He was coming alone."

Rodriguez gave Tessa a patronizing smile. "Oh, I know who she is. Wendy Monteith. Tyson's daughter. And a last-minute addition."

"Who approved her?"

Rodriguez had the decency to look abashed. "Sorry, Tess. It came from the president."

Tessa didn't bother to hide her annoyance. "Did *anyone* vet her?"

Carver had walked over to a computer while they were talking. He returned with the laptop turned toward her. "Wendy Monteith. Thirty-seven. Daughter of Tyson and Debra Monteith. Attended high school with the Carmichaels' daughter, Shelby."

Tessa scanned the write-up. It was painfully short. Looked like daddy dearest had pulled some strings.

*Don't scream*. She took a long, slow inhale and exhale. Carver handed the laptop to Rodriguez and stepped closer. He dropped his voice to barely a whisper. "Sorry, Tessa. It doesn't happen often. POTUS generally doesn't pull stuff like this. You see the security risk. I do too. But he doesn't. Monteith is a huge supporter and a frat brother. All the president sees is a friend who wants his daughter to have the opportunity to chat with the president and who's willing to pay a cool forty thousand to make it happen."

Tessa would never get used to the amount of money that flowed in the world of politics and campaigns. The idea of anyone dropping $40K on a meal and a photo op hurt her bargain-loving soul.

Monteith was on her list of possible suspects, and she'd hoped to have the opportunity to speak to him alone tonight. With his daughter in attendance, the odds of that happening went down considerably. Not that she was going to share any of that with Carver. "You're right, but I don't like it. We've had enough lunacy on this visit. I don't like finding out at the last minute that there's a hole in our defenses."

Rodriguez was still staring at the computer. "Wendy Monteith is hot."

Carver closed his eyes and gave Tessa an apologetic "What are you gonna do?" shrug. She understood. Rodriguez was a dog.

"Weird."

Tessa didn't want to ask, but she couldn't stop herself. "What's weird?"

"She never married."

"Rodriguez?" Looked like Carver had put up with all he could from Rodriguez. "What is weird about that?"

When Rodriguez looked up from the computer, all the smarminess had washed out of him. "Hear me out. She's an *extremely* attractive woman. She's the daughter of an *extremely* wealthy and influential man. Monteith is a gatekeeper."

Something about that set an idea spinning in Tessa's mind, but it flitted away before she could grab it.

"Wendy Monteith should have her choice of men." Rodriguez tapped the computer. "Money isn't everything. Ugly rich girls don't necessarily get their pick of men, but beautiful rich girls do."

For a fraction of a second, Tessa caught a glimpse of pain behind the deep brown eyes that until this moment had held nothing but flirtation. The pain disappeared, but the serious tone did not. "She may be here for something other than a night out with dad's old frat brothers."

Tessa would probably regret this later, but for now, she couldn't stay silent. "Being pretty, rich, and single doesn't set off the same alarm bells for me that it obviously does for you, Rodriguez. Probably because I'm thirty-five, unmarried, successful in my career, and no one has ever called me ugly."

Rodriguez, to his credit, didn't jump at that.

"Granted, I'm not an heiress or the daughter of a powerful man, but it's possible that Wendy Monteith is perfectly happy in her career and never wanted to marry in the first place. There's no rule that says pretty rich girls have to get married."

Carver chimed in. "Imagine that, Rodriguez. Wendy Monteith might have character and a spine and know that if she's going to fall in love, she wants to fall for a decent man who's attracted to her mind more than to her body."

Rodriguez rolled his eyes. "I get what you're saying. I do. But you don't understand this world the way I do. You're right. Money isn't an issue, and she wouldn't have been compelled to bother with men she deemed not worth her time. But I'm telling you, in this world, there's still a lot of pressure to marry well. And that goes for the men and the women. Something about this smells off. I'm going to do a little bit of digging."

With that, he took the laptop and found a spot at a table. Tessa turned back to Carver. "Did he just make a valid point?"

Carver looked as befuddled as she felt. "I think he did." Someone called to Carver. "Excuse me."

Tessa half expected to have to dodge Rodriguez now that she

was alone, but he was bent over the laptop and, for once, paying her no attention whatsoever.

That was weirdly good. She wouldn't be sad to see the back of Rodriguez when this visit was over, but Benjamin had said he was a good agent with good instincts. Having him keep an eye on Wendy Monteith wouldn't hurt anything. And it might even help.

**ZANE WAS FOCUSED** on the president, but part of that focus meant being aware of everyone in the room with him. He'd memorized the guest list over the past few days and knew which of tonight's attendees were more likely to monopolize the president's time than others.

The fact that three of those people were on his short list of suspects in Tessa's abduction was a bonus.

He'd joined the president at the airport, and the trip to the Carmichael estate had been without incident. Not one drop of red rain.

Now they were inside, and Zane caught himself checking every set of cuff links he could get a look at. It was unlikely that any member of the Janus society, as he and Tessa had taken to calling the shadowy group that might or might not exist, was a threat to the president.

But any man who would drug a woman and take her to a sketchy motel—

Zane cut off that line of thought before he lost his mind in a haze of fury. Tonight he had no room for anything but cool rationality.

"Mr. President!" The booming voice belonged to a man who had spent a few years too long in a tanning bed. Yancy McCloud was being trailed after by his wife, Daisy, a woman who was younger than McCloud's youngest son by three years. The profile they had on her indicated that while she appeared to be a gold digger on the surface, she was in fact a sharply intelligent woman who continued to manage an entire branch of McCloud's retail empire.

And they had a prenup that would leave McCloud a pauper should he ever do the same thing to Daisy that he had done to his previous wife. Of the three *M*'s, McCloud was number three on Zane's "most likely to have drugged Tessa" list. He didn't see the motive. But while he was the last one on the list when it came to Tessa, he was the first on Zane's list of men who shouldn't have easy access to the president. Something was very off about him. Zane couldn't prove it. On paper, McCloud was clean. But there was an edge to the man that didn't sit well.

The McClouds spoke to the president for five minutes before they merged into the crowd. Thirty minutes later, Wheeler Meadows and his wife, Laura, got their five minutes of face time. Laura Meadows was in her sixties, and her skin was flawless—if you didn't consider it a flaw that neither her forehead nor her upper lip ever moved. Zane found it disconcerting to watch her speak.

"She should fire her plastic surgeon," Ledbetter said as he watched them.

Zane didn't disagree, but the Meadowses interacted in a way that gave Zane the sense that they were very much in sync. It was possible that Meadows had gotten drunk and done something stupid with Tessa, but the longer Zane watched the man, the less he found that scenario to be likely. Meadows was largely unknown. He generally kept a low profile, but since the president had come into office, he'd become a huge financial supporter.

The Meadowses moved on, and the evening progressed. The meal was eaten. The president mingled inside and outside and posed for pictures with everyone there. Zane caught a few glimpses of Tessa, but always from a distance.

Carmichael was a charming host and had an easy way with the president that was rare to see. If he wanted something specific from the president tonight, he had yet to show his cards. So far, all he'd done was ensure the president had an enjoyable evening, including taking it upon himself to gently extricate the president from guests who wanted to monopolize his time.

The evening had hit the point where the guests were still fully engaged, but everyone from the agents to the president himself were running out of steam. This was a rare opportunity for 98 percent of the attendees, and they were making the most of it.

But Zane had lost count of the number of dinners he'd been to, and he'd only been on the PID for seven months. He couldn't imagine what it was like for career politicians.

Carmichael paused beside Zane. "Special Agent Thacker?"

"Yes, sir."

"I have a bit of an unusual request."

"Okay."

"I was wondering if it would be possible to have the president join me over by the painting on the far wall. The one we had restored."

Zane zeroed in on the painting. The three *M*'s stood in a semi-circle around the painting, facing Carmichael. The wives were nowhere in evidence, nor was Monteith's daughter, who'd been a late addition to the guest list.

"I'll see what I can do, sir." It took another ten minutes before Zane had an opportunity to pass along the request, but the president acquiesced immediately. "Monty!" The president pulled Monteith into a huge hug. "Where is your Wendy? I know I saw her earlier."

"She took off with Carmichael's butler, if you can believe it.

She used to play here as a kid and wanted to see if she could find a spot where she and Shelby drew on a doorframe or some such nonsense."

"Be sure you bring her over to talk to me before the evening is over. I don't think I've seen her since she was in college. How's she doing?"

"Great. Keeps me out of trouble."

The president roared with laughter, and it seemed genuine. Zane might not have noticed if it hadn't been so obvious to him that the laughter of the other two *M*'s was decidedly forced. Even Carmichael had tensed at the mention of Wendy Monteith.

Zane caught Ledbetter's eye. The man was the PID lead agent for a reason, and he'd picked up on the strange vibe.

Ledbetter took a few steps to the side and spoke into the com unit at his wrist. "I need eyes on Wendy Monteith. She's supposed to be with the butler and could be anywhere in the house or on the grounds, including areas otherwise off-limits to guests."

With that terse order, Ledbetter stepped back into his position. Anyone watching wouldn't realize it, but every agent in a five-mile radius was now on full alert. It could be nothing. But last-minute additions to the guest list who disappeared from the party and made people uncomfortable were not safe to ignore.

Carmichael reached into his pocket and pulled out a small box. "Monty. We have something for you. And since we're all here, we wanted to give it to you now." He handed the box to Monteith, then turned to the president. "You probably don't know this, but Monty here managed to lose a cuff link a while back."

Zane watched in a combination of shock, horror, disbelief, and disgust as Monteith removed the lid and pulled out a cuff link identical to the one that currently resided in a small box in Tessa's office.

# 30

TESSA COULD NOT BELIEVE she'd joined forces with Rodriguez. But when the call came over the coms, they had both moved toward the stairs.

"I got the sense that Graham was a straight shooter," Rodriguez said as they took the steps two at a time.

"I did too." Tessa had liked the guy. Right now, she was doubting everything.

"Right or left?" Rodriguez asked.

"Right."

The upper levels of the home were supposed to be empty. It shouldn't be too difficult to locate Graham and Wendy Monteith. Tessa moved down the hall toward Carmichael's office, Rodriguez a half step behind her. She kept her stride purposeful and swept the area with her gaze. She opened the first door on the left. Rodriguez entered while she stayed partially in the hall. It was a smallish bedroom, and Rodriguez was quick but thorough as he checked the closet, under the bed, and behind the curtains before he rejoined her in the hall.

He opened the next door, and she went inside. This was another bedroom. Significantly larger, and the decor screamed late-nineties teenager. The oldest Carmichael daughter had probably called this her own a few decades ago. Tessa checked the closet, bed, and curtains before moving into a Jack and Jill bathroom that connected to another room.

She was almost surprised to see a shower with an actual shower curtain. Most of the bathrooms in this house were large and had glass enclosures, but this one had so far escaped renovation. She yanked back the shower curtain and bit back a scream.

Graham lay in the tub. Blood pumped from a wound in his abdomen. "Rodriguez. Get in here now!"

But it wasn't Rodriguez who came through the door.

"There's a man dead in the hall!" Wendy Monteith screeched. Then she saw Graham's bloodied form, and her hand fluttered in front of her face. "What did you do to him?" This time her scream was filled with fury and fear, and she took three quick steps back. "I'm calling the police."

Tessa kept her mental focus on Wendy and deliberately bent toward Graham while she spoke into her wrist. "Rodriguez? Check—"

The pointed toe of a Louboutin heel came flying toward her temple, but Tessa was ready for it. She clasped her hand around Wendy's ankle and twisted hard. Wendy went down in the small space between the vanity and the door and cracked her head against the marble floor. The impact jarred a tiny handgun from her grasp, and it slid behind the toilet.

Tessa sent out an emergency code from a small device at her waist that she knew would alert the cavalry, but she couldn't let down her guard. Right now she had a guy dying in the bathtub, a guy who may or may not be dead in the hall, and a woman who had to be sporting a goose egg big enough to feed a small village but was now scrambling to her feet and coming at Tessa.

Hand-to-hand combat in a bathroom was less than ideal under the best of circumstances, but it looked like Wendy Monteith wasn't going down until Tessa put her in cuffs.

"Murderer!" Wendy screamed, and Tessa blocked a blow from the woman's fist that, if it had landed, could have put Tessa in the tub with Graham.

"I." A shove. "Didn't." Another shove. "Kill." Tessa kicked Wendy's shin before the woman could dig her heel into Tessa's calf. "Anybody."

The heel snapped on the other shoe, and Wendy teetered before falling onto the vanity. Tessa pulled her weapon from the holster she wore under her jacket and aimed it at Wendy Monteith. "Stop."

She half expected the woman to make a move, but instead, she raised her hands in the classic surrender pose and whimpered, "Don't kill me. Please. I'll forget I saw anything. Please. Just let me go."

They hadn't had a full dossier on Wendy Monteith, but nothing in what they did have had indicated that the woman was mentally unstable. Tessa had no idea what game Wendy was playing, but there was a look of cool calculation in her eyes that gave Tessa the creeps.

What was that about? Nothing gave Tessa the creeps. Snakes not withstanding.

A faint sound coming from the region of Tessa's neck alerted her to the earpiece that now dangled from her collar. She slid it back in and heard, "Reed, report."

"Upstairs bathroom, off second bedroom. One man injured. Rodriguez may be down, whereabouts unknown. Guest in the bathroom assaulted me and is convinced I'm a murderer."

The dead silence on the other end of the line would have been funny at any other time. When their communications expert for the evening spoke, she managed one word. "Copy."

Not helpful. "Where's my backup? And we need paramedics up here stat."

She hadn't forgotten Graham. Not for a second. But right now, she couldn't be sure what was the greater threat. Blood loss or Wendy Monteith.

Agents appeared in both doorways of the bathroom. "Ma'am, I need you to step outside."

Tessa didn't know the name of the agent who'd spoken, but she caught his eye and then flicked her gaze to the floor. "She had a gun. It's behind the toilet."

Those words were all the agent needed to know, and while he didn't manhandle Wendy Monteith, he certainly didn't treat her with kid gloves as she hobbled out of the bathroom.

As soon as she was gone, Tessa dropped to her knees and pressed a hand to Graham's neck and found a pulse, faint but there. "I've got a pulse."

She pulled a towel from the nearby rack and applied pressure to the wound. Graham moaned but didn't open his eyes. She turned behind her and caught another agent's eyes. "Rodriguez?"

The agent shook his head, expression grim. "I don't know. He . . . I don't know if he was breathing."

Tessa could have cried from relief when Luke and Gil ran into the room. "Tess!" Gil knelt beside her. "Are you hurt? Let me." He pushed her hands away from Graham's wound and held the towel against the man's abdomen.

Luke pulled her to her feet. "Are you hurt?"

"No. I'm fine. Where is Wendy Monteith?"

"In the next bedroom." That came from Carver. "Ledbetter is on his way up. The guests were told that the president had to make an immediate return to DC. He's already in the Beast, and they're all giddy because they think they've witnessed some top-secret something."

Which meant Zane was on his way to the airport and could be on his way to DC after that. Just because he was supposed to stay for several more days didn't mean it would happen. Not in unusual circumstances like these.

A low voice yelled from the doorway. "Everybody out so we can get to the injured man." Tessa allowed Luke to tug her from the room, but not before she got a good look at the men coming in behind them. Once she was satisfied that she recognized them as part of the security team for the evening, she walked into the hall.

Ledbetter walked by her. "Reed. With me. Now."

Luke and Gil gave her encouraging smiles as she followed Ledbetter into another room at the far end of the hall. That room proved to be Carmichael's office. Carmichael was watching a security feed, his jaw so tight he could crack a molar if he wasn't careful.

He glanced up when they entered but returned his focus to the video even as he spoke. "Special Agent Reed, I trust you are uninjured."

"I'm fine."

"And Graham?" His voice broke on the butler's name.

"Being tended to now. He had a pulse when I left him."

Carmichael had aged in the past fifteen minutes. Since she'd met him last week, he'd been the charming host, the angry home-owner, the delighted friend of the president, the mourning friend of the lost Janus painter, but never had she seen the lines that now bracketed his eyes, mouth, and creased his forehead. "I don't see anything, Agent Ledbetter. Graham and Wendy came upstairs. They were chatting. Friendly. Lots of smiles. They walked into my daughter's bedroom. There are no cameras in that room. And neither of them ever came back out."

"May I?" Tessa approached the desk, Ledbetter right behind her, and watched the video again. When it reached the end, she said, "Can you continue it? At some point, Rodriguez and I should be coming up the stairs." Carmichael fast-forwarded the video until Tessa appeared at the end of the hall. She watched as they cleared the first room. Then entered the next.

And then watched as Rodriguez frowned, took several steps down the hall, away from the door Tessa had entered, and pushed open the next bedroom door. Seconds later, he dropped to the floor in front of the door.

"What happened to him?" Tessa asked.

"I think it's time you and I had a chat with Ms. Monteith." Ledbetter pointed to the computer. "My people will need that footage."

"Of course."

"You should return to the guests. We encouraged them to stay. Until we know what's going on, we won't know if Ms. Monteith had an accomplice." Ledbetter paused. "For obvious reasons, should Tyson Monteith attempt to leave the premises, he will be detained."

When they returned to the hall, Ledbetter paused. "Your version of events in thirty seconds. Go."

Tessa did her best and relayed everything that had happened.

"Your take on Wendy Monteith?"

"She's neither in shock, nor is she the pampered society diva she attempts to portray herself to be."

Ledbetter's response was a grunt. Clearly not the most verbose agent she'd ever worked with. He paused at the door. "I'll talk, but don't hesitate to chime in."

"Sir?"

"Yes?"

"I don't want to hamper the investigation in any way, but for whatever reason, she's decided to call me a murderer and accuse me of causing the injuries to both Graham and Rodriguez. And based on that video surveillance, there's nothing to prove I didn't do it. It's my word against hers."

"Your point?"

"Should I go in there? Or should I stay outside?"

Ledbetter studied her for a moment. "Special Agent Reed, please don't take this the wrong way, but while I see your point, I don't have time to make this easy on her. If your presence incites her to violence or fits of temper, I'm okay with that. The more she talks, the more likely she is to give us something we can use."

"Fair enough."

They entered the room.

**THEY DIDN'T MAKE IT A FOOT** into the room before Wendy Monteith squealed and threw a shoe in Tessa's direction. Was this woman trying to make herself look unhinged? Because she was doing a decent job of it.

"Ms. Monteith"—Ledbetter stood across from the desk chair Wendy sat in—"we need to ask you a few questions."

Wendy rocked in the seat. "Scared. So scared. She's a murderer. She'll kill me." Then she straightened in her seat. "Is my daddy downstairs? He is. I need him. He'll take care of this."

Ledbetter turned back to Tessa and rolled his eyes. "Maybe you *should* wait outside for a few minutes."

Tessa left the room without argument. Something was very, very wrong, and Wendy Monteith was up to her pearls in it.

When she stepped into the hall, she spotted the agents standing post at the top of the stairs and Luke, Gil, and Carver located midway down the hall. The three men rushed her.

"What's going on?" all three asked.

"I have no idea." She leaned against the wall. "We came up here to look for Wendy. I'd kept an eye on her all night. Rodriguez had too."

"He said she smelled funny." Carver shook his head. "Not literally. But she set off his senses."

"Oh, he wasn't wrong." Tessa told them everything. "She's in there right now ranting about how I'm a murderer, but I think she shot Graham and did something to Rodriguez. And now she's trying to cover it up by blaming it on me and pretending to be the freaked-out victim. But what I can't make any sense of is why."

Luke tapped his phone. "Before Zane left, he sent me a text and said we need to check out the Monteiths. So I put a phone call in to Sabrina. She's working on it now." He looked at Carver. "We have access to Dr. Sabrina Campbell-Fleming. You may not have heard of her, but—"

"Oh, I've heard of her. She found some teenagers for us when I worked in the Dallas office. Kids were being trafficked, and she did some sort of voodoo with the paint in the hotel room and shadows from the curtains." Carver's expression was a mixture of confusion and awe.

"Sounds about right," Gil said.

"And you can just call her up on a Friday night?" Carver sounded impressed.

"Well, yeah. She's a friend." Luke turned back to Tessa. "The thing is, Zane was very clear that he wanted info on both of them. Not just Wendy." He held her gaze, and a prickle of awareness flitted down her spine.

"I understand." Could Monteith be her mysterious abductor? Maybe. But where did Wendy fit into this? Tessa's brain struggled to process everything going on. "Do we have the weapon that Wendy had?"

"Yes. They have it downstairs. Why?" Carver asked.

Tessa was already walking down the hall. "Because I don't believe for a second that she got that thing past our security sweep."

Luke and Gil followed her at a jog.

Carver called after them, "You go ahead. I'll stay here and pretend I'm doing something."

"If Ledbetter asks, tell him I'll be back in a minute. But I have to check this out. I have a hunch." Tessa jogged down the stairs. It took her less than two minutes to find Carmichael. Mainly because the suave host had turned into a reclusive hermit and was standing alone in a corner of the kitchen.

"Mr. Carmichael?" Tessa approached him gently. She could be wrong, but she didn't believe he'd known any of this was going to happen tonight.

"Special Agent Reed, how may I help?" The Southern gentleman in him rose to the surface, and he found a smile. "I'm afraid right now my mind is a bit scattered, but I will assist in whatever way I can. I was waiting for word about Graham. They haven't—" His eyes widened. "No."

"No, sir." Tessa hurried to his side. "No, sir. We haven't heard a word. I'm sorry to have frightened you."

"That's okay, dear." He patted her hand. "He's my oldest friend. And I sent him off with her . . ."

"That's what I wanted to talk to you about." Tessa knew she had to tread carefully. "You said she told Graham that she wanted to see if there was something she'd drawn in your daughter's room back when they were kids."

"Yes. Wendy and Shelby were great friends from elementary through high school. Not as much after that because they went to different colleges, but they'd still get together during the summer and over Christmas break. But then life took them in different directions, and they no longer do much more than exchange pleasantries when they happen to run into each other at a social event. Wendy has been in the DC area for at least fifteen years now, so that doesn't happen often."

Good enough friends that what Tessa was thinking was a possibility. Slim, but . . . "I was wondering, Mr. Carmichael, if by any chance your daughter owned a very tiny gun?"

Carmichael blinked at her, then frowned. "How did you know?"

Tessa hadn't known for sure. "Sir, would it be possible for you to contact your daughter and find out if she has that gun in her possession?"

"You want me to call her now?"

"Yes, sir. It would be most helpful."

To his credit, Carmichael didn't argue. If anyone was in shock in this home tonight, it was him. Poor guy was going through the motions, but it was clear he wasn't fully engaged. He dialed a number and waited as it rang. He put it on speaker without them asking. "Hey, Daddy. Is everything okay? I thought your big party was tonight." Her voice was soft and Southern, and when Carmichael didn't respond immediately, it lowered and there was confusion mixed with concern when she said, "Dad?"

"It was. It is. I'm fine, darling, but I need to ask you something, and I can't explain right now. Maybe later."

"Dad?" The voice had sharpened. "What's going on? Are you sure you're all right?"

"I'm fine. But I need to know where that tiny gun is. The one I gave you for your sixteenth birthday."

"What? Oh. Wow. It's probably still in the safe in my room. It's funny that you would ask me that now. I haven't thought about that little thing in years, and you're the second person to ask me about it this week."

"Ask her who else." Tessa mouthed the question to Carmichael.

"Who else asked you?"

"Wendy Monteith. She called yesterday, or maybe the day before, and wanted to catch up. Said she was coming to the party, wanted to know if I would be there, and we got to talking about old times. Have you seen her tonight?"

Carmichael looked to the ceiling and shook his head even though his daughter couldn't see it. "Yeah, baby. I have."

"So, do you need the gun or something?"

"No, baby. I don't need it. I was thinking we should put it in the gun safe."

"Right. That's a good idea. But Dad—"

"I'm afraid I have to go. I'll call you later, okay?"

"Sure. Love you."

"Love you too."

Carmichael's hand shook as he ended the call. "Did Wendy shoot Graham with a tiny 9mm?"

"I can't prove that yet, sir." Tessa kept her tone gentle. "But I can tell you that she tried to shoot me with one."

# 31

AN HOUR AFTER LEAVING the Carmichael estate, Zane ran up the driveway and wove through the people still in the main entertaining area. Part of his brain noted that agents were chatting with the guests in a nonthreatening way before allowing them to depart.

Another part of his brain noted that Monteith, Meadows, and McCloud were huddled together in one corner of the room and three agents were too close for it to be a coincidence.

But a solid 99 percent of his brain was focused on one thing and one thing only. The woman who stood at the back of the room and, at least in his imagination, had eyes only for him. He didn't stop moving until he was two inches away. "You're okay." His hand reached for her, and he managed through sheer force of will to be content with a gentle squeeze to her elbow.

"Yes." Her voice was low and a little raspy. "I'll fill you in."

"Not yet. I need to tell you something first." This time he pulled her back into the command center for the evening and bent so he could speak in her ear. "Monteith."

"Yes. Wendy Monteith."

"No. Tyson Monteith."

"What are you taking about?" Tessa shook her head in obvious confusion.

"I witnessed Carmichael, Meadows, and McCloud give Monteith a replacement for his Janus cuff link. Right in front of the president."

Tessa's eyes widened, then she blinked rapidly. "It can't be."

"Why not?" Monteith had been one of Zane's top contenders all week.

"No. It's not that." Tessa filled him in on what had happened upstairs.

"So Wendy Monteith suckers Graham into taking her upstairs on the possibility that her buddy from two decades ago hadn't cleaned out her safe?" he asked.

"We found the safe open, and we also found a jet injector of insulin in her purse. That's how she took out Rodriguez."

Zane dropped his head. "If she had a prescription for it, and it was sealed and in her purse, the agents wouldn't have taken it from her."

"Oh, it had her name on it." Tessa's rage burned with the force of a supernova. "But Wendy Monteith isn't a diabetic."

"And injecting insulin into anyone who doesn't need it—"

"Can kill them," Tessa finished his thought. "We called the hospital and told them what we suspected. Rodriguez should be okay, but it was a close call."

Zane took the time to process everything he'd heard. "Where's Wendy Monteith now?"

"Still upstairs. They want to wait until all the guests have left to take her out of the house. They're trying to cut down on the scandal."

"Has anyone questioned Tyson Monteith yet?"

"No. The focus has been on trying to keep everything casual

down here. But he won't be leaving until he has a sit-down with Ledbetter. By the way, Ledbetter is seriously ticked about having to stay here. He promised his kids pancakes in the morning. I wouldn't want to be Monteith right now."

"Tessa?" Zane hated what he was about to say, what he was about to do, but it had to happen. "I think you need to tell Ledbetter about our suspicions about Monteith."

She dropped her head. "If I tell him, my career is over."

Zane wanted to tell her she was wrong. And she might be. But she might be right.

"But the coincidences are too great not to make sure he's aware of the full situation." Tessa straightened. "Wish me luck."

Before he could say a word to encourage her, she slipped away. Luke, Gil, Benjamin, and Jacob converged on him. "What's going on?" Jacob asked.

When Zane told him where Tessa was headed, Jacob looked at them and said, "Gentlemen, if you'll excuse me, I have an agent to defend."

"Godspeed." Benjamin clapped him on the back as he walked past them.

The four of them were left staring at each other. "Now what?"

Zane wanted to run up the stairs, hold Tessa's hand while she bared her soul, and make sure Ledbetter treated her with respect, dignity, and professionalism. Then he wanted to personally deliver both Wendy and Tyson Monteith to the loving embrace of the Raleigh Sheriff's Office Detention Facility. Not that Tessa wanted or needed him to do any of those things. She was more than capable of taking care of herself. She was also quite possibly the bravest woman he'd ever known. She was willing to not only face and conquer her demons, but when the consequences of the past came charging into the future, she tackled them with grace and dignity.

She would never see herself the way he saw her. And that was okay. He'd tell her every day how extraordinary she was.

"Earth to Zane?" Luke waved a hand in front of Zane's face.

Zane pulled himself back to the present. "Now we do our jobs and wait to see what happens." With that, they split up and kept busy doing everything from interviewing the guests who were ready to leave to making a run to the kitchen for bottles of water.

It was almost midnight when Tessa, Jacob, and Ledbetter came downstairs. Ledbetter nodded to Carmichael, who stood in the middle of the room and clapped his hands. "Ladies and gentlemen. It's been a glorious evening, but our friends in the Secret Service and the other law enforcement branches would love to get home to their families, and they can't do that until everyone else goes home!" He said it in such a way that the majority of the people chuckled and moved to gather purses and suit jackets from where they'd been draped over chairs. "Thank you for coming!"

As Zane watched, Ledbetter walked to the corner where the three M's stood talking, along with their wives. He couldn't hear what was said, but a few moments later, the wives were being escorted out. The men were being led toward a small sitting room at the back of the home. Ledbetter caught Zane's eye and jerked his head in a "come on" gesture. Zane didn't wait to be told twice.

"Are you prepared to back up what Agent Reed told me?" Ledbetter asked.

Zane answered without hesitation. "Yes, sir."

"What if she lied?"

"She didn't."

Ledbetter rolled his eyes. "Are you and she a couple?"

"Yes."

"Does she know that?"

"Before this week? No. But as of this week, yes."

Ledbetter huffed, but there was amusement in the sound. "Lucky for you, I'm a romantic."

Zane was unable to hide his shock at that statement. "I had no idea, sir."

Ledbetter spoke with a touch of arrogance. "I'm single-handedly responsible for at least ten happy marriages. When you're ready to propose, come talk to me. You can't just get down on one knee. That's not how it's done anymore. And if you think you have a chance with Special Agent Reed, you're going to have to up your game and plan to keep it elevated for the next sixty years."

"I'll keep that in mind."

"Good. Now, let's go see if we can make the world a better place by taking some of the vermin out of circulation for a while."

TESSA STOOD at the back of the room.

She stared hard at Monteith when he entered, but no matter how much she tried, she couldn't remember anything about him. But when he caught her staring, his face went slack and his stride faltered. Every bit of his body language screamed that he did not want to get anywhere near her.

Jacob edged a fraction closer to her. His lips barely moved as he said, "Funny. He doesn't look happy to see you."

"I did just arrest his daughter."

Jacob chuckled. "True. But he doesn't know that yet. Wait until he finds out."

Monteith, Meadows, McCloud, and Carmichael all took seats in the four chairs that circled a small coffee table. Ledbetter entered a few seconds later, with Zane right behind him. Ledbetter pulled a chair from a small game table and put it in front of the men. Zane strode around them and came straight to Tessa. He took a position on her other side, with his arm brushing against hers. "Everything okay?"

"Not sure." She'd explained everything to Ledbetter. At one point, she truly believed his head was going to explode, and she was so thankful for Jacob's steady presence nearby. But when she was done, Ledbetter shook his head and said, "This is why my daughters are never dating. They're also never going to the beach with their friends on Spring Break. Or leaving home. I'll get them tutors. Who needs college?" Then he'd asked where Monteith currently was.

Jacob leaned around her and said, "It went fine. She's fine. Ledbetter's a good man."

They fell silent when Ledbetter cleared his throat. "Gentlemen, it's been quite an evening."

Carmichael's nostrils flared. Ledbetter needed to hurry, because Carmichael was going to take Monteith down if he wasn't arrested soon.

"Right now, we have Ms. Wendy Monteith upstairs. She's in custody."

Tyson Monteith jumped to his feet. "What? Why? You have no right—"

"Your psychopath daughter shot my butler and injected a Secret Service agent with insulin." Carmichael was on his feet with his finger in Monteith's face. "Why would you bring her here in the first place, Tyson? We all know she's nuts, but what could have possessed her to do something like that?"

And that's when it happened. Monteith's gaze flicked to Tessa, and everyone in the room saw it.

"Do you have a problem with Special Agent Reed's presence, Mr. Monteith?" Ledbetter asked.

"No." Monteith sat. "Wendy wouldn't have done what you say she did. I'm sure there's an explanation."

"Oh, I'm sure there is." Ledbetter sat back and steepled his fingers. "Right now, I need to direct our conversation away from Ms. Monteith for a moment." When Tyson made as if to object, Ledbetter hurried to say, "Oh, don't worry. We won't forget about her. Not for a second. But before we can go on, I need to ask you gentlemen about the present you gave to Mr. Monteith this evening."

Carmichael frowned. "What are you talking about? The cuff link? What does that have to do with anything?"

"I'm afraid it may be the key to everything, Mr. Carmichael, so I ask your indulgence. What can you tell me about the significance of the cuff link?"

Carmichael shrugged. "There was a group of us in college. We were sitting around one night, talking and drinking beer. We were giving the president a hard time. He was determined to run for office, and we were razzing him about how he'd better let us stay in the White House. But Monteith"—Carmichael nodded in Tyson's direction—"said he didn't want to be the one to hold office. He wanted to be the one with the real power. The power to open doors, a gatekeeper type. Someone people would come to when they wanted to get stuff done."

McCloud and Meadows nodded their agreement with Carmichael's version of events. "It was a bunch of guys sitting around doing some male bonding, but that night was when we agreed we'd always support each other. Someone said we should come up with a name for who we were. One of the guys was a Classics major. He told us about Janus, and it seemed like a perfect fit. We figured most people would assume it was an acronym. But those who knew about Janus would get it."

Meadows snorted. "I was so drunk that night that I had to look it up the next day to see what I'd agreed to."

McCloud leaned forward and rested his forearms on his legs. "We were young and stupid, but I've never regretted the decision to be part of Janus. We were selective about membership, but we continued to accept new members for another fifteen years. At that point we felt that we had the group we needed and made the decision not to add anyone else. That's when we decided to get the cuff links made. I didn't wear mine tonight, but I wear them a lot. We all do. But Monty here lost one a few years ago, so since we were going to be together, we thought we'd get him a replacement."

Monteith looked like he'd swallowed an ice cube.

"How did you come to lose that cuff link, Mr. Monteith?" Ledbetter asked.

"I, uh, don't recall." Monteith's face was red, and he was acting like his collar had grown too tight around his neck. "Look, what does it matter about an old cuff link? My daughter is upstairs—"

"Mr. Monteith, if you wish to have this discussion at the local sheriff's office, that can be arranged." Ledbetter's expression hadn't changed, but he was exuding menace in a way that made Tessa think it would be wise to never ever make him angry. "Otherwise, I suggest you let me ask the questions, and you provide answers. So again, the cuff link. Where did you lose it?"

"I don't recall."

"Oh, I do." Meadows leaned toward him, his face eager. "Don't you remember, Monty? We all went out to that bar. What's the name of that place? Gino's? Yeah. That's it. I remember because it wasn't Memorial Day weekend, but it was the weekend after that. It was a Friday night, and we all went out. You hooked up with some chick and lit out of there."

"I can't say if I remember the specifics the way Meadows does." McCloud gave Ledbetter a smile that was close to authentic but didn't quite hit the mark. "But with all due respect, there's no law against getting drunk in a bar. And Monty here hasn't been married in years. If he can find a beautiful woman willing to leave with him, that's his business."

"You are correct." Ledbetter turned to Monteith. "Are your friends' memories jogging yours?"

"Like they said, I was drunk. I may have left that night with someone. I honestly couldn't say."

"Do you make a habit of that?" Ledbetter leaned back, his face an expression of concern.

"Of what?"

"Getting drunk and leaving bars with beautiful women you don't remember."

"Mr. Ledbetter—"

Everyone in the room looked up as the door at the back opened. Luke slipped in and handed a piece of paper to Ledbetter, then slipped back out. Ledbetter scanned the page, and his lips tightened into a grimace. "Mr. Monteith, at this point, I'm going to ask you a question, and I suggest you think about it before you answer."

Monteith glared at him.

"Would you like your friends to remain in the room while we continue this discussion? Or would you prefer they leave?"

Tessa could almost see brain cells colliding in Monteith's mind as he tried to figure out the best way to proceed. He obviously wanted to avoid doing anything that would make him look bad in front of his friends, but he also didn't want to make himself look guilty in front of the Secret Service either. "I'm sure they're ready to go home."

"We aren't going anywhere, Monty. Something weird is going on here tonight," Meadows said.

McCloud settled himself in his chair and crossed his arms. He wasn't going anywhere either. Ledbetter smiled, and it was a smile that would make hardened criminals flee in terror.

Monteith looked at him and said the words Tessa had been expecting since the conversation began. "I'm done talking to you, Special Agent in Charge Ledbetter. If you have something to charge me with, do it. Otherwise, I'm leaving. I'm a US citizen. A personal friend of the president. And a guest in this home. You cannot detain me." He turned to his friends. "Let's go."

Ledbetter tapped the paper on his knee. "Yeah. See. I'm afraid since you put it that way, I'm going to have to go ahead and charge you with kidnapping, attempted rape, and"—he held up three fingers—"three counts of attempted murder."

# 32

THE AIR IN THE ROOM CRACKLED with enough energy to blow the roof off the place. Zane's gaze circled from Monteith to Meadows to McCloud to Carmichael.

At the words *kidnapping and attempted rape*, Monteith had flicked his focus for a mere fraction of a second to Tessa. It wasn't an admission of guilt and wouldn't stand up in court, but Zane had the sense deep in his bones that Monteith was their man.

Meadows couldn't have been more stunned if someone had shoved his face in ice water. He gaped at Monteith in disbelief.

McCloud's lips flattened so thin that tiny white lines flared out from his mouth.

Carmichael was the first to find his voice. "Special Agent Ledbetter?"

"I'm sorry, Mr. Carmichael. Right now, I'm going to have to take Mr. Monteith and Ms. Monteith into custody. I can assure you we will be in touch tomorrow." Ledbetter turned to McCloud and Meadows. "Consider yourselves warned. This goes nowhere. You don't share it with your Janus buddies. You don't talk about it with your lawyers. You do not say a word."

Meadows bobbed his head in understanding.

McCloud's response was a curt, "Of course."

"Special Agent Reed?" It was the first time Ledbetter had looked at Tessa. "Would you care to do the honors?"

"I'd be delighted." Tessa pulled the handcuffs from her belt and walked to Monteith. But before she could ask him to put his hands behind his back, he struck out. The blow would have left her with a black eye if it had landed. But Monteith was far too slow. Tessa caught his arm and twisted it behind him before Ledbetter, Jacob, or Zane reached her. "We'll go ahead and add attempted assault on a federal officer to the list." Her voice was ice.

"I want my lawyer." Monteith growled the words and turned his gaze to Tessa. "You'll never win."

She tilted her head to the side, and there was no hostility, no simmering cauldron of rage in her expression. Instead, she gave him a faint smile that held a hint of compassion. "Sorry, Monty. But I already did."

The click of the handcuffs echoed in the otherwise silent room. Zane and Jacob took positions on either side and slightly behind Tessa as she escorted Tyson Monteith from the room all the way to the patrol car outside.

Moments later, Wendy Monteith emerged, handcuffed, with Luke on one side and Gil on the other. She took one look at Tessa and started shrieking. "You'll never get away with this! You're a murderer! I'll take you down!"

Tessa ignored her, and they climbed the stairs to the wide front porch. Wendy was still screaming when Luke closed the door of another patrol car in her face, shutting her inside.

He and Gil joined them on the wide front porch. "She"—Luke widened his eyes—"is going to make their night extra fun. I need to call Morris and give him a heads-up to be careful. She's trying to pull off crazy, but cunning is a more appropriate description."

"Agreed." Gil quirked an eyebrow at Tessa. "You okay?"

She sighed. "Maybe? I'm not sure what's going on." She turned to Luke. "What was on that paper you handed Ledbetter?"

Luke gave her a smug smile. "Nothing much. Just proof of Monteith's involvement."

"How—"

"Sabrina came through." Luke pulled his phone from his pocket. "When you sent her the name, she started digging. She said she isn't done, but she found a video from social media that shows you sitting at the bar with Monteith."

"What?" Tessa sagged against the porch rail. "It's too far back—"

"People put so much up on their public profiles these days. Sabrina said it was a bachelor party. She was searching for anything from that date and that location and found it. Then she worked her magic to enhance it and says there's no doubt that he was with you. And here's the best part—he left the bar with you, and it's clear on the video that you're not yourself."

"Drugged." Zane bit the word out.

"There's no evidence, yet, of him putting anything in your drink, although Sabrina says now that she has something to work with, she may find it. Regardless, it places him at the bar with you and shows you leaving the bar with him."

"It's still circumstantial." Tessa clearly wasn't satisfied.

"It is, and he'll probably never go to court for what he did to you, but what do you think the odds are that you were the first?" Luke reached out and squeezed her hand. "Or the last?"

"It's enough to launch an investigation, but that's not all she found." Gil pointed to the patrol car driving away. "Turns out Wendy Monteith isn't just the daughter of Tyson Monteith."

"Who is she?" Zane had a feeling Wendy was the key to everything.

Luke held Zane's gaze. "Sabrina said she found a description of her that seemed fitting: 'She's a figment of your imagination right until she slices your throat with a very real blade.'"

"Bottom line," Gil said, "Wendy Monteith is a fixer. She's the one people go to when they've messed up. She makes their problems go away. She commands a high salary, chooses her clients with care, and while she doesn't make a habit of it, she's willing to use extreme measures when necessary."

"Right now, she's trying to fix this mess by blaming me for shooting Graham and harming Rodriguez." Tessa glared into the dark. "And if she has those kinds of connections, she might manage to slither out of this."

"I think she messed up this time. She lives in DC and rarely ever works in Raleigh. And Carmichael"—Luke pointed to the house, where Carmichael could be seen talking to Jacob and Ledbetter—"is furious. He won't let this go. Whatever loyalty Monteith might have been able to call on disappeared when Wendy shot Graham. Carmichael won't just let Monteith swing, he'll tie the noose."

FOUR ENDLESS HOURS LATER, Zane opened the door to Tessa's apartment. Only after the door closed behind them did he tug her toward him. She rested her forehead against his neck and placed her hands at his waist while he ran a hand up and down her spine. "Do you think it's really over?" she whispered into his shirt.

"I honestly don't know," he said against her hair. "Let's get some sleep. We won't figure anything out until we get some rest."

# — 33 —

TWO WEEKS LATER, Tessa walked into Luke and Faith's home and found that she was the last one to arrive. The entire gang was in attendance. Everyone from the Raleigh office was there. Emily and Liam had driven down from DC, and the Carrington investigators had come from Carrington for the afternoon.

It didn't always happen this way, but tonight it looked like the group had split along gender lines. The men were in the backyard sitting around a firepit or huddled near the grill.

The women had commandeered the back deck. Faith sat beside Hope. Emily sat squeezed in between Faith and Ivy. Benjamin's wife, Sharon, was talking to Sabrina Fleming-Campbell while Leigh Weston Parker and Anissa Bell-Chavez chatted with Leslie Martin and Jacob's wife.

One person was missing, and he was the one she missed the most. They hadn't been able to spend any time together after the president's visit. Zane had been called back to DC on Saturday morning while she was being interviewed by Detective Morris at the Raleigh sheriff's office.

In the time since, they'd talked, texted, and FaceTimed, but it wasn't the same. She'd missed him before, but it was so much worse now. Tonight he was with the president at another dinner in another state, and he didn't have a free weekend on his schedule for two more weeks. Thankfully, Emily had invited Tessa to stay with her in DC anytime. And now that things were wrapping up in Raleigh, Tessa fully intended to take her up on the offer.

Tessa gave hugs and cheek kisses to all the ladies, then pulled a sparkling water from the cooler before joining the men. Luke made a spot for her, and she sat beside him. He leaned toward her. "He misses you. You know that, right?"

"I know." None of the others had gone through this. Benjamin and Sharon had been separated for a few months after they started dating again, but it was with the knowledge that Benjamin was moving back to North Carolina soon. Tessa was still several years from moving to DC, and the thought of a lengthy long-distance relationship made everything inside of her want to find a dark corner and pout.

The meal was fabulous as usual. Between Gil and Leigh, the food was guaranteed to be spectacular. Luke and Faith had put the tables together so they could talk, and it wasn't until dessert was served that the conversation turned to work. This time, Ivy and Emily remained where they were. There was no need for them to excuse themselves. Everything was public record.

Luke raised a glass and said, "I'd like to propose a toast." Cans of soft drinks, bottles of water, and cups filled with sweet tea were lifted into the air. "First, to our very own Tessa for understanding the minds of the whack jobs who wanted to douse people with bleach."

"To Tessa!" Everyone said with a few hoots of laughter and snide remarks about whether Tessa should actually be proud of such an accomplishment.

"And to Sabrina," Luke continued once everyone had taken a

sip. "For working your magic and placing Tyson Monteith in the bar with Tessa and all you've done in the past two weeks to hunt down all the perpetrators in the attacks on Tessa."

"To Sabrina!" Tessa fought the tears that threatened to spill down her cheeks.

Sabrina waved a hand and refused to look at anyone until the dust had settled.

Emily raised a hand. "Any chance of getting a breakdown of the events for those of us who aren't in Raleigh?"

Luke pointed to Tessa. "It's your party."

She cleared her throat. "First, I want to say thank you. To all of you. You stood by me when I didn't have the ability to stand up for myself. You never wavered in your friendship. You prayed for and accepted me, flaws and all, and I'm so very thankful that God led me to Raleigh. I believe he knew this is where I needed to be in order to finally overcome my addictions and heal."

Faith, who was sitting beside Tessa, reached out and squeezed Tessa's hand. Tessa continued. "As for the case. What we know now is that Tyson Monteith has drugged and assaulted at least three other women. All before he tried it with me. But he was never arrested, or even formally accused. The women who refused to press charges were either paid off or warned off. And Wendy was the one who took care of that."

"How could she do that? I mean, he's her dad, but seriously, he's creepy." Emily scrunched up her nose like she smelled something foul.

"Turns out Wendy had an aptitude for fixing things way back in college. She caught Tyson's friend doing something, and when she confronted him, he thought she was blackmailing him. But instead, she had him pay her to make it go away. She did the same thing for Monteith. She started small, but over the years her influence and connections grew, and it eventually became her full-time job. So far we've found at least thirty well-known men and women who have used her services to help them get out of everything from a DUI to a pregnant girlfriend to tax evasion."

"How does she do that?" Ivy asked.

"Usually by blackmailing or bribing the people who are in a position to make things disappear. She has a network of informants all along the East Coast who tell her all sorts of juicy information. She pays well and never gives up her sources." Tessa looked at Luke. "Turns out when Bruce was telling us that he was hearing stuff on the wind, he was talking about Wendy's network."

Luke blew out a breath. "How is Bruce?"

"He's okay. I checked on him this morning. He recited a sonnet that was so beautiful I cried." Tessa had begged him to let her reach out to his family, but he wouldn't hear of it. So she'd had to let it go. For now.

"So Wendy's a fixer, and she fixes the messes Tyson gets in. And she has a reputation with his Janus buddies?" Emily asked.

"Yes. As far as we can tell, she mostly fixed stuff within the Janus group for the first five years or so after going all in with fixing as her profession. Tyson would send his people to her to sort out when they'd fouled up. But eventually she got really good at it, and now she has clients all over the country, and more than a few of them are senators or congressmen."

"But what turned her attention to you?" Hope asked. "You still don't remember him. If she'd left it alone . . ."

"Yeah. I have no clear memory of that night. And even the videos that Sabrina managed to find from that evening haven't broken anything loose. We would have had our suspicions, of course, because of the cuff link. And after what Zane saw and heard, we would have started investigating Monteith after the president's visit, but we might not have ever had enough to take him down. And we wouldn't have had a clue what Wendy was up to."

"She hired people to come after you? All those attacks were her idea?" Sharon asked.

"Yes and no. She was responsible for the attacks. She started with some low-level informants. People who genuinely had no idea who they were taking orders from. All the way up to the guy who attacked me in my apartment. He was a manager in the security firm that operated security on my building and eight other high-end apartment complexes in the southeast. She had used him before to help her—he'd erased video footage, planted evidence, that kind of thing—using the same method he used to enter my apartment. He created a second keycard, used it after disabling the cameras, and got right back out before anyone knew. He kept his mouth shut until she rolled over on him. Then he sang like a nightingale in exchange for a reduced sentence."

"So no one who came after you had a personal issue with you? They were all people who had been hired in some way by Wendy Monteith?" This question came from Leslie.

"As far as we can tell."

"Then where does Hank and the candy basket fit in?" she demanded. "Because that was creepy."

Luke answered. "Hank won't be pestering Tessa anymore. We finally got him to confess that he followed her to a talk she did at a high school. One of the kids there asked her about her favorite things outside of work, and she told them she loved candy. She and the kids batted around their favorites for about five minutes. He showed me the footage."

Tessa groaned. "I didn't even remember that the kids and I talked about that."

"Why would you?" Faith said. "You've only done that talk

about twenty times in the past year. If Hank hadn't been stalking you and recording everything you said, he wouldn't have known."

"True. But Wendy did pay Hank a visit after he showed up at the property and ran his little newscast. He claims she got him talking about me and he shared about my hatred of snakes and a few other things she used to set up the attacks."

"Wow. So Hank is just a creep. And that candy wasn't poisoned?" Gil shook his head in dismay. "Think of all that candy, Tessa."

She shuddered. "Anyway, Wendy and Tyson are both in jail while the investigations continue. We suspect that part of her performance the night of the president's visit was to try to get herself to a psych ward. If she'd managed to do that, she would have disappeared. But because no one believed she was as crazy as she was trying to act, she went to jail and stayed there. She's such a flight risk that her bond is higher than Tyson's."

"How are the two men who were injured?" Leigh asked. "Bullets to the abdomen and insulin injections into bodies that don't need insulin are both extremely dangerous." And she would know, having worked in the Carrington County Hospital emergency department for the past several years.

"Graham is home and recovering under the watchful eyes of the Carmichaels." Tessa had gone to see them this morning as well. "He's very frustrated that they won't let him get the door. It's hilarious. As for Rodriguez, he's back to work. Zane says he got a visit from a woman who looks like the girl next door. Apparently she was a trembling mess in the hospital corridors as she asked to see him."

Benjamin whistled. "What's this? I hadn't heard this story."

Tessa grinned. "It's not common knowledge. Zane said she's supercute, supersweet, and not at all Rodriguez's known type, but he allowed her to come into his room and she didn't leave until visiting hours were over. Rodriguez came back to work this week, and when Zane asked about her, all Rodriguez would say was, 'You got your girl, leave mine alone.'"

Everyone laughed, but when the room grew quiet, Sharon swirled her tea in her glass and said, "There's something about this that still doesn't make sense to me. I get that they were worried about you recognizing Monteith, but I don't understand why Wendy came after you at the Carmichaels'. What was so important that she would take that kind of risk?"

Tessa pointed to Sabrina. "You want to take this one?"

"Sure," Sabrina said. "That loose end rubbed me the wrong way too. So I kept digging. Turns out that five years ago, McCloud and Wendy reached an agreement. McCloud is wealthy and influential, but Monteith was the true Janus. He knew everyone, was liked by everyone, and had the charisma that made people think the best of him. Meadows had no clue about Monteith's predilections, but McCloud did." Sabrina paused. "We were able to get warrants, and we found a record of a phone call from McCloud to Wendy Monteith at 2:30 a.m. on the night of Tessa's abduction."

"So he knew what Monteith was up to, knew what he might do, but still let him leave?" Sharon asked.

"It appears so. We're still putting the pieces together, but we think McCloud got some dirt on Wendy, and then turned the tables on her. Her father was never to know, but she no longer answered to him. She answered to McCloud about Tyson's behavior and actions. McCloud paid her and paid her well. Her responsibility wasn't just to get her dad out of trouble, which she'd been doing for years. It was to keep him out of trouble. So that night, while Meadows was blissfully enjoying another bourbon, McCloud suspected what Monteith was up to, called Wendy, and told her to shut him down."

"So, what? She drove to Raleigh and got her dad out of the room?" Emily asked.

"No. We think she called him and told him she knew what he was doing and he left on his own."

"But that still doesn't explain why she was so determined to take Tessa out on the spot," Leslie said.

Sabrina let out an aggrieved sigh. "She's claiming now that McCloud threatened to kill her father if Tessa walked out of there alive."

"What?" A chorus of feminine voices asked.

"Apparently the original plan was to kill Tessa with a dose of insulin. Graham was never supposed to be in danger, but he caught Wendy with the gun. According to his version, he told her she needed to hand it over. Instead, she shot him and stashed him in the bathroom."

"I thought she was some big bad fixer," Leigh said. "She sounds like an idiot."

"Part of why she was good was because she left the dirty work to others. She'd never shot anyone, and when she did, the whole thing spiraled out of control. Before she could come up with a new plan, Tessa went upstairs with Rodriguez and found Graham."

Tessa took over the tale. "Monteith told the investigators that he'd recently changed his will. Apparently daddy dearest wasn't quite as dumb as Wendy and McCloud thought. He didn't know the specifics, but he knew something was hinky. So he added a clause that if he died under mysterious circumstances, or by foul play, Wendy's inheritance would go to a charity."

"So if she didn't take you out of the equation on Friday night and McCloud followed through on his threat, she'd be without an inheritance." Sharon summarized the situation but pressed for more. "Okay. I get that. But why did McCloud insist on taking Tessa out?"

Luke answered. "Our best guess is that he saw the writing on the wall and decided that Monteith could survive the scandal if Tessa wasn't alive to plead her case. But if she recognized him, it would be all over."

**ZANE STOOD INSIDE THE DOOR,** listening to every word. No one but Luke and Jacob knew he was here. He'd planned to run out there and pull Tessa into his arms, plant a kiss on her lips, and drag her away from everyone else so he could have her all to himself tonight. But then she'd started talking, and he decided to wait. He didn't want to steal her moment.

"What does the president have to say about all of this?" Sabrina asked. "Monteith was his friend, after all."

"He's a politician. And he has enough distance from Monteith that it won't blow back on him, so my guess is he plans to keep it that way. Nothing has leaked so far. If we can keep Hank Littlefield away, hopefully we'll be able to keep a lid on everything. And the president's relationship with Carmichael is solid. When I visited today, he told me the president has called him three times to check on Graham and to see if he needs anything."

"Have the protestors backed off any?" Ivy asked.

"Yes and no. They've tried a few things, but because of what happened here, the Secret Service has the authority to eject them from any event, prevent them from entering any venue. So everyone we have listed on the records as a supporter of Calvin Cross can't get close, and they can't do anything about it." Tessa looked up. "And I got an email today asking me to be involved in developing a drone prevention procedure."

Everyone laughed at that, and Tessa threw up her hands. "As if I want to spend any more time learning about UAVs." She scooted her chair away from the table. "And now, if you'll excuse me—"

"Wait! I have another question." Luke jumped to his feet.

"What more is there to answer?"

"Inquiring minds want to know. What's the deal with you and Zane?"

Tessa spoke so low that Zane had to strain to hear it. "I think I've been in love with him since the first day I walked in the office. Then I messed everything up. And then I spent a lot of time thinking that I wasn't good enough for him. And I still think that."

Multiple protests came from around the table, and she held up her hand. "But that doesn't mean I'm not going to love him forever. If he's too dense to realize he can do better, who am I to convince him otherwise?"

Zane couldn't take it anymore. He jogged to her. "What kind of foolishness are you spouting, Princess? You're too good for me. Always have been. Doesn't mean I'm not going to love you forever."

"What are you doing here?" Her initial delight faded and her eyes narrowed. "Wait just a minute. What"—she overenunciated the word—"did you call me?"

He couldn't stop himself from grinning like an idiot as he pulled her into his arms. "Oops."

Tessa didn't put up any resistance as he lowered his head to hers. "How do you feel about kissing in front of our friends?"

"Depends."

"On?"

"Who I'm kissing."

"Me. Only ever me."

Tessa pulled him closer. "Then I have no objections."

Based on the smiles on the faces that surrounded them, their friends had no objections either.

TWENTY MINUTES LATER, Jacob stood and cleared his throat. "I need to head home, but before I do, I have an announcement to make."

Everyone turned toward him. Tessa barely moved from where she sat with her head against Zane's shoulder, their fingers laced and hands resting on his thigh. Zane pressed a kiss to her head.

"Since we're all here," Jacob said, "this seemed like a good time for me to share some news I received earlier today."

Tessa sat up and gave Zane a questioning look, but he had no answers to give her.

"It turns out that the DC crowd was impressed with our work a few weeks ago. Agent Ledbetter sang your praises and folks were listening." He turned toward Tessa and Zane. "Special Agent Reed."

Tessa sat straight and said, "Yes, sir?"

"This happens sometimes, and I'm not gonna lie. I hate it for myself. But something tells me you won't feel the same way."

"Sir?"

"Your presence has been requested in DC."

Tessa's hand gripped Zane's thigh. He fought to keep from jumping up and down like a three-year-old who just consumed a swirl of cotton candy. "What?"

"Like I said, you made an impression. They want you in DC where the bigwigs can keep an eye on you. My guess is you'll be fast-tracked for the PID, but for now they want you in the DC field office." Jacob crossed his arms. "You can turn it down. No one here would complain if you stayed. But something tells me we'll be saying goodbye sooner rather than later. Congratulations, Tessa."

"I thought for sure they'd fire me. Or leave me in Phase 1 forever. Or . . ."

Jacob shook his head. "We all have a few skeletons in our closet. It takes far more bravery to pull them out and own them than it does to keep them hidden and pray they never come to light. Ledbetter told his superiors they'd be nuts if they didn't keep you happy, and he somehow got the idea that DC would make you happy." Jacob turned a fake glare on Zane. "I can't imagine how he came to that conclusion."

Tessa squeezed his arm, and Zane turned to her. "You told him I'd want to be in DC?"

Zane's heart stuttered. "Don't you?"

"Yes. More than anything."

"Then?"

She looked down. "I wasn't sure if *you* wanted me in DC. But I guess you do."

This woman was going to make him insane. "What will it take to convince you that I love you and I'm never letting you go?"

"Getting me moved to DC is a good start."

He certainly hoped so. The second part of his plan would begin as soon as she was settled. He hated to admit it, but Ledbetter was a genius.

# 34

## A LITTLE MORE THAN FIVE MONTHS LATER

Tessa propped her bike against a tree and pulled her helmet from her head. Zane followed behind her and did the same. They locked their bikes to a tree and took a seat on a bench. It was shady here but relatively warm for a March morning.

She and Zane had been on a mission to ride every bike trail in the greater DC area. While there were quite a few to choose from, her desire to decorate Zane's home, along with competing work schedules and winter weather, had conspired against them. Today was only their third ride since she'd moved to DC four months earlier.

As far as Tessa was concerned, it had all been worth it. After months of sporadic purchases and random evenings spent painting and decorating, Zane's house was finally ready for visitors. The living area was warm and inviting. The kitchen was a showstopper. Even the bathrooms reflected Zane's personality. And maybe a little bit of hers as well. It couldn't be helped. She wasn't ever going to decorate a room and not throw in some pops of color, and Zane had said for her to do whatever she wanted. So she had.

Tessa had moved in with Emily Dixon, but now that Emily was married to Liam, Emily's apartment was Tessa's. And now that she had Zane's place set up, it was time to turn her attention to her own place. Especially since she planned to be here for a long while. She loved DC, but the truth was that it had absolutely nothing to do with DC and everything to do with the man who made living here worthwhile.

She missed her Raleigh friends so much it was a kick to the gut every time she thought of them. But the past four months had been a revelation when it came to Zane. Their relationship had been rock-solid, their friendship secure, long before they took things to the next level. Now? She had no idea how she'd ever done life without him. They talked every morning while they were getting ready. Texted throughout the day. Spent most evenings together. Fought a little, laughed a lot.

She was happy at a level she'd honestly never allowed herself to dream was possible. She hoped her dad could see her. Hoped he knew she'd fought her battles, faced her demons, and come out the other side bloody and weary but whole and able to love fully and without fear.

"Tess?" Zane tucked her against his body, his arm around her shoulder. She leaned into him, her head on his chest. "Do you know what today is?"

Tessa shook her head. "Tuesday?"

He pretended to growl at her. "Other than that?"

"I have no idea."

"What am I going to do with you?"

Her mind raced. What was significant about this day?

"Stumped?" He looked pleased with himself.

"Yes."

"This is the six-month anniversary of our first kiss."

"Is it really?"

"It is. And I was thinking that a day like this should be commemorated."

"We did commemorate it. We went on a ride. Maybe we should do that every year on the six-month anniversary of our first kiss."

Zane didn't seem impressed with her idea. "Yeah. Maybe."

"Okay." She drew out the word. "What did you have in mind?"

"I was thinking of something a little bit . . . bigger." Between one heartbeat and the next, a beautiful princess-cut diamond appeared between his fingers. "Will you marry me?"

Part of her brain registered the sparkle of the diamond and the question he had asked, but the rest of her brain functions had focused all their attention on keeping her breathing. It took a few seconds for her to successfully form words. Well, one word. "Yes."

He slid the ring on her finger. "Look at that. A perfect fit." He leaned toward her. "I want to get married today."

She almost choked. "I don't think that's legal."

"Tomorrow?"

Tessa grinned. "What about next weekend?"

## SEVEN MONTHS LATER

Tessa checked her watch for the fiftieth time.

Zane had been gone for ten days, but he would be home any minute now.

She took in the room. When she was done with it, it would be perfect. But this was a good start.

A chime floated on the air, signaling that a door had opened, followed by Zane's "Tess? Where are you?"

She tried to keep her voice steady. "In the office."

His voice moved up the stairs. "Is everything okay? I was kind of expecting you to be in the garage." Which was where each of them had been every time either one returned from a trip since their wedding six months ago.

"I wanted to mix it up a little." Her attempt at casual confidence had failed dramatically. But it didn't matter. He was here.

**ZANE FROZE IN THE DOORWAY.** When he'd left ten days earlier, this was their home office.

No one would mistake this space for an office anymore.

The diplomas and awards had been replaced with neutral prints of baby animals—lions, tigers, and rhinoceroses.

Tessa stood beside a rocking chair, holding a fluffy elephant.

Was this really happening? "Princess?"

"Welcome home. You're going to be a daddy."

# Epilogue

### *Welcome to Gossamer Falls*

The small sign, freshly painted and lettered in an elegant script, was tucked into the mountain laurels on the side of the twisty road that Tessa and Zane had been traveling for thirty minutes.

"That's the smallest welcome sign I've ever seen." Tessa had turned in the passenger seat so she was facing Zane as he maneuvered through the curves. "How did anyone ever find this place before GPS?"

"From what I gathered, not many people *did* find their way to Gossamer Falls, and the people who live here would prefer to keep it that way." Zane tapped the phone. "This says we'll be at the police station in two minutes."

Tessa flipped down the visor mirror. "Well," she said as she applied some lip gloss and settled back in her seat, "it's lovely here. And isolated. I can see why the president thinks it would be a good option for their anniversary trip."

"I'd prefer he stay at Camp David." So did the rest of the Secret Service.

"Camp David is safe, but it isn't romantic."

"True, but Camp David isn't hours away from civilization either. And FLOTUS isn't exactly the 'roughing it' type."

"Asheville's not that far. The First Lady likes Asheville."

"Princess, this is the part of North Carolina where a person could hide out for months. Years even. There could be any number of criminals hiding in these forests."

Tessa patted his arm. "I don't think we have to worry about a criminal element in Gossamer Falls. If they're hiding, they're not going to show their face when we flood this mountain with Secret Service agents."

Zane snagged her hand and laced his fingers through hers. "Even if there's no danger, I don't see FLOTUS being happy with anything less than five-star accommodations, dining, and spa services."

"According to the information they sent, The Haven has all of that." Tessa pulled the fifty-page, high-gloss, full-color booklet from her bag.

"I'll believe it when I see it. And taste it." Zane still couldn't believe they were in Gossamer Falls, NC, on official Secret Service business. He could only imagine the field day the press would have if they knew that government resources were being used so he and Tessa could spend a weekend at The Haven. No one had ever heard of the place, yet it claimed to be a resort that catered to the highest echelons of society.

But before they visited The Haven, they needed to check in with the police chief—who was expecting them—and explore the town, hopefully without anyone being the wiser about their real purpose. Zane pulled to a stop in a visitor space in front of the building with a sign proclaiming it to be the Gossamer Falls Police Station. "This can't be right."

"It's adorable." Tessa grinned at him.

Zane bit back a growl. "Police stations aren't supposed to be adorable."

"And yet . . ." Tessa waved a hand toward the small mountain bungalow. "I could see this being featured in *Southern Living* as the newest trend in stylish law enforcement options."

He jogged around the SUV and opened Tessa's door, then took her hand and held it until she was on her feet. But instead of stepping away, he rested his other hand on the slight bump where their son grew inside her. "How's our boy?"

"Happy to be out of the car."

Tessa leaned into him, and he claimed a lingering kiss. "Have I told you today how much I love you?"

His wife—he took a second to savor that thought—tilted her head, and her smile stole his heart all over again. "You may have mentioned it, but I never get tired of hearing it." She brushed her fingers across his lips. "But if we get caught making out in the police station parking lot, it's going to be all kinds of awkward. Let's go talk to the chief so we can get the lay of the land."

Five minutes later they were ushered down a small hallway and into a spacious office that Zane knew had been decorated by someone other than the man sitting behind the desk. He popped to his feet and met them halfway. "Grayson Ward. I'm the police chief here in Gossamer Falls."

Tessa shook his hand. "Tessa Reed Thacker."

Zane shook his hand next. "Zane Thacker."

Ward's eyebrows rose. "You're both Thackers?" Ward directed them to a small, handcrafted table on the side of the room. "Is that just for this weekend?"

Tessa laughed, and Zane held her chair for her to sit. "Definitely not. I'm keeping him." Her hand fluttered over her stomach, something she did multiple times a day, but Zane didn't know if she even realized she did it. Her protective instincts were already in overdrive when it came to their son. A son who would know his mother loved him every second of his life. A son who would know his father loved his mother. Their kid was already the luckiest boy in the world.

Ward's eyes went from Tessa's hand to Zane's face. "I didn't know there were any married Secret Service agents. I mean, married to each other."

"There aren't many. But it certainly works to our advantage for an assignment like this one."

"I should say so."

They settled into their seats and made small talk for a few minutes before Chief Ward, who insisted they call him Gray, leaned back and said, "So, what can I do to help you this weekend?"

Tessa took the lead. "We're staying at The Haven for two nights. It would be great if you could fill us in on what to expect there. As well as give us any insights into your town and how a presidential visit could impact the area."

"I'm happy to talk about Gossamer Falls, but I can't give you much on The Haven. Normal people don't drop that kind of cash for a weekend getaway, much less a weeklong respite or a three-week retreat."

Zane recognized the verbiage as coming directly from The Haven brochure.

Gray leaned toward them. "Here's what you need to know. The people who live here are some of the best folks around. They're devoted to family, have a phenomenal work ethic, and walk the talk when it comes to their faith. They like what they have here, and if it'd been possible, they would've gladly remained hidden from the world. No one in Gossamer Falls wanted anyone else to ever find this place, and some folks were pretty adamant about it. But over the years there was a push to do what a lot of small towns in the mountains around here have done and play to the tourists."

Gray pointed to a map of western North Carolina on his wall. The Gossamer Falls jurisdiction was outlined in black. "There are two prominent families in Gossamer Falls. The Quinns and the Pierces. Both are descended from the original European settlers to this area. Both families own huge swaths of land, and both are protective of Gossamer Falls. The Quinns are doctors, dentists, and teachers and have built half the houses in a fifty-mile radius. The Pierces developed The Haven."

"How do the families get along?" Zane poured a glass of water from the pitcher on the table.

Gray shrugged. "Apparently they got along great until the Pierces developed The Haven. Now? Not so much. But it's nothing to worry about for your purposes. It's all very civilized. We don't have the Hatfields and McCoys here. There's no overt feuding. If the Quinns and Pierces meet in public, they nod and move on. I know the Pierces still take their sick kids to Dr. Shaw, and she was a Quinn before she married."

"But is she the only doctor in town?" Tessa asked.

"Well. Yes." Gray grinned, then his expression shifted. "It was before my time, but my understanding is that the Quinns were sure the Pierces were ruining the town with The Haven. And the arguments were intense and long-lasting. But so far, The Haven hasn't brought harm to the community. It's so exclusive that almost no one knows it exists. A lot of the people who come to The Haven never venture past the resort property lines. The few who do come into town find Gossamer Falls to be charming and quaint, but a bit too rustic for their delicate sensibilities."

"So the town retains its identity and the townspeople have a good place to work?"

Zane's conjecture was met with a wink and a nod from Gray. "Exactly."

"How did you wind up here, Gray?" Tessa pointed to the office. "And who decorated your office?"

Gray had tensed at Tessa's first question but relaxed at the second. "You're assuming I didn't. And you're correct. I don't have the time, energy, inclination, or budget for it. But the Quinns are a force of nature. Meredith, she's the dentist here in town, saw my office not long after I settled in and declared it a travesty. Next thing I knew, there was a committee and the whole space had been revamped." He tapped the table they sat at. "This was a gift from her cousin, Callum Shaw."

"Any relation to the doctor?" Tessa ran her hand over the table's smooth surface with veins of bright blue running through the wood.

"He's her son. Cal and I served in the Marines together. He makes everything from vases to bookmarks. You'll see some of his smaller pieces in a few shops in town."

Gray pointed to his window. "Gossamer Falls is small and doesn't want to be big. But we have some nice shops. A florist. A bookstore. A coffee shop. A delicious diner and a great pizza spot located inside the grocery store."

At Zane's snort, Gray held out his hands. "I don't know why it's in the grocery store. But the pizza is fabulous."

Gray ran a hand over his face. "We have a couple of bars that don't give me too much trouble. Small but good schools. And while it feels like we're in the middle of nowhere, we really aren't that far from Asheville."

"Sounds ideal." Zane didn't believe any place could be this perfect.

"Don't get me wrong." Gray grimaced. "We have our issues. Alcohol abuse. Drug addiction. The occasional ornery guy who doesn't think the law applies to him." Something in Gray's expression set off Zane's internal warning system. There was a story behind that comment.

"But," Gray continued, "the pace here is slower. The pressures lighter. Most folks don't lock their doors. Kids run around from house to house without fear. It's ideal for families or for people who just want off the hamster wheel."

"Are you one of those people? Who wanted off the hamster wheel?" Tessa asked.

"Definitely. I'm not cut out for city life anymore." Something about his tone made it clear that Gray wouldn't be sharing any more on the topic.

Zane stood and offered his hand to Tessa to help her to her feet. "Gray, thank you for taking the time to fill us in. We'll wander around town for a little while before we check in at The Haven."

Handshakes were exchanged all around. "I'll keep your purpose here to myself, but do me a favor and give me a heads-up if it's really going to happen. I don't have much in the way of manpower, but I'll help any way I can."

"We'll do that."


"WE AREN'T IN KANSAS ANYMORE." They'd spent an hour wandering around Gossamer Falls, and Tessa loved the small town. But as they paused at the entry to The Haven, she had to stop herself from gaping. The wrought-iron gate was at least fifty feet high and set into stone columns. There was a twenty-foot-high fence surrounding the property, but it was mostly hidden behind a wall of greenery. The security guard at the gate checked their reservation information in seconds, provided them with a map and verbal directions to their private cabin, and encouraged them to relax and enjoy their stay. A five-minute drive later, they found a valet and a concierge awaiting them at their parking space.

"Welcome to The Haven." The concierge walked them inside as the valet removed their bags from the SUV. "I've provided a complete schedule of optional activities for you this weekend. There's a guided hike to Gossamer Falls tomorrow morning. Please be aware that Gossamer Falls is on public property, so if you choose to participate, we cannot guarantee your privacy. We also have a guided hike to several waterfalls on The Haven property if you prefer."

The concierge pointed out various features in the cabin, including heated tile floors, towel warmers, and blackout shades that could be put on a timer. He turned on the TV, confirmed their couples spa appointment for the next day, and didn't leave until both of their phones were connected to the complimentary Wi-Fi.

When they were alone, Tessa settled onto a cozy sofa and Zane joined her. "I fully expected him to unpack our suitcases and then hold our hands as we walked to the dining room."

"He probably would have if we'd wanted him to." Zane looked at the activities list. "Almost every class can be held privately by making a call to the concierge. Or you can attend an open session."

"I vote we attend an open session." Tessa leaned over Zane's arm to read the list. "No archery or marksmanship options. Pity."

Zane laughed and tapped the paper. "Our couples massage isn't until four. We have time to go on a hike in the morning, check out a class after lunch, then the massage, then dinner."

"That works for me."

BY THE NEXT AFTERNOON, Tessa had concluded that the First Lady would love The Haven. The meals were extraordinary, the waterfall tour on the property included snacks and beverages carried by the resort staff, and their cabin was an oasis of calm elegance.

She and Zane had enjoyed their morning hike but decided to forego a group class in favor of exploring the resort before their massage. They wandered into a gift shop filled with everything from two-hundred-dollar sweaters with The Haven's discreet logo embroidered on the chest to gourmet treats that could be shipped anywhere so patrons could take a piece of The Haven home with them. But it was the pottery on the back wall that captured Tessa's attention. She examined the pieces. Each one was a small work of art.

A sales associate approached from behind a row of sweaters. Her name tag declared that her name was Courtney and she was a Gossamer Falls native. "May I help you?"

Tessa pointed to the wall. "Is the pottery made locally?"

"Oh, yes." The young woman's eyes lit up. "Our in-house artist created all these pieces."

"Does she teach the classes you offer?" Zane asked.

"She does. And she offers private lessons if you'd be interested in that option."

"Not on this trip, I'm afraid." Zane gave Courtney an apologetic smile. "We don't have time, but perhaps on our next visit."

"Just be aware that her private lessons fill up fast. When you book your stay, be sure to go ahead and get on the schedule."

"Thanks for the tip."

"My pleasure."

Courtney excused herself, and Tessa lifted a coffee mug from the shelf. "Seventy-five dollars."

Zane frowned. "Is it gold-plated?"

"I don't think so. I mean, it's beautiful, but . . ." She turned it over. "Hmm."

"What?"

"It isn't signed."

"Should it be?"

"Yes. There's a small anchor and the date. But that's it." She replaced the mug, then picked up a vase, then a bowl. No names on anything. "You'd think pieces this expensive would be signed and numbered."

"Well, when we come back, you can ask about it." Zane pulled her away from the shelf. "But for now you'll have to wait until we go back into town to pick up a Gossamer Falls mug for ten bucks."

"That will be great. And I also want a bookmark from the local woodworker who made Gray's table."

Zane dropped a kiss on her forehead. "We'll get them tomorrow."

They wandered out of the gift shop without making any purchases and spent another thirty minutes exploring, their focus shifting to the areas that would be easily defensible, as well as what they might have to do to make it safe for the president.

"Well, what do you think?" Zane asked as they walked back to their cabin.

Tessa paused at the door. "I don't think everything is as postcard perfect here as the good people of Gossamer Falls and The Haven would like us to believe. But the president and First Lady will love The Haven. And regardless of what they decide, I'd like to visit Gossamer Falls again. Soon."

Read on for a sneak peek at
Lynn H. Blackburn's novella from *Targeted*,
**AVAILABLE AS AN EBOOK SOON!**

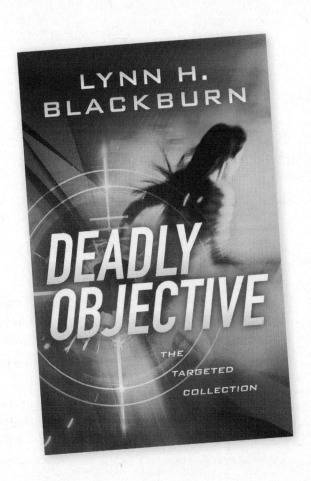

In *Deadly Objective*, physical therapist Emily Dixon and Secret
Service Agent Liam Harper are committed to keeping their relationship
professional. But when the vice president's son enters the crosshairs of
a killer, some lines will have to be crossed in order to keep him safe.

EMILY DIXON NODDED at the Secret Service agent standing post inside the front door of the vice president's home. She handed him her bag and waited for him to examine the contents, the same way she had three times a week for the past six months. Before he finished, another agent approached from the long hallway to her right. Red hair, blue eyes, freckles, and a baby face that made him look like a college student and not the seven-year-veteran agent he was.

He stopped well into her personal space, crossed his arms, and loomed over her. "You're early today, Ms. Dixon. This is going to mess up the schedule."

Her Southern accent usually lingered around the edges of her voice, but she layered it thick on every word as she replied, "Good morning to you too, Special Agent Harper."

Liam Harper developed an immediate and intense fascination with his shoes, but not before she caught the twitch of his lips. He made no reply until Emily's bag had been returned to her and they were behind the closed doors of the small room designated for her to treat the vice president's son. She and Liam had been on a first-name basis for months, but not in public. The only person who'd picked up on the way their relationship had been sliding from professional to personal was Mason Lawson. Her patient. Liam's protectee.

"You really let the East Tennessee fly this morning." Liam grinned at her, his words coming in a slow, low-country drawl that she didn't ever get tired of hearing.

"My East Tennessee can take your South Carolina any day, and we both know it."

"All kidding aside . . ." He leaned against the door, arms crossed, ankles crossed, accent gone—well, mostly. "Do you need me to get Mason early?"

She dropped her bag onto the octagon-shaped table to the left of the door and pulled out the exercise bands and massage gun she needed for today's session. "There's no rush. I hit the traffic jackpot today. I've never managed this trip in under forty-three minutes. Today was thirty-five."

Liam waggled his eyebrows. "Right. That's your story, but I know the truth."

"Which is?"

"You couldn't wait to see me."

Emily made a show of pondering his words before giving her head a slow shake. "No. That's not it." The words were true enough. She'd been lucky with the traffic today. But they were also a whopper of a lie, because somehow over the past few months, her three-times-a-week therapy sessions with Mason Lawson had become the highlight of her week.

And it certainly wasn't because of Mason. The teenager could be a nightmare when he was in a mood. Emily and her twin, Gil, had gotten into their fair share of trouble as children, but Mason Lawson was like a Tasmanian devil in three-hundred-dollar khakis and four-hundred-dollar polo shirts.

For the most part, the press left the VP's kid alone, but that didn't mean Mason hadn't earned a nickname. It was unclear who'd started it, but rather than referring to Mason as a royal pain in the rear, someone had dubbed him His Royal Hiney.

It was ridiculous, but it stuck. Probably because while the VP was on the campaign trail during the previous election, four different agents were assigned to Mason on a one-week-on, one-week-off rotation. No one could put up with him for more than a week at a time.

Enter Special Agent Liam Harper. The only agent on the VP's detail who could keep Mason in line. He'd been assigned to the VP's son for almost a year, and while Mason could still be moody, he reined it in when Liam was around. And after a rocky start, he'd also settled in with Emily. She suspected Mason might have a wee bit of a crush on her. She suspected the same of his favorite agent.

Liam pulled his phone from his back pocket and tapped on the screen. "I'll have him come down. Do you want him longer or to finish up early?"

"How's his mood?"

Liam cut his eyes to her but didn't respond to the question before returning to his text. Awesome. Mason was in a mood.

She hadn't fully appreciated the "Liam effect" until her third week of working with Mason. Liam was on vacation, and by the end of the last session that week, Emily told her practice manager she "would never see that brat again unless Liam Harper was available to run interference."

Her displeasure had been communicated, and since then she'd never seen Mason without Liam being present. Over the past few months, she'd discovered that she and Liam were polar opposites. He was an outdoorsman. In fact, the week he'd been on vacation, he'd been in Wyoming. Hiking, camping, living off the land, with the frequent use of a compass to navigate.

Emily, however, had never met a hotel, mall, or nail salon she didn't like. The only time she wanted to be outside was when the temps were in the low seventies, humidity was nonexistent, and there were no bugs. Or dirt. So, basically, she had about a five-hour window in spring and another in the fall.

If she'd been interested in pursuing a relationship with Liam, they might have been able to get past that. But she was not interested. At all. He was an agent who would literally take a bullet for someone else. She didn't date agents. Ever. Some women were attracted to men like that. Not her.

Liam frowned at his phone as he spoke. "I'd say let's get it over with. The family has an appearance this afternoon." Mason hated public appearances. "If he has a few extra minutes before that, he'll be happy to take them."

"You make it sound like he'll be happy or there will be consequences. And based on the length of the text you're sending, I'm suspicious that you might be laying out those consequences in detail."

Liam grunted but continued texting.

Not for the first time, she caught herself staring. With his head bent over the phone, she had a perfect view of his thick red hair. Before she met Liam, if anyone had asked her if she found redheads attractive, she would've said she'd never thought about it. But Liam had great hair. It suited him.

"Emily, I would never threaten my protectee."

She waited.

"I would, however, remind him of promises made and the rewards coming his way if he holds it together, but that will be lost to him if he screws up."

Liam had a great voice that made her name sound like music. He was quick to laugh, but he never laughed at anyone, only with them. And when he cared about something, or someone, his devotion was off the charts. He cared about his job. He cared about his family. He even cared about Mason Lawson, and unfortunately, unless they were a blood relative, not many people did.

All those things would've made Liam someone she would

at least entertain the possibility of considering. But he was an agent, so she'd friend-zoned him on day one, a move she didn't regret. Much. She understood the life. Her brother was up to his eyeballs in it. It had almost gotten him killed several times, and worrying about Gil was all her heart could handle. Gil had had her heart from the womb. Caring about him and for him was literally in her DNA, so she'd learned to live with the constant fear.

But there was no way she could hand her heart over to someone else and risk losing them.

**LIAM FINISHED HIS TEXT** and pushed away from the door. "Mason's en route. How can I help today?"

Emily flashed him the smile he liked to think she reserved for people she really, really liked, but he reminded himself, as he did every time she was here, that the only reason he was in this room was to protect Mason Lawson.

"I'm good, thanks. Just need the man of the hour." She pulled a few more exercise bands from her bag. "Did you try the Thai place I told you about?"

"I did." They spent the next ten minutes in easy conversation. Everything about Emily was easy. She was easy to look at. Easy to talk to. Easy to make laugh. The one thing that wasn't easy? Getting out of their easy camaraderie and into something . . . more.

The kind of more where they'd be trying new restaurants together as opposed to telling each other about them and trying them separately.

Mason slouched into the room. The agent with him didn't say a word, but her eyes spoke volumes before she touched her fingers to her head in a small salute. Liam acknowledged it with a chin lift. Mason was now his responsibility. And he knew everyone in the house breathed a collective sigh of relief.

Mason knew the drill, and he took a seat in the chair while Emily asked him questions about how his shoulder felt and if he'd done his exercises yesterday.

Mason grumped a few words, and Liam cleared his throat. Mason sat up straighter and spoke politely.

Better.

At only sixteen, the kid could be a handful. There was no way around it. Mason approached all new relationships with bluster and attitude, and most people let him get away with it because they didn't think it would be appropriate to correct the vice president's son.

Liam had no such issues. It wasn't his job to correct the kid, but it also wasn't his job to be his best friend. It was his job to protect him, and he'd made that clear to Mason on their first afternoon together.

He'd also figured out fast that Mason Lawson was like those yappy little dogs who talk a big talk but have nothing to back it up. Establishing boundaries and enforcing them had been huge.

"So, is everything a go for your camping trip?" Emily asked the question right as she pulled Mason's arm into a stretch the kid hated. She had a knack for finding the right time to ask a question that would give Mason something to think about other than the discomfort.

"All packed." Mason hissed the words between clenched teeth.

"The weather looks good for it." Emily counted a slow ten count before releasing Mason.

Liam couldn't agree more. "It should be perfect. Chilly mornings, pleasant afternoons, sunshine."

"When do y'all leave?" Emily continued to move through what Mason dubbed the "torture routine."

Mason glared at Emily but managed to say, "Tomorrow."

"Mason here tried to get out of all his classes tomorrow, but Mrs. Lawson vetoed that. She did approve an early dismissal, so we're hitting the road after lunch."

"Trying to throw your rabid fans off the scent?"

Mason flushed bright pink at her question.

The press left Mason Lawson alone. But that didn't mean he didn't have a devoted, some would call it obsessive, following of teenage girls who made it their mission to track Mason everywhere he went. It was an overly excited group of teenage girls that led to his shoulder injury.

Liam knew the torture routine well by now, and he grabbed a small green exercise band from the table. "That would be a bonus, but it's mostly so we can get there and set up before dark." He handed her the band with a wink.

Emily took it with a nod of thanks, their private choreography having settled into a comfortable pattern at this point. Her expression altered, and Liam braced for what was coming. He knew that look. It was her "I'm up to something" look.

"I don't know." Emily nudged Mason until he looked at her, then wrinkled up her face and shook her head. "Mason, weren't you here when Liam told us he could put a tent together blindfolded?"

Mason's expression cleared of pain, and he nodded with overdone solemnity. "You know, Emily, I do believe I heard those very words come out of his mouth."

"Must not be true." Emily's eyes were wide, and she shook her head sadly as she dropped her voice to a stage whisper. "Go easy on him this weekend, Mase. This may be why he's held off on taking you. He claimed it was because your shoulder needed to heal. But the truth is going to be revealed. I'm going to need a full report from you on Monday, so maybe you should take notes."

Mason sucked in a deep breath as Emily twisted him up like a pretzel, but he managed to gasp out, "I'll do that."

"If I were you," Emily continued in her stage whisper, "I'd make myself scarce during the tent setup. That way he won't be embarrassed."

"Oh no." Liam gave them both a wide and completely fake smile. "I think Mason needs to be there every step of the way. So he can document this and report back to you later."

Emily released Mason and gave him a small shrug. "I tried."

Mason grinned, actually grinned, back at her. "It was a great effort. I appreciate it."

The session continued for another twenty minutes, and now that the worst of the treatment was over, Mason gabbed about hiking, fishing, and the potential for animal sightings. He was particularly hoping for a bear.

"Liam, please tell me you're not going anywhere near bears. Or mountain lions." Emily didn't sound like she was joking.

"Yes, ma'am."

That earned him a spectacular eye roll, complete with a head shake and hands raised in a "What am I going to do with him?" gesture. Mason rolled his eyes at Liam and muttered, "Man, you keep poking the Tiny Tyrant with that ma'am stuff. When she finally snaps and attacks you with a massage gun, I'm taking her side."

Emily wasn't large, but she also wasn't tiny. After one particularly tough therapy session, Mason had referred to her as the Tiny Tyrant and the nickname stuck, although now it was said with what Liam knew was genuine affection, not belligerent exasperation.

"I wouldn't bother with the massage gun." Emily positioned the gun on Mason's shoulder and moved it in tight circles. "I'd grab some of the massage balls out of my bag and take him down."

Mason snorted. "You think that would work?"

Emily's expression grew smug. "It worked for David against Goliath. And I have excellent aim. My brother almost went pro in baseball, and I learned to pitch right along with him."

"No way."

"I assure you, it is the truth."

Now it was Liam's turn to share an exaggerated eye roll with Mason.

"Right." Liam reached for Emily's arm and squeezed her bicep. "You know how to pitch?"

Her back went straight, and her voice was frosty when she said, "Are you doubting my skills?"

Mason laughed, and Emily winked at him.

"Why didn't your brother go pro?" Mason asked the question with a hesitancy that surprised Liam. Maybe the kid was learning some tact. Finally.

"Injury."

Mason's entire body reacted to that one word. His injury had threatened to end a promising golf career. "How old was he?"

Emily didn't make eye contact with anyone as she spoke. "Seventeen. Senior year. Scouts had followed him for years. He was going to be drafted straight from high school."

"That must have been awful." The total absence of sarcasm in Mason's voice testified to how strongly he was responding to this revelation.

"It was." Emily continued to work Mason's shoulder. "He was devastated, and he was in a dark place for a while."

"Is he okay now?"

Was Mason genuinely concerned?

Emily smiled at Mason. "Oh yeah."

"How—" Mason cut himself off with a frown, and Emily gave

his arm a gentle squeeze. It must have given Mason what he needed to continue to ask his question. "How did he get better? I mean, from being depressed about it."

"It took a while. But he found other things he enjoyed doing."

"Like what?"

"Guitar, music, cooking."

"Cooking?"

"Yep. He's amazing. His coworkers buy groceries so he'll cook for them."

"What does he do?"

Liam watched the interaction, fascinated by the way it was playing out. Emily continued to drop crumbs. And as she did, Mason continued to follow them.

"He's an agent."

"What kind?"

She shrugged and glanced at Liam. "Secret Service."

"What? Do I know him?"

"No. He's in Raleigh. If he stays in, he'll probably be on a protection detail in a few years."

"Why wouldn't he stay in?"

Liam lost the thread of the conversation. Emily's brother was a Secret Service agent in Raleigh? That would explain how easily she'd adjusted to the protocols and extra hoops she had to jump through to take care of Mason and meet the strict safety measures he lived under.

"Why wouldn't he stay in?" Mason asked again, oblivious to the tension that now emanated from Emily.

"He has a woman in his life now. They're solid, but her job will keep her in Raleigh."

That wasn't the real answer. It wasn't a lie, but it wasn't the whole truth. Mason didn't know what Liam knew—that the Raleigh office had nearly been decimated the previous spring. Of the five surviving agents, only two had avoided injury. Then last month they'd had a major malware case that somehow had led to a shootout in an agent's house.

The Raleigh office was small enough that there was no way Emily's twin hadn't been involved, at least at some level. It wouldn't be surprising for an agent to want to find safer employment after surviving that. And if her brother had been injured recently, that might also explain why she kept Liam at arm's length.

A sharp rap on the door interrupted his thoughts. Liam opened the door, his body blocking the view into the room. The Second Lady's chief of staff, Lisa Goldman, glared at him from the hall. "Are they done yet?"

"No."

"I heard she was early."

"Emily was. *He* wasn't."

Lisa frowned at her iPad. "I need him ready for the road in thirty minutes."

"They'll be done in fifteen. He won't need more than fifteen to change. His clothes are already prepped."

"If he's late, it's on you."

It took all Liam's restraint to keep his face still when every muscle itched to contort into a grimace. But this new chief of staff had a reputation. She tolerated no dissent, no attitude, and no disrespect, especially from anyone she deemed beneath her. And those beneath her, in her mind, included the agents assigned to protect the Second Family.

"It won't be a problem." Liam moved to close the door.

Before he succeeded, an explosion shook the house.

**Lynn H. Blackburn** is the award-winning author of *Unknown Threat* and *Malicious Intent*, as well as the Dive Team Investigations series. She believes in the power of stories, especially those that remind us that true love exists, a gift from the Truest Love. Blackburn is passionate about CrossFit, coffee, and chocolate (don't make her choose) and experimenting with recipes that feed both body and soul. She lives in Simpsonville, South Carolina, with her true love, Brian, and their three children. Learn more at www.lynnhblackburn.com.

If you loved *Under Fire* by
Lynn, don't miss any of the other books in the

# DEFEND AND PROTECT SERIES

# Plunge into the enthralling cases of
# DIVE TEAM INVESTIGATIONS

 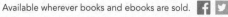

# MEET LYNN

WWW.LYNNHBLACKBURN.COM